PENGUIN BOOKS

MUSUNGU JIM AND THE GREAT CHIEF TULOKO

Patrick Neate is a 28-year-old freelance journalist. He lived in East Africa for a couple of years before settling in West London. *Musungu Jim and the Great Chief Tuloko* is his first novel.

Musungu Jim and the

Great Chief Tuloko

Patrick Neate

PENGUIN BOOKS

For Caroline

PENGUIN BOOKS

Published by the Penguin Group
Penguin Books Ltd, 27 Wrights Lane, London W8 5TZ, England
Penguin Putnam Inc., 375 Hudson Street, New York, New York 10014, USA
Penguin Books Australia Ltd, Ringwood, Victoria, Australia
Penguin Books Canada Ltd, 10 Alcorn Avenue, Toronto, Ontario, Canada M4V 3B2
Penguin Books (NZ) Ltd, Private Bag 102902, NSMC, Auckland, New Zealand

Penguin Books Ltd, Registered Offices: Harmondsworth, Middlesex, England

First published in 2000
10 9 8 7 6 5 4 3 2 1

The Acknowledgements on p. 377 constitute an extension of this copyright page

The moral right of the author has been asserted

Set in 9.25/13 pt Monotype Sabon
Typeset by Rowland Phototypesetting Ltd,
Bury St Edmunds, Suffolk
Printed in England by Clays Ltd, St Ives plc

Contents

Preface: 'The Zamba' by Edison Burrows III
(Author's preface to the 1993 edition)

1. *A myth must never be interpreted on one level only. No privileged explanation exists, for any myth consists in an interrelation of several explanatory levels.*
2. *A myth must never be interpreted individually but in its relationship to other myths which, taken together, constitute a transformation group.*
3. *A group of myths must never be interpreted alone but by reference: (a) to other groups of myths; and (b) to the ethnography of the societies in which they originate.*

Claude Lévi-Strauss

Since the initial publication of my humble ethnography The Zamba *in 1965, much has changed, both in the theoretical slant of cultural studies and, of course, in Zambawi itself. I do believe (although I'm sure many of the* enfants terribles *of anthropology departments across the world would beg to differ) that* The Zamba *has stood the test of time. However, I accept that it now serves more as a historical documentation of anthropological approaches long dismissed than any cutting-edge theory (as an ageing anthropologist – a former student of Radcliffe-Brown, no less! – I am all too aware that the cutting edge soon becomes as uncomfortable as any university chair). Was I really so interested in the abstraction of political, gender and kin structures? If I were to carry out my fieldwork among the Zamba today, I would certainly be less concerned with my own hypothesizing than with listening to what the people themselves had to say. But I maintain that this is less a* shift in theoretical leanings than one of experience; age certainly teaches one to listen.

Of course, it would be naive to suppose that the timing of this second edition of The Zamba is driven by anything other than the political upheavals in Zambawi of recent years. Since 'the shit hit the fan' (as my agent so charmingly puts it), I have guested on numerous radio and television programmes (billed on one occasion as the Cambridge Professor of Anthropology – long since a pipe dream!) and my kind editor has been pressing for a new study of the Zamba. Grandchildren and good health permitting, this new work (tentatively titled Myth and Meaning: The Primary Dialectic of Identity) will be completed some time in 1995. However, this preface is not meant merely to trail the unwritten. It is also an opportunity to include the Zamba myth below, both to imbue the ethnography that follows with something approaching modernity (reluctantly succumbing to the pressures of academic fashion) and to provide an interesting adjunct to recent events in Zambawi. I point out that the quotation of the great Lévi-Strauss's three guidelines for the interpretation of myth is used with tongue firmly in cheek. Clearly I offer this myth to the reader on one level, in isolation and prior to the ethnography. But I also offer no interpretation of my own. Instead I leave any analysis to the reader. You may wish to return to this preface when you have finished the book or you may not; but I suggest that you keep Lévi-Strauss's most excellent rules in mind throughout.

The myth of Tuloko and the Totems (my title) was told to me in May 1964 by a young witchdoctor in the Zimindo Province of Zambawi. What follows is an exact transcript of my recordings, translated from the original Zamba.

The Great Chief Tuloko (the Traveller, the Child of the Horizon) led the people (under the authority of Father Sun, with the guidance of Cousin Moon) from the time of the melting of the shamva for more than ten generations. This was a time of great prosperity and the people made sacrifices to Tuloko of food, precious stones and ritual objects that you would not understand.

Of course, there were wars to be won (with the shamva and the Men with the Spears between Their Legs) and there was the flooding of the Great Lake in the West That Cooled the Traveller's Feet and the sickness of the Years of the Dreaming (eventually cured in the ritual of the belabe shuffle). But, all in all, the reign of the Great Chief Tuloko was a happy one in which babies rarely cried and the mboko would vault on to the backs of black bulls even up to the age of 125, when their bones were as brittle as the branches of a baobab tree. Indeed, many times a mother would have to slap her docile child just to know it was still breathing. And many times Tuloko or one of his zakulu would have to mend the broken limbs and broken pride of an over-ambitious geriatric. During this period, the Zamba population grew and spread out from the plains of Zimindo and Maponda to cover all the land of the present day, from the Mountain in the East That Kissed the Sky to the Great Lake in the West That Cooled the Traveller's Feet.

Only when Tuloko was as old as the sand did the time of prosperity draw to an end. As his skin began to crack and blister, so the land dried and ruptured. As his spine curved, so the maize crop wilted. As his eyes paled, so the days shortened and the nights lasted for weeks at a time. The Zamba realized that Tuloko was soon to die and they began to gossip about who his successor might be.

At that time, it was common for most Zamba to take more than one wife. In the age of plenty and strength, even the poorest and weakest man could afford a minimum of four wives (these days such extravagance is unusual since the land is so poor and the women so expensive). But the Great Chief Tuloko married only once, to Mudiwa. Some people said this was because Tuloko wanted to ensure the unity of the Zamba. Others suggested that Mudiwa was the only person Tuloko feared. Most agreed that Mudiwa's famous appetite for gulu gulu left Tuloko with little energy for other women.

One of Tuloko's many gifts, granted by the will of Father Sun, was the ability to transform himself into any creature of the earth (although only at night). And when Cousin Moon rose in the sky, the Great Chief would come to Mudiwa in the marital hut in all manner of guises. Sometimes he came as shumba and their love-making was a frenzied as a kill and Mudiwa would find claw scars on her breasts and hips. Sometimes he came as gudo and Tuloko's whooping would wake the whole village. Generally Mudiwa liked such variety. Although the spines of pfanje made her uncomfortable and the size of nzou left her sore for a week.

In the ten generations of the reign of the Great Chief Tuloko, Mudiwa had many sons and they were named for the creatures of their conception. These names have become our totem ancestors and they speak of who we are as clearly as our own faces. However, when Tuloko was soon to die, these totems were a cause of much disagreement among his sons. The eldest sons believed that they surely had the right of succession. But all of Tuloko's sons were now centuries old, so questions of age and experience no longer mattered. Instead, therefore, the sons argued over the merits of their totem names.

Shumba claimed that he should succeed the Great Chief because no one could deny that he was the greatest warrior. Nzou claimed the right was his because he was as strong as fifty men. Boka Bird said that he should be chief because he could fly high into the sky and see what lay in store for the people. Every one of Tuloko's sons defended the value of his own totem and soon it seemed that they would fight for the right to be chief. Tuloko was very worried and he called them all together on the plains of Zimindo before the people.

'My sons,' Tuloko said, 'my time draws closer and Cousin Moon prepares a soft bed for me in a place I do not know. A successor must be chosen who will lead our people with a strong arm and a gentle voice. Yet all you do is argue with the arrogance of saplings that stand tall in a powerful wind. I tell you that my love is equal and, for all your different totems, my heart beats inside each one of you. But there can only be one chief. Shumba, in a time of war, you would lead us bravely into battle. Gudo, in a time of exchange, you would be a cunning businessman. Mbudzi, in a time of need, you would bring plenty. But I tell you this, a true chief must be as many things as the people require. So I have decided to set you all a test and he who completes it will be my successor.

'I am Tuloko. I am the Traveller and the Child of the Horizon. I came to this land from far beyond the Great Lake in the West That Cooled My Feet, the offspring of earth and sky. The test for you, my sons, is to journey to the horizon, my birthplace, and tell me what you find there. Whoever first reaches the horizon will become chief (under the authority of Father Sun and with the guidance of Cousin Moon) and all of you will accept his judgement.'

When the Great Chief Tuloko finished speaking, the noble brothers looked at one another in some confusion. 'Where is the horizon?' they said and then they sharpened their spears and packed knapsacks of mealy biscuits and maize cobs in preparation for their journey.

Shumba stretched himself to his full height and looked into the distance. He said to himself, 'I see the horizon! It is right there. At the base of that baobab tree.' And he quickly set off to get a head start on his brothers.

Before he began his quest, Gudo climbed a tree and shielded his eyes with his hand, so that he could look far to the west. 'There it is!' he exclaimed. 'The earth meets the sky at that hill beyond the river.' And he was sure that he would be the first to complete his father's test.

Of course, Boka Bird had the best view and he saw beyond the baobab tree and the river and the hill; beyond even the Great Lake in the West That Cooled the Traveller's Feet. 'There is the horizon!' he whispered. 'Where Father Sun rests his head for the night.'

Soon all of the Great Chief Tuloko's sons were racing across the plains of Zimindo, eager to fulfil their father's wishes. And Tuloko (the Traveller, the Child of the Horizon) watched their shrinking backs with a heart as heavy as maize porridge made with the milk of mbudzi. Tuloko was about to return with Mudiwa to his kraal when he realized that one of his sons had not moved. He was called Zveko Ant, the youngest of all his sons (only 183 years old), conceived when Mudiwa was tired of childbirth and gulu gulu.

'My son,' Tuloko said. 'Do you not wish to complete your father's test?'

'Oh, my father,' Zveko Ant replied, 'you are the Great Chief Tuloko and I wish you no dishonour. However, I am the smallest and most humble of all your sons and I was named for the smallest and most humble creature. I am not even worthy to call myself your descendant. I cannot see the distant horizons of Shumba or Gudo or Boka Bird and there is no point in my searching for something I can never see. I am so small that I live for ever on the horizon. The horizon, my father, is here.'

Tuloko looked at his youngest son and a smile as bright as Father Sun himself spread across his face.

'And what do you find on the horizon?' Tuloko said, and Zveko Ant thought for a moment and looked around himself.

'I find myself and I am not worthy to be called your descendant. I find the people in need of a chief. I find the Great Chief Tuloko in need of a successor.'

'My son,' Tuloko exclaimed, 'you are the first to complete my test and you shall be my successor and the chief of the people. For, as Father Sun himself once said to me, what is a descendant but a man whom you trust?'

That is how the Great Chief Tuloko's youngest son succeeded his father as the chief of the Zamba. That is why the Zamba chiefs are chosen by the zakulu (under the authority of Father Sun and with the guidance of Cousin Moon) on the basis of both age and totem but, above all, character.

Kotto, E. (1991), 'Gentleman Jim', Sunday Times, 17 November

Kotto, E. (1991), 'Musungu Takes the Myth', in Rose, A. and Lash, S. (eds), New African Outlooks, New York: Camstead Press

Lévi-Strauss, C. (1968), 'Religions comparées des peuples sans écriture', in Problèmes et méthodes d'histoire des religions: mélanges publiés par la section des sciences religieuses à l'occasion du centenaire de l'école pratique des Hautes Études, Paris, Presses Universitaires de France

Preston, T. (1981), A Colonial State of Mind, London, Black List Publishing

1 : How Jim Tulloh lost his innocence

What the hell am I doing here?

It was a sultry afternoon in early summer and Jim Tulloh was composing a letter to his grandmother. He stared blankly at the piece of paper on his desk. So far, all he had managed to write was the date (21 September 1991) and his address in the top left-hand corner: 'St Oswald's School, PO Zimindo, Zimindo Province, Zambawi, Africa'. Jim sighed. After 'Africa', he wrote 'The World'. Then he wrote 'The Solar System' and he sat back in his chair. He chewed on the plastic end of his ballpoint for a moment before he remembered that this was his last one. God knows where he'd find another. 'The Universe', he wrote.

What the hell am I doing here? What the hell am I supposed to say?

In ten years of living with his grandmother, they had never had a proper conversation. She asked him if he was warm enough. She asked him if he was hungry, if he'd finished his homework, if it was time for him to go to bed. But they never actually talked about anything beyond his superficial well-being. So what the hell was he supposed to say now that he was on the other side of the globe?

Besides his grandmother was seventy-five years old and mad. She lived on a diet of sausages, boiled potatoes and ketchup. She wore electric blue leggings. She smoked 120 cigarettes a day. She rented martial arts movies from the local video shop. She owned two cats named Diane and James Senior after Jim's parents. On Sundays she visited their grave with a Thermos and a packet of chocolate biscuits and she poured hot tea into the soil around the rose bush Jim had planted and crumbled the biscuits over the simple headstone. Then she came home and wept through the night to Monday morning.

Jim lit a cigarette and looked out of his window. The sun was behind him, so that shadows of his house stretched ludicrous lengths across the dusty scrub land and long *kiba* grass. At this time of day, the sky turned the most wonderful shade of indigo. One of the first things Jim had noticed on arriving in Zambawi was the way the sky changed colour throughout the day. In the mornings the countryside was washed in golden light, slightly unreal, like a touched-up old photograph. By midday the sky was white with heat and the scorched earth reflected it like a mirror. As the afternoon wore on, the colours ran across the spectrum from blue to indigo, then purple and black. The first time he saw this he had been astonished by its beauty. But now he was unmoved. It seemed strange that he could take such exquisite nature in his stride when he still found the day-to-day realities of his life in Zambawi – the heat, the food, his job, the pitch nights – so difficult to manage.

Some of the boys from Jim's GCSE class were playing football beyond the teachers' washing block. He thought about joining them, but he remembered what had happened the previous day and concluded that his ego wasn't sufficiently recovered for another pounding. They had divided into two teams and, though the boys laughed at his scrawny chest and skinny legs, Jim started pretty well. He even scored a goal, prompting shouts of '*Musungu! Musungu!*' from his team-mates. But then the opposition complained that Jim's trainers were an unfair advantage and he agreed to go barefoot like the rest of them. As soon as he was shoeless, Jim sprinted after a loose ball and straight into the middle of a patch of *zvoko* thistles. Screaming in pain, with inch-long thorns embedded deep in the soles of his feet, Jim was carried back to his house by the cheerfully laughing pupils to rhyming chants of '*Musungu longa ku maponga!*' As he gingerly extracted the needles from his skin, he irritably asked what this meant. 'The white man has feet like a baby!' he was gleefully told.

What the hell am I doing here? How the hell did I get here?

Jim ran a hand through his sandy hair and wrinkled his forehead in a frown. Then he winced. The taut sunburnt skin on his face was still tender enough to make any expression painful. His fair complexion wasn't cut out for the African sun.

In the three weeks Jim had been in Zambawi, he'd spent a lot of time trying to figure out how the hell he'd got there; trying to piece together the chain of events that had led him from completing his A-levels at a small comprehensive school in rural Dorset to teaching English in Zambawi in the space of four months. After all, he'd never *meant* to come to Africa. Not really. He had intended to go straight to college, until his exam results had gone so badly awry and he'd had to defer his university applications.

Jim remembered going to visit his school's careers master some four months previously. It was the day after the results were published and it was pouring with rain. Jim wished he'd remembered to use the phrase 'pathetic fallacy' in his English paper. Maybe that would have bumped him up a grade.

The careers master sat Jim down in his monochrome office with the buzzing striplight and put an aptitude test in front of him. The first question required him to describe himself in no more than ten words. Jim began seriously enough – it wasn't like he intended to be so facetious – but he was feeling down on himself and flippancy seemed to be the easiest way out. Besides, Jim soon found that all the words he was scribbling on the rough paper began with 'in' or 'un' and so he challenged himself to complete a list of ten. Indolent. Unambitious. Incompetent. Unassuming. Inconspicuous. Unprepared. Inconsequential. Underachieving. Indecisive. That made nine and Jim had to think for a moment or two before coming up with the tenth. Unintelligent. That was a good one since it began with both 'un' and 'in'.

The careers master read Jim's answers with rising eyebrows and a twitching nose while Jim watched. The patter of the rain on the office window was beginning to nag his bladder.

'OK, Jim,' the master said at last. 'Maybe you should do something worthwhile for a year.'

'Worthwhile?'

'Exactly. Have you ever done anything worthwhile?'

'No,' Jim conceded, 'I don't think I have.'

The master then dazzled him with glossy brochures of opportunities for vocational work. An autistic school in Port Regis? Too close to home. An orphanage in Calcutta? Too depressing. Viaduct construction in El Salvador? Too much like hard work. Teaching in Zambawi? Well. OK, then.

As the daylight faded and the sky began to purple and Jim contemplated his unwritten letter, he began to wonder exactly what constituted 'worthwhile'. So he had committed himself to a year's English teaching in Zambawi. So what? What was so worthwhile about that? And, more to the point, whose 'while' was it 'worth'? Not his pupils', that was for sure. The simple truth was that Jim was an unambitious, incompetent, unassuming, inconspicuous, unprepared, inconsequential, underachieving, indecisive and unintelligent teacher, much worse than his African counterparts. His one advantage – that he spoke fluent English – was easily outweighed by the fact that he spoke no Zamba and few of the children understood what he was saying. There didn't seem to be anything very worthwhile about sending a naive, monolingual school leaver whose qualifications ran to ten damning adjectives to feed the minds of knowledge-hungry rural Africa.

Maybe it was worth *his* while. Maybe. But he couldn't see it right now. He figured that this was the kind of experience that you looked back on in later life and described as 'character building' when what you really meant was that you were completely overwhelmed from start to finish; inundated with experiences that left you with a whole lot more questions than answers. 'Inundated': that could be his eleventh adjective – 'in' and then 'un'.

A fly settled on Jim's lip and he slapped at it. The fly easily evaded his fingers and hovered for a second around his nose before reclaiming its spot. African flies were remarkably ballsy and had none of the neuroses – no doubt induced by decades of flypaper and insect repellent – of their British peers. The fly began to stroll casually across his cheek. He scrunched up his face but the fly surfed the undulating waves of his skin with sure feet. Again he slapped his face – harder and faster – and this time he caught the insect in a glancing blow, sending it nose-diving into his lap. For a few seconds the fly writhed in the throes of an elaborate Hollywood-style death before it finally breathed its last. Jim felt momentarily guilty and then he blew on his fingertips as if they were a smoking gun. 'Rule Number Ten,' he muttered. 'You do what you gotta do. The rule to end all rules.'

The Ten Rules of Africa.

Jim flicked the miniature corpse from his lap and found his mind rewinding two months to the training course on the Isle of Skye. Three days roughing it in the back of beyond with thirty other would-be teachers was a precondition of his acceptance for the Zambawi programme. Jim had hated every second of it and the memories made him light another cigarette straight from the last. He would be turning into his chain-smoking grandmother if he wasn't careful.

He remembered three days of driving rain, sinking mud and enthusiastic yomping to 'build team spirit'. He remembered the sadistic survival exercises, the childish role plays and the songs around the camp fire – like he was a boy scout! And, most of all, Jim remembered feeling very out of place. The other school-leavers divided neatly in two: self-confident public schoolboys with lazy hair and slippery voices on one side and worthy types with velvet bags and hessian shirts (never the other way round) on the other. Jim fitted into neither category. Nor did he want to.

The course was run by an extraordinary man, an ex-marine called Terry Lamberton (or Lambo for short). A squat, muscular frame with bulldog neck, insane eyes and crew cut, Lambo was billed as an 'Africa expert'. It was only later that Jim realized that this was a euphemism for 'mercenary'.

There was no denying that Lambo cut an impressive figure, inspiring awe among the public schoolboys and abject terror among the worthies. He lectured the group three times a day about the challenges they might face, continually returning to his Ten Rules of Africa. His language was bizarre, part squaddie and part marketing man; he sounded like a terrace hooligan who'd swallowed a self-help manual.

'All right, ladies!' he would say. 'Let's blue sky about sex for a moment. And we're talking opportunity cost.'

He always addressed the whole group as 'ladies'. In fact, he never referred to anyone as anything but female. The women were sneered at as 'skirt' or 'little miss' and the men were harangued as 'you big girl' or 'you blouse'.

'Sex,' Lambo said. 'Come on, you girls! Who remembers Rule Number One? SWALK – Sealed With A Loving Kiss. Sex With Africans Leads to Krap. All right, the acronym's not perfect but you get the picture.

'I know you lot. You're all horny little girls, aren't you? Yes you are. I can see it in your faces, your hormones are in overdrive. You're eighteen years old and you blouses have been tugging yourself around the house for the last five years! What? Don't be shy, little miss. I'm sure you've been there with the long-handled hairbrush.

'So listen to what I'm saying. Sex with Africans leads to crap. Rule Number One. We're talking disease and pregnancy and all kinds of other crap. You may look like a sorry bunch of ladies to me, but to a rural Zambawian you're the richest meal-ticket in town. So don't get yourself into a compromising situation. Don't offer a pupil of the opposite sex some extra classes after school, don't invite them into your house, don't fall for one of the other teachers, and – for God's sake, you big girls! – give the local hookers a wide birth because they'll have more wildlife in their knickers than the Insect House at London Zoo.'

Lambo paused for a moment and then produced a condom from his pocket, stretching it out in front of his attentive audience.

'And if you really can't keep your privates private, then make sure you use one of these! If you're going to screw an African, make damn sure there's a floppy on the hard drive before you start pushing the buttons, all right?'

As much as Jim despised Lambo and his macho bullshit, he could remember the Ten Rules of Africa verbatim. Rule Number Five: A-B-C. Always Be Cleaning. A clean house is a healthy house. Rule Number Seven: The Three Ds. Diarrhoea = Dehydration =

Drink Fluids. And so on and so forth. He had even stashed a bumper pack of floppies in his rucksack.

A knock on the door awoke Jim from his reverie. He jolted upright in his seat and realized with some surprise that his eyes had been shut. How long had he been dozing? Inky night was closing and the light in Jim's house was dusk murky. He rubbed his eyes with his knuckles and stretched his back. He drew his writing paper up to his face as if he expected the letter to have written itself while he was snoozing. No such luck. There was a second knock at the door.

'Come in,' Jim called.

The door opened and, peering through the half-light, Jim could just make out some smiling white teeth. He had forgotten that he'd asked Innocence Murufu, one of his Form Two pupils, to deliver the class exercise books to his house.

'Innocence?'

'Mr Tulloh.'

'Just put them here on my desk.'

Innocence nervously walked into the house, shutting the door, and deposited the books on the desk. Jim smiled gratefully and thanked his pupil before picking the top book from the pile and flicking through its tatty pages. Innocence didn't move. After a minute or two, Jim looked round to see what his pupil was doing and he found that Innocence had her skirt raised to her navel.

'You want *gulu gulu, musungu*?' Innocence asked.

How the hell could I have been so stupid?

Jim's adventures in Zambawi were less than a month old and he was already in danger of breaking Lambo's Rule Number One. But this potential transgression was the product of ignorance rather than intent. For the truth was that Jim had yet to learn to distinguish the close-cropped head of one pubescent black African from another. In fact, he hadn't yet learned to distinguish with any certainty between a pubescent black African boy and a pubescent black African girl. Instead, Jim treated all his pupils with an even hand and did his best to avoid the potential embarrassment of gender-specific pronouns.

How the hell didn't I notice her skirt?

Jim pushed his chair backwards, away from the little girl, but Innocence Murufu kept coming, her skirt held high, her twelve-year-old's hips swinging as provocatively as she could manage. '*Gulu gulu!*' she kept saying, pouting her lips and wriggling her tongue in a suggestive way. This was the last thing Jim needed, a Zambawian Lolita, and he cursed her parents for christening her with such a sexually undecided and decidedly inappropriate name.

Jumping to his feet, Jim side-stepped Innocence and made his escape. He threw open his door and there, standing on the step, was Paul 'PK' Kunashe, the headmaster of St Oswald's. Despite the fading light and the little girl's desperate attempts to hide her modesty, PK surmised the situation in a flash and an eerie smile spread over his face.

'A word please, Mr Tulloh,' he said.

'Of course, headmaster,' blustered Jim.

2 : The rubber balls

The Zambawian President, Zita Adini, was playing with his rubber balls. Adini knew this wasn't a very statesman-like thing to be doing. But he countered this thought with four others. One: no one knew that he was doing it. Only General Bulimi was in his office and he couldn't see what Adini was up to behind the ornate mahogany desk. Two: he was the President and could do as he pleased. Three: he doubted whether any other world leader had rubber balls. Therefore to describe the action of playing with said balls as 'unstatesman-like' was irrelevant. And four: his scrotum *was* extremely itchy. He didn't remember his natural-born testicles being quite so irritable.

This was how Adini tended to think, in numbered order. And he felt that it was a positive sign of a tidy, logical mind.

So tidy is my mind, Adini thought, that if I ever did my own shopping, I would not have to write a shopping list.

This hypothesis had yet to be tested.

General Bulimi was beginning to stumble over his words. He knew that Adini's mind – however tidy – had begun to wander and he also knew that this tended to inflate the President's noted testiness. As Adini slumped lower in his chair and his pot belly popped another inch above the desk, Bulimi wished he was somewhere else. Why couldn't Adini at least allow him to sit down in his presence? He remembered the days of the independence war, when the pair of them fought shoulder to shoulder, driven by shared purpose and fading moral certainty. They discussed ideology in whispers around the camp fire; they watched each other's backs on moonless nights in the African bush, when succumbing to sleep was a life-and-death gamble; Bulimi wrote revolutionary poetry on tatty scraps of paper and Adini peppered his comrade with classical quotations. Hadn't they been friends? Twenty years of devoted, character-breaking service, ten years of independence and still he hadn't won the right to a chair.

I am too tired to spend hours standing to attention as rigid as a lamp-post. I am just thirty-seven years old. But what does an arbitrary measurement of age mean when I have experienced enough to fill a dozen lifetimes? I am too tired; as tired as the Traveller himself.

The general cleared his throat and, knowing that Adini had not been listening, decided to begin again.

'The Black Boot Gang have struck again, sir,' the general repeated. 'In Simba Province. The usual M.O.'

'Modus operandi, Bulimi!' spat the President in his unnaturally high voice. 'For goodness' sake! Do you have to be so lazy with your Latin?'

'It was the usual modus operandi, sir. They marched into a village and handed out thousands of leaflets of treacherous propaganda. I have one here, sir, if you would like to see.'

Bulimi handed his president a cheaply printed piece of A4 paper. Across the top it said 'Africa for the Africans!' in bold type above a rough sketch of a curious four-legged beast. Adini snorted in disgust.

'What's this strange animal?' he asked.

'Sir?'

'This!' said Adini, waving the leaflet irritably. 'This strange animal! It looks like a zebra with a deformed head.'

'I think it is supposed to be you, sir.'

'Me?' the President squeaked. 'Why?'

Bulimi shifted uncomfortably from foot to foot, licked his lips and wrinkled his nose.

'I think it's satire, sir,' he said. 'I think the implication is that you are like a zebra, half black and half white. Because you won't resolve the "land issue", sir. Because you have allowed the *musungu* to keep their land.'

For a moment, it looked as though Adini might explode. His pot belly rose and fell with quickened breath, his bug eyes popped further from their sockets and he ran a brooding hand across his mouth. But he was distracted by the smell on his fingertips; part sweat, part rubber, like a squash court at the end of a busy day.

Realizing the President's distraction, Bulimi blustered on.

'The Black Boot Gang, sir,' he said. 'They also procured some items from the villagers.'

'Procured?'

'Yes, sir. I have the local constable's report right here.' The general leafed through the papers in his hand. 'I quote: "The Black Boot Gang procured on behalf of the Democratic People's Republic of Zambawi fifteen sacks of maize, nine chickens, one cow and a Sony Walkman."'

'A Sony Walkman?'

'Apparently it belonged to the son of the local headman.'

'What would the Black Boot Gang want with a Walkman?' ruminated Adini.

He squeezed a dent into one of his rubber balls and waited for the little rush of pleasure that would come when it sprang back into shape. The general couldn't see this and he felt the emptiness of the moment's silence.

'Perhaps it was a gift, sir,' the general said.

'What?'

'The Walkman. Perhaps it was a gift.'

'For goodness' sake. Don't be so ridiculous! And what I want to know is where the hell were our boys when all this was going on?'

'They were on the scene within half an hour, sir. They just happened to be on exercises in the area. But an extensive search of the surrounding terrain uncovered nothing. These Gangers, sir, they just strike and disappear into thin air. Frankly a few of our boys are beginning to get scared. They're saying that the Gangers have the ancestral spirits on their side. They vanish into the scenery like baboons into the tree tops, like shadows retreating from the midday sun.'

'Like what? For goodness' sake, general! Are you a soldier or a poet?'

'A soldier, sir.'

'Well, start instilling some bloody courage into our army, would you? They should be ready to give everything for their country. They should be ready to make the ultimate sacrifice. *Moriamur et in media arma ruamus*. That must be their battle cry just as it was ours in the independence war! Is that understood?'

'Understood, sir,' Bulimi said. And with that he clicked his heels, saluted and goose-stepped out of the President's office, his footsteps echoing on the hard wooden floorboards.

It was common knowledge, or at least urban myth in Zambawi, that President Adini was a nut or two short of a full lunchbox. The story was that the future President had had his testicles removed in a colonial torture chamber during the early months of the decade-long independence war. This was not true. However, the story so enhanced the President's patriotic credentials that, embarrassing though it was, he did nothing to deny it. In fact, ten years after independence, Adini had fleshed out this story with such care that he found he could actually remember the moustache on his fictitious persecutor and the small flecks of spit that sprayed his face under questioning. He thought it would make rather a good film.

The truth of the President's missing testicles was far more prosaic and dated more than twenty years. It had been a cold night outside Brasenose College in Oxford where the young Zita Adini was studying on a Livingstone Scholarship. He had been dining at formal hall with a delightful young lady who later went on to be the MP for Bicester. Adini drank a port or two too many and, high on a brief kiss, decided that it would be a good idea to vault on to the second-hand bicycle that he had bought only that day. He did not notice that someone had stolen the saddle.

The future President awoke from his anaesthetic in the Radcliffe Hospital, Oxford, to find a kindly surgeon looking down at him.

'Mr Adini,' the surgeon said delicately, 'the good news is that we have managed to save your testicles.'

'Thank God!'

'The bad news is that we were not able to save them *in situ*.'

'What do you mean?' Adini asked, with a growing sense of trepidation and, indeed, emptiness tugging at his scrotum.

'Well, we thought you might like to keep them,' said the surgeon sheepishly, producing a small jar from the pocket of his white coat. At the sight of his pickled balls, Adini passed out.

3 : Gar

Although it only took Jim three weeks to tread on the toes of
Lambo's Rule Number One, he was none the less surprised when
he actually broke Rules Two and Three (concerning alcohol and
drugs respectively) in such quick succession. But he was soon so
drunk and stoned that he couldn't care less. And when, at the end
of one evening, he transgressed Rule Number Four (the one about
respect) by throwing up all over the headmaster's floor, he didn't
give it a second thought.

It was a warm night and the air was clinging and uncomfortable.
Jim was sitting in the living room of P K Kunashe's house. He was
cross-legged on the floor with his back to the breeze-block wall
and a beaker of overproof millet brew in his hands. Being the
headmaster's, P K's house consisted of two rooms rather than one.
But Jim was surprised to find that the headmaster's residence was
more sparsely furnished than his own. Along one wall, hundreds
of exercise books were stacked into neat piles, in one corner there
sat a small petrol stove, and in the middle of the room an upturned
cardboard box carried the flickering stub-end of a tired candle.
And that was about it. This was not what Jim had expected.

Nor had Jim expected P K to be quite so friendly. After all,
P K had greeted the *musungu*'s arrival at St Oswald's with curt
resignation and had acknowledged any previous meeting with no
more than a brusque nod. What's more, Jim had been summoned
to the headmaster's house this evening to discuss the Innocence
Murufu incident. So P K's new-found open manner and easy smile
came as something of a shock.

P K pulled a rolled newspaper from the waistband of his trousers and sat down next to Jim. He was still wearing his one pair of teaching trousers (threadbare blue pinstripe), but otherwise he was naked. The muscles on his torso were unusually flaccid for those of a rural African. His toes were grotesquely long and irregular like the tendril branches of an ancient *bola* tree.

PK waved the newspaper in front of Jim's face. The grin on the headmaster's face was, Jim thought, verging on the manic. Jim sipped tentatively at his drink.

'Do you know what this is, Mr Tulloh?' PK asked.

'It's a newspaper, headmaster,' said Jim.

'Indeed, Mr Tulloh, you are right. It is a newspaper. But it is more than that. It is *the* newspaper. It is the *Zambawi National Herald*, the only newspaper that is available in this great country of mine. I'm sorry. *Of ours*. It is owned by the government.'

'Oh!' Jim said.

'You did not know that? No matter. There is no reason why you should. In UK they call the newspapers "the fourth estate", do they not? In our country "the fourth estate" is the President's winter retreat on the shores of Lake Manyika. That is far to the west of here. The Great Lake That Cooled the Traveller's Feet.'

'That cooled the traveller's feet,' Jim repeated. 'Right.'

PK carefully laid the front page of the newspaper out on the concrete floor, folded it in two and tore along the crease. Jim noticed that the headmaster stuck his tongue out slightly as he concentrated. Like a child doing sums.

PK pointed at the large picture that took up the majority of the front page.

'Do you know who this is, Mr Tulloh?' PK asked.

'It is the President,' said Jim.

'Indeed, Mr Tulloh, you are right. It is President Adini.' PK nodded seriously. 'And can you read the headline?'

'ADINI OPENS RESTAURANT.'

'Indeed, Mr Tulloh,' said PK, 'Zambawi must be a very successful country, don't you think? For there is no bad news to report. Only the opening of a new Wimpy restaurant. We have no political conflict, no economic problems, no crime, no scandal. But we do have the Home of the Hamburger.'

PK looked at Jim and his smile seemed curiously misshapen. Jim looked back at PK and found himself blinking. From the pocket of his trousers, PK produced a large leather pouch. He curled the beaming face of President Adini in the palm of one hand and sprinkled the contents of the pouch evenly over the picture.

'Do you know what this is, Mr Tulloh?' PK asked.

'Marijuana?'

'Indeed, Mr Tulloh, you are right. It is grass, herb, weed, Mary Jane. But in this great country of ours, we call it *gar*.'

'*Gar*?'

'Exactly!'

PK bent his head over his work and wrapped President Adini's features around the extravagant quantity of *gar*. His fingers worked with nimble dexterity and within a minute he had concocted the biggest reefer Jim had ever seen. Jim's experience of drugs was limited to the odd puff at parties he'd sneaked into uninvited. But he knew that this mighty spliff was special. It looked, he thought, more like a weapon than a source of recreation. PK struck a match, lit his fabulous construction and sucked deep, with his cheeks hollowing until his dark features seemed to assume an almost translucent quality.

'I tell you something, Mr Tulloh,' gasped PK. 'There is no finer way to relieve the stresses of the day than to burn the fucking eunuch. It is a symbolic combustion.'

'What? You mean, like voodoo?'

'Voodoo?' PK chuckled emptily. 'Indeed not, Mr Tulloh. It is merely a personal symbol of contempt for that fucking eunuch. Just as we used to burn the White Horse in the days of the independence war.'

'The White Horse?'

'Yes, the Manyikaland flag, when Zambawi was called Manyi-kaland.'

PK exhaled expert smoke rings that tickled their way up Jim's nose and made him feel giddy. Jim swallowed a mouthful of his drink and tried not to choke as the millet brew burned the back of his throat.

'So, Mr Tulloh,' said PK at last. 'How does teaching find you?'

'Inadequate,' said Jim glumly.

'Indeed? Do not be downcast! It is an honour for us to have a future student of the famous Oxford University on our staff. And what is it you will be studying?'

'Actually, headmaster, I'm not going to Oxford. It's Oxshott. Oxshott College.'

'No matter!' said PK generously, before adding with a cryptic twist, 'These are all Ivy League establishments, are they not? Of course they are.'

PK handed Jim the club-like reefer with a flourish. Jim accepted its moist tip between nervous fingers.

'What's it called?' Jim asked. 'I mean, what's the Zamba word for this?'

'I told you, Mr Tulloh. It is *gar*. *Gar*. G-A-R.'

'*Gar*? What does that mean?'

'It means marijuana.'

'No. I realize that. I meant, where does it . . .'

Jim found his sentence curtailed by his first inhalation of the pungent weed. It was not an unpleasant sensation, like a lizard licking his brain. But then, after a good ten seconds or so, Jim realized with some dismay that he was no longer breathing and forced out the smoke with a mighty effort: '*GAR!*'

'It is good shit, Mr Tulloh?' said the smiling PK.

'Good shit,' mouthed Jim. And, though he could propel no words from his mouth, he did manage to let rip with a fart of artistic proportions. He handed the joint back to PK and the headmaster showed no signs of noticing his anal verbosity.

'So, Mr Tulloh,' PK began, propelling dozens of perfect smoke rings towards the ceiling. 'This incident with Innocence Murufu, is there anything you would like to say?'

There was indeed much that Jim wanted to say, but a direct link had been established between opening his mouth and opening his bottom. Open mouth: pop! Mouth open: parp!

'Indeed, Mr Tulloh,' said PK dryly. 'Your arse has put forward a cogent argument.'

PK leaned forward through the smoke and looked at Jim intently. For the first time, the bizarre smile had passed from his lips.

'But seriously, Mr Tulloh – for this is a serious business – I should warn you of the possible consequences of your actions. There are two – what's the word? – scenarios: either Innocence will tell her family nothing, or she will tell her family that you made her *gulu gulu*. And I must tell you that to make a girl of *chinjuku* age perform *gulu gulu* is one of the most terrible crimes for the Zamba! If she says nothing, then I will back you to the hilt and I will say nothing also. If she tells her family, then they will kill you and you are on your own.'

Now Jim had to speak.

'But I didn't do anything!' he gasped. He was barely audible over the rhythmic tattoo that shot from his anus.

The headmaster shrugged.

'Life is very unfair,' he said. 'But keep a stiff upper lip, as you say in England.'

Jim was more concerned with the rigidity of his lower ring than his upper lip. But he managed to get some words out to a chorus of approval from his arse. 'What should I do, headmaster?' he asked.

'Do? There's nothing you can do,' PK replied calmly and he tugged on the spliff again before handing it on to Jim.

'Mr Tulloh, I have four things to tell you about Zambawians that will be useful to you. In the first place, we love the Englishman. In the second place, we hate the Englishman. In the third place, we are very fickle. Do you understand?'

'No. No, headmaster, I don't.'

PK sighed and tutted as if bored by an especially dull student.

'What I'm saying is that you must cross your fingers and hope.'

'Oh!'

'OK?'

'OK. And the fourth?'

'The fourth?'

'The fourth thing to tell me.'

'Ah yes! The fourth. The fourth thing you should know, Mr Tulloh, is that we Zambawians know how to hold our wind when smoking *gar*. The trick in our society is to suppress your gas until the *gar* is finished and then let it out in one swift voice of appreciation. Here, let me show you.'

With that PK rocked back where he sat and lifted his knees to his shoulders, cradling his legs in arms.

To compare what happened next to a fart would be like comparing whitebait to Moby Dick. From somewhere deep in the posterior of the grinning headmaster, a rumbling Leviathan announced its coming and Jim wondered if he was dreaming. Then the mighty beast surfaced with an angry roar. 'There she blows!' shouted PK.

It was a fart that would scare babies and leave little boys in awe. It was a fart that could warm a pensioner's flat for a chill winter month. It was a fart that deserved its own name, like 'Hurricane Nancy' or 'Typhoon Clara'. And the smell! The smell invaded Jim's nose with the texture of lumpy gravy. And it pushed him from the crow's nest of frailty that he'd sat in for the preceding half-hour, and his dinner of green vegetables and maize mash jumped out of his mouth like the whalers abandoning the *Pequod*. Jim bolted for the door with puke streaming down his front.

'I'm sorry, headmaster,' he gobbled. But PK was lost in reverence to the magnificence of his creation, as spent and deflated as a used floppy.

4 : The Poet (one)

General Indigo Bulimi was conceived in the year when the Zamba first began to unify in their fight against colonial rule. Perhaps, therefore, he might have been born to be a soldier. But he was not.

People are rarely born to an identity. People are not, for example, born to a particular nation (as much as nationalists – African and European alike – might argue otherwise). When someone says, 'I am English', it refers to an evolution rather than a state, an ongoing, unchosen process of osmosis and consumption. A fluid soul, desperately seeking a vessel in which to contain itself, may even plead, 'But I am English by birth!' But, contrarily, this refers less to the facts of their personal history than their current state of mind – barely more revealing than an analysis of what they ate for lunch. It is an unsatisfying business.

The Englishman grows up in the hope of discovering who he is, only to rise one morning to find that a laconic worrier with a passion for comfortable shoes has assumed his form and it was the process of discovery that made him this way, and now it's too late for wilful change. For most people, therefore, identity is a wild goose chase.

It is similarly rare for people to be born with a vocation. The Zambawian subsistence farmer, for example, was never called to farm. This is evident from the extreme variety in the skills of agriculture and animal husbandry that can be seen in any Zambawian village. For every dozen competent smallholders, there are at least a dozen more lazy farmers whose goats' udders are painfully distended. There are forgetful farmers who lose chickens to the baboons for the sake of an open gate and weedy farmers who take orders from their cows. In rural Zambawi, farming is not a vocation but a prescription. It is not a way of life but life itself.

For the rare exceptions to these given uncertainties, life should be as easy as a sneeze, as natural as a piss, as satisfying as a marvellous shit. But – since life is unfair – those who are born to be themselves are rarely comfortable with the role.

General Indigo Bulimi was not born to be a soldier. No. But Indigo Bulimi, an only child from a colonial backwater, *was* born to be a poet. It was his identity and his calling. It was his downfall and his redemption. Poetry was who he was.

When Indigo Bulimi was born, his father was forty-two years old and his mother thirty-eight. At least that's what their permits said, though the colonial authorities were far keener to compile the appropriate lists than to ensure their accuracy. The couple had married two decades before, in the year when the Great Lake That Cooled the Traveller's Feet burst its banks. Father Bulimi paid a hefty brideprice for the buxom girl from the *gwaasha* and he hoped that the flood was a sign from the ancestors of her great fecundity. But it was not.

After three years of barren marriage, Zamba tribal law entitled Father Bulimi to return his bride to her homestead to the shame of herself and her family. This was what his parents had wanted.

'My son,' they said, 'a childless man can never attain respect. Who will look after you when your back stoops and you can no longer lift a plough? Who will pack dung on to your elbows when the skin begins to crack and sore?'

But Father Bulimi could not bring himself to divorce his young wife. For when she washed, the water droplets glistened in her hair like tiny beads of sun; when she fetched water, the upward curve of her coccyx tickled his groin; and when she scolded him for drinking too late, her mouth would split into a helpless smile that he felt in his navel.

Instead, Father Bulimi took his wife to live and work in Mutengwazi, on the outskirts of Queenstown. Mutengwazi was euphemistically designated a 'high-density suburb' by the colonial government. In fact, it was an overpopulated slum with a heartbeat of fist fights, a circulatory system of open sewers and alcohol on its breath. It fed houseboys, gardeners, pool attendants and the like to the Queenstown elite.

Father Bulimi was large, strong and willing and he soon secured a job as a security guard for the Kellys in the upmarket Chisipite area of Queenstown. Mr Kelly was a civil rights lawyer with an approximate conscience, and the extra five dollars of guilt that this brought every month enabled the young couple to rent a one-room brick house between the Queenstown bus stop and a large *shabeen*. Every night Father Bulimi would return home late and say, 'I just stopped for a quick drink on the way.' And every night his wife would frown at this definition of 'on the way'. But she looked at the honest lines that creased Father Bulimi's tired face, her mouth split into that helpless smile and the couple made passionate, fruitless love by the light of the gasoline stove.

Often, when Father Bulimi was drinking in the *shabeen*, some troublemaker or other confronted him with ribald wit. 'I see the crop has failed for another year,' the wag would say. 'You must sow the seed deeper than two inches.'

When Father Bulimi was challenged in this way, his friends watched him nervously, expecting a reaction. But Father Bulimi was a peaceful man who dealt with life's inequities with great serenity and he answered all such mockery with the same slow smile and easy catchphrase. 'We are hoping for the ancestors to smile,' he would say.

Over the years his unshakeable faith landed Father Bulimi with the nickname 'N'dgo'. It does not have a direct English translation. Roughly it means 'one who expects'. However, the word is imbued with a taste of false hope.

By the time he was forty everyone called Father Bulimi 'N'dgo'. Everyone, that is, except his wife. Mother Bulimi was so used to hearing her husband referred to by his nickname that she often found the word forming on her lips. But she always caught it just in time. Although she loved her husband and knew that he loved her, they no longer talked about their infertile marriage.

When Mother Bulimi finally fell pregnant, therefore, her husband didn't know what to say. Indeed, his first thought – that the child simply couldn't be his – left him feeling so ashamed that he drank in the *shabeen* for three nights and two days from the Friday on which he heard the news. He leaned against the bar and supped millet brew straight from the bucket. His friends nodded to one another and commented that 'N'dgo has never looked so unhappy.'

On the Monday morning Father Bulimi headed straight from the *shabeen* to the bus stop. He did not look up as he passed by his own front door. Only when he boarded the Queenstown bus did he realize quite how hungover he was and that his security guard's uniform stank of rancid alcohol.

Standing at the gate to the Kellys' residence, Father Bulimi spent the entire day reflecting on the change in his fate. He realized that he wasn't pleased by impending parenthood and this realization puzzled him.

It is strange, he thought. It seems that if you wish for something long enough, when it finally arrives you have forgotten why you wanted it in the first place.

At around 6 p.m. that day, Mr Kelly pulled into his drive. As he passed Father Bulimi, he wound down the driver's window and beckoned him over. Father Bulimi wondered what he had done wrong. But Kelly had a broad grin on his face.

'Boy!' Kelly said.

'Yes, boss.'

'Boy, today I have won the most important case of my career.'

'Yes, boss.'

'The two nationalist revolutionaries – you've seen it in the *Herald*, I suppose? – I have had their death sentences commuted to life. It's been a hard struggle but we won in the end.'

Father Bulimi chewed the inside of his mouth. He felt nervous. He didn't understand. 'That is good, boss,' he said.

'Good?' Kelly laughed significantly. 'Yes. It's good for you people.'

The two men looked at one another. They both felt uncomfortable. Kelly reached over to the passenger seat and picked up a tissue-wrapped package.

'Look,' Kelly said. 'I have bought Madam a gift.'

He tore open the package to reveal a length of the most beautiful cloth that Father Bulimi had ever seen. It was rich blue satin with delicate beading embroidered in intricate patterns along the hem. The blue, Father Bulimi thought, was deep enough to embarrass the sky. The beading reminded him of his wife's wet hair.

'What is that called, boss?' Father Bulimi asked.

'It is indigo,' Kelly said. 'Indigo is her favourite.'

When Kelly spoke that word – 'indigo' – a weight lifted from Father Bulimi's heart as if an evil spell had been broken. Indeed, when he looked back on that moment, this is exactly what he believed. For years after, Father Bulimi did not know what 'indigo' meant. Sometimes he thought that Kelly had been mocking him with that slight mispronunciation of his nickname, N'dgo. But mostly he believed that while N'dgo was Zamba for 'one who expects', so 'indigo' must be English for a special kind of gift at the end of a long struggle. And it was a coincidence that he enjoyed. And he resolved to call his child 'Indigo', for the word was magical and perfect and his child was a special kind of gift too, the kind that would be his favourite.

That night Father Bulimi didn't stop in the *shabeen* on his way home and his wife was surprised but pleased to see him an hour earlier than usual. She was even more pleased to find that the honest lines that creased his tired face had vanished. His forehead was as smooth as the skin on her slowly stretching stomach. And when they made love by the light of the gasoline stove, Mother Bulimi giggled as her husband's hot breath tickled her ear with 'indigo'. And she agreed that it was a magical and perfect word and thanked the ancestors for answering her expectations with such a special kind of gift.

5 : St Ignatius' College

While the future President of Zambawi was tongue-twisted with the future MP for Bicester in a smoky Oxford combination room, in a small rural clinic in the south-west corner of Manyikaland (as Zambawi was then called), the future President's wife was just going into labour. And two hours later, when Adini had his feet in stirrups to facilitate the removal of his testicles, so Mrs Sally Adini had her feet in stirrups to facilitate the birth of their son.

The next day, Adini spoke to his wife on a crackling long-distance line. Generally, since he was already a known nationalist intellectual and suspected revolutionary, Adini's phone calls were tapped by Manyikaland's secret service. However, on this occasion, since he was telephoning from the surgeon's office in the Radcliffe Hospital, the conversation went unrecorded, which is a pity. Because it must have been worth hearing.

As for President Adini himself, all he could remember of this conversation was his wife's attempts to comfort him for the loss of his manhood. 'Don't think of it as losing your testicles,' she had told him. 'Think of it as gaining a son.'

That sentence stuck in his mind. And now, more than twenty years later, he could not look at his son without feeling that he was somehow to blame for the rubber balls that needed constant scratching.

Of course, it didn't help that Enoch Adini was, in his father's eyes, such an utter waste of space. Adini had been absent for much of Enoch's childhood: first completing his degree, then learning to use a gun at the expense of the sympathetic Soviet government and finally as a battalion leader in the ZLF (the Zambawi Liberation

Front). In fact, Adini had barely spoken two words to his son before the end of the civil war. Then, as they paraded victoriously through the streets of Queenstown with the triumphant ZLF forces, he had turned to the ten-year-old Enoch. Adini remembered it clearly.

'Well, my boy,' Adini said. 'How does it feel to be free?'

Enoch looked at him for a moment before picking his nose and saying, 'Can we get a telly now?'

The original idea had been that Enoch should follow in his father's footsteps: St Ignatius' College, Queenstown, followed by Brasenose College, Oxford. But it soon became apparent that Enoch had no intention of doing any such thing. For starters, Enoch was in constant trouble at St Ignatius' from the time he started at thirteen to the day he was expelled three years later.

St Ignatius' was a school on the British model; i.e. its credo – as Adini like to call it – was a system of education that had not existed in Britain since the late nineteenth century. It was staffed entirely by monks of the Order of the Ark, a bizarre puritanical sect that upped sticks from Britain some time after the First World War and now existed solely at St Ignatius'. The official reason for their departure from Britain was missionary: a desire to bring their peculiar brand of Christianity – not so much 'muscular' as 'violent' – to the dark continent. In fact, they were eased out of their home country by the established church. Long uncomfortable with the methods of the Order of the Ark, Canterbury put its foot down after an unfortunate incident in a theology lesson in one of the Order's schools. The Archbishop simply wouldn't accept that the best way to explain the suffering of Christ was to crucify a pupil on a hockey goal.

So now the monks were in exile in Africa, a climate which did nothing to improve the comfort of their abrasive sackcloth habits. Enoch Adini often used to wonder if it was the constant sweaty chafing that provoked the monks' own abrasive habits. And, sometimes, during morning prayers in the school chapel, he would look at the crucifix before which the monks bowed their heads and think that it should really be replaced as an object of worship by the three-foot *shambok* that every 'brother' carried at all times.

One master in particular – his Latin teacher, Brother Angelo – had it in for Enoch. Enoch never quite figured why but he suspected that it might have something to do with his appearance. Because, even as an adolescent, Enoch was exceptionally tall, full-chested and sculpture-beautiful, while Brother Angelo was an extraordinary-looking man: squat and middle-aged with a stomach that touched his knees, an arse that nudged his ankles and a bulbous beetroot face that sat atop an incongruously long and scrawny neck. From the chest down, his weight seemed a slave to gravity, so that his bizarre upper vertebrae appeared to be desperately climbing to freedom. Looking as he did, he could never have been anything but a monk. Looking as he did, he could never have been anything but an ogre.

Brother Angelo's 'difficulties' with Enoch started in their very first lesson together. Enoch questioned – not unreasonably – the value of learning Latin instead of the indigenous Zamba. For a moment Brother Angelo's face turned an even deeper shade of purple and Enoch thought his head might burst. But then he said with quiet menace, 'My study. After school.'

When he knocked on the monk's door at 4.15 p.m., Enoch didn't know what to expect. He'd been through a few scenarios in his head but nothing could have prepared him for what was to follow.

Brother Angelo was tapping his *shambok* on the desk.

'Take off your trousers and underpants,' he said.

'I'm sorry?'

'I'm going to beat you.'

'Why?'

'Bend over.'

'No,' said Enoch and backed towards the door. But, surprisingly swift for a middle-aged tub of blubber, Brother Angelo got there first. And he locked the door.

'Hold on,' said Enoch lamely. 'Do you know who my father is?'

'Indeed I do, Mr Adini. Now I am going to beat you. Remove your trousers and underpants or I will remove my cassock.'

'What?' screamed Enoch.

'One of us must be naked for this punishment,' said Brother Angelo calmly, as if it were the most obvious thing in the world, and he began to lift his habit.

'No!' shouted Enoch. 'Wait! Christ!'

'Blasphemy, Mr Adini,' said Brother Angelo. 'That will be another two strokes.'

'Shit!' said Enoch. He looked at the mad monk in front of him, imagined the horrors of his naked body and furiously began to tear at his flies, dropping his trousers to his ankles and his underpants to his knees. Brother Angelo swallowed and his Adam's apple bobbed the full length of his giraffe-like neck. He licked his lips and his fingers folded tightly around the *shambok*.

Thereafter Brother Angelo beat Enoch at least once a week for the next three years (excepting school holidays). And the routine was always the same. Only once did Enoch dare suggest that Brother Angelo should be the one that would bare all. But never again. The terrifying sight of the monk's genitals – the bulbous head, skinny shaft and gargantuan balls bore an uncanny resemblance to the man himself – left poor Enoch with enough imagery for a lifetime's nightmares.

Of course, Enoch complained about the beatings to his father. But the President was less than sympathetic.

'So he beats you?' Adini said. 'It's good for the character.'

'But Dad! The man's a pervert.'

'A pervert? For goodness' sake! Of course he is. It's the perversity of private education that formed the greatest characters of the British Empire. Besides, it never did me any harm.'

And Enoch would look at his father, consider his contrary misanglophile ways – part paranoid African dictator, part *nouveau riche* English gentleman – and take no comfort at all.

Enoch was one of only three black students at the school (the others were the sons of the ministers for tourism and defence). And, of course, President Adini had a word or two to say about that too.

'I was the first black boy to go to St Ignatius',' he said. 'I was bullied. I was an outcast. They called me kaffir, munt and nigger.

But the words just strengthened my political resolve. And look who had the last laugh! These men now come to me to protect their farms and protect their exports. St Ignatius' is grooming you for greatness, my son.'

'You don't understand, Dad,' Enoch replied. 'Times have changed.'

And he was right.

During his time at St Ignatius', Enoch Adini was never bullied because of his colour. Not physically anyway. However, he did discover that his proximity to so many white adolescents drove him to the edge of despair. His *musungu* schoolmates inflicted a mental cruelty upon him that left him wishing for a bit of good old-fashioned kaffir-bashing.

Enoch did not like to stereotype. But the *musungu* Zambawians were simply so *uncool* that he couldn't stand their company. Perhaps it was their clipped, starched accents, their obsession with rugby football as a marker of machismo, or the idea that alcohol-induced vomiting was the height of sophistication. Or perhaps it was the way they cut their hair: cropped on top with long, greasy straggles snaking down between their shoulder blades. But most of all it was their music. By the time he was fourteen, Enoch had suffered the osmotic assimilation of the lyrics of every Meatloaf, Guns N' Roses and Bon Jovi song ever recorded. And it drove him to distraction.

He would walk into his dormitory to find a dozen screwed white faces lost in an ecstasy of two-finger keyboards and screaming guitar solos.

Some would be thrashing out the chords on their tennis rackets, others would be 'dancing' – substituting frenzied activity for any rhythmical movement – and still others would just lie on their beds with agonized expressions on their faces and their hands delving deep into their pyjama bottoms. Enoch would look at his peers with a mixture of pity and contempt before retreating to his corner bed with his fingers in his ears and tears of frustration pricking at his eyes.

Enoch had nothing against the *musungu* in theory. However,

he did feel that five minutes spent in his dormitory might teach his father why his post-independence policy of reconciliation was doomed to failure. Enoch could excuse 100 years of white colonialism without too much trouble (after all, he could barely remember the pre-independence Manyikaland). But their music was unforgivable. Sometimes, at night, he would imagine a second civil war with the whites chased out of Zambawi, ducking low as their CD collections of trad-rock and soft metal whizzed over their heads.

It was music that finally led to Enoch's expulsion. One Sunday afternoon, he had walked into the dormitory. To his relief it was empty and quiet. He had dropped to his hands and knees and retrieved his suitcase from under his bed, where he kept a secret stash of 'his' music: Jamaican reggae and American hip hop and R 'n' B. With a reverence born of neglect, he selected a Public Enemy album and dropped it into the communal tape deck.

'The number! Another summer. Get down! Sound of the funky drummer.'

Enoch lay back on his bed, closed his eyes and for a moment or two he lost himself in the James Brown rhythms and the aggressive polemic of rapper Chuck D.

The song reached his favourite bit – 'Elvis was a hero to most but he never meant shit to me . . .' – when the music abruptly cut out. Enoch opened his eyes to find two of his room-mates, Grant Walker and Horst Van De Horse, rugged farm boys from Zimindo Province, standing over the stereo.

'What the fuck is that shit, Adini?' said Horst and threw Enoch's beloved tape across the room.

At the same time Grant slipped a replacement tape into the deck and, within seconds, Enoch was being tortured once again with the bizarre hyperbolic sounds of Joey Tempest and Europe with its whoopee-cushion bassline and orgasmic vocals.

'It's the final countdown!' sang the stereo and both the white boys picked up their tennis rackets and began to strum as if their lives depended on it.

Even in retrospect Enoch Adini struggled to come to terms with what happened next. He wasn't by nature an aggressive person, but the sound of a curly-permed Scandinavian in skin-tight PVC trousers seemed to inspire him with new levels of hatred and spite. Calm and purposeful, Enoch retrieved his tape from the floor, replaced it in its box and marched over to the stereo system, unseen by the furiously head-banging white boys. He picked up the offending stereo and with one fluid movement propelled it out of the dormitory window with a triumphant, tribal shout worthy of the Great Chief Tuloko himself. 'Fuck off!'

'It's the final countdown!' blared the stereo as it flew in a graceful parabola towards the ground. And Brother Angelo craned his prehensile neck skyward just in time to catch the corner of the heavy box square in the forehead. The autopsy noted that the monk's top five vertebrae had been crushed and he had lost three inches in height. In fact, only on the pathologist's table, with his neck squashed into shoulders, did Brother Angelo assume something approaching a normal human shape. It was the closest to normality that the mad monk ever came.

Of course, Enoch hadn't been thinking about where the stereo might land. So the fact that it landed on Brother Angelo was mere good fortune. But the school didn't see it that way. The police were called, Enoch was expelled and President Adini had to flex his totalitarian muscles to keep the story out of the *Zambawi National Herald* and his son out of prison.

Enoch was thrilled to leave St Ignatius'. But his father never forgave him. For now, in the President's eyes, Enoch was not just a castrator but a murderer too. And on the rare occasions that the first family sat down to dinner together, the President would occasionally catch himself sitting with one hand on his crotch and his eyes flitting towards the ceiling for fear of a falling weight.

6 : Headless chickens

The late afternoon sun shone through the imported jacaranda trees that bordered the Commissioner's residence before shimmering on the surface of the gently lapping Olympic-sized swimming pool. The dogs were chasing bees among the rainbow colours that populated the flower beds and two baby geckos played hide-and-seek in the crevices on the veranda. The lush smell of freshly cut lawns hung in the air like an ambrosia syrup and nothing could be heard but the occasional chink of ice against glass. Alistair Digby-Stewart, CBE, the British High Commissioner to Zambawi, sat back in his sun lounger, sipped on his gin and tonic and reflected, with no irony at all, that life was a bitch.

'Thomas!' Digby-Stewart called. 'Thomas!'

He didn't look round. He didn't have to. He knew that the houseboy would never be out of earshot. And, sure enough, Thomas's smiling face and pristine white servant's jacket appeared at his side within seconds.

'Another gin and tonic,' Digby-Stewart said.

'Yes, sir.'

'And Thomas?'

'Yes, sir.'

'Go easy on the gin this time.'

'Less gin. Yes, sir.'

'And Thomas?'

'Yes, sir.'

'How about a spot of dinner? Out here on the veranda.'

'Yes, sir.'

'Whatever cook has to spare.'

'Yes, sir.'

'And Thomas?'

'Yes, sir.'

'This Black Boot Gang.'

'Yes, sir.'

'You've heard about them?'

'Yes, sir.'

'Do you think they'll stage a coup? I mean, what do you think would happen if they staged a coup? What would be their attitude to the British? What I mean to say is, what would be their attitude to me?'

'To you, sir?'

'Yes, Thomas.'

'I think you would be the first against the wall, sir.'

For the first time Digby-Stewart looked directly at his houseboy. But he couldn't detect any perceptible change of expression except, perhaps, a slight widening of the smile. Or maybe he was just getting paranoid too.

'Chicken, sir?' asked Thomas.

'What's that?'

'Cook was planning to kill a chicken.'

'Yes. Thank you, Thomas.'

Thomas retreated into the palatial Commissioner's house and Digby-Stewart lay back once again. He reached under the lounger with one hand and retrieved his revolver. He flipped open the barrel and checked that it was fully loaded. He then replaced it on the grass within easy reach. You can't be too careful, he thought.

He looked down his body at his pinking torso and thighs. He liked what he saw.

'Not bad,' he said aloud. 'Not bad for a fifty-year-old, Alistair old chap.'

Then he noticed a few white hairs sprouting from the dense shrubbery on his chest and he spent a minute or two plucking each offensive sign of age between thumb and forefinger until he was satisfied there were none left. Next, he picked up his sun cream from beside the gun and began to massage it, absent-mindedly, into his chest. He closed his eyes, rested his head and thought of England.

Alistair Digby-Stewart was worried and he was angry. He was angry partly with himself and partly with the civil service that had posted him to Zambawi just two months previously. A career diplomat, he had spent more than half his life in the trouble spots of the world: Beirut, Baghdad, Tehran and Tel Aviv. But never in sub-Saharan Africa. Digby-Stewart had seen his step up the civil service ladder to the top job in Zambawi as little more than a sinecure. How hard can it be? he had thought. Just the odd fawning dinner party, the occasional tactful speech about the perceived dangers of a totalitarian regime and perhaps an annual role as independent monitor-in-chief of a rigged election or two. No trouble.

He hadn't recognized that he was walking into a potential *coup d'état*, and he cursed himself for not paying attention to the sniggers that echoed around Whitehall on his acceptance of the post.

What's more, he realized with some trepidation that he had failed to spot the key issue of his latest appointment. While Zambawi was not a noted war zone, it had been a British colony until relatively recently. When the shit hit the fan in Lebanon, Iraq, Iran or Libya, it was always the Yanks who got the blame. But in Zambawi? He could already sense a rising bitterness directed towards the former colonial power.

As far as Digby-Stewart was concerned, Zambawi's President Adini was a pretty good egg. A curate's egg at worst. He was a dictator, of course. But Digby-Stewart had no inherent problem with that. As dictators went, Adini was really rather a nice chap: an Oxford croquet blue, a eunuch and a gentleman. Unlike many of his fellow African heads of state, he had never mentioned the notion of reparations, never caused a fuss in the Commonwealth, and he only killed his political enemies when absolutely necessary.

But the trouble that was now brewing stemmed from Adini's post-independence policy of racial reconciliation, a policy that was given the full support (and full development subsidies) of the British government. After the civil war white Zambawians had scuttled to the airports like rats to the bilges, fearing for their land and their lives. However, Adini – on the carefully worded advice of Downing Street – had proved to be less of a tyrant than the whites had feared. Few whites lost their land, none lost their lives and now, ten years later, the white minority (currently down to around three per cent) still owned eighty per cent of Zambawi's prime agricultural land. This, Digby-Stewart conceded, could be construed as somewhat unjust. However, the whites also contributed ninety per cent to the nation's GDP and ninety-four per cent of its foreign exports (mostly tobacco and sunflower seeds). So the fact that most whites managed to live the lifestyles of – well – colonial plantation owners was, Digby-Stewart concluded, only right and proper.

Indeed, the new British High Commissioner's first public airing had been on Zambawian state radio to defend this position in a live debate with one of the (then) surviving opposition leaders. In retrospect this seemed like less of a good idea – not least because his opponent was blown up on his toilet a fortnight later – but Digby-Stewart was adamant that he had said nothing wrong.

'We live in a totalitarian state,' the opposition leader had said. 'All we want is a true democracy and a free market of opportunity for all Zambawi's citizens. How can this be achieved when three-quarters of the land is still held by our white oppressors? How can this be achieved when three-quarters of the population still lives below the poverty line?'

Digby-Stewart felt he had handled the situation admirably. He scoffed when scoffing was called for, he questioned the value of statistics and he noted that 'a free market that strips the profits of the successful is no free market at all'. Indeed, President Adini himself had rung him to congratulate him on his stirring performance. However, Digby-Stewart was forced to concede that the President couldn't have been that impressed if he still felt the need to explode his opponent on the bog.

And now, as Digby-Stewart explained to the Foreign Office, the natives were restless. The mysterious Black Boot Gang were rampaging through the Zambawian bush, distributing their 'Africa for the Africans' propaganda and looting all manner of consumer goods. What's more, the Zambawian security forces had not managed to capture a single member of the infamous gang, which led Digby-Stewart to suspect a degree of army support. The number of attacks was increasing, the tension was rising and Digby-Stewart found himself in the strange position of wishing for the good old days of Tehran and the hostage crisis. Back then all you had to do was stand in front of a camera and make veiled, threatening reference to Islamic fundamentalists.

'The trouble with this country,' Digby-Stewart said to himself, 'is that there's no sense of order.'

At that moment a piercing shriek shattered the peace of the Commissioner's garden. Digby-Stewart's eyes shot open and he instinctively fumbled for his gun. The first thing he saw was his cook running towards him across the lawn with crazed eyes and a meat cleaver in hand. Then he saw the object of the cook's aggression: a chicken bearing down on him with blood spurting from where its head had once been.

'Headless chickens!' said Digby-Stewart and he took aim and fired. Seeing his boss raise the gun, the cook yelped and leaped into the swimming pool. The bullet winged the bird and it stopped still for a second. 'Don't fuck with me!' Digby-Stewart shouted. But the bird had no eyes, no ears and no brain and still it kept coming like a zombie. Now it was just a few feet from the sun lounger and the Commissioner unloaded the remaining five chambers into the persistent poultry. Bits of chicken – feathers and feet – were thrown into the air and the remainder crumpled to the ground like a burst pillow.

'Headless bloody chickens!' said Digby-Stewart and he lay back once again, closed his eyes and wished it would all go away.

7 : Gulu gulu

Unfortunately for Jim, Innocence Murufu did tell her family that her *musungu* teacher had made her *gulu gulu*. So he woke up the next morning to a banging hangover in his head and a banging fist on his door. Jim was confused. He could remember little about the preceding evening and only when he looked at his reflection in his small shaving mirror and saw the particles of puke clinging to his chin did the memories come flooding back.

'Oh God!' Jim groaned and reached for his bucket of water. He dipped into the bucket and was about to dab his face when he saw that his hand was also covered in puke. He looked into the bucket. More of the previous night's vomit coalesced into globules of vile matter in the rancid water. Jim promptly dry-retched.

The banging on the door continued.

'Who is it?' Jim shouted.

'It is I.'

'Who?'

Jim pulled on a pair of pants and lit a cigarette. Through his haze he noticed that the smell of smoke seemed to purify the stagnant air of his room.

He stumbled to his door and opened it. Immediately the sun blinded him.

'Shit!' Jim said and put his forearm over his eyes. Gradually he became accustomed to the light and he was confronted by a stranger. A small man. An old man. A smiling man. A small old smiling man who was brandishing an enormous machete.

'Fuck!' Jim said and slammed the door shut again.

For a moment there was silence. Jim pressed his back to the

door and his head was rushing. He realized with some distraction that his life was flashing before his eyes. He was less distracted by the narrative.

The banging started again.

'Mr Tulloh!'

'Who are you?'

'It is I, Mr Tulloh. Taurai Murufu. I want to speak with you.'

'You've got a machete!'

'A what?'

'A machete. A big knife.'

'Ah yes, Mr Tulloh! A big knife. A very big knife.'

'You're going to kill me.'

'Yes, Mr Tulloh.'

'Then I'm not letting you in.'

There was a moment or two's silence. Then a moment or two more. Jim put his ear to the door. Nothing. He put his eye to the keyhole. Nothing. More silence. Slowly Jim opened the door a crack. There was a small old smiling man with a big machete.

'Shit!' said Jim and slammed the door once again.

'Mr Tulloh?'

'Yes.'

'You cannot stay in there for ever.'

'Yes I can.'

'I am not going to kill you today, *musungu*.'

'Then why have you got a fucking machete?'

'Machete? Ah. My big knife. I just wanted you to see it.'

'What? Are you some kind of sadist?'

'Sadist?'

'Yeah. A sadist. Are you trying to torture me?'

'I don't understand, Mr Tulloh. My English is not good.'

'I said, are you playing games with me?'

'Games? Like football? This is not games, Mr Tulloh.'

Jim sighed. The smell of his room was beginning to make him queasy again. He needed to let in some air.

'Look,' Jim said, 'are you going to go away?'

'No, Mr Tulloh. I need to speak to you.'

'Do you promise you won't kill me?'

'I will not kill you today.'

'That'll have to do,' said Jim and opened the door. 'Come in.'

'Thank you, Mr Tulloh,' said the small old smiling man and he bowed his head slightly, raised his hands in front of his face – machete and all – and began to clap, a Zambawian custom of respect when entering someone's house that Jim found bizarre. Especially from his would-be murderer.

'There is a strange smell in here,' said Taurai Murufu.

'Yeah,' said Jim. 'Vomit.'

'Vomit? What is that?'

'It doesn't matter.'

For a moment or two Murufu stood uncertain in the middle of Jim's room. Jim took the opportunity to look him up and down and considered that, as hitmen went, Murufu was less than threatening. He couldn't have been more than five foot two, couldn't have been less than seventy-five years old and his battledress consisted of a threadbare jumper, outsized jeans that were tied at the waist with a piece of rope and an ancient pair of flip-flops – hardly all-terrain footwear. What's more, Murufu was rather unsteady on his feet, so Jim grabbed his only chair and thrust it towards the old man.

'Have a seat, Mr Murufu,' Jim said.

'Thank you,' said Murufu and sat down. Jim propped open his front door, deciding that the darkness had to be sacrificed for some fresh air, and sat, back to the wall, opposite his guest.

'Mr Tulloh,' Murufu began, 'you have come to Zambawi from overseas to teach our children the English tongue. You are a good man.'

'Thank you.'

'I am sorry that I am going to have to kill you.'

'So am I. Look, Mr Murufu, I don't know what Innocence has told you, but I swear to you, on my life, I did not do anything.'

Murufu looked at Jim and nodded slowly. Jim tried to distinguish the meaning of the old man's gaze and began to nod as well. Then Murufu started to shake his head. Jim shook his head too.

At last Murufu spoke. 'I think . . .'

'Yes?'

'I think I believe you, Mr Tulloh.'

'Thank God!'

'This makes it harder.'

'What?'

'Mr Tulloh, I am so sorry that I am going to have to kill you.'

'What? But I didn't do anything.'

'I know that, Mr Tulloh. But my daughter says that you made her *gulu gulu*.'

'But you said that you believed me! I didn't do anything. Your daughter's lying!'

Again Murufu shook his head sadly from side to side and his tiny frame shrank further into the chair. He looked almost embarrassed.

'I know, Mr Tulloh,' he said. 'Daughters. They will do anything to cause trouble. But who am I to believe? My daughter or a *musungu*?'

'But . . .'

Jim didn't know what to say. He felt helpless. He would have pressed his innocence harder but for the fact that he had no idea what *gulu gulu* was. And part of him was scared that he might actually be guilty. 'But she's lying!' he pleaded feebly.

'Of course, Mr Tulloh. But there is an old Zamba saying that I find helpful in this situation: *Vaurai enyu da zvalanaka, amai manganani, amai noka, ne amai mazinga chittingdingu.*'

Murufu paused, allowing the weight of his words to sink in. So Jim had to prompt a translation.

'What does that mean?'

'A daughter is like diarrhoea. She leaves you drained and empty but when she calls you have to answer.'

'Great!' said Jim. 'So you are going to kill me because your daughter says I made her *gulu gulu*. Even though I don't have the first clue what *gulu gulu* means and we're both agreed that she's lying.'

Murufu beamed from ear to ear.

'Exactly, Mr Tulloh. I am so glad that we understand each other.'

Jim suddenly felt very tired and the light that reflected off the old man's machete was beginning to give him a headache.

8 : Rujeko Tula

For three months after her arrival in Zambawi, Rujeko Tula, daughter of the exiled President of Mozola, did not leave the room she was allotted in the house that President Adini had given her father on the outskirts of Queenstown. She sat at the small desk with the brass-knobbed drawers and she stared at herself in the mirror for hours at a time. Sometimes she bared her teeth and looked at the small gap that a succession of governesses had described as 'charming'. Sometimes she opened her mouth as wide as it would go and watched the way her uvula dangled like an upside-down question mark. Sometimes she scraped her braids back from her forehead and tilted her chin as if posing for a photograph. Sometimes she stared into her own eyes so hard that she was sure she could make herself cry. But she never did.

She remembered her two years spent at a private boarding school in England and the way the white girls used to look at their reflections more than they looked at their books, as if only a mirror could affirm who they were. She remembered how, before one school disco, she had tentatively applied some eyeliner. One of her room-mates looked over her shoulder and said, 'You don't have to make yourself pretty. You're black.' Rujeko had never understood what that meant.

Before the coup toppled her father and the details of his atrocities (the genocide of the Ikbo in particular) shocked the Western media for the best part of two days, Rujeko Tula had been the face of Mozola. Her picture had appeared on banknotes and coins; it had hung in post offices and classrooms and hospitals; it had featured on a popular line of Java print above the words 'Rujeko – light of the world'.

On the day that she was evacuated from Mozola she was driven to the international airport through screaming crowds who burned the Mozolan flag and chanted 'Die! Die! Die!' Rujeko covered her ears and stared blankly at the fury while her father sipped a gin and tonic from the limousine's minibar and waved a dismissive dictator's hand. At one point a burning photograph of her face blew up against the limousine's windscreen and was held in place by the forward motion. Rujeko saw her features bubble and blister against the glass.

When Rujeko arrived in Zambawi, she learned that her twelve stepmothers and her twelve stepbrothers had been executed in Mozola by the rebel leadership. Even President Tula's favourite wife, a stone-eyed fifteen-year-old (three years younger than Rujeko), had suffocated with her mouth stuffed full of her own jewellery. When she heard this Rujeko felt no sorrow. But she was relieved that her mother had been put to death by her father six years previously for an accused but unproven infidelity. At least she had escaped the shame that Rujeko now felt.

One night, in her bedroom in her new Zambawian home, Rujeko was woken by a faint scratching sound in the bedroom. She switched on her table lamp and found a small gecko trying to climb the sheer surface of the mirror with its sticky feet struggling to grip. For every step the creature took up the smooth glass, it seemed to slide down two. On three occasions it slid all the way back to the desk. But it wouldn't give up its struggle and in the end it made it to the very top of the mirror's frame before darting up the wall. Rujeko watched it in fascination, the way the gecko's reflected stomach puffed and fell with effort, the way its tongue flicked in and out of its mouth in apparent concentration. Rujeko remembered that her mother used to call her 'Gecko' too. But since her execution the nickname had fallen out of favour. Rujeko decided to revive it there and then and vowed that 'Gecko' was how she would be known. In the morning she painted simple gecko shapes all over the mirror in bright pink lipstick until she could no longer see her face.

In the fourth month of her exile in Zambawi Gecko had to get out of the house and she travelled into Queenstown every day and sat on the lawns of Independence Square. She stared at the sky and wondered what it meant to be African, to be black, to be her. She listed the defining characteristics of Africanness in her mind and realized two things: that these characteristics were imposed rather than chosen and that they hardly applied to her. She wondered if she was the only African who found it strange to be black; not in a bad way, just something of a surprise. She wondered if blackness was really just a question of skin colour. And, if not, did she still qualify? And did she want to? She thought about what meanings could be rescued from her position as the daughter of an African Stalin (or the 'Butcher of Ikbo', as her father had been christened). And she couldn't think of any. Though she had always hated her father (for the murder of her mother and his arrogance and ignorance too), she had never known the full extent of his evil. Now that she did know, was there anything left of herself that could be reasonably salvaged? Probably not.

When she sat in Independence Square, Zambawian men approached her, making kissing noises through their teeth and saying, 'Hey, *sisi*!' and blunt passes in lewd Zamba. Gecko, though beautiful enough to make old men feel nostalgic, was not used to the attentions of the opposite sex because she was the daughter of President Tula and had therefore spent her adolescence off limits. Now that men were showing an interest, at first she didn't understand why. And when she realized why, she also realized that she didn't like it. As if they knew who she was! As if they knew what she was like! As if they knew anything about her!

For the next couple of months Gecko decided that she wanted to be an actress. She had acted at her English school – as a witch in *The Wizard of Oz* and the raven in an adaptation of the story of Noah – and though she was never the leading lady, her teachers always told her she had talent. Gecko liked the idea of assuming the personalities of another's imagination and she practised her

expressions in front of the mirror: anger and shyness and embarrassment and shame. When she pulled these faces, she sometimes
thought that she looked like a real person. Not like herself at all.

During this stage Gecko began to make compromises for her
father. She accompanied him to his meetings with important
businessmen and politicians who might support a counter-coup.
She sat demurely in the corner of luxurious offices while fat men
stared at her over their coffee cups and licked cream from their
lips. She dressed up in sequinned cocktail dresses for boring parties
in five-star hotels that were all attended by the same small group
of Queenstown's elite. She took her father's arm as he shook the
hands of cabinet ministers and lusted after their daughters, and
she smiled sweetly when the cabinet ministers lusted after her.

At one such party Gecko met two Zambawian sisters who wore
glossy red lipstick and identical, straightened bob wigs. They spoke
in quasi-American accents and tapped her repeatedly on the arm
to illustrate their every point. They talked of nothing but the merits
of men and the failings of women, and Gecko soon began to feel
irritable and claustrophobic. But they wouldn't leave her alone.

Towards the end of the evening Gecko noticed a commotion at
the doorway of the reception room and she found herself caught
by each elbow by the excitable sisters as they pointed and squealed.

'Tha's Enoch Adini sugar!' one squeaked. 'The President's son!'

'He sho's lookin' fine!' the other squawked.

At the doorway Gecko saw a tall, bored-looking young man
with his hands in his pockets. He was, she conceded, handsome.
But he looked so uninterested that she concluded he couldn't
possibly be interesting. He was surrounded two-deep by fawning
women, like piglets suckling a sow. And when he lit a Chesterman
cigarette the women cooed as though he'd done the cleverest thing
in the world.

Is this what I am? Gecko thought.

She found herself overwhelmed with revulsion and spite. She
caught sight of her father, who was staring down the cleavage of a
young woman who enjoyed such attention and she hated him more
than ever. She wiped her lipstick roughly from her mouth, she

unstacked her braids and scattered them down her back, she kicked off her high heels and marched out of the party. Gecko felt a new sense of release and remembered that she wasn't stupid at all.

After six months in Zambawi Gecko began to press her father to allow her to go to university in England. But her father's eyes turned the colour of storm clouds and he said that he needed her at his side. So Gecko began to buy books from a Queenstown bookstore to ensure that she wouldn't forget how to learn. The first book she bought was called *A Colonial State of Mind* by a Jamaican writer with a forgettable name. Much of the book seemed to be about the Zambawian independence war and the rest was about cricket and Gecko found it boring. However, she loved the introduction and she soon knew the twenty-page chunk near verbatim. She loved this section not because it gave her a new perspective but because it seemed to express her own thoughts with greater clarity than she possessed. And this, Gecko concluded, was what learning was all about.

She particularly liked the story of the five little boys in the sweet shop that was told under the grandiose heading 'The Pick 'n' Mix Theory of Identity':

Every day five little boys went to their local sweet shop to buy their quarter pound of treats from the pick 'n' mix counter. The first boy arrived promptly at 9 a.m. and, though his selection was limited by the treats on show and the amount of pocket money he'd been given by his mother, he thought he was the king of the sweet shop. He felt the excitement of his choice (however illusory) and if he wanted only jelly babies, he would say, 'I'll have what I damn well please!'

The other four boys arrived at the sweet shop at closing time, when the choice at the counter was depleted. The second boy bought a bag of discarded leftovers (either foul-tasting or broken) because he didn't realize what he'd missed. But the third and fourth and fifth boys saw the near-empty trays and were angry. They decided that they would rather go hungry than accept the sweets that no one else wanted.

One day, the five little boys all arrived at the sweet shop in the morning. The first boy made his customary selection even though he was now so fat and unhealthy that he could barely keep his balance. The second boy too made his customary selection because he was so used to his disgusting sweets that he thought they were what he wanted. The third boy saw the breadth of choice available to him and immediately spent all his money on all manner of sweets. Despite the first boy's ill health, the third boy desperately wanted to have everything he had. The fourth boy was still too angry to buy sweets, so he decided to go hungry again. And as for the fifth boy? The fifth boy looked at the wide selection of sweets available and realized that he didn't actually want any of them. So he put his pocket money back in his wallet and left the shop.

When the little boys were all grown up, the first man went to work for his father, who owned the sweet factory. His father immediately made him a director, although the man was now so fat that he couldn't fit into the lift and his father had to build him an office on the ground floor. The second man also went to work for the father. But he was given a job on the factory floor and he was happy because he didn't know any better. The third man applied to the father for a job in management. But the father wouldn't give him a job because he was now too fat to fit into the lift. The fourth man didn't want a job in the father's factory, so he stood at the factory gates instead and insulted the workers who were going in and out. And the fifth man? The fifth man opened a factory of his own with all the money he'd saved instead of buying sweets. His factory produced fresh fruit and soon everybody realized that fresh fruit was healthier than sweets and they all wanted to work for him.

In the seventh month of her Zambawian exile Gecko took to walking the streets of downtown Queenstown where the unemployed men openly beat their wives and the prostitutes stood on street corners laughing like the happiest people in the world. She saw the *musungu* farmers, in the city for the tobacco auctions, pay twice the going rate and skulk through the alleys with their faces rigid with disdain. She saw the legless veterans of the Zambawian independence war wheel themselves through the gutters on make-shift skateboards and roll enormous joints from the pages of the *Zambawi National Herald.* She saw the suited owners of small businesses, whose hard noses told of a ruthlessness learned in a *musungu*'s employ. She saw street kids by the dozen who scavenged the dustbins and took more kickings than the stray dogs.

Eight months after arriving in Zambawi Gecko began to avoid the downtown and walked straight to Queenstown's Mbave Bus Station instead. She liked to watch the bustle of the crowds, the smiling faces of people who were going somewhere else or had just arrived, the diligent hawkers who sold mangoes from tin bowls and the feisty bus conductors who touted for business. She wondered at this vibrant economy and concluded that poverty must be the natural concomitant of such hard work. Either that or the economic structure of post-colonial Zambawi was still geared to benefit the minority, be they black or white.

Sometimes the bus conductors would approach her where she sat on a wooden bench. '*Munondipe, sisi?*' they asked. And she under-stood the question because her Zamba was improving all the time.

'I'm not going anywhere,' she would reply.

On one occasion, however, she was approached by a scruffy young Rastafarian who had descended from the Zimindo Province bus. As soon as he jumped off the bottom step, the man walked directly towards her as if he thought she'd come to meet him. Gecko's heart skipped a little; she felt nervous and irritated.

'*Munozva kape, sisi?*' the man asked and his voice was bewitch-ing, deep and vibrant enough to give the simple question an almost moral weight.

'Mozola,' Gecko replied without thinking.

'*Ne munondipe?*'

'I'm not going anywhere.'

'Ah! You speak the English mother tongue! "Long is the way and hard, that out of hell leads up to light" – Milton. We are all going somewhere, my sister.'

And Gecko realized that he was right and she was enchanted by the archaic lilt of his language and the profundity of his tone. Sitting on the wooden bench, Gecko talked to the young Rastafarian for two hours and he told her all about the Black Boot Gang.

9 : Cultural Venn diagrams and the inspiring effects of terminal boredom

Enoch, the President's son, was bored. Enoch was always bored. Enoch was so bored that he barely knew he was bored any more. Enoch's boredom was more a chronic condition than an acute pain. Kind of like colour-blindness. Enoch had been bored for so long that he didn't know what he was missing.

The trouble was, Enoch reflected, that it was hard being young and rich and black in Queenstown. It was the combination that was the killer. Young and poor and black was fine: you were like everyone else, one of the crowd, unremarkable. Old and rich and black was fine. So you stood out? So what? You had a twelve-foot electric fence, a pack of Dobermanns and a sub-machine-gun in the gazebo. And any kind of white was fine because you were too busy relishing the chips on your shoulders to notice your repetitious lifestyle. But young and rich and black was deadly.

Your social circle was so claustrophobically small. There were about 500 young, rich, black people in Queenstown. Of those, half could be ruled out at a stroke because they wanted to be white. 'The Noses', they were called. Because they spoke in those ridiculous starched *musungu* accents, looked down their noses at you when they talked and went to *musungu braais* to eat red meat and apologize for the state of the nation.

A further 100 could be ruled out as too old (over twenty-five) or too young (under sixteen). If they were too old, then they could remember the civil war. Perhaps they had even fought in it. This was bad since it imbued them with something more boring than boredom itself: political consciousness. The twenty-five-to-thirties would have meetings conducted entirely in Zamba (even though it was generally their second language) to discuss the application of Marxist thought to post-colonial Africa. And Enoch noticed that these young, rich, black people didn't have 'friends' but 'comrades', not 'opinions' but 'ideologies', not 'lives' but 'agenda'. And it was boring. And the under-sixteens? Well, their lack of sexual experience rendered them intrinsically boring. But, on top of that, with no memory of independence or colonialism at all, Enoch would say that they had been 'born to Nose'.

So that left only 150 like-minded young, rich blacks for Enoch to choose from. But the whittling process hadn't finished. Of those 150, you had to lose at least fifty more to sundry other discriminations. At least ten had tried to solve the boredom through marriage (in Enoch's opinion, a risky business), another dozen suffered from *torpor neurosa* (clinical boredom severe enough to constitute madness) and maybe a further twenty were sullied by some kind of sexually transmitted disease (everything from AIDS to pregnancy). Was that it? No. What about the six young, rich blacks who had driven across the border into the war zone of Mozola in search of boredom relief and found nothing but a landmine? What about the young, rich, black queens who hung out in the cabaret bars of Queenstown's five-star hotels?

You could go on whittling for ever. Of the remaining 100, nature dictates that fifty were women. And of those fifty, Enoch must have fucked and chucked half of them. And the other half were the first half's friends. So there were fifty young, rich, black men left for Enoch to hang out with and that was before he'd even considered whom he might actually like. Damn! It was no wonder he was so bored.

But even if you managed to come to terms with the fact that there was no one to do it with, you had to deal with its twin dilemma: that there was nothing to do. You could work. But why work when you were so rich? You could study. But learning for learning's sake? It didn't appeal to Enoch. His minimal experience of education had been less than rewarding, all *shamboks* and *schadenfreude*.

Sex. Now sex was something Enoch had tried to pass the time.

But even that had accompanying problems of its own. Once you had fucked your way through all the young, rich blacks who would have you – a trial in itself (see above) – you were left with very few options. Of course, there were plenty of prostitutes. But that was like playing Zambawian roulette with your penis, with five out of six chambers holding a lethal STD. Then there were the tourists. But *musungu* women, in Enoch's experience, simply didn't know how to have sex. They would push you on the bed and bounce up and down, whooping like demented baboons. Enoch remembered that the colonial *musungu* thought that blacks were closer to apes. And he wondered if these white men had ever had sex with their own women before coming to such a conclusion.

So that left drink and drugs. And you could only get so drunk before making yourself sick. And you could only get so high before you farted yourself to a dead faint.

Surely, Enoch concluded, there was nothing for it but to get the hell out of the country. But for that he would need his father's help.

Enoch had been considering all these weighty issues of age and wealth and race as he drove his BMW back towards the presidential residence on the outskirts of Queenstown. He had been drinking at the Barrel, the bar attached to the Queenstown Sun Hotel. He was depressed to realize that he had been drinking in this bar for every night of the previous week. Question: was there anywhere else to go? Answer: no.

Enoch pulled up to the gates of his dad's house and waited for them to open. When they did not, he hooted his horn irritably at the pill box next to the gate, revved his engine and squinted his eyes to look for Isaiah, the guard on duty. Suddenly there was a tap on the window next to him. Enoch started and looked round to be confronted by a man in a balaclava. And a gun. An AK47. Army issue.

'Fuck!' Enoch said.

'In the name of the Black Boot Gang and the Democratic People's Republic of Zambawi, get out of the car!' the man snarled.

'No.'

'Get out of the car!' the man shouted.

'No.'

'Get out of the car!' the man pleaded.

'Why?'

'Because I've got a gun.'

Enoch looked the man square in the eye. He could see another shadowy figure standing behind and he noticed, for the first time, an old Volkswagen Combi parked just up the road. Where the hell were the presidential guard?

At that moment Enoch discovered the single greatest consequence of acute boredom. He realized that he was so bored that he was reckless. And he found that recklessness was only one step away from courage. Enoch reached into his pocket and pulled out the novelty cigarette lighter that General Bulimi had brought him back from the Commonwealth conference in Edinburgh. It was in the shape of a Walther PPK, complete with an ornate bone butt and realistic chrome barrel.

'So have I,' Enoch said.

'Get out of the car or I'll shoot you.'

'No,' Enoch said. 'I'll shoot you. Why do you want me to get out of the car?'

'We're going to kidnap you.'

'Well, then, I'm definitely not going to get out of the car. What happened to the guard at the gate? Where's Isaiah? Isaiah happens to be a friend of mine and if you've hurt him, I swear I will fucking shoot you.'

'Oh God!' the masked man said. 'I knew this wouldn't work.'

The would-be kidnapper backed away from the car to consult with his partner in crime. They appeared to argue. Enoch realized that he still had the engine running and he could easily drive away: either crash through the presidential gates – which would be entertaining – or spin back into Queenstown. But he decided to stay where he was. He hadn't had this much fun in years. So instead he shouted at the men, 'This is the most incompetent kidnapping I've ever seen! Fuck! You two are useless! You two couldn't get laid in a brothel!'

Now he had them riled and the second man grabbed the gun from the first and approached the window. He smashed the butt feebly into the driver's window. Not a scratch.

'Bullet-proof glass,' lied Enoch smugly.

'Get out of the car, sir!' the second man shouted.

'Sir? Well, at least you're polite. Hold on a minute. I know you. Take off that balaclava. Go on. Take it off.'

The second man shuffled back a step or two and let slip a distinctive high-pitched giggle that clinched it for Enoch.

'All right, then,' he said. 'Have it your own way. But I'd recognize that silly laugh anywhere. I know it's you, Isaiah. So what the hell do you think you're playing at?'

'I am not Isaiah,' said Isaiah with an unconvincing change of accent. 'I am Dubchek of the Black Boot Gang.'

'Of course you are Isaiah,' Enoch said. 'Look. Just open the gates, let me go to bed and we'll say no more about it.'

Enoch was getting cocky. He lowered his electric window, lent out of the car and pointed his cigarette lighter between Isaiah's eyes.

'Look, Isaiah. You need me alive, whereas I'll happily kill the pair of you. So just open the fucking gates before I decide to shoot you.'

For a moment the two men looked at one another. Enoch was loving every minute of it. Isaiah was shitting himself. 'Yes, sir,' he said and went to open the gates.

As Enoch drove into the presidential grounds past the bizarre sight of two saluting Gangers, he leaned out of the window again. 'Thanks, boys,' he shouted. 'You've made my night. Try again tomorrow?'

10 : Just because you're paranoid, they're still out to get you

President Zita Adini was feeling lonely and angry. This was not a new state. He was permanently lonely and angry and he was used to it. But he couldn't help but wonder if these troubled times were beginning to intensify the feelings. And this thought was depressing and made him feel lonelier and angrier still.

He lit his pipe, opened his smoking jacket and slipped a hand through the fly of his paisley nightshirt. With dexterity born of years of practice, he began to circulate his balls around the flat palm of his hand with rhythmic movements of his fingers. Five years previously, at the World Environment Summit in Tokyo, Adini had noticed the Chinese delegates doing something similar with brightly painted metal globes that chimed as they touched. A relaxation technique, they had said.

Adini had adopted a modified version with his testicles. It wasn't much help on the relaxation front – there was no sonorous tinkling for starters – but it did at least grant his rubber testicles a sense of purpose that he cherished. Although that didn't stop him wishing that their function was more sexual than executive toy.

Adini was angry because the Black Boot Gang had had the temerity to attack his presidential home. He was angry because the Gangers had terrorized his trusted gateman to such an extent that Isaiah had put in a request for transfer. He was angry because the Gangers didn't understand the complexity of the 'land issue'. He was angry because of Enoch.

Adini was lonely because the failed attack had left him feeling more isolated than ever. He was lonely because, with Sally eight years buried, he had nobody to talk to. He was lonely because only he understood the complexity of the 'land issue'. He was lonely because of Enoch.

He sucked on his pipe and sighed heavily. He had a lot to think about but the state of his mind was in danger of becoming as messy as the state of the nation.

'In the first place, my mind keeps wandering,' he said aloud.

But before he had even finished that sentence, he found himself reflecting on the incompetence of the presidential guard. And then on the death of his wife. And then on the land issue. And then on his troublesome son. And he didn't even list these anxieties in numerical order.

His thoughts went something like this: 'How the hell did the Gangers manage to get so close to my home? My home, for goodness' sake! They tie up Isaiah, steal his gun and try to force him to open the gates. For goodness' sake, where were the rest of the presidential guard? *Quod erat demonstrandum*. It smacks of an inside job. You can't trust anyone these days. Except Isaiah. A gun to his head, his life on the line and still he stays loyal to his President! I must send him a gift or some such thing. Perhaps a promotion. No. A chicken or a side of beef would be more appropriate. A personal token.

'The guard. Are they incapable or insidious (from the Latin: *insidia*, meaning "ambush")? They are certainly incapable. What about Sally's funeral? Dear Sally! A wife that put up with everything: from a good-for-nothing son to good-for-nothing testicles. But the guard even managed to make a mess of her funeral. Dear Sally! Such jokers! All I wanted was a volley over the grave! The eyes of the world on Zambawi and my elite guard put four of the cabinet into hospital. For goodness' sake! Such an embarrassment! Thank goodness nobody was killed! Thank goodness they missed the Prince of Wales!

'I must visit the grave. Heroes Acre. It is good for the people to see my sensitive side. It makes them feel patriotic. Reminds them of the war.

'But I hear that Heroes Acre has been appropriated by the townships. Who was telling me this? General Bulimi. I have known him twenty years and I can see that his resolve is faltering. He was never going to cut it as a soldier. He should have remained a poet.

'And now they turn Heroes Acre into a vegetable garden. For goodness' sake, imagine that! The townships are growing rape and tomatoes on my dear wife's plot. It is not good enough! Poor Sally!

'It is all about land. All these questions come back to land. A nation three times the size of the UK and still we argue about land. What am I supposed to do? I seize land from the whites – how I would love to do that! – and we lose all our ForEx, investment and the support of Downing Street, for goodness' sake! But I do nothing and people start to listen to the Black Boot Gang. As if they could do any better! If only I knew who they were. The cowards! How am I supposed to deal with political opposition if I don't know who to kill? And they say that *I* have no balls!

'It is Enoch's fault. My own son and he brings me nothing but shame, gallivanting around Queenstown as if he owned the place! Drinking with his friends all day, bringing loose women to my house all night, and now he plays childish tricks on me. Me! The President! The boy needs a sense of responsibility. But what is a father to do?'

At that moment a knock at the door of the presidential office disturbed Adini from his rambling daydreams and, without waiting for an answer, in strolled the main object of his anger and the cause of his loneliness. Adini pointed at his son.

'You!' he spluttered. 'You have no respect!'

'All right, Dad? What's up?'

'Don't you "all right, Dad" me! We have a situation here and you can do nothing but try to ridicule me! Don't you have any responsibility? Already many people are calling for my head over the "land issue" and you want to make more trouble for me with your childish tricks.'

Enoch sat down in a leather-backed chair and tried a conciliatory smile. He was feeling a lot stoned and a little guilty. But he hadn't believed that the President's entourage could fail to notice the wide bumper sticker he'd affixed to the presidential limousine – 'Just because you're paranoid, they're still out to get you.'

It wasn't his fault that it had remained in place through a full day of presidential engagements. It was only a joke.

'It was only a joke, Dad,' Enoch said.

'Well, Mr It-Was-Only-A-Joke, I tell you. Life is not just a pint of beer, you know. Do you want to give my opponents more fuel for their engines? What am I to think when I cannot even trust my own household?'

'Quite,' Enoch said. And he sighed. He hated listening to his father like this, all pompous passion and poor metaphors. He pressed his knuckles into his puffy eye sockets. He was tired and the bright lights of the office were beginning to quicken his smoky heart rate.

'Look at Isaiah . . .' the President began again.

'What about him?'

'He puts his life on the line for the presidential person. And yet my own son is nothing but a troublemaker!'

'Look, Dad, I'm sorry about the sticker, OK? It was only a joke. But I wouldn't put too much faith in Isaiah if I were you.'

'What? You criticize the man who saved my life? And yours too, I shouldn't wonder.'

'No, Dad. All I'm saying . . .'

'I don't want to know what you're saying. You think you understand the life of the politician? You do not understand anything. I have to stand up for what is right. I have responsibilities. One: to myself. Two: to my people. Three: to my partner governments. Four: most of all, I have a responsibility to the truth. You cannot even imagine how that feels. I have to stand up for what is right and all you can do is say that I am paranoid!'

For a moment Adini and his son stared at each other. And for a moment they shared the same thought. Can this really be my son, thought Adini, with no sense of honour, shame or modesty? Can this really be my father, thought Enoch, with no sense of humour, sham or modesty?

Enoch wanted to answer his father. He was always astonished by the ease with which his father could trot out these political platitudes. He didn't actually believe them, did he? Surely not. The only responsibility to truth that his father felt was to ensure it never came out. And yet he spouted this kind of bullshit so often that he made it sound quite convincing.

Enoch was considering his reply – along the lines of 'Look, Dad, you're my father and all that but, let's face it, you're nothing but another two-bit African dictator with more Swiss bank accounts than sense and a paranoia born of thieving' – when the *gar* he had been smoking in his bedroom finally penetrated his bowels.

'Look, Dad,' Enoch began and pressed his buttocks deep into his chair to try and muffle the pernicious gas that was seeping silently from his arse. But Adini's nose was already twitching.

'What's that smell?' the President snapped.

'Smell?' asked Enoch innocently. 'What smell?'

'That smell. It's disgusting. Oh God! Quick!'

And, with that, President Adini suddenly dropped to his knees, cupped a hand over his mouth and began to crawl across the polished floorboards towards the door. Enoch watched his father, nonplussed.

'Dad!' Enoch said, trying to ignore the tickle of the hot wind escaping across his buttocks, 'What on earth are you doing?'

'Gas!' Adini cried. 'They're trying to gas me! Can't you smell it? Quick. We must get out of here! Stay low!'

Enoch stayed exactly where he was and watched the roll of his father's backside as he hurried on all fours towards the door. Was this really happening? Or was he just stoned? He began to giggle, silent but helpless. Now his father's nightshirt had ridden up and he could see the famous prosthetic testicles bouncing around in their sack as only rubber balls could. He began to cry with laughter and his head buzzed as the smell of his fart swelled and filled the President's office.

'And you're not paranoid?' spluttered Enoch at his father's disappearing arse.

11 : The Poet (two)

From the moment of his birth Indigo Bulimi was a remarkable child. But nobody realized this because he couldn't speak. Attendant neighbours at the birth *were* astonished to see that baby Indigo emerged with his eyes open. However, they put this down to the age of his mother.

'She is thirty-eight years old,' they said to one another. 'Of course, the baby's eyes are open. He has been waiting for this moment for more than two decades.'

Maybe the more sensitive adults looked down into Indigo's alert, wildly curious eyes and noted an unusual degree of enquiry. But, if so, they never said anything. And Father and Mother Bulimi certainly never picked up on it.

If Indigo had been able to speak from birth, you can bet he would have been asking questions. Of course he would. But the questions would have been extraordinary and disturbing. As the old woman cut his umbilical cord, Indigo's screams were not merely fuelled by natural fear of the unknown. No. Indigo screamed in frustration at the wordless impressions that filled his raw mind, impressions of detachment, classification and self. And as the old woman's rheumatoid fingers knotted his belly button, so Indigo felt that she was tying him into something he'd had no part in choosing. No wonder he screamed.

In the early months it was the questions of classification that bothered him most. Not for Indigo worries about his next meal or shit or burp. He was desperate to disassemble the world around him. What was the difference between milk and piss? Why was *his* food served through soft flesh? Why were the fawning adults blessed with different names when he could distinguish them only by smell? Why did the floor and wall deserve different words, when the roof – for all its angles – was known simply as 'roof'? Sometimes, as Father Bulimi bent towards him, Indigo would reach up his little hands and, though this was not what he wanted, his father would pick him up. Indigo just wanted his hands to make sense of the features that were so confusing to his eyes. Sometimes it all got too much for him and, as he sat on his mother's lap, he would try and burrow his way back where he had come from. But his limbs were so weak and unresponsive to his will.

One would have expected such a precocious child to begin speaking sooner than the average. In fact, quite the opposite was true and the infant was a full two years old before he uttered his first word: 'Indigo'. Father and Mother Bulimi worried that this late development was some sign of retardation. Actually Indigo had learned numerous other words – from 'Dad' to 'roof' – a year previously but he had not wanted to label anything else before he could label himself, and 'Indigo' proved to be a tricky word on which to cut his milk teeth. So Indigo bided his time and practised his name at a whisper when his mother was not looking.

As a toddler, Indigo liked nothing better than to play in the communal toilet ditch that had been dug directly behind the Bulimis' house. When his mother was hanging out the washing, he would stumble to the ditch, sit down on its lip and allow himself to slide forward into the mass of smelly excrement. Indigo felt sorry for shit. It was so formless.

Of course, Mother Bulimi was after him in a flash and dragged him out by the arms with a cross word and a slap. But not before Indigo managed to award names to a few of the more consistent turds.

Almost thirty years later, when General Indigo Bulimi looked back at his childhood, he could remember little of its resonances, still less of the detail. And, with his parents long buried, there was no one to confirm or deny the frustrating, wordless impressions of youth that filled his cooked mind. Of course, he did not remember that he had been born with his eyes open; nor his development of the word 'Indigo' on soft, childish lips; nor even the joy he'd found in his games in the lavatory ditch. And he would often reflect on the inconsistencies of memory, as formless as a shit and not so satisfying.

So much stuff in my head, he thought, and yet it is all as unchosen as life itself. That is why it is so important to classify! To classify! To classify! Why is it that I can remember the precise location of every battalion from the Great Lake in the West to the Mountains in the East? As if soldiering has done me any good! Why is it that I can remember every last word of Wole Soyinka:

– Fruits then to your lips; haste to repay
The debt of birth. Yield man-tides like the sea
And ebbing, leave a meaning on the fossiled sands.

As if poetry has done me any good!

When he thought these things, General Bulimi always felt guilty. He felt guilty that poetics now had all the acuity of a *zvoko* thistle in a rhino hide. He felt guilty that he could not remember his middle-aged mother's fading days of beauty.

In fact, Indigo's earliest defined memories came from around the age of three, when Father Bulimi used to take him into the *shabeen*. This was the deal that Father Bulimi had struck with his wife: he was granted a weekly drink in return for a child-free evening.

Father Bulimi would chat away the day with the other men and their melancholy eyes would briefly clear. They moaned about the intransigence of their boss; they giggled coyly at tales of glimpsing Madam in the shower; they laughed heartily at the tantrums of their wives when they returned home late and drunk. Indigo was not interested in such conversations and he played on the floor among the discarded bottle tops, chicken bones and corn snacks.

Sometimes, however, when the night ran late and the beer more freely than his father intended, the local men gathered around Father Bulimi in a cosy ritual that fascinated the child.

'N'dgo,' the men would say, 'tell us one of your stories.'

Indigo's ears pricked up at the sound of what he thought was his own name and he picked his way through the tree-trunk legs to where Father Bulimi sat on the one bar stool. His father drained his beer, shook his head and gathered Indigo up on to his knee.

'No,' Father Bulimi would say with a smile. 'It is time I put my son to bed. His mother will be worried.'

But the drunken men would continue to press and encourage. 'Are you ruled by your wife, N'dgo?' they would ask. And a fresh beer was thrust into Father Bulimi's willing grasp.

'All right! All right!' Father Bulimi would concede. 'Just one story and that's your lot!'

And the men sat quietly around the bar stool like eager children while Indigo bounced on his father's knee.

Father Bulimi must have known a dozen stories. No more. And it wasn't long before Indigo had heard them all a dozen times. But the deep tone of his voice and the implacable gravity of his face never failed to keep his audience in rapt attention. He told how the mountains in the East came to kiss the sky. He told how Tuloko – the Traveller, the first great chief, the Child of the Horizon – had travelled to Zambawi on the back of a mighty eagle from far beyond the Lake in the West That Cooled the Traveller's Feet. He told how the rivers of Zambawi tried to drown Tuloko for betraying them to Father Sun.

Sometimes, as Father Bulimi spoke, Indigo would watch the assembled faces and see the way some men mouthed the words of each story as if they were singing along. But nobody ever interrupted.

On those late nights Indigo would lie awake for hours, snug between the beery heat of his father on one side and the soft perfume of his mother on the other. Usually Mother Bulimi scolded her husband for an hour or more before her anger dissolved once again into devoted love. But Indigo never listened to such disagreements; they were no more than soundtracks to the cinema of his imagination.

As he stared up into the pitch blackness, Indigo repeated his father's stories word for word through silent lips. And as the words breathed from his lungs, so their substances materialized in the darkness above him: great warriors with skin that shone like polished stone, spears that whistled as they flew, and the noble chief, Tuloko, with his high forehead, proud chin and generous eyes.

Gradually, as the stories came to him ever more easily, Indigo began to add his own signature to each twist and turn. At first this meant no more than the odd word, added detail or sentence of description. But, in time, Indigo would reorder his father's tales into a more pleasing rhythm so that they fell from his mouth with the reassuring beat of raindrops on the roof. He added characters to each tale, sidekicks and lovers and treacherous uncles. He concocted sub-plots and cul-de-sacs that teased his mind with their possible significance. He made up stories of his own.

Thirty years later General Indigo Bulimi could still remember the first story he told. It was a summer day in the middle of October and all of the children of Mutengwazi were sweeping the dust from their houses. But it was too hot for work and one by one the children gave up their chores and began to mill around in the shade beneath the *shabeen*'s Coca-Cola sign, next to the Bulimis' house. The children were restless and irritable. It was too hot even to play and the water in the pipes was tepid and unsatisfying.

Indigo had never told one of his stories aloud before. He had never wanted to. However, that day, there was something almost magical about the silence of the choking heat and the dust that spun in eddies between the houses. And as Indigo laid down his broom and sat among the other children, he knew that the time had come. He had just turned ten years old.

'I am going to tell you a story,' he announced.

'You?' one of the children said. 'I don't want to hear your story.'

'Yes, you do,' Indigo said confidently. 'It is a story of the Great Chief Tuloko that you have never heard before. So there.'

Slowly the other children quietened down and arranged themselves in an orderly circle around him.

'Many years ago . . .' Indigo began.

'How many years?' interrupted an older girl with her hair in corn rows.

Indigo wasn't very good with numbers and he had to think for a moment.

'What is the highest number you know?' he asked.

'Eight hundred and forty-three!' said the girl proudly.

'Well,' he said, 'the time I tell you about was long before 843 years ago.'

The girl looked impressed and Indigo relaxed a little.

'Many years ago,' he began again, 'when the Great Chief Tuloko was still a young man – younger than all your fathers, before he married Mudiwa – a great trouble came to his village. It started one night in the rainy season when the wind howled like a spirit, rivers fell from the sky and Cousin Moon offered no comforting light. The villagers huddled together in their houses, fearful that they must have offended the ancestors.

'In the morning, when Father Sun rose and made the mud smoke like a fire, a terrible discovery was made. One of the girls' houses was completely destroyed and all the children were gone. At first the villagers thought that the spirit of the wind had carried them away. But, in the rubble where the house once stood, the Great Chief Tuloko found a *shumba*'s claw the length of a hunting knife. "There is a rogue *shumba* on the prowl," Tuloko said.'

'How many girls were taken?' asked the girl with the corn rows.

'Three,' said Indigo.

'How old were they?'

'It was a *chinjuku* house,' Indigo said. 'They were your age.'

The girl shivered and Indigo felt a tingle of excitement in his stomach.

'Great Chief Tuloko addressed the men of the village. "My brothers!" he said. "We must hunt this *shumba* down before he kills any more of our families. We do not know who will be next. But every *shumba* returns to the scene of its last kill. Who will come with me?"

'But the men of the village were afraid. "Tuloko," they said, "Father Sun appointed you chief of our people and he protects you. So you must protect us." And they refused to join the hunt.

'That night the air was still and silent and Cousin Moon shone down and the villagers huddled together in the dark corners of their houses. The fearful villagers stayed awake all night and nothing could be heard but the echoing snores of the Great Chief Tuloko. And yet, when Father Sun rose in the morning, another villager had been seized by the terrible rogue *shumba*, a widow called N'tendu.

'Again the Great Chief Tuloko appealed to the men of the village to join him on the hunt. Again they refused. "Tuloko," they said, "you are protected by Father Sun, but who will protect us?" But as the men hid their cowardice behind their words, a small boy came forward. His name was N'kimwi. He was the widow's son.

'"Great Chief Tuloko," N'kimwi said, "five winters ago my father was taken by disease. Now my mother is gone too. There is nothing left for me in this village. Allow me to accompany you on this hunt, for I am entitled to vengeance."

'The Great Chief Tuloko looked at the small boy and admired the courage that fired his eyes and the pride that straightened his spine.

'"Your heart beats well, N'kimwi," Tuloko said. "Stronger than that of any man in this village. But I cannot take you on this hunt, for you are just a small boy and the last of your line. Think how angry your ancestors would be if you too were killed! No! I must hunt alone."'

'How old was N'kimwi?' asked the girl with the corn rows.

'He was *temba*,' Indigo said. 'About the same age as me.'

'That's the same age as me too!' said Comfort, the skinny child who lived in the house opposite the Bulimis. Strangely Indigo had never spoken to him. But he knew his voice well enough from the screams he heard when Comfort's father administered his daily beating.

'The same age as most of us,' Indigo said conspiratorially and he turned his head around the attentive faces, revelling in their wide eyes and bitten lips.

'When Father Sun drew himself up to his full height, the Great Chief Tuloko took up his spear and his hunting knife and packed himself a small knapsack of mealy biscuits and fruit. "I will kill the *shumba*," Tuloko said, "or I will die in the attempt!" And he marched into the bush in search of the rogue *shumba*. The sun was unbearably hot but Tuloko, the Great Chief, the Traveller, was accustomed to such hardship.

'All day Tuloko marched, following the *shumba*'s trail. He hoped to catch the *shumba* sleeping off the widow in the heat of the afternoon sun. But the trail wound on until even Tuloko, even the Traveller, found himself in unfamiliar country. Indeed, the Great Chief Tuloko was about to return home, for the shadows were biting his ankles, when he heard the *shumba*'s roar. Ahead of him on the path he saw the rogue *shumba*, as tall as a house, as wide as the Queenstown bus, with a mane that was as silver as a waterfall at dawn. The air was heavy with the smell of death.

'The Great Chief Tuloko stopped still and drew his hunting knife. But already the terrible beast was charging towards him. "Father Sun!" Tuloko cried. "Grant me the strength of the light!" But Father Sun had reached the doorstep of the West and could not hear him. "Cousin Moon!" Tuloko cried. "Grant me the cunning of the night!" But Cousin Moon was not yet risen in the sky.

'Before he knew it, the *shumba* was upon him. The Great Chief Tuloko threw his spear, but it bounced from the *shumba*'s muscular flank. He thrust his hunting knife towards the *shumba*'s face, but the beast struck him down with a paw, like a grown man swatting a mosquito. In seconds the rogue *shumba* had pinned the Great Chief to the ground and its claws cut five long gashes across his chest. Tuloko could smell the scent of the *chinjuku* girls on its breath and he could taste the blood of the widow on the saliva that dripped on to his face from the *shumba*'s mouth. "Oh, my people," the Great Chief Tuloko cried, "have you deserted me?" And he prepared himself for death.

'Suddenly another voice cut through the murky light like the striking of a match. "Stop!" There, at no further distance than a small boy could piss, stood the widow's child, N'kimwi. "Stop!" he said again.

'For a second the *shumba* paused and turned his attention to this intruder to his kill. The *shumba* showed N'kimwi its teeth. It showed N'kimwi the confident wag of its tail and the evil terror of its eyes. But N'kimwi did not run away.

'"You do not scare me, *shumba*!" N'kimwi said. "For you are nothing but a foolish animal. You have taken my mother, but you do not scare me. You have captured the Great Chief Tuloko, but you do not scare me. For you have no honour. Your ancestors do not protect you, for you cannot pray to them. Your family do not respect you, for you can tell them nothing of your fighting and your conquests. Your descendants will never sing praise-songs to the glory of your courage. Your blood is as thin as the water of a *shamva* river, your life as joyless as a stagnant pond, your existence as meaningless as a shallow puddle that vanishes in the morning sun. You do not scare me, *shumba*, for one day you will die and nobody will mourn. Your corpse will be eaten by the jackals, but they will leave your heart because it is blackened stone. Your eyes will be pecked out by vultures, but they will leave your heart because it is blackened stone. The maggots will strip your bones, but they will leave your heart because it is blackened stone. Even the smallest of the creatures of Father Sun will find no sustenance in your heart and it will be the only monument to your life until the summer winds blow and cover it in dust. Then you will be nothing."

'When the *shumba* heard this, it let out a roar so terrifying that it could be heard by the cowardly villagers a full day's walk away. The villagers looked at one another and said, "What can this mean?" But N'kimwi wasn't scared. And as the *shumba* roared, the Great Chief Tuloko saw his chance. Taking up his hunting knife, he plunged it deep into the *shumba*'s neck and, before the *shumba* fell dead in the dust, the roar was strangled in its throat. And, for just one instant, it sounded like a screaming child.'

Even so many years later General Indigo Bulimi remembered the excitement on the other children's faces as the story built to its climax. And he remembered countless other afternoons over the next two years and countless other stories, told in the shade of the Coca-Cola sign. But that first story remained his favourite, with its quickening beat and thrilling conclusion. Many years later Indigo had tried to translate the story into English – for English was the language he loved – but, curiously, he found that the translation seemed to strip the tale of all its childhood passion.

Every now and then General Indigo Bulimi would recite his first story to himself on lonely evenings. He would return to his small apartment on the Queenstown barracks, strip off his uniform and relax into his favourite chair. Then he wrapped himself in the comforting texture of his childish words, watching the characters play out his narrative in the cinema of his mind's eye, just as he had on those sleepless nights so many years before. Sometimes these memories led to others. Sometimes he remembered the day of his twenty-third birthday, when he had stopped being a poet and become a soldier. Sometimes this memory made him cry.

12 : How Jim Tulloh took the piss

Jim looked around the laughing faces and felt like an outsider.

There's no two ways about it, he thought, I just don't fit in. I don't speak the same language; I don't wear the same clothes; I have nothing in common with these people. We are from different worlds.

The Barrel was packed with expatriate teachers. Once a fortnight all of Jim's peers would bus into Queenstown from their various rural postings to meet for a drink and a gossip. They would share stories of the horrors of their school – the snakes in the washing block, the time they ran out of candles, the dilapidated classrooms and the troublesome headmasters – they would show off their smatterings of Zamba; they would compare diseases like trophies; and they would get drunk and cop off with one another in cheap hotels. In spite of himself Jim always looked forward to these meetings and he always turned up. And he always regretted it.

One thing he couldn't help but notice was the strange degeneration in his fellow teachers' appearance. Take the public schoolboys, for instance. Where once their hair had been a precise composition of unkempt style, now it was knotted into ropey, matted dreadlocks. Their crumpled chinos had been replaced with curious Java-print loon pants with capacious crotches that billowed as they walked. Their pinstriped shirts by Raith of Bond Street had given way to extraordinary tie-dye smocks bearing slogans like 'Samora Machel: Aluta Continua'. Clearly the posh kids were trying to go native, but their bizarre choice of garb was more eco-terrorist than rural African and provoked nothing but looks of bemusement and amusement from the local Zambawians.

Jim found it all a bit weird and he looked down at his jeans and cheap trainers with some uncertainty.

That the worthy half of his peer group had gone the same way was less of a surprise. After all, they had established their ethnic credentials all those months ago on the misty Isle of Skye. However, the public schoolboys' new-found love of all things crusty had driven the worthies to ever-greater extremes of collective individualism. So now they wore studs in their noses and carved primal tattoos into their forearms with a penknife and a cartridge of black ink. They walked barefoot through the streets of Queenstown, leading mangy dogs on fraying lengths of rope. The worthy boys grew dirty beards and the worthy girls shaved their heads and they sat in Queenstown's Independence Square reading Bruce Chatwin and Claude Lévi-Strauss.

At these occasional meetings in the Barrel conversations soon gave way to competition as every young teacher regaled the rest with ever more incredible tales of their own unique experience. On this particular day a public schoolboy called Josh started the bidding with his life-and-death battle with malaria, when all that had saved him was a two-litre bottle of quinine tonic water. But this was soon dismissed as small change when baby-faced Johnny lifted his intricately woven tunic to show where a *putsi* fly larva had embedded itself in his stomach. Then a shy-looking bald girl whose name Jim had forgotten told of her confrontation with the rampaging guerrillas of the Black Boot Gang and she blushed as she spoke. Then a loud-mouthed Etonian called Bruiser regaled the group with his harrowing fantasy of beating a black mamba to death with a hockey stick. 'Do you remember? Lambo said that the mamba is the deadliest snake on the continent!' he kept saying. 'The absolute deadliest.'

The conclusion of Bruiser's garrulous lies left a brief lull in the action as each teacher tried to conjure the next level of bullshit. Jim wondered if he might contribute the death threats of Mr Murufu. But, at that moment, a worthy, portly girl called Hannah walked into the bar and trumped the lot of them. For she was holding the hand of a tall Zambawian man.

'Everyone!' she said smugly. 'This is King!'

None of them had actually fucked a Zambawian before and so, on Hannah's appearance with King, all bets were off.

With no other space available in the crowded bar, Hannah sat down next to Jim and nodded a greeting. They had barely spoken before. Jim vaguely recalled a strange conversation by a Scottish camp fire. 'Are you socially aware?' Hannah had said. 'I am. I am socially aware.' And for a moment or two Jim had wondered what she meant, until she began to batter him with the names of every creditable organization of which she was a member: Amnesty International, the Refugee Council, the ANC, CND, the League against Blood Sports, Kick Racism out of Football.

'What about you?' she had said again. 'Are you socially aware?' And Jim had thought for a moment or two before conceding meekly, 'No. No, not really.'

So now that he found himself sitting next to this intimidating paragon of all things righteous, Jim didn't know what to say. He licked his lips and gulped his beer and was disturbed to find Hannah staring at him over the tilt of his bottle.

'Better red than dead,' Jim said lamely.

'What?'

'I said, "Better red than dead." Support the frontline states. Football's not all black and white.' Jim's words were beginning to stumble. 'Amnesty International. It is. Are you? The ANC. Just for the taste of it. The Refugee Council. The home of the hamburger.'

Jim ground to a halt. Hannah stared at him as if he were mad. She didn't know what he was on about. But she didn't care either.

'We met at my school,' Hannah said conspiratorially.

'Oh!' said Jim.

'King is the caretaker.'

'Oh, right,' said Jim.

'We couldn't help ourselves.'

'Oh. Right. That's nice,' said Jim.

'He doesn't speak English. We communicate with the sense of touch.'

'Right,' said Jim. 'Fuck.'

Maybe it was the beer or maybe it was the company or maybe it was the image that gate-crashed his mind of this horrible woman playing Braille with her new African boyfriend, but Jim was suddenly overwhelmed with a heady sense of disgusted detachment. So much so that he stood up and lurched over to the bar, away from his compatriots. At that distance he watched the group for a moment or two – the gargling voices, the couples tangling tongues and dreadlocks, the silly giggling – and, passive soul though he was, he felt a stir of irritation. Looking around the bar, he noticed for the first time a small group of smartly dressed Zambawian men whose eyes were fixed on the slobbering Brits and his irritation turned to shame. He had to take time out. He made his way to the lavatory.

Jim unzipped his fly, but he didn't need a piss. Instead he lent his forehead on the white tiles of the pristine urinal, enjoying the cooling, calming sensation.

The door of the gents banged and, realizing he had company, Jim pulled back and strained his bladder into an unwanted leak. He sidled a coy look at the man next to him and saw a strapping, handsome Zambawian in a Calvin Klein T-shirt, sharp slacks and immaculate black brogues. This man pissed magnificently, a gushing waterfall of urine that steamed and frothed and made Jim feel inadequate.

Suddenly, noticing Jim's sideways glance, the man altered his trajectory and began to piss on Jim's feet. Jim looked directly at the man, but now he had thrown back his head and shut his eyes in ecstatic concentration. This had to be an accident, hadn't it? Not wanting to cause a fuss, Jim edged away, further up the urinal, only to discover that the stream of urine followed his feet, landing on the uppers of his shoes with a gentle pitter-patter.

'Excuse me,' Jim said, 'but you're pissing on my feet.'

The man opened his eyes and looked at Jim. He seemed annoyed at the disturbance in his fabulous excretion.

'Yes?' the man boomed.

'I said, you're pissing on my feet.'

'Yes,' the man acknowledged. 'And you piss on my country.'

For a moment the two of them stared at one another. Then Jim blinked, zipped up, snagged his foreskin, yelped and hurried back into the bar, chased on his way by the man's bawdy laughter.

By now Jim's group of teachers were well out of hand and there was no way he was going to rejoin them, especially with the fraught state of his nerves and the smell of piss on his shoes. So instead he propped himself against the bar again, ordered another beer and watched his national shame grow by the second.

Several of the worthies were involved in a noisy, drunken argument about the cancellation of third-world debt; Hannah was rubbing herself unerotically up and down King's placid thigh; and Bruiser was loudly plotting the exact details of his snake hunt with two beer bottles and an ashtray. 'The snake was here, I was here and the hockey stick was over there. The deadliest snake on the continent!' No one was listening.

Meanwhile the rest of the public schoolboys had hijacked the ancient jukebox and were chorusing along to clumsy rock records of the last decade: Aerosmith, Bon Jovi and Europe.

'It's the final countdown! Da-da-dah-dah! Daddle-la-da-dah!'

At that point the piss artist walked out of the lavatory. For a moment he stood and watched the degenerating mayhem. Then, slowly, he walked to the jukebox, shrugging aside a couple of blundering *musungu*, and put the toe of his polished brogue through its glass front, immediately silencing both the music and the half-cut happiness. The teachers stared at the man and one said, 'Steady on!' But the man took no notice. He extricated his foot and ambled confidently across to the bar with all eyes fixed on him. He stood next to Jim.

'Sorry I pissed on your foot,' he said.

'That's OK.'

'It's just you English . . .' he said and left the sentence unfinished.

'I know,' said Jim and nodded earnestly. 'Why did you kick the jukebox?'

The man looked at him and thought for a moment before replying.

'I fucking hate that record,' he said.

13 : Number 17

St Oswald's School in Zimindo Province was a fair distance from Queenstown; 100 miles due south down the Lelani tar road, followed by twenty miles west on a winding dirt track. While many of the buses that served rural Zambawi had romantic names hand-painted on their flanks like Second World War bombers, the bus that served the school and surrounding villages was simply called 'Number 17'. Of course, there was no 'Number 16' and no 'Number 18', so a passenger at Mbave Bus Station in Queenstown would usually find their bus to St Oswald's sandwiched between 'White Lightning' and 'Painted Lady'. Number 17 belonged to the Mapondera Bus Company and the rumour was that the prolific Mr Mapondera had named this bus after his seventeenth child. Since most of the staff of the bus company were relatives of Mr Mapondera, Jim had always hoped to meet the unfortunately named Number 17. But his delicate questioning of the drivers, conductors and loaders who milled around Mbave had yet to succeed.

Number 17 – the bus, that is – was a rickety contraption that never passed fifty miles an hour on the road and ten on the dirt. And since the driver insisted on a bottle-store beer stop every thirty minutes or so, the journey could take anything up to five hours. What with the length of the journey, Mapondera's pack 'n' stack philosophy and the terror of a merrily drunk driver swigging from his beer bottle and driving with his knees, Jim generally found the trip back to his school on a Sunday afternoon after a weekend in the capital to be a wearing business. However, the day after his encounter with Enoch in the Barrel he was remarkably laid back.

He found a seat by the expressively labelled 'Emergency Kick-Out Panel' – something he always liked to do – and he rested his small plastic bag of spare socks, toothbrush and the like between his feet. He didn't flinch when a large Zambawian lady deposited a wet-nappied child in his lap; he made no comment when the goat in the seat behind began to nibble at his hair; and, when the driver briefly dozed off at the wheel, sending the coach careering off road for a moment before he came to, Jim found his heart rate remained even.

Jim was lost in his thoughts. He couldn't believe that he had met the son of the President of Zambawi. The President's son, he thought, pissed on my feet! And though, at first, he wasn't sure that this meeting and his new state of mind were directly connected, he realized that, for the first time since arriving in Zambawi, he was beginning to be comfortable with his situation.

After Enoch had pissed on Jim's feet, after he had put his foot through the front of the jukebox, after he had placated the hotel staff with a raised eyebrow and a 'Do you know who I am?', the pair of them had talked at the bar for a further hour. And they found that they had much in common. Or at least as much as was possible between two young men of such different races, cultures and backgrounds. Or at least they revelled in their shared distrust of Jim's fellow teachers. Or at least they had got drunker together.

'Shall I tell you what fucks me off?' Enoch had said.

'Tell me. Tell me what fucks you off.'

'These *musungu*. . . children . . . kids . . . no offence . . .'

'None taken.'

'These *musungu* kids turn up in Zambawi to teach in our schools like they are Bob fucking Geldof or something, come to save Africa from itself, come to save Africa from the Africans.'

'But Zambawi does have a shortage of teachers.'

'Of course. Of course we do. But if we have a shortage of teachers, then why does my government employ English kids who speak no Zamba, have no experience and couldn't teach a fish to swim? Why?'

'I don't know.'

'I'll tell you why. Because in the first place it is a good public relations exercise with the British government – Dad is worried he'll murder one political activist too many for Downing Street. And in the second place it is because you are cheap. No Zambawian with A-levels wants to teach in a rural school with no electricity or running water for the pennies that the Ministry of Education pay. Of course they don't. Just as the UK looks to India to fill its sweatshops and Africa to staff the fucking trains, so we in Zambawi look to the British bleeding hearts to fill the menial posts that no one else wants. That is the truth of the matter.'

'So what am I doing here, then?'

'I can't answer that! I don't know. I suppose you are here for your memories. You are here so that when you are watching television with your friends at university and the news turns to another drought, famine or civil war, you can look off into the distance with a misty-eyed expression and your friends will nod to one another and say, "He was in Africa."'

'The headmaster at my school said that there were three things to know about Zambawians. One: they love the English. Two: they hate the English. Three: they are fickle.'

'Your headmaster is a wise man. But is that not true of all nations' attitudes to one another?'

'You're a cynic.'

'Of course.'

'You should follow your father into politics.'

'No! Things will change in this country soon. Dad will not survive for ever on the back of winning independence and losing his testicles. And when the revolution comes, my life will not be worth anything. I will be forced to go to the Underground.'

'What do you mean?'

'What do you mean, what do I mean? I will be forced to go to the Underground. I will go to London and train as a driver or a conductor.'

'We don't have conductors.'

'Then I will be a guard and wave a flag. I am good at waving flags. I have been waving flags at every one of Dad's rallies since I was ten years old.'

As Jim shut his eyes and moved the soggy baby from one damp knee to the other, he concluded that it was indeed this conversation that had given him a new sense of hope. Previously he had felt like a failure; he had felt like an outsider who was never going to fit in to his African surroundings. And, though those feelings hadn't changed, his attitude to them had transformed. So I'm a failure? he thought. Of course I am! So I'm an outsider? Of course I am. Not for me any notions of worthy do-gooding!

At that moment Jim's contented thoughts were broken as the bus screeched to a sudden, skidding halt. The passengers were thrown forward and he struggled to hold on to his little infant package. He gathered the child into his chest just as a frenzy of hooves and horns flew over his shoulder to land on his knees. As the bus came to a standstill, the goat was wailing like a baby. And so was the baby. The goat thrashed its legs, catching Jim full in the face. 'Shit!' Jim said and his eyes began to water.

Now the terrified beast was snapping its teeth around Jim's crotch. With great presence of mind, Jim whipped the nappy from around the baby's midriff, stuffed it between the chomping jaws and deposited the goat into the cluttered aisle with a swinging forearm.

While all this was going on, Jim was vaguely aware of raised voices at the front of the bus. He caught a glimpse of the driver shouting angrily. But he couldn't see the object of his aggression and he was too concerned with the smooth baby shit that was now trailing down his chest to bother craning his neck for a better view.

Jim was just mopping at the mess on his front with his dirty socks when he heard a voice that he recognized, and his head shot up and he understood the reason for the bus's sudden halt and the subsequent commotion. Standing in the aisle just a few feet away from him was a small, old, smiling man brandishing an enormous machete.

'Mr Tulloh! I am going to kill you.'

Behind Mr Murufu Jim could see the bus driver looking

extremely agitated. He barked something in Zamba and a few of the other passengers nodded in agreement. Jim hoped that they might intervene. But then the driver merely returned to the wheel and the engine spluttered into life. Clearly he was just keen to get going. Now the baby's mother was behind Murufu, pressing to get to her child. Jim's mind was racing.

'Look, Mr Murufu,' Jim said. 'At least pass this baby to its mother. Then you can kill me.'

Jim offered the baby to Murufu and the old man accepted it into one arm, the machete in the other. Just as Murufu took the child, it began to vomit and the old man let out what could only have been a Zamba curse. Seeing his distraction, Jim grabbed his chance. He stood as tall he could in the cramped conditions and launched himself head first at the Emergency Kick-Out Panel. Jim's head hit the panel square on and extremely hard. However, in all the years of Number 17's service, the supposed escape route had never been kicked, let alone butted, and it barely dented with the impact. Jim collapsed to the floor, clutching his skull, with his ears ringing and blood seeping through his fingers.

'Fuck!' he shouted and he was blinded for a moment with a mixture of blood and tears. But he had no time to recover. On seeing the treachery of his intended victim, Murufu let out a furious yell and leaped forward with his machete raised above his head. Jim's vision cleared just in time to see the gleaming blade poised over him.

'Oh fuck!' he shouted again.

For the previous minute or two the voracious goat had been sprawled in the aisle, somewhat dazed and uncertain about the epicurean merits of its nappy sandwich. But now, as Murufu moved forward, the goat was confronted by a juicy cut of trouser leg and he sank his teeth into the would-be murderer's kneecap. Murufu screamed and brought down his machete with a threatening swish that ended in the goat's neck. There was blood everywhere, angry shouting from the goat's owner and, as the stricken animal's jaw relaxed, Murufu struggled to disengage his weapon.

But Jim was long gone, stumbling up the aisle, crying and

laughing and bleeding and dropping shitty socks in his wake as if they were landmines that might aid his escape. He reached the front and realized, to his horror, that the bus was now moving once again. But there was nothing else to be done. Jim looked at the driver, screamed 'Number fucking 17' at the top of his voice and threw himself out of the open door.

14 : It was Lord Byron who wrote that truth is stranger than fiction

Jim had learned little on the Isle of Skye. Or so he thought. He had learned Lambo's Ten Rules of Africa – though not well enough to keep them – and not much else. He could remember vague, dull lectures about diet and disease, given by middle-aged men with glasses and Open University beards. But he couldn't remember what had been said. Mostly he remembered playing endless hours of bizarre games devised, Lambo claimed, 'to build some trust among you ladies'. In particular Jim recalled a long afternoon spent on a Skye clifftop. The group had split into pairs and Jim had been unlucky enough to end up partnering the public schoolboy called Bruiser.

This game of trust had been simplicity itself. All you had to do was cross your arms over your chest and fall backwards, where your partner would catch you. Then your partner would step back a foot and you would do it again, falling further each time. The rules were straightforward and unmistakable. However, Bruiser seemed to delight in getting them wrong. He would catch Jim the first time and step back. He would catch Jim the second time and step back. Then, on the third occasion each round, Jim would fall back and Bruiser would let him slip through his hands to smack his head and shoulder blades into the hard rocky outcrop.

Jim protested. Of course he did. But Lambo merely said, 'S'all about trust, in'it?'

'But I don't trust him!' Jim complained.

'Exactly, you big girl! So get your dainty little arse back to it until you do.'

So Jim was forced to spend the next three hours banging his

head until night closed and Bruiser's amusement finally wore thin.

This experience taught Jim a great deal about trust. And even more about how to fall as painlessly as possible.

Therefore, when Jim threw himself out of Number 17's open door to bounce across the dust and land in a road-side ditch, he managed to keep himself relatively unscathed. Sure, the fall left him with a few bumps and bruises, and his head was bloody and aching from its encounter with the immovable Emergency Kick-Out Panel, and his T-shirt was covered in baby shit, and his mouth and eyes were full of dust and dirt, and the palms of his hands were skinned and raw, but, all things considered, he wasn't feeling too bad. And, as he struggled gingerly to his feet, he recalled Bruiser's harsh lessons with something approaching affection.

I might have broken my neck, he thought. I could have knocked myself silly.

And he spat out a mouthful of small pebbles and rubbed the stinging grit from his eyes. His vision slowly cleared and he was confronted by the most extraordinary sight.

There, in front of him, stood a small boy. This was not extraordinary in itself. Nor was the fact that the small boy was naked. That the boy held a piece of string that was fastened around the neck of the biggest bull that Jim had ever seen was verging on the unusual. And that the bull was carrying on its back what appeared to be a Rastafarian, complete with red, gold and green cap, poking dreadlocks, wide smile and *gar*-filled pipe, was extraordinary indeed. Jim suddenly felt peculiar and wondered if he had, in fact, been knocked silly after all. 'Hello,' he said weakly and he smiled a wan smile at the little boy. The boy smiled back, revealing a mouthful of point-sharpened teeth. Jim fainted.

Jim wasn't sure what finally woke him up. It could have been the smell of rancid carpet, the gentle rocking motion or the curious cold sucking sensation that sent tingles through his forehead. Slowly he opened his eyes and found himself staring at the night sky through what seemed like an ivory picture frame. A shooting star shimmered and faded like a cheap firework. Then another.

Perhaps I'm dead, he thought.

'Ah, Mr Tulloh! Finally you have awoken.'

Jim looked round and saw the head of the strange Rastafarian, level with his own.

'Generally, Mr Tulloh,' the Rastafarian said, 'it is advisable to disembark from the bus at the bus stop. Hence the name: bus, stop.'

The Rastafarian issued a throaty laugh that bubbled out from his stomach. He sucked on his *gar* pipe and the sickly sweet smoke tickled Jim's senses.

'Would you like some?' the Rastafarian asked.

'Thank you,' Jim said and the oaky barrel of the pipe was pressed between his lips. He sucked hard and began to cough. His head raced and fizzed.

'Where am I?' he asked.

'You are on the back of my bull.'

And Jim suddenly realized that he was six feet off the ground. The curl of the bull's horns was the frame that bounded his view. The bull's fur was the rank smell that troubled his nose.

'Who are you?' he asked.

'I am Musa,' said the Rastafarian.

'Where are we going?'

'To my home.'

'I need to get back to St Oswald's School. Do you know it?'

'I do.'

'Can you take me there?'

'Do not worry, Mr Tulloh.'

Jim was feeling distinctly confused. He tried to sit up, but the roll of the bull's back made it difficult. He tried to look at Musa again, but the Rastafarian had disappeared from view. And what was this cold sucking sensation on his face? He lifted a hand to his forehead and felt a chilled fleshy substance attached to his skin. Next to it was another. And a third. He pulled one off between his fingertips and it came away with a popping noise. He examined the object. When he realized he was looking at an enormous leech, he promptly screamed and fell off the back of the bull with a thump that compounded his feelings of fragility.

'You put fucking leeches on me!' he shouted, tearing manically at his face. His senses had returned with a rush and he found himself scrabbling around in the dirt at Musa's feet.

'Today is your day for falling off,' Musa observed.

'You put fucking leeches on me!' Jim shouted again.

'A panacea. Very good for a bump on the head.'

'Fucking leeches!' Jim said and started to stomp off into the bush. After about ten yards he stopped. 'Fucking leeches!' he said. It was pitch black and Jim didn't have the faintest idea where he was or where he might go.

'Where are you going, Mr Tulloh?' Musa asked.

'How do you know my name?'

'I know many things about you, Mr Tulloh. You are from England. You teach at St Oswald's School. You made a *chinjuku* girl perform *gulu gulu*.'

'I did not!'

'No matter. Will you walk with me a while?'

'How the hell do you know so much about me?'

'I am Musa,' said Musa and he then adopted a tone of appropriate gravitas. 'I know many things, for I am a witchdoctor.'

Jim looked at him and felt a hot wind blow up his shirt and tingle his spine. For a moment he was disquieted. But it was only the *gar* working its magic on his bowels once again.

It took about an hour to reach Musa's homestead and there was little chit-chat on the way. This was OK by Jim. Though he had a thousand questions to ask, it gave him time to gather his confused mind into something approaching coherence and observe the witchdoctor at his side.

Musa was a tall man in his late twenties. Jim had no conception of how big or old a witchdoctor should be, so this posed no problems. However, the rest of Musa's appearance did not sit so comfortably with Jim's imagination. Surely a witchdoctor should wear nothing but a leopard-skin loincloth? Surely a witchdoctor should have shrunken skulls hanging from his neck, a long stave that beat the ground as he walked and mad hypnotic eyes that drew you in with their intensity? Somehow a Rasta hat, baggy jeans, trainers and an affable manner didn't quite fit the bill. The bull, Jim thought, was a nice touch. Likewise the pocketful of leeches. But where was the naked, razor-toothed boy? He seemed to have disappeared and Jim wondered if he had ever existed. Weirdest of all was Musa's language. He spoke perfect English but with a precision and vocabulary that seemed to have been lifted from a fictitious English past. When Jim asked him how far they had to walk, Musa replied, 'It is but one league hence.' When Jim remarked that he was tired, Musa sniffed before saying, 'Fatigue is the bedrock of a healthy character.'

Eventually they approached Musa's kraal and it was little different from any of the other homesteads Jim had visited: a collection of small, circular buildings, fenced into a dusty yard, surrounded by rickety animal pens housing goats and chickens, and cultivated squares of land that sprouted sickly maize and rape. There was, however, a notable absence of women and children, and none of the accompanying hubbub of family life. And the silence of the buildings and the incomparable darkness of the Zambawian night made Jim feel slightly uneasy.

'This way,' Musa said and he ducked his head inside the largest, central building.

Jim found himself in a typical Zambawian living room. Almost. A small fire in the middle of the building gave off plenty of smoke and heat and very little light. Around the edge of the room, a low clay bench was built into the walls. The walls were painted with stylized images in pale grey slip: angular geckos, snakes and rotund lions. All of these features were commonplace in Jim's experience. However, above the clay bench at about head height, a wooden shelf circled the room and it was fully stocked with books. And these weren't just any books but beautifully bound hardbacks with ornately embossed spines and metal-tipped corners. Jim tried to read the titles, but the atmosphere was too murky. Musa noticed his fascination.

'Take one down,' Musa said and Jim selected a beautiful book with a marbled cover. He held it up to his eyes. *Tales from Shakespeare* by Charles Lamb. Despite the filthy air, it was in near-pristine condition. On the inside leaf was written a perfect calligraphic inscription: 'St Oswald's Mission School, February 1948'.

Jim carefully replaced the book and sat down. His eyes were streaming in the smoke and he couldn't ignore the sudden stench of baby shit that rose from his front.

'Welcome to my home, Mr Tulloh,' Musa said and Jim coughed and spluttered and thanked him. It took a minute of two to get used to the potent atmosphere. He rubbed his eyes with his knuckles and tried to hold them open for more than a second before the smoke blurred them once again. On the other side of the fire Jim saw his headmaster, PK Kunashe, grinning back at him.

'Hello, Mr Tulloh!' PK piped cheerfully.

'Mr Kunashe!'

'You look like shit.'

'It's a long story.'

Musa was busying himself around the room. Jim couldn't see what he was doing. Now he hung a heavy black pot over the fire and sat down next to PK. Musa and PK smiled at one another. Jim's sense of unease grew.

'I heard that Mr Murufu was looking for you,' PK said. 'I thought that Musa might be able to help. He is a witchdoctor.'

'He told me,' said Jim.

Musa smiled at Jim, took off his cap and shook his long dreadlocks down across his face and shoulders.

'Hold on a minute!' said Jim and, to his surprise, he felt his temper rising.

I've had a tough day, he thought. And he pointed an accusing finger at Musa.

'Hold on a minute!' Jim said again. 'You told me that you knew so much about me because you were a witchdoctor!'

'Yes, Mr Tulloh.'

'But PK must have told you!'

'Indeed, yes; because I am a witchdoctor.'

'But that's . . .' Jim stuttered. 'That's cheating!'

There was a heavy moment of silence, broken only by the

bubbling of the pot on the fire. Eventually PK spoke. Very quietly.

'Mr Tulloh,' PK said, 'I warn you. It is a mistake to insult a witchdoctor. Especially in his own home.'

'There is no problem, PK,' said Musa. 'He is not cognizant of our culture. An Englishman has "scorn of irregular perquisites" – *Decline and Fall*.'

'But you put leeches on my head!' protested Jim.

'Mr Tulloh,' said Musa firmly, 'would you like some tea?' He tipped the contents of the cooking pot into three tin mugs and a pungent, acrid aroma filled the room. 'It is *gar* tea. Very strong. But it does not make you fart.'

Jim took the mug and nervously sniffed its contents. He took a sip.

'Mr Tulloh. I put leeches on your head. Does your head ache? It does not. PK informed me of Mr Murufu's intent and yet, by curious good fortune – curious good fortune, Mr Tulloh! – you escaped from Number 17. Then, by some bizarre happenstance, you exited the bus at precisely the point where I had taken my position. And I promise you that Murufu's desire to unseam you from the nave to the chaps shall never be fulfilled!'

Musa drank thirstily from his mug. Jim didn't know what to say.

'So, Mr Tulloh,' Musa continued, 'as the great Sherlock Holmes himself so eloquently opined, once you have eliminated the impossible, whatever remains, however improbable, must be the truth.'

'But . . .' Jim began. 'But . . . I'm sorry but I don't believe in magic.'

'I am not asking you to believe in magic, Mr Tulloh. For the truth cares not one jot for your beliefs.'

As Musa spoke, Jim supped from his mug and found that he was becoming very stoned. However, he felt certain that it was more than *gar* tea that enveloped his mind in cosy soft packaging. Musa's voice – his explicit intonation and exact language – bathed Jim's thoughts in the warm liquid of each syllable until Jim felt his brain seep up through his skull like hot water through a tea bag to reach a new eidetic plain

Fuck! Jim thought as he looked down on his head from where he floated, level with the bookshelf. I'm flying!

And the names on each book spine resonated in the air like poetic stanzas: Kipling, Doyle, Robert Louis Stevenson. Hughes and Tennyson; Waugh and Byron. And he spread his wings and soared around the circular room in long swooping arcs until he was out of breath. And he thought it was weird that he should be out of breath when he no longer had a body. And he looked down at his face and he found that his face was watching him. And he looked down at Musa and he found that he was watching him too.

'Let me tell you a story, Mr Tulloh, so that you may understand the truth,' Musa said, addressing himself to Jim's floating, disembodied mind.

15 : The story Musa told

A long time ago, when the land was unsettled and swam in the ocean like maize porridge in the cooking pot, and bad men were swallowed into the ground for the theft of a chicken, and the spirits of the dead and the yet to live floated free in the air like whirlpools of dust, Father Sun ruled the earth in eternal light through his soft-footed descendants. These were righteous chiefs, *shamva*, who were merciful in their authority and just in their judgements. It was a time of great prosperity for all people. From the Mountain in the East That Kissed the Sky to the Great Lake in the West That Cooled the Traveller's Feet, the homesteads would make sacrifices to the *shamva*: food, precious stones and ritual objects that you would not understand. In turn, the *shamva* would make sacrifices to the sun. And the sun, in his benign power, would heat the land until it coalesced and held the farmer's seed tight in its womb.

But as your prime minister Benjamin Disraeli once wrote, 'All power is a trust.' So it was in this land. It was a trust of sacrifice between the people and the *shamva*. It was a trust of sacrifice between the *shamva* and Father Sun.

Millennia passed and, though the people continued to sacrifice to the sun's descendants, the *shamva* themselves were not so regular in their own sacrifice to the sun. Like the people of today, the *shamva* had forgotten their ancestors or thought that the history of their birth from the heat of the sun was nothing but a legend. The *shamva* thought that the sacrifice made to them was their birthright. However, they did not understand why they should make sacrifice to the sun and so they kept the people's food, precious stones and ritual objects that you would not understand for their own uses.

Over the following months the *shamva* became very fat because they ate all the ritual food and they could no longer work, so weighed down were they by the precious stones and ritual objects that you would not understand. At first Father Sun continued to shine. However, soon he became angry and he went to the *shamva*.

'Why do you no longer make sacrifice to me?' he asked.

The *shamva* were very afraid because the sun had not spoken to them for many centuries.

'Because the people no longer make sacrifice to us,' they replied.

'Then the people must be punished,' said the sun.

From that day forward the sun beat down on the land with all its might. Soon the land no longer swam in the ocean like maize porridge in the cooking pot but turned into dry crust, like porridge that has been left over. All the seeds were hidden in the womb of the earth and her stomach was so strong that they could not break free. The people began to starve.

Now at this time there was a young man who lived on the land whose name was Zamba. This name is where our language, Zamba, comes from – it has come to mean 'language of the gods' – and also the name of our land, Zambawi.

Zamba saw that the *shamva* were eating his family's food, wearing the precious stones and performing rituals with the objects that you would not understand. He saw that the *shamva* were getting fat as his family slowly starved to death. So Zamba travelled to the East where the mountain kissed the sky to talk to Father Sun and expose the *shamva*'s treachery.

'Oh Father Sun!' Zamba cried. 'Do not punish us, your people, any more. For we still make sacrifices to your descendants, the *shamva*. It is they who keep our sacrifices from you.'

When the sun heard Zamba speak in this way, he was very angry.

'Who are you who dares speak to me?' asked the sun. 'You ask me to believe the word of a mere farmer over that of my own descendants? Be gone, presumptuous fool! I banish you to eternal cold!'

And with that, the sun turned Zamba to stone and threw him across the land into the Great Lake in the West That Cooled the

Traveller's Feet. For two whole months, Zamba lay at the bottom of the lake. For one further month, Zamba struggled to reach the surface, swimming as fast as he could and catching rides on the back of passing *kapenta*. All the while, the people of the land continued to starve.

At the end of the third month, Zamba was just below the surface, swimming for all his might. As he approached the surface, he saw the sky darken above the water. With every stroke he made, the sky darkened a little more until he broke the surface. He sucked the air deep into his lungs and the sky turned to black. This was the first darkness.

Zamba was tired. He had swum from the very bottom of the Great Lake in the West That Cooled the Traveller's Feet and his stone limbs were heavy. However, when he finally reached the water's skin, the air was so thin that he fell upwards into the first dark sky. He looked down upon the land and he was amazed by the beauty of the darkness and he cried shining stone tears that fell upward around the sky. Zamba became the moon, and his tears the stars that decorate the darkness.

When Father Sun saw what Zamba had done, he was very angry and, for months, the sun and moon fought. One moment it was dark, the next it was light. One part of the land was dark, another was light. And all the while the people starved.

Now. Are you listening? Good.

When Zamba was first thrown into the Great Lake in the West That Cooled the Traveller's Feet, his family sent word to the Traveller, who just happened to be a cousin of Zamba by marriage. The Traveller was the Child of the Horizon, a great warrior who lived far to the West where the earth and heavens meet, beyond even the Great Lake That Cooled the Traveller's Feet. His name was Tuloko.

As soon as he heard what had happened to his cousin, Tuloko came to the land. At night, he travelled to the East where the mountain kissed the sky.

'Oh, Cousin Moon!' Tuloko cried. 'This war cannot continue because the people are still starving.'

'But what can I do?' Zamba replied.

Tuloko stayed where the mountain kissed the sky until the sun rose angrily in the heavens.

'Oh, Father Sun!' Tuloko cried. 'Do not punish your people any more. For they still make sacrifices to your descendants, the *shamva*. It is they who keep the sacrifices from you.'

When the sun heard Tuloko speak in this way, he was very angry.

'Who are you who dares speak to me?' asked the sun. 'You ask me to believe the word of a mere nomad over that of my own descendants?'

'Wait, Father Sun!' Tuloko cried. 'Look at the *shamva*! See how fat they grow! That is your proof!'

However, the *shamva* were ashamed of what they had done and hid in the parts of the land where the moon ruled the sky and the sun could not see them.

Now Tuloko stayed where the mountain kissed the sky and called to the warring parties.

'Oh, Father Sun! Oh, Cousin Moon!' Tuloko cried. 'This war cannot continue because the people are still starving. You must see the treachery of the *shamva*. Oh, Father Sun! You must allow Cousin Moon to control the whole sky so that the *shamva* believe they are safe. Oh, Zamba! Then you must allow Father Sun to control the whole sky to reveal the *shamva*'s treachery.'

The sun and the moon agreed to Tuloko's proposal and the first night swept over the whole of the land and the people were very afraid, even though Zamba's smiling face and the beauty of his tears reassured them that he was good. After some hours Zamba, the moon, withdrew and the sun shone down on all the land.

Immediately the sun saw the *shamva* and he saw how fat they had become. He was very angry and, with one turn of his face, he melted the *shamva* into liquid and they washed through the land, moistening the womb of the earth and allowing the seeds to break free. And so the *shamva* became the rivers that fertilize Zambawi.

When he saw all the good that Tuloko had done, the sun decided that he should replace the *shamva* as the chief of the land.

'How can I do so?' Tuloko replied. 'For I am not your descendant.'

'What is a descendant but a man whom you trust?' said Father Sun. 'But this must not be allowed to happen again.'

Father Sun turned to Zamba.

'Oh moon!' the sun cried. 'You have behaved with great honour and from now on we shall share the sky as equals. The people will make sacrifice to Tuloko and he will make sacrifice to me. However, he shall never speak to me again. Instead your descendants shall live among the people and they shall speak to you, oh moon, and you shall speak to me. In this way chiefs of the land shall never be able to lie to me again.'

And so the sun and moon shared the sky as day and night. And the word *shamva* came to mean river. And the descendants of Tuloko became the chiefs of the land. And the descendants of Zamba are known as *zakulu*. In English, that is 'witchdoctor'.

16 : Losing battles

Grant Walker fingered the cluster of melanomata that he was collecting on his forehead and pulled ruefully on the loose tobacco of his maximum-strength cigarette. Since he'd been diagnosed with skin cancer – albeit curable – he had lost interest in trying to cut down on his sixty-a-day habit. Besides, as a white Zambawian, he was supposed to smoke. All white Zambawians smoked.

If that fool Adini could wait a year or two, Grant reasoned, he wouldn't have any kind of 'land issue' to worry about at all, so decimated would the *musungu* population be by heart disease or one kind of cancer or another.

Grant was standing in the massive rambling garden of the massive rambling farmhouse on his parents' massive rambling farm. The day was hot and clear, the beer was cold, the meat on the *braai* was fresh kill and the Walkers' fertile land stretched out to the horizon. But, for some reason he couldn't finger, Grant was feeling unsettled.

Next to him stood the hulking form of Horst Van De Horse, his oldest friend, all barrel chest, puffed features and leather skin. They had grown up on neighbouring farms in this southernmost tip of Zimindo Province and lived their childhood as brothers, loving and hating each other in equal measure. They shot their first baboon together; they camped in the bush and learned to find water in the bark of a baobab tree. They mercilessly tortured Horst's ancient houseboy with scorpions in his shoes; they had their arms splinted, side by side, after an accident roping cattle; and at the age of thirteen they packed their trunks into the back of the Walker family flatback and headed off to boarding school at St Ignatius' College in Queenstown. Seven years later they were both back on their family farms as estate managers. Horst loved the post-colonial, neo-colonial lifestyle. But, these days, Grant wasn't so sure.

'That's it! Go for his bloody eyes, mun! That's it, Chip! If the bastard can't see you, then he can't hit you.'

Horst was shouting at his little brother, Chip, as he beat the living crap out of Scott, Grant's own younger sibling. But this was no boyish horseplay, for white Zambawian kids never 'played' at anything: they roped real cattle, fought real fights and shot real guns.

'Jesus, mun!' Horst laughed to his friend. 'Who'd have thought your Scott would be as much of a little pussy as his big brother?'

Grant looked at Horst and remembered the numerous beatings he'd taken at his hands. Although the same age, the Afrikaner had always had at least half a stone on him and he'd lost count of the number of times he'd lain wrist-pinned to the ground while Horst knelt on his chest.

'Give?' Horst used to say.

'Give,' Grant would concede immediately. But this provoked nothing but fury in his friend. Generally Horst then spat in his face.

'Give?' he would say again.

'Give,' Grant would repeat.

And Horst would clear his throat and spit and the process was repeated until Grant was forced to attempt a struggle, thereby opening the moral door in Horst's warped excuse for a mind to further physical beating.

All these memories flooded Grant's mind as he watched his little brother take another full-knuckle punch on the chin. Grant winced as Scott crumpled to the ground like an empty tobacco sack. Now Scott appeared to have given up. He just curled himself into a tight ball and began to sob audibly.

'Fucking pussy!' spat Horst at Grant's side.

For a moment or two Chip off the old block stood back and stared at his defeated victim as if unsure how to proceed. But then he perceptibly shrugged, drew back his leg and repeatedly sank his safari boots into the quivering midriff of the prone Scott.

Grant thought he should do something. He looked round to find the gnarled walnut face of his father, Old Man Walker, at his shoulder. He too was smoking a cigarette and his tobacco-stained fingers shook as he pressed the butt between his lips.

'Shouldn't we do something?' he said.

'Ach, mun!' his father said. 'The boy's got to learn.'

Grant watched as Chip Van De Horse kept kicking what was now an eleven-year-old dead weight.

'What's he learning?' Grant asked.

He thought it was a reasonable enough question, but it provoked no more than an exchange of indulgent smiles between Horst and his father.

'That's it, Chip!' Horst shouted. 'Pretend the bastard's a *ter*!'

Oh God, thought Grant.

Later, as the parochial party of about twenty friends, family and neighbours (some of whom, by virtue of the size of their farms, lived hundreds of miles away) tucked into the beefburgers, *boerwors* and juicy kudu steaks, the talk turned to the 'land issue' and the threat of the Black Boot Gang and a new civil war. As usual, Grant noted, the white farmers could never discuss the specifics of the problem for very long. Unsurprisingly, for a group who saw the world in black and white, the conversation always degenerated quickly into a primitive dissection of the African psyche and a bizarre, melancholy hankering for the 'good old days' of the colonial war against the black *ters*.

So the conversation went something like this:

OLD MAN WALKER: Ach! I tell you something, mun. If Adini turned up here after my land, the only thing he'd be leaving with is an arse full of buckshot.

HORST: And now there's a new prime minister in the UK. At least with Thatcher you knew where you stood.

OLD MAN WALKER: You're right there, mun! But don't forget that she sold us down the line in the end. We were toe to toe with the *ters* before she started her bloody sanctions. That's the trouble with the UK. You can't trust them any more either.

HORST: Too much pressure from the Jews.

OLD MAN WALKER: Exactly, mun.

GRANT: But you can see how the Africans feel, can't you, Dad? As far as they're concerned, we own all the best land and they're left to farm the sand.

OLD MAN WALKER: Ach! You're right, mun. But why's it sand? Over-farming, that's why. The African has no sense of planning, no sense of business. All he thinks about is where his next meal's coming from. It's his nature, isn't it, mun?

 Desertification, that's the biggest problem facing this country. And whose fault is it? Not ours. We look after our land while the population of Afs just grows and grows. Ach! Shit, mun! Imagine if we gave up our land to the government. In five years this country would be nothing but a sandpit.

MRS WALKER: Lottie Terreblanche tells me that they give away free condoms down at Queenstown General and none of the Bush Africans will take them.

OLD MAN WALKER: Of course they won't. Your average Af thinks that twenty babs means he's got more lead in his pencil, even if he can't feed the little bastards.

MRS WALKER: You want some more meat, hon?

OLD MAN WALKER: Put it on my plate. This is some *lekher braai* you've cooked up.

MRS WALKER: Don't smoke while you eat, hon!

OLD MAN WALKER: Stop your fussing, woman! I've been smoking all my life and it's never done me any harm yet.

GRANT: But Dad, you can see that the Africans think they were here first, can't you?

OLD MAN WALKER: Here first? Jesus, Grant, mun! You don't half talk some commie shit! When your great-grandfather came up on the first wagons, there was no one here at all. Maybe one million Afs in the whole bloody country! Now there's five million. And you know why? Because we brought European medicine, that's why.

HORST: Anyway, I'm not letting any of my family's land go to a corrupt bastard like Adini. How much of our money do you think he's already got stashed in some Swiss bank account or other? That's the trouble with Afs. They're like baboons . . .

GRANT: Horst!

HORST: What? They are, mun! You get one hard old bastard dominating and he'll take the rest of the troop for all he can until some young bull knocks him off his perch. Then it all starts again. It's true, mun!

OLD MAN WALKER: Wasn't there that business with Adini's son when you were at St Ig's, Grant?

GRANT: Yeah, mun. Enoch. But he was nice enough . . .

HORST: Nice enough! He killed Brother Angelo with a bloody stereo system!

MRS WALKER: And you never saw that in the papers.

HORST: You can bet your bloody life you didn't.

OLD MAN WALKER: That's the trouble with Afs. Terrible tempers and no sense of justice. It's not their fault. It's not in their natures.

GRANT: Dad! You can't say . . .

OLD MAN WALKER: Can't say what? I tell you something, son; I can say what the fuck I like in my own home! Are you telling me I'm a racist? I'm not a racist. I'm not a racist, am I, Horst?

HORST: No, Mr Walker. Nobody treats the Afs better than you, mun!

OLD MAN WALKER: Am I a racist, woman?

MRS WALKER: Of course not, hon.

OLD MAN WALKER: So do you think I'm a racist, Grant?

GRANT: No, Dad.

And so the conversation concluded, as it always did, in a paranoid guilt-fest in which all reassured one another of their liberal racial sensitivity. So Grant bowed out. Not because he couldn't stand the hypocrisy of Horst or his father – he didn't see it like that – but simply because he'd heard it all before. Too many times.

The main problem, he figured, with being international pariahs – a loathed minority bounded by skin colour, contemptible throwbacks to colonialism – was that it provoked the most intense navel-gazing. And yet, as pariahs, this self-examination involved a great deal of defensiveness and very little progress. And so you always ended up saying the same thing until you were the most boring people in the world. In fact, Grant supposed, maybe one day the international community will have forgotten their original reason for despising white Zambawians and they will only hate us as dull dinner-party guests.

Grant wandered off down the garden and left the party to defend one another from the threat of the accusing fingers that kept them awake at night. He sucked in the hot air, enjoyed the carpet lawn beneath his bare feet and looked up to the sky, shading his eyes against the brilliant sun. Whatever you thought of white Zambawians, he considered, it was obvious why they'd chosen to stay after independence. Grant had visited the UK on one occasion and, as soon as he got out of the plane, he'd felt claustrophobic. It wasn't the skyscrapers and narrow streets that provoked these feelings – though they didn't help – but the apparent proximity of the sky. It looked as though it might fall on to your head at any moment and envelop you like the cloth of a parachute. By comparison the Zambawian sky seemed breathtakingly high, a gargantuan blue canopy that gave you a heady sense of vertigo and possibility, as if you could fly away if the mood took you. And you couldn't help but be intoxicated by the space.

He reached the prim white fence separating the garden from the acres of fallow paddock that fell away behind and took a couple more deep breaths. He leaned forward on his elbows and sparked up another cigarette. Out of the corner of his eye he saw that Scott was sitting in the flower bed of African violets to his left, his knees tucked up to his chest, sobbing his eyes out. Without turning his head Grant spoke to his little brother.

'What are you doing, Scotty?'

'Nothing.'

Grant nodded and swigged from his bottle of beer, enjoying the cool tickle of the liquid against the back of his throat.

'Come here, Scotty, and I'll give you a sip of beer.'

'I can't,' Scott sniffed.

'Why not?'

'Because Chip said I had to stay here or he'd put a snake in my pants.'

Grant turned round to look at the snivelling child. He was shocked. Even Horst had never threatened to put a snake in his pants.

'Come here, Scotty,' he said. 'And if Chip comes to the bottom of the garden, you can leave him to me.'

Scott got reluctantly to his feet and tottered gingerly over to his brother. His nose was snotty, his sandy hair was matted with blood and his lip was fat and quivering. Grant handed him the beer bottle and he glugged like a pro.

'You know what, Scotty?' Grant said. 'You need to learn to fight.'

Scotty looked at him and began to cry again. 'That's what Dad says. You've got to fight like a man, he says. Keep your hands up, your chin tucked in and don't let him see you're hurt. That's what he says. But Chip's so much bigger than me.'

'Come on, Scotty!' Grant said. 'Don't cry, mun! I'm not talking about Dad's kind of fighting. I'm not talking about boxing. The only way to fight someone like Chip is to find his weakest point and go at it again and again. When you fight Chip, this is what I want you to do: don't worry about defending yourself, don't worry about hitting him in the face; just grab hold of his privates, pull as hard as you can and don't let go.'

'But that's not fair fighting!' Scott protested.

'Fair? There's no such thing as fair fighting! Chip's bigger than you, isn't he? Well, that's not fair either. The only fair fight is the fight you win, Scotty. Trust me!'

'But what if he holds my hands?'

'Then kick him in the privates. And if he holds your legs, then you use your teeth. OK?'

'OK.'

Grant looked at his brother and wiped his nose and a tear stain from his cheek with the sleeve of his shirt. The little boy looked a little more cheerful and he drank from the beer bottle again before handing it back.

'Thanks, Grant,' Scott said.

'No problem.'

'Will it work?'

'Of course it will.'

'Grant?'

'Yeah, Scotty?'

'Who are those men?'

Scott was pointing over his brother's left shoulder. Grant turned quickly and was astonished to find thirty to forty black men standing on the other side of the flimsy white fence. Although they wore an anonymous jumble of civilian clothes, they were drilled four across into company formation and wore full webbing across their chests, with Soviet assault rifles slung over their shoulders. Despite the state of his clobber, each man was shod in army regulation black boots. Grant sucked nervously on his cigarette as their apparent leader broke rank to approach the fence.

'Are they *ters*, Grant?' Scott asked.

'Shut up, Scotty!'

Grant stubbed his cigarette and walked as nonchalantly as he could to meet the captain of this particular company of the Black Boot Gang. The man looked faintly ridiculous beneath an aged floppy hat with bobbing corks, Aussie style. But his drawn pistol stopped Grant from smiling. The man took off his hat and Grant was surprised to find him grinning sheepishly.

'Greetings from the Democratic People's Republic of Zambawi.'

'Yeah, yeah,' Grant said. 'What do you want?'

The captain holstered his pistol, fingered the brim of his hat nervously and his smile widened.

'We're heading for the main Zimindo township,' the captain said.

'Yeah? So what, mun?'

'We're lost,' the captain said and an incongruous, high-pitched giggle escaped from his mouth.

'It's west,' Grant said shortly. Then he turned on his heels, grabbed Scott by the hand and started back towards the farmhouse. He could now see Horst and his father running towards them down the garden. Shit! he thought. The captain spoke again and stopped him in his tracks.

'The thing is, sir,' the captain began, 'our compasses are broken.'

'So look at the sun,' Grant said.

The captain pointed off into the distance with an uncertain finger.

'That's east,' said Grant shaking his head. Slowly the man reversed the indication of his digit. Grant nodded.

'Look, mun,' Grant said. 'I don't want any trouble, right? So if I were you, I'd get the fuck out of here.'

But it was too late. Grant was suddenly deafened as a shot rang out over their heads. Some of the Gangers hit the floor and the captain had redrawn his pistol in a flash. Grant turned to find Horst training his hunting rifle on the *ter* company, just ten yards behind, with his father standing, arms crossed and defiant, at his side. Horst looked somewhat bizarre: shirtless, fat and sunburned with his sunglasses pushed back on his forehead. His father looked much older than his fifty years. Grant felt sick.

'What the bloody hell are a bunch of *ters* doing on my farm?' Old Man Walker shouted.

'It's all right, Dad, they're lost,' Grant said. Then he whispered to Scott. 'Go on, Scotty. Run back to your mum.'

Scotty sprinted back towards the farmhouse.

'Too right they're lost, mun!' his father shouted. 'They're on my bloody land!'

The captain barked a command in Zamba and the Black Boot Gang had their guns to their shoulders in a second, trained on Horst. Horst didn't flinch but adjusted his sights to aim at the Captain. Grant was stuck in the middle. His heart was racing and his legs were heavy, useless, immobile.

'This land belongs to the Democratic People's Republic of Zambawi,' the captain said.

'Just get off my fucking land, mun!' shouted Old Man Walker.

'Look, Dad. They're going,' Grant said and he turned to the captain. 'Aren't you? You're going, aren't you? West.'

The captain raised an eyebrow and giggled his unlikely, nervous giggle once again.

'We will go,' the captain said, 'when boss puts his gun down.'
Grant turned back to Horst.

'Horst! Just put your fucking gun down!'

Horst's eyes shifted to Grant for a second. He sniffed, cleared his throat and spat on to the ground in front of him. His fingers fidgeted on the barrel of his rifle and he flipped the safety catch.

'No way, Grant, mun!' he said. 'They put their guns down first.'

'Horst! There's thirty of them and only one of you! Just put the fucking gun down!'

'Just get out of the way, mun!' Old Man Walker said contemptuously. 'You always were a little pussy. Do you think we'd have won the war last time if we'd all had your attitude?'

'But, Dad . . .' Grant said.

He was about to point out that they had in fact lost the colonial war but he was silenced by another shot from Horst's gun. The bullet whistled past Grant's leg and spat dirt between the captain's feet.

'I'm not telling you again,' Horst shouted. And Grant noted a slight break in his voice. Maybe he was scared after all. 'Get off this property!'

The captain remained impassive. Despite possessing an absurd nervy laugh and no sense of direction, he was a cool customer. He turned to the closest gunman of the company. '*Saurayi mabhuku enyu!*' he said.

'Ach! What are you saying, mun? Speak fucking English!'

'Fire!' said the captain and a bullet bit into Horst's thigh.

'Shit!' Horst shouted and his leg buckled beneath him. But Horst was never going to be one to give up on a losing battle and, as he sank to his knees, he raised his rifle to his shoulder once again.

'I warned you!' he shouted.

'Fire!' said the captain and Horst's whole body kicked as a second bullet embedded itself in his shoulder. Horst swayed for a moment or two. Grant could see that his eyes were glazed.

'You want some, do you?' Horst squeaked. But he couldn't lift the rifle any more and his head turned towards Grant for a moment. 'Ouch!' he said pathetically before falling forward into the lush grass.

Grant was rooted to the spot. So was his father. So was the captain. They all looked at one another. They all looked at Horst's prone form. He was still breathing. In fact, but for the exit wound of the bullet from his shoulder, he looked, Grant thought, like he was sunbathing.

Suddenly Old Man Walker's face contorted into a vicious snarl. 'You kaffir bastards!' he shouted and bent for the fallen gun.

'No, Dad!' Grant screamed. He swung around and screamed again – 'No!' – at the Black Boot Gang captain. But the captain focused only on his father and the 'F' of the word 'Fire' pulled his lower lip beneath his front teeth. No sound came out. Instead Grant heard a spluttered yelp from Old Man Walker and he turned to find his dad clutching his chest, his legs rigid and his eyes wide. For a second Grant didn't know what was going on. And then the captain spoke.

'I think boss is having a heart attack,' he said.

17 : The Poet (three)

Father Bulimi hated his work for the Kellys. Sometimes he had to stand at the gate of their house for eight hours at a time and his heavy wooden truncheon left a circular impression in his belly, just below his ribcage. Sometimes, depending on his shift, he patrolled the expansive garden when the night was at its blackest and his heart thumped in his ears because this was at the beginning of the independence struggle, and the nationalist *ters* had started to raid *musungu* households. Even in Queenstown.

In every bush Father Bulimi saw the glint of a gun barrel and a hammer was cocked with his every footfall. He took to repeating his son's name – 'Indigo! Indigo! Indigo!' – as if it were a magic word.

I am fifty years old and they call me a deterrent, Father Bulimi thought. What do they expect me to do? Do they expect me to beat away the bullets with my wooden stick? Do they expect the *ters* to surrender from respect for an elder?

Maybe Father Bulimi did act as a deterrent, maybe the nationalists decided to spare a *musungu* civil rights lawyer, or maybe the word 'Indigo' really was a magic shield; but the *ters* never did attack the Kellys' home. But Father Bulimi didn't have the benefit of such hindsight, so he never stopped being scared.

Every Friday at 4 p.m. Father Bulimi stood with the other garden servants (as opposed to the house servants) in an orderly queue outside the back door. They took it in turns to approach the doorstep, hat in hand, and Madam handed each worker a small envelope containing five Manyikaland dollar bills. Each worker then made his or her mark on a small piece of paper, beneath where Madam placed her finger. Sometimes Mrs Kelly allowed her son, Tom, to pay the servants. Tom would say, 'Here's your envelope, boy. Don't spend it all on beer.' Just like his mother.

When Father Bulimi returned home to Mutengwazi on a Friday evening, he bought presents for his family: a juicy yellow stick of sugar cane that Indigo sucked all weekend and a pouch of tobacco for himself that lasted him the best part of a week. Sometimes he bought his wife a small bottle of groundnut oil that she rubbed into the cracking skin of her elbows. Otherwise he bought her a length of the latest Java print that she wrapped around her head to look like Mudiwa herself.

On one occasion Father Bulimi bought his wife a small cake of soap that had been individually wrapped with a picture of a rose on the paper. Mother Bulimi had been delighted with this gift and had washed with the soap that very evening. In bed that night, however, Father Bulimi had been disturbed by the sweet, cosmetic smell. His wife smelled unnatural, sexless, like a *musungu* woman. He never bought Mother Bulimi soap again and she never asked for it. But when the bar of soap was finished, she did keep the wrapping in the small wooden box that lived behind the loose brick in the wall beneath the window.

The small wooden box also contained Indigo's school money. Father Bulimi would make a weekly contribution to the fund from his wages; sometimes fifty cents, sometimes more, often less. By the time Indigo was twelve years old Father Bulimi had saved 300 dollars for school fees, enough for a place at the state boarding school, five miles outside Mutengwazi.

It was a cold morning in late August when Father Bulimi told his son of the plans for his education. Father Bulimi was washing by candlelight from the shallow metal basin, the water so cold that it burned his back, while his wife laid out his uniform, gloves and woollen balaclava next to the gasoline stove. Indigo was still in bed, burying himself in the warm imprints left by his parents.

'My son,' Father Bulimi said, 'I have something to tell you.'

Indigo heard the seriousness of his father's tone and sat up in the bed, pulling the blankets tight round his neck. He liked watching his father wash. There was something secure about it; the ritual of face, then shoulders and armpits last of all. He liked the way his father's toes rucked the reed matting as beads of water slid down between his shoulder blades.

'I have decided that it is time for you to go to school,' Father Bulimi said.

'Why?'

'Because I am a security guard, Indigo. Because I cannot read and write. Because this is a *musungu* world. Because sometimes I accompany Mr Kelly to the bank and he is given money at the desk by a black man. Because every Friday I make my mark on a piece of paper and I don't know what it means. Because some of the house servants say that I am signing away my life for five dollars a week. Because I am getting old and one day soon Mr Kelly will realize that I am as toothless as a pet dog. Because you are young enough to live in this *musungu* world. Because you are young enough to be a clerk or a state officer.'

'What are they?'

'They wear neckties and spectacles and earn more than ten dollars a week. You will be the best clerk or the best state officer in the whole of Mutengwazi.'

'But, Dad! I don't want to wear a necktie! I don't want to be a clerk or state officer!'

'How do you know what you want, Indigo?'

'I want to be a storyteller. Like you.'

'I am not a storyteller. I am a security guard.'

'I want to be a storyteller like you!'

Father Bulimi stopped washing and rubbed the bone-soap from his eyes with the back of his knuckles. He realized that his underpants were wet and clinging transparently to his buttocks. He felt embarrassed and irritated, and looked to his wife for support.

'Speak to your son!' he said.

'Indigo!' Mother Bulimi said. 'You will listen to your father. You will go to school and that is final.'

'But Mum! I want to be a storyteller.'

'Then you shall be the best storyteller in the whole of Mutengwazi,' Mother Bulimi said and she smiled to reassure him that everything was going to be OK.

The state boarding school did not have a name. This was the first thing Indigo noticed two months later when he stepped off the Coppertown bus that ran right past the school gates. There was a large, decrepit wooden sign that hung off the tall iron fence: 'State Boarding School 063, Mutengwazi Province'.

Indigo looked at the sign and he looked at the school beyond the sign. He had never seen a school before and he didn't know what a school should look like. But this wasn't what he'd imagined. Beyond the fence a long gravel path arrowed across dusty scrub land to a village of uniform rectangular buildings that were painted a dull yellow. There wasn't a single boy in sight. In fact, there wasn't a single living thing to be seen: not a tree, not a bush, not even a blade of grass. State boarding school 063 looked like a concentration camp – though Indigo didn't know it.

For a moment or two, Indigo was frozen to the spot. He looked at the school and he did not know how to describe it. He looked down at himself – his maroon blazer, the matching necktie that choked him with its implications and the ankle socks that chafed his skin – and he no longer knew how to describe himself. He remembered something his father had said to him.

'The state boarding school,' Father Bulimi had said, 'prepares black boys for the *musungu* world.'

Maybe that was why he couldn't describe what he saw. Maybe that was why he couldn't describe who he was. This is a nothing place, Indigo thought. It is neither one thing nor the other.

The first person Indigo saw when he made his way into the grounds turned out to be the headmaster, Mr Kola. He was a tall man with thick spectacles and defiantly negroid features that depressed him when he looked in the mirror.

'Are you a new boy?' Mr Kola asked.

'Hello,' said Indigo.

'I said, "Are you a new boy?" Yes or no?'

'*Zvedu bolaka enyu*,' Indigo said. '*Faurai museka lanje, mai zamba, mboko?*'

'Speak English, boy! It is the school rule. You must speak English at all times within the school grounds.'

'I speak English bad, *mboko*,' Indigo said.

Mr Kola appeared to be angry and he took Indigo by the hand and marched him to his office at the end of one of the rectangular buildings. There, he stood Indigo against the wall and slipped his belt out from around his waist. He then thrashed Indigo across the back and shoulders.

'You! Will! Speak! English! At! All! Times!' grunted Mr Kola, punctuating each word with a stroke of his belt.

Indigo didn't understand what was going on. He didn't understand what Mr Kola had said. His mind raced with every gesture he'd made and every word he'd spoken. What could he have done wrong? Indigo yelped with pain as the leather belt stung his back for the seventh time. He tried to turn round to apologize to Mr Kola for his unknown misdemeanour and the belt's heavy buckle caught him full in the face. Indigo collapsed to the floor, spitting snot and blood and teeth and tears. He looked up at Mr Kola in disbelief and the headmaster hit him again. Indigo buried his head in his hands and curled his body into a tight little ball. His father's words echoed around his brain like a curse – 'The state boarding school prepares black boys for the *musungu* world.'

During his first month as 'a 63' (as the pupils were known), Indigo was beaten by Mr Kola at least twice a day. At first Indigo was beaten for speaking Zamba, though he thought that he was being beaten for merely speaking. Then Indigo was beaten for refusing to answer a teacher. Then he was beaten because he spoke such poor English. Then he was beaten for refusing to answer a teacher once again. By the end of that first month, Indigo's English was as certain as his hatred of the headmaster.

Although English was the source of all Indigo's punishment, this never translated into a hatred of the language itself. In fact, quite the opposite. The way Indigo saw it, English was the one weapon at his disposal in his struggle to get by in such a vicious environment. Initially from self-preservation, then with a growing sense of curiosity, Indigo would secrete himself away in a corner of the school's dilapidated library and pore over the enormous tatty dictionary that harboured the entire English language. At first, of course, Indigo couldn't read. But this didn't seem to matter. He would simply stare at the shapes on the page, the intricate detail of individual letters and the undulating waves of the two-column format.

One day, when he was hiding behind the dictionary's bulky shape, a thought occurred to Indigo and he whispered it softly to the tissue-thin pages. 'This book must be the most powerful book in the world,' he said, and at that moment he vowed that he would not look at the dictionary again until he was able to understand its contents. As if it were a book of magic spells.

It soon became apparent that Indigo was an exceptionally quick learner with a nimble mind that took to a new language with the agility of an acrobat. So, within six weeks, he could not only speak passable English but also form the letters of the alphabet with some confidence. He could even spell his own name. By the end of the first term he could write simple sentences and read most of the words that the English teacher spelled out on the blackboard. 'You are learning well, Indigo,' said the English teacher, Mr Kiba (whom the boys nicknamed 'Strawhead' on account of his name and the wiry tangles of his hair). 'Now you must begin to read books.' But there was only one book that Indigo wanted to read.

It was a Friday afternoon in early December when Indigo rushed to the library. The sun burned through the windows and bathed the room in hazy, dusty light as he flicked excitedly through the pages of the heavy dictionary.

evacuate. fly. gear. gutta-percha. incumbent.

And there it was. His name. *Indigo*. His heart raced and his eyes blurred as he focused in on who he was.

indigo. adjective. deep violet-blue.

Indigo stared blankly at the page. What did this mean?

colour between blue and violet in the spectrum.

What does this mean? Indigo thought. Why did my parents give me such a name? I am neither one colour nor the other. But blue? But violet? Maybe it's the blues that the old men sing in the *shabeen*.

Maybe it's the violets that survive any heat and wind to bloom in summer. But no! It doesn't make sense!

Indigo's eyes scatted across the page. Before *indigo* came *indignity*. After *indigo* came *indirect*.

indignity. noun. embarrassing or humiliating treatment.

indirect. adjective. done or caused by someone or something else.

Indigo watched the page for a minute or two. It was as if he expected the definitions to change before his eyes. But nothing happened. He noticed that his finger was shaking where it marked the spot and his lips were dry and chapped. He felt the sting of tears in the corner of his eyes. What was Father Bulimi's nickname? N'dgo. One who expects. But the expectation had died. What was it his father used to say? 'Indigo, my special kind of gift from the ancestors.' But there was no mention of anything special here.

Slowly all the definitions began to coalesce for Indigo into a new and confusing sense of self. He was an uncertain colour; neither one thing nor the other. He was caught between humiliation and someone else's plans. And all these images fitted together with an astonishing degree of coherence.

It is true! he thought. I am the child of my parents' humiliation. I am an indirect consequence of indignity. I am neither one thing nor the other. Could I live at home, knowing what I now know? But could I possibly fit into the *musungu* world? I am dislocated, alienated, an observer. I am truly a storyteller! But how can I tell stories in a language that is so precise? These words have no culture for me! A story with no culture is no story at all. This English is the language of science for me: deprived of any nuance, bursting with painful meaning with words like spears. This is not the language of stories. Its truth is too accurate, its emotion too vivid, it is as clear as the outline of the Mountain in the East That Kissed the Sky. Surely it is the language of . . .

Again Indigo bent over the dictionary and flicked furiously through the pages to the letter P. His eyes scanned up the words.

poetry. noun. the art or work of a poet. poems collectively. a poetic or tenderly pleasing quality.

poetic. adjective. of or like poetry or poets. written in verse. elevated or sublime in expression.

poet. noun. a writer of poems. a person possessing high powers of imagination or expression.

Indigo sat bolt upright in his chair so that the shafting sun caught his eyes and blinded him for a second. He threw his hands out, as if begging for mercy.

'It is the language of poetry!' he shouted. 'And I am a poet!'

But the library was empty and nobody heard him.

That night, when the rest of his dormitory was asleep, Indigo lit a candle and made his way to the library. The summer night was blessed by Cousin Moon and the pale light cast on the deserted school buildings a new dignity. The hot wind whispered across the courtyard and Indigo was sure that the Great Chief Tuloko himself was encouraging his mission. 'Learn, my little poet,' he said. 'Find meaning where you can.'

Indigo opened the dictionary at the first page and began to read. Immediately he was lost in the words that twisted his lips and tongue; innumerable images filled his mind with a clarity he'd never known. Not even in his stories. Indigo read all night, at superhuman speed. And by the time Father Sun was winking on the horizon, he had read the entire dictionary.

As the pupils began to file into the courtyard for morning assembly, Indigo finally looked up from the pages and got to his feet. Although he had been sitting in the same position all night, there was no stiffness in his limbs, nor any torpor in his soul. Indigo's mind was acute with purpose and new life. He strode through the gathering boys to Mr Kola's office. He knocked on the door and entered without waiting for a reply. Mr Kola was standing behind his desk, gathering together some papers. Indigo could see the headmaster's shining belt buckle at his waist and he felt his mouth sneer in contempt.

'*Iwe!*' he said. '*Musu neva!*'

'What do you want, boy?'

'*Musu neva! Musu neva!*'

The headmaster smiled, as if enjoying this confrontation. One hand stroked the belt at his waist.

'You know the school rules, boy!' Mr Kola said. 'Speak in English!'

'You!' Indigo said again. 'Black man!'

The headmaster unbuckled his belt and began to slide it between the loops on his trousers. But Indigo seemed to relish this development and he approached the wooden desk, leaning his weight on to his hands and staring up at the headmaster's hated face.

'You do not scare me, headmaster, for you are nothing but the *musungu*'s foot soldier. "Speak English," you say. "You must speak English." As if you understood the weight of language! You think that English empowers you? No! It is the tool of your slavery, the chain that shackles you. Divide and rule! By language, by aspiration, by overreaching ambition. You will never be *musungu*! You will never be a white man! Give a black man a gun, point him at his brother and tell him to pull the trigger. In one instant they make you a murderer and keep you in their debt for life. You are an eviscerated black man! Do you know what that means? You speak English, don't you? It means that you are gutted. Disembowelled. Your very essence has been cut from your belly like an alley abortion and the stench of the death of your very soul makes me nauseous.

'Your ancestors do not protect you, for you cannot pray to them in an unknown tongue. Your family do not respect you, for you can tell them nothing of your beatings and your pedantry. Your pupils will not sing of England's green and pleasant land at your funeral. Your blood is as thin as the water of a *shamva* river, your life as joyless as a stagnant pond, your existence as meaningless as a shallow puddle that vanishes in the morning sun. You do not scare me, headmaster, for one day you will die and nobody will mourn.

'As for me, headmaster, I am a poet. Do you know what that means? When you hand a poet the *musungu*'s gun, he will take it with a confident grip and train its sights between your eyes. When you beat a poet with the *musungu*'s belt, every lick of pain will scar his back with deeper cuts of truth. For a poet can only speak the truth. And the truth is that your days are numbered. As a poet, I tell you that. And when the wordless roar of freedom bursts from my heart with the unarguable wisdom of a screaming child, I will show you no mercy. You will be impaled upon my tongue and riddled with my words and consumed by my truth. And when a final phrase of Zamba, a desperate prayer for forgiveness, exhales in your last breath, even the Great Chief Tuloko will not be able to hear you. For you shall be gagged by my contempt!'

Indigo hadn't finished speaking. But as soon as his breath died, Mr Kola crashed his belt around Indigo's face and proceeded to beat him with any object he could lay his hands on. Ten minutes later, when Mr Kola walked out into the courtyard to conduct morning assembly, Indigo was crumpled on the floor with broken ribs, jaw and nose. But he was happy.

I am a poet, he thought.

18 : Ten years of independence

'Vood zur keer vor zum moor shampine?'

Enoch looked at the elderly black man in white tie and tails and tried to see if his eyes were laughing. They were not.

'I'm sorry?' Enoch said.

'Vood zur keer vor zum moor shampine?' the waiter said again and he swivelled his wrist to offer Enoch the tray that he carried at shoulder height.

'Oh!' Enoch said. 'Some more champagne! Yes. Indeed, sir would.'

Enoch took a champagne flute and knocked it back with a wince and a shiver. The waiter turned to go but Enoch called him back.

'Hold on, *mboko!*' he said.

The waiter ignored him. Enoch had referred to the old man as 'grandfather' as a mark of respect. But his pidgin Zamba invested the word with unintended condescension.

'*Mboko!*' Enoch called again. But now the waiter was servicing a group of men that Enoch recognized as the delegation from the Russian embassy, shady-looking characters with narrow eyes, Mafia connections and vodka miniatures in their pockets. One of them looked in his direction with a frown. Enoch buttoned his lip and held back for the waiter to reappear from their midst. These were the last people he wanted to piss off. Even as the President's son.

'*Garçon!*' Enoch called when the waiter emerged. And this time the elderly man turned as if by remote control.

'Zur?' he said.

Enoch used one hand to lift the narrow stems of two more glasses from the tray and he smiled at the old man.

'Save you coming back,' he said. But the old man remained impassive and took a wide circle into the main body of the party.

'Oh, for fuck's sake!' Enoch whispered to himself and he ran an irritated finger around the restrictive collar of his dress shirt. There was nothing for it but to get drunk. These presidential functions were so fake! With their colonial dress codes, fixed smiles and pseudo-Gallic *oncle Tom* waiters.

Even the sham-pagne was iffy! On the President's orders the kitchen staff had soaked off each bottle's label to leave them with the vintage potential of anonymity. But Enoch knew that the champagne was cheap own-brand plonk that a UK supermarket had given Adini to sweeten a deal for Zambawian sugar-snap peas. Still, it was better than the sparkling home-brew that his father usually served up.

Enoch remembered the sugar-snap deal all too well. And not just for the champagne. The story had made the front page of the *Zambawian National Herald* – of course it had – with a picture of the President shaking hands with a bespectacled English supermarket buyer. Below the picture Adini had been quoted: 'This deal guarantees that Zambawian produce will be sold in eighty per cent of "Stir-Fry Selections" available in the UK'. The ecstatic headline ran 'More Peas Please!' Enoch had been embarrassed.

Similar feelings of embarrassment recurred as Enoch cast his eye over the packed marble hall of the presidential residence. Hundreds of Zambawi's leading lights from the business community mingled and small-talked with various expatriate bureaucrats. They discussed the worry of the 'land issue', the threat of the Black Boot Gang and the merits of Lake Manyika as a holiday destination. They kissed each other's wives on both cheeks, they lusted after each other's daughters and they slapped one another heartily on the back. They admired the decorative banner that hung from the landing of the soft-carpeted double staircase. 'TEN YEARS OF FREEDOM!' it announced.

This is just so unreal, Enoch thought. This is just so out of touch.

He wished that he was somewhere else. But, still feeling guilty for the prank with the bumper sticker, he had promised his father that he would see the party through to the end.

Enoch scanned the room for some kind of entertainment. His eyes flitted from woman to woman in a vain search for one to relieve his boredom. There was the French under-secretary's daughter with the suggestive eyes and inconsolable frigidity. There was the young English journalist who couldn't hold her drink. There were the Murewa sisters who had returned from American university with Oprah values and accents to match. There was the German ambassador's wife with the appetite for oral sex. There was Shingai, pretty but dumb, and Enoch considered approaching her. But she was surrounded by five or six fellow Noses who talked in loud, twanging voices and smoked their cigarettes through the very end of their fingertips.

Briefly Enoch wondered what the collective noun for Noses should be. 'A tissue of Noses', perhaps. Or maybe 'an olfactory'.

Enoch decided that the trouble was once again one of ever-decreasing social circles. The nepotism of the Zambawian elite meant he was related to at least half the women in the room and the rest had already been kissed and dismissed.

He spotted his father on the far staircase. Adini looked every inch the African dictator in an absurd scarlet dress uniform that was weighed down with dozens of medals for valour that he'd been awarded by the army's Supreme Commander – i.e. himself – a decade ago. He was talking animatedly with an elderly man, the exiled President Tula of Mozola, who had sought refuge in Zambawi following last year's coup. Enoch suddenly felt nauseous and downed another champagne to steady his stomach.

Enoch could remember Adini's state visit to Mozola some six years earlier. He had returned full of praise for his Mozolan counterpart. It had been during the school holidays and Enoch recalled sitting down to breakfast with his father opposite, at the other end of the enormous mahogany table in the presidential dining room. Enoch had listened in awe as his father described the reception he had received.

'The finest wine, Enoch! Cases of it from Tula's own cellar.

From his own cellar, for goodness' sake! Sweet cakes made by the pastry chef from the Paris Ritz, Chinese prawns imported from China, Bombay duck from Bombay, fried chicken from Kentucky and finger sandwiches made from English Marmite. The floor of the reception room featured a 5,000-piece marble mosaic of Tula's face that was laid by Venetian craftsmen. There was a string quartet from London's Royal Academy. They had been flown in for the occasion, for goodness' sake!

'And the rest rooms! For goodness' sake, Enoch, the rest rooms! Golden taps and marble basins. Every fragrance, talc and moisturizer you could imagine. Delicately scented toilet paper embossed with Tula's totem crest. Servants to hand you towels, servants to soap your hands, servants to warm ÿour seat.

'I tell you, Enoch, that man knows how to throw a party!'

And Enoch had been duly impressed – though not as impressed as his father – and felt honoured to be the President's son. Only last year, with the coup, did Enoch discover that Tula had amassed a personal fortune equivalent to Mozola's national debt and was wanted for human rights atrocities by the International Court of Justice.

Thinking about this, Enoch's face contorted with disgust. There was his father talking to a man who had ordered the ethnic cleansing of the minority Mozolan Ikbo tribe, a man responsible for genocide, a man with a taste for luxury and blood. And his father was prepared to fly in the face of the international community and offer this frail monster refuge!

Yet he didn't consider his father a bad man. He was arrogant, aloof, greedy, paranoid and – strange for a President, this – a terrible social climber. But he wasn't a bad man. He murdered his rivals, so he had blood on his hands. But he wasn't a bad man.

Enoch found himself mouthing the words 'not a bad man' and he wondered who he was trying to convince.

Everyone has blood on their hands if they are prepared to look for it, he reflected. And at least Africans only bathe in African blood.

Enoch despised the smug piety of the West and the ease with

which the British and Americans could condemn 'African atrocities' with no pinprick of conscience for their own evil part in the dark continent's holocaust.

Across the room he saw Tula gesticulating wildly with one hand, trying to catch someone's eye. For a moment he could not spot the object of Tula's attention but then a young woman appeared on the step beside him. Enoch was surprised he had not noticed her before. Unlike the other women at the Independence Day party, who were decked out in imported finery, this girl was wearing quasi-traditional African dress: a long Java-print wrap in delicious reds and blues and a matching headdress. Tula bent to kiss her – this must be one of his famous harem, Enoch thought – but the girl pushed him away and stalked back into the crowd.

As she descended the staircase, she stepped directly into Enoch's line of view and for a split second their eyes met. Her face was a cold and beautiful story, her full lips spoke of unformed kisses and her eyes said, 'What the fuck are you looking at?' Enoch was jolted from his reverie. He one-swallowed his umpteenth glass of champagne and turned quickly away.

Immediately his attention was caught by a commotion at the front door of the great hallway. There he saw General Bulimi arguing with a tall white man. Although the argument had subdued the crowd to a murmuring silence, all curious whispers and straining ears, Enoch could not make out was being said. He did not recognize the white man. But he looked pompous and had a large nose, and Enoch thought he must be English.

Perhaps it is the new British High Commissioner, Enoch thought.

Now the two men appeared to be involved in some bizarre kind of dance. One moment they would square up to each other, then the white man would crab to the left. Bulimi would quickly follow this movement and they would square up to each other again. Now the white man would step to the right. Bulimi would follow. And so on. It took Enoch a second or two to figure out that the white man was trying to get past and speak to the President.

Eventually the white man brushed Bulimi aside and approached his father with a purposeful stride. Adini appeared to smile and then frown and then shrink. His gaudy scarlet uniform suddenly looked under-filled and blushing. Enoch was intrigued. Bulimi had now caught up with the white man and led him up the stairs and into one of the conference rooms on the first floor. The President followed with his chin on his chest.

Enoch was disappointed to see the door slammed shut, for his boredom quickly returned. But now he saw the mysterious Mozolan woman heading out through the front door and his heart quickened.

'Oh well,' he thought. 'Nothing ventured . . .'

And he followed her.

19 : Ambushed and kidnapped

President Adini was staring at his feet through the conference room's glass tabletop. He shifted uncomfortably in his seat and adjusted the medals on his chest to try and stop the irritating chafing against his left nipple. He clasped his hands across his stomach and watched his fingers fidget nervously on his pot. His fingertips had an unthinking desire to slip down to the comfort of his groin but Adini desperately resisted the temptation. One: fiddling with his balls would send out the wrong signals to the British High Commissioner. Two: the heavy brass buckle of his uniform's belt precluded any such intrusion. Three: his testicular shortfall was a tool of popular consciousness that required gentle manipulation rather than brazen scratching.

Besides, he hoped to shake plenty more hands before the Independence Day party was over and he needed to keep his palms clean and dry.

Sir Alistair Digby-Stewart was haranguing Adini from the other side of the table. He jabbed an accusing finger, sneered and pointed his jumbo nose somewhere over Adini's left shoulder. As the British High Commissioner got angry, so he would turn his head slightly to the right and confront the object of his anger with one staring eye. And the angrier he became, the further his head turned until he was facing the window that overlooked the presidential gardens.

Adini caught the gist of what Digby-Stewart was saying but he wasn't really listening. He thought instead about how well the party had been going, how former-President Tula had appeared impressed by his little soirée and how this interruption could not have come at a more embarrassing time. He wondered how his counterfeit testicles managed to call so seductively to his fidgeting fingertips. He stared at the Englishman's bizarre physiognomy and the bright red veins that lined his left nostril. He pondered the recent reduction in his attention span and he concentrated as hard as he could on the High Commissioner's polemic.

Frankly he wondered what all the fuss was about. So a *musungu* farmer had died at the feet of the Black Boot Gang? It was unfortunate. But, for goodness' sake, what was all this talk of an 'international incident'?

General Bulimi stood rigidly to attention by the door of the conference room. He wasn't listening to Digby-Stewart either. He just stared at the spare chair on the far side of the table, resented his discomfort and remembered sunny afternoons he had spent beneath Coca-Cola signs and flag poles. He wished he were still a poet. Reading or writing, poets got to sit down.

'For God's sake, Adini,' Digby-Stewart was saying, 'are you actually listening to me?'

This was the first time that he had paused in his heated discourse and it brought Adini's drumming fingers to an abrupt halt. There was a moment or two of silence as Adini sniffed, sucked his cheeks and prevaricated.

'Would you care for a drink, High Commissioner?' he asked. 'We're drinking champagne from my cellars and I'd value your nose.'

'What? My nose? No, I do not want a drink. I want to know what we are going to see you do about this heinous act of terrorism.'

'Terrorism? Indeed. It was a most unfortunate incident and you can be sure that the perpetrators will be hunted down and punished accordingly. All your points have been noted with interest and we – that is, I – appreciate the concerns of the British government. However, I should like to highlight two points of my own. One: the Black Boot Gang did not actually "kill" anybody. My sources tell me that Mr Walker died of a heart attack. Two: the death of a Zambawian citizen is a matter of internal concern and internal security and, as such, will be dealt with internally.'

Adini spoke calmly. He was pleased with the authoritative

timbre of his voice. While he wished he could drop it an octave or two, there was no denying its commanding tone.

But Digby-Stewart's reaction soon put paid to the President's complacency. His face reddened and his head turned even further on its axis in an almost impossible twist. In spite of himself Adini felt his hand slide between his legs and cup itself around his testicles as if they were some kind of comforter.

'Have you actually heard a word I said, man?' Digby-Stewart bellowed. 'Mr Walker was not a Zambawian citizen! You hear me? Unfortunately for both of us, the stupid blighter still held an English passport! So I am investigating the murder – and yes, I mean it, MURDER – of one of my country's citizens in your sovereign territory. This is no longer an internal matter of internal security and it cannot be dealt with internally. Do I make myself clear?'

'Oh!' Adini said. 'Yes. Indeed. Very clear.'

Adini turned to look at General Bulimi.

'Why wasn't I informed of this?' he asked.

Bulimi saw the buck being passed his way. But he was standing to attention with his hands behind his back and he refused to accept it.

'Because we did not know, sir,' he said.

'Didn't know? Well, why didn't you know?'

'We did not know, sir,' Bulimi said again with detached finality.

Adini turned back to look at the British High Commissioner who stared at him from the corner of one eye. Cupping his rubber testicles in the material of his trousers Adini began to knead them between his fingers until he realized that Digby-Stewart's eye was focused through the table to his groin. Adini was embarrassed. This was bad. This was all very bad.

'This is bad,' Adini said and Digby-Stewart untwisted his torso so that he could lay his wrists on the table and look directly at the President.

Digby-Stewart sighed. He had been in Africa for less than four months and he was already fed up with the place. It was intolerably hot, the food was monotonous and the dust played havoc with his sinuses. What's more, he found the people unbearably cheerful. And somehow their cheerfulness in the face of terrible poverty just made them all the more irritating.

But worst of all was the politics! African politicians seemed to have no concept of the nub of the process and the Zambawian bureaucracy seemed to think that inefficiency was an end in itself. How naive! Any British civil servant worth his salt would tell you that inefficiency was merely a means to an end. If you were inefficient for the sake of it, then you were merely inefficient. But with carefully considered incompetence? Well! Then you could pull the cat out of the bag at the last minute, you could encourage greater investment and – best of all – you could preserve the sanctity of the status quo. But the Africans understood none of the basics of political management. And so Digby-Stewart found himself faced with a full-blown international incident.

He continued to look at Adini and his face was now as impassive as it had previously been impassioned. How long had he been silent? A minute? Maybe two?

Come on, man! he thought. Stop playing with your balls and ask me your question. I haven't got all night.

'What should I do, High Commissioner?' Adini asked.

Thank you! Digby-Stewart thought and he hummed and hawed for a moment – just for effect – before launching into his answer.

'Look, Mr President. It seems to me that you have two choices. Either you do what you have suggested, hunt the perpetrators down and punish them accordingly; or . . .'

'Or what?'

'Or you do nothing.'

The British High Commissioner nodded to the wisdom of his own words. And he soon had Adini nodding along too.

'I see,' Adini said. 'And which course of action would you suggest?'

'I'm sorry to be pedantic, Mr President, but only one of my options is a course of action. And I suggest you take the other. If you hunt down the terrorists, then, rightly or wrongly, Downing Street will see the first steps down the road to civil war. And such a perception will cause all kinds of problems. The charitable lobby will press for more aid, Whitehall will press for sanctions, the UN will press for . . . well, God knows what they'll press for, but they're bound to press for something. And British holidays, Mr President! The government will be forced to set up helplines, issue travel warnings and evacuate scared tourists. And revisionist historians will appear on the television news and describe your nation as "an accident waiting to happen". The National Union of Students will demonstrate outside Westminster and expatriate Zambawians will lobby the parliamentary Black Caucus. And, worst of all, the Americans will get involved and . . .'

'Why will the Americans get involved?'

'Because the Americans always get involved! And when they're involved, the Russians will have to stick their noses in too. And the Chinese. It will be a disaster, Mr President!'

Digby-Stewart paused for breath. He was pleased to see Adini fumbling with his testicles again. The President looked physically sick. So his speech had had the desired effect.

'So you're saying I should do nothing?'

'Mr President, if you do nothing, the same consequences may occur. Now this is your nation and ultimately it's your call. But . . . may I speak bluntly?'

'Go ahead.'

'Frankly, Mr President, what you do is irrelevant compared to what you are seen to do.'

'I don't understand.'

'Let me put it this way. You must be seen to do something by those who care, while those who know will not care that you do nothing.

'What I suggest is this: you call a meeting with the leaders of the Black Boot Gang and the Democratic People's Republic of Zambawi Party and it will be chaired by me. It will be an informal, open-ended affair that can last for weeks, months, years even. It doesn't matter. It just has to last long enough for everyone to forget about this nasty little episode – three weeks or so should suffice – after which you can hunt down all the terrorists you want. In this way you satisfy the interested parties' desire for action and Downing Street's desire for inaction. And, best of all, you and I look like models of modern diplomacy. What do you say?'

The High Commissioner slapped the table in front of him with the flat of his hand to mark the conclusion of his wisdom. For a moment or two Adini looked quite excited. He liked this idea. Sucking up to the British by doing nothing slowly sounded too good to be true. And he especially liked the part about being a model of modern diplomacy. Former-President Tula could put that in his hand-crafted Bavarian pipe and smoke it! He, President Zita Adini, would be a 'model of modern diplomacy'!

But then Adini realized something and his face fell.

'There is just one problem,' he said.

'What's that?'

'I do not know who the leaders of the Black Boot Gang are. Nor those of the Democratic People's Republic of Zambawi party.'

'What do you mean? You must know who your opponents are! It's the first rule of politics!'

'I know who they *were*. But I killed them all.'

President Adini shook his head and looked, shame-faced, across the table. He was perturbed to see the High Commissioner's head begin a slow turn to the right.

'What? All of them?' Digby-Stewart asked incredulously.

'Yes. I blew the last one up while he sat on his toilet.'

'But that was two months ago! Surely somebody has emerged since then.'

'Not really,' Adini reflected glumly. 'I think that they are scared to admit who they are these days. But you have to kill them as soon as they appear because they breed like rabbits. Isn't this just typical? What do you call it? Sod's law. You can never find a good enemy when you need one.'

That was it! Suddenly Digby-Stewart exploded in a hail of snot and indecipherable groans. For a full thirty seconds, the corner of his left eye pinned Adini to his chair and he began to shake with fury. His nose flared and twitched, his cheeks blotched and reddened, and his chest swelled with inflating anger. And then it all burst out. Three months of sleepless sweating, three months of a red-meat diet, three months of blocked noses and infuriating sunny smiles, and three months of utter incompetence.

'You. Fucking. Prick!' He bellowed, and droplets of spittle rained on to the window that his head was now facing. He had plenty more expletives where those came from. But they were cut short by what he saw in the presidential garden.

A young black man was walking beside a young black woman. At first glance they looked like lovers. But then Digby-Stewart saw the gun that she pressed into the young man's temple. The High Commissioner wanted to say something. And he did. But all that came out of his mouth was 'Fucking Africans!'.

20 : Of the cowardice of lust

Despite his best efforts it took Enoch a full five minutes to make it down the stairs, across the crowded hallway and out of the door of the presidential residence. He easily ignored dull Shingai and the lascivious lips of the German ambassador's wife were avoided with a shimmy and a sidestep. But at the bottom of the stairs he was accosted by one of the Murewa sisters. He didn't know which one. Since they had got back from the States, he couldn't tell them apart.

'Enoch!' the Murewa sister exclaimed, as if she was surprised to see him. 'Enoch, baby! Damn! It's sho been a long time.'

'Hi,' Enoch said. 'How are you?' And he tried to brush past before she had time to answer. But Murewa Sister Number One was too quick and caught him by the elbow.

'I's fine, baby! Damn! It's sho good to see you. Just got back from NYC. So watchasayin'?'

Enoch shrugged. His eyes were impatiently focused on the front door to see if the beautiful Mozolan woman with the cold eyes would reappear. But Murewa Sister Number One took no notice. Instead she regaled him with tales of her last term at New York State, where she had majored in Media Marketing, which sounded like a Mickey Mouse course if ever he'd heard of one.

She told him about the African American Dance Society of which she had been treasurer; she told him about the dorm room she had shared with two white girls from Arkansas – Kelly and Kelly-Sue; she told him how she had been voted 'person most likely to succeed' by her fellow graduands; she told him how she had starred at the campus party to celebrate Kwanzaa; she told him that her shoes came from Bloomingdales and that her foundation was 'All-Butter Pecan' from a range by a black American super-model. But Enoch wasn't listening. His eyes flitted from the helmet-bob wig that topped her head to the door behind and he wondered vaguely whether all trace of Africa had been squashed for good.

Eventually Enoch managed to break away. 'I gots to go to the bathroom,' he said and checked the way her weird transatlantic accent appeared to be catching.

Outside Enoch nodded to the two presidential guards on either side of the impressive double door. They stood rigidly to attention and puffed out their chests. It took Enoch a second or two to accustom himself to the dark after the harsh glitz of the hallway. He was worried that he might have missed his chance with the Mozolan woman, so he was relieved to spot her immediately, sitting on the bonnet of a Mercedes, smoking a cigarette. Close-up, she looked even better than he'd expected. Enoch admired her stacked African headdress, the elegant length of the neck that supported it and the smooth curve of her breast beneath the loose Java-print wrap. He noticed the way the circular Mercedes insignia protruded between her knees.

'Do you mind if I join you?' Enoch asked.

The Mozolan woman looked at him coolly with her cold eyes and blew smoke in his face.

'It's a free country?' she said.

Enoch noticed the questioning tone of her voice. But he thought nothing of it and sat down.

'I'm Enoch,' Enoch said and he offered her his hand. She didn't take it. Nor did she look at him. He was about to add 'the President's son'. But he thought better of it.

'Rujeko,' Gecko said.

'Rujeko? That's a cool name,' Enoch said and he nodded for a moment or two. 'What does it mean?'

'What do you mean, "What does it mean?"'

'I'm sorry. I meant, where's it from? I haven't heard that name before.'

'It's Mozolan,' Gecko said. 'It means "light of the world".'

Enoch laughed.

'And are you?' he asked.

'Am I what?'

'The light of the world.'

'Fuck off.'

Gecko pulled deeply on her cigarette and blew perfect smoke rings into the air. Enoch watched them rise and reflected that this conversation wasn't going according to plan.

'So what does Enoch mean, then?' Gecko asked.

'Enoch? It's biblical, isn't it? Enoch and Esau. Esau and Enoch. I saw Esau on the see-saw.'

Enoch regretted saying this. It sounded very foolish and Gecko looked at him as if he were a fool.

'Just a joke,' he said and he took out a cigarette and lit it to hide his embarrassment.

'You smoke Chesterman?' Gecko asked.

'Yeah. I get them imported,' Enoch said casually. 'Do you want one?'

Gecko inverted her lips and her mouth made a small popping sound that Enoch didn't understand.

'No,' she said. 'Shall I tell you something about Chesterman?'

'Sure.'

'Did you know that eighty per cent of the tobacco used in Chesterman cigarettes is exported from Zambawi?'

'Of course I did. It's one of the country's main sources of ForEx.'

'Right.'

Gecko turned to look at him. He met her eyes placidly. Was it his imagination or had her cold eyes cooled?

'Did you know,' she continued, 'that Chesterman pay the Zambawian plantation workers the equivalent of two cents an hour?'

'I didn't know that,' Enoch admitted.

'How much did you pay for those cigarettes? Three US dollars? There's twenty cigarettes in a packet. So that makes fifteen cents a cigarette.'

'So?'

'So? So fifteen cents is seven and a half man-hours of Zambawian labour. So a full day of hard-earned foreign currency has just gone up in smoke because you're too much of a Nose to smoke local cigarettes!'

Gecko turned away and flicked her own cigarette butt into the night. Enoch watched the last of its tobacco glow, fade and extinguish on the gravel path.

'But . . .' Enoch began. But he didn't have anything to say. He felt uncomfortable and his mind was racing. He resented being described as a Nose but he didn't have any defence. This wasn't going very well at all. He sniffed and, in his embarrassment, lit another cigarette without thinking. Gecko popped her mouth once again.

'Might as well be hung for a sheep as for a lamb,' Enoch said and he tried to laugh but no sound came out. Gecko looked at him and the hint of a sneer played around her lips. She jumped off the Mercedes and strode away across the pristine carpet of the presidential lawn.

Fuck it! Enoch thought and he felt his temper rise. He wasn't used to taking criticism from a woman that wasn't of the 'Why haven't you called me?' variety. And the fact that Gecko was so obviously right only made him angrier still.

'Hold on a second,' Enoch said as he set off in pursuit. 'Where the fuck are you going?'

He caught her by the shoulder, but she turned with such ferocity that he immediately retracted his hand. And she marched off deep into the garden, away from the light of the doorway and the rigid armed guards. She strode across the ornate Chinese bridge, past the Graecized statue of a semi-clad Zamba warrior and down the path that led through the perfectly landscaped flower beds of African violets and snoozing mesembryanthemums. Enoch followed.

'Now just wait one fucking minute!' Enoch said. 'Look. You're right. I'm sorry. I can take criticism as well as the next man and I swear I won't smoke another American cigarette. OK? But it strikes me as a bit rich having to take that whole Afrocentric, Afreconomy, Africa-for-the-Africans bullshit from you. You of all people! One of *mboko* Tula's own little harem! A dictator so vicious that he makes Stalin look like an ageing nanny-goat!'

Rujeko stopped so abruptly that Enoch, following at a trot, bumped into the back of her. For a second his hands were on her shoulders until she spun round. For a moment her eyes blazed before she recaptured her poise. And Enoch's heart skipped.

'One of Tula's harem? Is that what you think? How dare you? How *dare* you?'

'I'm sorry. I just assumed . . . I saw you with him . . . and . . .'

'He's my father!' Gecko Tula cried and her voice cracked a little.

The two presidential offspring looked at one another in silence. Enoch was surprised to find that he was short of breath. Gecko's chest was heaving too.

Eventually she said quietly, 'I did not choose to be born to a murderer, you know. I cannot take responsibility for the actions of my family but that does not mean I should lose consciousness, does it? That is why I joined . . .'

'Look,' Enoch interrupted and he tried a baby smile. 'It's funny really. You and me. Talking like this. I didn't mean to be rude. It's just you were so uptight. I just wanted you to let your hair down a little. You see. Actually. I'm Enoch Adini.'

He said these last words with such weight that he expected some reaction. But Gecko offered him none.

'The President's son,' Enoch tried again.

'I know who you are,' she said and she stepped a little closer to him, so that she was looking up at his face.

At this angle, Enoch thought, her eyes do not look so cold at all.

He could feel the warmth of her breath on his neck and the sweet smell of the African violets made him feel quite light-headed. Gecko lifted her hands and, just for an instant, Enoch thought that she might be about to touch him. Instead she dexterously untied the knot in her headdress and began to unwrap the luxurious blues and reds from around her scalp.

What is she doing? Enoch thought. Does she think I meant she should literally let her hair down?

But he did nothing to stop her and his mouth was dry as she unravelled the swathes of Java print. It felt like an intimate moment to Enoch; as if she were baring her soul or indeed the whole of her body. He blinked and ran an unconscious tongue across his lower lip. Then he caught sight of some dark metal among the colour.

'Wou wave . . .' he began. And then paused to retract his tongue.

Next thing he knew, she had retrieved a semi-automatic pistol from the heavy cloth of her headdress and was pointing it directly at him.

'You have,' Enoch began again, 'a gun in your hair.'

'How else was I supposed to get it into the President's house?'

Enoch shrugged numbly. Gecko shook out her hair and it fell into long plaits down the length of her back. In spite of himself Enoch thought she looked more beautiful than ever.

'Rujeko?' he asked. 'What are you doing?'

'My name is not Rujeko. I am Lieutenant Gecko Tula of the Black Boot Gang and I claim you as my prisoner on behalf of the People's Democratic Republic of Zambawi.'

'You're kidnapping me?'

'Yes.'

'But you're President Tula's daughter!'

'Karl Marx said that the proletariat must be drawn from all classes of the population.'

'You're a Marxist?'

'No. But I studied it for A-level.'

'Why me?' Enoch protested. 'I haven't done anything.'

'Exactly.'

'Look. Rujeko. Gecko. Lieutenant. If that gun goes off here, you'll have the presidential guard swarming all over you before you can blink. You don't want that, do you?'

'If this gun goes off, you'll be dead. You don't want that, do you? Now come on. We've got to get going.'

Enoch looked into Gecko's beautiful cold eyes and tried to laugh. But the sound that came out of his mouth was stilted and unconvincing. He realized with some surprise that he was scared and the fear pricked his bladder and the corner of his eye. And he cursed Gecko for attracting his interest and denying him the reckless courage he'd found in boredom.

'Put your hands in your pockets!' she ordered.

'Why?'

'Just do as I say. Now bend forward slightly. More. That's it.'

Enoch obeyed Rujeko's commands and, with his head at a more manageable height, she pressed the barrel of her pistol into his temple.

'If your hands move from your pockets, I'll blow your brains out,' Rujeko whispered. 'Now walk!'

The two of them strolled slowly towards the service entrance at the back of the presidential residence, where they were met by two men in combat fatigues and balaclavas. Propped against the wall next to the thick iron gate, a loyal presidential guard was dying slowly. His blood-stained hands were clasped peacefully across the gash in his stomach. His eyes looked sleepy-bored. The corners of his mouth were decorated with delicate red bubbles. Swelling and popping. Swelling and popping. And the Black Boot Gang had claimed their first intended victim.

At the sight of the corpse Enoch felt the gun barrel relax slightly against his face. He glanced at Gecko and saw that her bottom lip was quivering and her cold eyes looked like a misty morning. Enoch cupped his hands around his testicles and squeezed them for reassurance, just as he'd seen the President do so many times before.

21 : The Poet (four)

On those quiet, lonely nights when there was nothing to do but think and no company but his past, General Indigo Bulimi would often sit back in his favourite chair and reflect on his conversion from poet to soldier. His twenty-third birthday! Oh God! His twenty-third birthday! Still the vivid memories haunted him like totem ancestors. And maybe that's what these memories were too, ancestors. Because they were responsible for making him who he now was.

Sometimes, however, Indigo looked that fateful twenty-third birthday squarely in the face, unflinching and brave, and he wondered if he was conning himself. Could a single event really be so powerful in its meaning? Could a man's nature really be overwhelmed by one vision of horror that paralysed his throat and emptied words of their potency? As a rule, Indigo saw the soldier in him as diametrically opposed to the poetic essence that was buried deep beneath the rubble of that one destructive moment. But perhaps his present self was really the product of generations of memories rather than one, just as he was the product of generations of ancestors. Perhaps a poet and a soldier were not so different after all: obedient to forces that they did not understand, playthings of ideology, ready to reinvent history with their chosen weapon (be it pen or gun), ever dreaming of intangible and unworkable truth. Certainly Indigo had to admit that the poetry that first ignited his soul was the poetry of revolution, heroic and bloody.

Even all these years later Indigo could still remember something that his English teacher, old Strawhead, said to him. They were reading *The Three Musketeers* aloud in class and Indigo, for all his enjoyment of the swashbuckling action, bemoaned the story's dawdling among the heroes' endless romantic trysts.

'You must understand,' Mr Kiba said, 'that Dumas was writing in French and French is the language of love.'

The language of love? This idea fascinated the young Indigo, as if hot breath and passion and meaningful gazes could be secreted in the very words themselves. And if French was the language of love, then English was the language of poetry riding on the wheels of precision. And poetry was the language of revolution, precision the solder's tool.

At state boarding school 063, it was commonly agreed that Indigo's talent as a wordsmith was unique. Unfortunately it was also undisputed that he was a schoolboy troublemaker of the most pernicious kind, the clever boy who has discovered his own mind but is yet to find the balance of despair. Even though Mr Kola, the vicious headmaster, had long since resigned – worn down by the razor tongue and insatiable appetite for pain of his nemesis – still Indigo made trouble. His discovery of the English language – his discovery of its poetry – had been like a dam bursting in his soul and the release of passion was unstoppable, washing away any lesser intellect that dared to stand in its way. No teacher escaped the examination of Indigo's rigorous mind. And no teacher passed. Only the foolish teachers dared accept the viscous challenges of logic that Indigo threw down; the wise resigned themselves to the privilege of the company of such an exceptional mind.

Indigo completed six O-levels at the age of fourteen (two years early), achieving nothing but top marks and A grades. Thereafter he began to refuse to attend any lessons in the subjects that formed the basis of the curriculum. It wasn't that he denied their value *per se*, but Indigo knew that he was a poet and, as far as he was concerned, that was that. So science and mathematics were dismissed as 'a game within a game. As pointless as a crossword,' and he abandoned history with a shrug, turning to the class and asking, 'Are you really interested in *musungu*'s dirty underpants?'

Instead Indigo set up camp in the library, reading voraciously and churning out page after page of original verse. At first he was determined to explore his chosen medium and his poetry lurched between styles. He wrote blank and rhyming verse, iambic pentameters and disorderly masterpieces; he wove love poems around a simple thread and tied satirical knots in the colonial government; he concocted tip-of-the-tongue aphorisms and obtuse puzzles; he wrote sonnets and haiku and limericks.

Gradually, however, Indigo found himself drawn to a polemical, epic style and he settled into regular structures and revolutionary content. He felt the beat of the war drum in his rhythms; the marching songs of an army resounded in his rhymes and the oppression by the *musungu* reverberated through every line.

And they colonize our minds with slippery intent,
    Commercialize our senses,
      Leave our backs bent.
They suck blood from our women's breasts, emasculate our men.
    They undermine our gods
      With Jesus. Amen.

To the other 63s Indigo was a hero. They hung on his every word, marvelling at his knowledge and the brilliance of his cheek. So devoted was Indigo's following that the teachers often used to wonder who was actually in control of state boarding school o63. Mr Kiba used to look out of the staff-room window at the crowds of boys surrounding Indigo. 'That young man!' he would say, shaking his head in bewilderment. 'He could start a revolution!'

Most days, at lunchtime, Indigo sat down on the base of the concrete flagpole in the middle of the school courtyard and held forth. He enjoyed the irony of sitting below the ubiquitous Manyikaland flag – a white horse on a green background – and he loved the lullaby sound of its material fluttering in the wind. The 63s of all ages would gather round him and Indigo tested his latest verses on their eager ears, just as he had told stories to the local kids as a ten year old beneath the Coca-Cola sign. He recited epic narratives of the victories of the Great Chief Tuloko; he launched scathing invectives against the abuses of the colonial *musungu* and irresistible rallying calls to arms.

Sometimes he eschewed poetry to allow his rhetoric free reign.

'Tell me!' he said. 'Why is it that you attend this school? Let me guess. You wish to obtain qualifications to prepare for the *musungu* world. You wish to be a clerk or a state officer, to earn more than ten dollars a week, to wear spectacles and a necktie. How ridiculous! The ten dollars you earn each week has been stolen from your brothers. The spectacles are just goggles that make you see the world like a *musungu* and the necktie is the colonial noose that chokes you. An officer? The word is overseer. You will oversee the oppression of your fellow men. Is that what you want?'

Generally Indigo's words provoked animated debate, often in Zamba. But Indigo cut short any such discussion with a furious exclamation.

'Speak English!' he declared. 'For the sake of the Great Chief Tuloko, speak English!'

'But Indigo,' the boys would reply, 'surely English is the language of the *musungu*!'

'It is his language and his greatest weapon! It is the source of our oppression! You cannot fight a gun with a spear! You must steal the gun and turn it on its owner! Kaffirs! Niggers! Munts! Savages! Make those words your own and feel their injustice echo through your skulls like an owl hooting in a cave! Read the small print! Dispute the contract! Know the law! Choke the *musungu* bastards on every syllable of apartheid! And when liberty is finally ours, make sure you know what it means!'

Few of the teachers had any inkling of Indigo's oratory – although a later inspector's report on state boarding school 063 did note the remarkable degree of literacy among the boys and Mr Kiba, as head of the English department, received a Queen's Commendation for the excellence of his teaching.

After Indigo's refusal to attend any lessons other than English, there was some talk in the staff room of a possible expulsion. But the majority of the teachers were wise enough to realize that genius has its own agenda and they hoped – for the pride of the school –

that Indigo might be the first pupil in Manyikaland to attend the one native university.

Certainly Indigo would have fulfilled their ambitions for him if it hadn't been for the loss of his father and mother. It was the third term of the school year and Mr Kiba had already begun to prepare Indigo's university application in secret. Indigo was seventeen years old.

Indigo first learned of his father's arrest in a message brought from his mother by the driver of the Coppertown bus. The message was vague and incomplete, but Indigo managed to piece together some picture of what had happened with the help of the gossip of the other passengers. It turned out that Mr Kelly had been murdered outside the Manyikaland High Court after the conviction of a known nationalist *ter* whom he had defended. Masked gunmen had pulled up next to him in a battered Citroën and pumped six bullets into his chest and face before speeding off. The assassins had not yet been caught. The next day, plain-clothes internal security officials had turned up at the Kellys' home to question all the victim's staff. Only Father Bulimi was taken into custody.

When Indigo arrived home in Mutengwazi, he found Mother Bulimi sitting on the doorstep. As he approached she didn't look up, and he had a good few seconds to digest the shock of her appearance. His mother looked so old! Her hair was white, coarse and unkempt; her fingers were as thin and brittle as twigs; her breasts rested lazily on her stomach; slowly, continuously, involuntarily, she shook her head from side to side in a strange autistic manner.

'Mum?' Indigo said.

'My son!'

Mother Bulimi stood up and embraced Indigo passionately. Her meagre frame fitted snugly into his chest.

'What's happened to Dad?'

'My special gift! The ancestors' blessing! How tall you have grown! Your eyes are clear and bright, your arms are strong, your shoulders broad. You are as handsome as your father. More handsome, even.'

'Mum! Talk to me!'

Mother Bulimi pushed Indigo gently away. Tears were streaming down her face, sliding over the taut skin of her cheeks before finding pathways in the wrinkles of her chin.

'Oh, my son!' she said. 'What have you done?'

'What do you mean?'

'They will not let me see him! They took him away in handcuffs; they beat him with their *shamboks*. They say that he is an accessory. What does that mean? And they said – oh, Indigo! – they said that his son was a terrorist sympathizer!'

'What?'

'They said that you are a terrorist sympathizer. They knew all about you. They said that you were recruiting for the ZLF.'

A cold wave of nausea upturned Indigo's stomach. Was he responsible for his father's arrest? A terrorist sympathizer? Of course he was. But how could they know? Did they have spies in the playground? Suddenly Indigo was consumed by fear; fear for himself but, most of all, fear for his poor father.

'When did they take him?' he asked.

But his mother was now sobbing so hard that she couldn't answer.

'Mum! This is important! When did they take him?'

'Exactly one week ago today.'

By the time Indigo arrived at Queenstown central police station with his mother, he was high on a cocktail of fear, anger and bubbling nerves. His heartbeat was irregular and his hands were shaking as he rang the bell at the front desk. An obese police sergeant with a tomato face and indulgent moustache read a newspaper in a glass-fronted office behind. Briefly he looked at Indigo, then he yawned and went back to his reading. Indigo bit his lip and rang the bell again. The sergeant sighed, got to his feet as slowly as he could and sauntered to the front desk.

'What do you want, boy?' he growled. His moustache was decorated with spittle and the odd crumb.

'I have come to collect my father. He is being released today.'

'Name?'

'I'm sorry?'

'His name, boy! What's his name?'

'Bulimi.'

The sergeant started. For the first time he raised his eyes to Indigo's face. Indigo tried to keep his cool and smiled placidly. The sergeant picked up a telephone and dialled, keeping his eyes fixed on Indigo all the time. He muttered something into the phone before returning the receiver to its base. He leaned forward so that he was barely an inch from Indigo's face.

'Wait here,' he said. His breath smelled of eggs; cooked by 'cook', delivered by 'houseboy'.

Almost immediately a door opened behind Indigo and Mother Bulimi and a tall white man in a pristine grey suit appeared. He wore heavy-framed square spectacles and his lank hair was neatly parted on the left. His mouth seemed to be trapped in a permanent half-smile, toothless and creepy.

'Mrs Bulimi? I am Detective Pienaar,' the man said and he offered Indigo's mother his hand. Mother Bulimi retreated, as if she expected Detective Pienaar to hit her. 'And you must be N'dgo?' he said and Indigo shook his hand. His skin felt as dry as paper.

'N'dgo,' the detective repeated. 'Ach mun! That's a strange name. I've not heard it before. What does it mean?'

'Indigo. It is the colour between blue and violet in the spectrum.'

'No. But it's Zamba, right? What is the translation in English?'

'It is a special kind of gift from the ancestors,' Indigo said.

Detective Pienaar led him and Mother Bulimi into a sparse room with a desk and a few chairs. He sat down on one side of the desk and invited the two of them to sit opposite him.

'Now,' he said brightly, addressing Mother Bulimi. 'What can I do for you?'

'My mother doesn't speak much English, Detective Pienaar,' Indigo said. 'We have come to collect my father. He is being released today.'

Detective Pienaar stared at Indigo for a moment and then leaned forward on to his elbows, clasping his hands together.

'You do realize, Indigo, that your father is being held in connection with a very serious crime. You do understand that, mun?'

'Yes, Detective Pienaar, I understand that.'

'And it is important to our ongoing investigation . . .'

'Have you charged my father?' Indigo interrupted.

'Not yet.'

'Then he must be released.'

Detective Pienaar licked his lips and raised one eyebrow.

'Indigo, I don't expect you to understand this. But under the national state of emergency, we are fully entitled to hold a suspect without charge.'

'For seven days,' Indigo said. 'You are entitled to hold a suspect without charge for seven days. The National State of Emergency Act, clause four, paragraph two. Let me quote it for you. "The state is entitled to detain, without charge, any adult citizen whom it believes constitutes a threat to national security for no longer than seven consecutive days." Your time is up, Detective Pienaar. You must release my father.'

Detective Pienaar removed his spectacles, breathed mist on to the lenses and began to polish them on his tie. How young he looks! Indigo thought.

'You're a bright young man, Indigo,' Detective Pienaar said coolly. 'Your father will be released.'

'Today.'

'Yes, today. Now then, let me ask you something. May I do that?'

Indigo shrugged.

'How do you know Zita Adini?' Detective Pienaar asked and his eyes narrowed.

'I don't know that name,' Indigo replied truthfully.

'We will release your father. I have said that. But what if I said to you that we will arrest you in his place?'

'On what charge?'

'We don't need a charge.'

'Detective Pienaar, let me ask *you* a question. What part of the National State of Emergency Act is it that you do not understand? Let me quote it for you again. "The state is entitled to detain, without charge, any adult citizen whom it believes constitutes a threat to national security for no longer than seven consecutive days"'.

'What is your point, boy?' Detective Pienaar asked and Indigo enjoyed the shift in his terminology. He was rattled.

'Clause eight of the Manyikaland constitution states that a citizen reaches majority at the age of eighteen. I believe this applies to both blacks and whites alike. I am seventeen years old, detective. Therefore I am not an adult.'

'You realize that I could make you and your family disappear, boy?'

'Indeed, you could. When will my father be released?'

'No one would even know that you were gone.'

'You would know, detective. Are you entirely comfortable with such barbarism?'

'I'm sure that I would sleep easy knowing that utilitarian principles . . .'

'Utilitarian principles!' Indigo exclaimed, raising his voice for the first time. 'Utilitarian principles dictate that any action shall be done for the greatest good of the greatest number. Tell me, Detective Pienaar, of which greatest number are you a member? Exactly! Now. When will my father be released?'

'I will be watching you, mun.'

'Good. When will my father be released?'

'This conversation is over,' Detective Pienaar said and he stood up and headed for the door.

'When will my father be released?' Indigo insisted.

'Take your mother home, boy. We will let your father out today. We'll even deliver him to your bloody doorstep.'

'No thank you, Detective Pienaar. We will wait right here.'

It was only when Indigo and his mother arrived home with Father Bulimi that they began to discover the extent of his suffering. When he had first appeared at the back entrance of the police station, he had seemed relatively unhurt. Of course, his face was badly marked – wounds clumsily stitched up – his hands were swathed in bandages and he moved with evident discomfort. But at least he walked unaided and he greeted his wife and son with a degree of recognition. He didn't speak at all, but Indigo assumed this was the temporary shock of the ordeal.

At their house in Mutengwazi, however, Indigo and his mother soon realized the full horror of Father Bulimi's incarceration. And as the heavy drugs that he had been dosed with began to wear off, Father Bulimi began to realize it too. He started to weep and rant and scream at the top of his voice. He may have walked out of prison on his own, but he had done so with ten broken toes, crushed by ten, individual, sadistic blows of a hammer. On removing his shirt, Indigo found that the torso he knew so well was scarred beyond recognition; long, ugly welts patterned his back and his chest was branded with two triangular burns that blistered and pussed. Unravelling the bandages from his hands, Indigo found that every knuckle had received the same treatment as every toe; what's more, every one of Father Bulimi's fingernails had been torn out.

As he and his mother bathed the wounds in warm water, Indigo had to check the revulsion he felt from showing in his face. Father Bulimi looked up at him with meek, vacant eyes. 'Indigo,' his father whispered. 'No more stories.'

The worst came that night. Father Bulimi was sitting on the household's one chair, naked apart from his underwear, while his wife spoon-fed him a smooth, milk-based maize porridge. Suddenly his legs straightened, his back arched and he began to scream in pain. Indigo and his mother frantically searched this body to try and find any injury they had missed. Desperately Father Bulimi began to tug at the waist of his underpants. Indigo dropped to his knees and, with his throat closing and gagging, began to ease the material over his father's buttocks. At first Indigo could see nothing wrong. Then he glimpsed the circular wound that cut deep around the base of his father's penis. Indigo forced himself to swallow mouthful after mouthful of bitter vomit as he used one tooth of a small fork to cut the triple-twisted elastic band that was embedded deep in the wound. His father's penis had almost been severed.

In retrospect Indigo concluded that it had been the discovery of this horror that had finally killed his parents. The vision of Mother Bulimi standing with her blood-stained hand to her mouth, her eyes wide with terror, had lived with him ever since. And Father Bulimi wept like a child, his eyes screwed shut, his face awash with the paradoxical innocence that can only come from such experience.

The next morning Indigo was not surprised to find that both his parents had died in their sleep. If anything, he was surprised to see the peace in their faces. His mother's head was resting on her husband's chest; Father Bulimi's mouth was slightly open, as if in the midst of a final declaration of love – love to the grave. They did not, Indigo decided, die of broken bones nor broken dreams nor broken hearts. They died simply because they were broken.

Indigo never returned to state boarding school 063, nor, in fact, to Mutengwazi. He transported his parents' bodies back to the Bulimi *gwaasha* in the Tribal Trust Lands and, as soon as the funeral rituals were completed, set about looking for the man that Detective Pienaar had mentioned, Zita Adini. Indigo knew nothing about him other than his name, but he reasoned that anyone who attracted the interest of the Manyikaland security forces would know how he could join the ZLF.

In fact, it did not take Indigo long to track Adini down to a small village in Chivu Province (clearly the security forces were as incompetent as they were brutal) and, twenty years later, he remembered his first meeting with Zambawi's future President as clearly as if it were yesterday.

Indigo arrived in the village late at night and headed straight for the lights of the local *shabeen*, where he could hear the noise of men drinking. As soon as he entered, the boisterous conversation of the dozen men stopped. But Indigo expected this. He went through the usual greetings rituals, clapping and bowing, before ordering a bucket of millet beer for the assembled company. Gradually, cautiously, he fell into conversation with the other men, telling them everything about himself, a deliberate tactic to breed trust. He told them that he came from Mutengwazi; he told them that he had just buried his parents; he told them that he had recently left school. And when they asked him what he was going to do next, he replied, 'Ah! What is there to do in Manyikaland when the *musungu* owns all the land from the Mountain in the East That Kissed the Sky to the Great Lake in the West That Cooled the Traveller's Feet.' The men nodded sagely in agreement.

All the time Indigo spoke he noticed that the man serving at the bar did not join the conversation. Instead he watched Indigo through narrow eyes. Clearly this was the man that Indigo needed to meet. Eventually the barman spoke up.

'So tell me, city boy, what is it that brings you to our little village?'

'I am looking for a man,' Indigo replied. 'Zita Adini.'

Immediately Indigo spoke the name the *shabeen* was silenced and the men began to shift from foot to foot, looking at one another uneasily.

'What do you want with him?' the barman asked.

'I thought that he might give me a job. Do you know him?'

'I have heard the name. Adini is a very important man in Chivu Province.'

'I believe he is an important man in the whole of Zambawi.'

'Surely you mean Manyikaland?'

'I know what I mean.'

'So you wish to speak to Adini? I am told he is a difficult man to find. He will not talk to just anyone.'

Indigo smiled and spread his arms in a devil-may-care gesture.

'So it was for Zamba himself when he went to talk with Father Sun. But a brave heart has no fear of difficulty.'

'And he was cast to the bottom of the Great Lake in the West That Cooled the Traveller's Feet.'

'He was,' Indigo nodded. 'But a man's fate is unknown to all but the ancestors and the *zakulu*.'

Gradually the men around Indigo began to relax once again and, though none of them would admit a personal knowledge of the mysterious Adini, they now talked about him freely, their words laced with reverence and pride.

'Did you know that Adini was the first black man to attend St Ignatius' College in Queenstown?'

'Of course! And he was the first Zambawian to attend Oxford University in England!'

'He has visited Russia! He has spoken with the man called Brezhnev!'

'They say that Adini has killed more than forty *musungu* with his bare hands!'

'And he has the wisdom of the Great Chief Tuloko.'

'The *musungu* arrested him too, Indigo. Just like your father. And they tortured him unbearably with . . .'

'But we do not talk about that!'

Suddenly Indigo was aware of a breeze on his back that prickled his neck. He spun around and there was a man standing in the doorway. Dressed in khaki battle fatigues, with a sub-machine-gun slung over his shoulder and a pipe hanging from his mouth, he was tall and muscular and handsome with angular cheekbones and a proud, high forehead. He couldn't have been more than twenty-three – just six years older than Indigo – but his bearing spoke of experience and authority and charisma. To Indigo he looked like a vision of the Great Chief Tuloko himself.

'I hear that someone is looking for me,' the man said and his words rang out above the buzz of chatter and the men quickly quietened down. If Indigo hadn't been so awestruck, he might have laughed, for – despite the authority of his tone – this man's voice was extraordinarily high-pitched and unlikely, as clear and delicate as a woman's singing.

'It is me,' he said nervously, standing as tall as he could.

'Who are you?'

'I am Indigo Bulimi.'

'N'dgo? So what do you expect, my friend?'

'No. My name is Indigo. The English. It means . . .'

The man laughed and waved Indigo's explanations aside.

'I know what it means. Don't worry, Indigo. In this colonial state we are all defined by our colour. You haven't answered my question. What do you expect?'

'I expect nothing, sir. I hope to join you.'

'To join me? In what?'

'In the ZLF. In liberty.'

'And what can you do, Indigo? What have you got to offer?'

'I am a poet.'

Again the man laughed and Indigo began to feel uncomfortable. Although the night was cold, his hands were clammy and the air seemed close and unsatisfying.

'A poet!' the man exclaimed. 'I think you'll find, my colourful friend, that the laws of conflict make little allowance for a poet.'

Indigo bristled.

'And I think you'll find, sir, that, as a great philosopher once wrote, "Laws are inoperative in war."'

'Cicero! You know Cicero! *Mens cuiusque is est quisque!*'

The man bounded towards Indigo and wrapped him in a passionate embrace as if he were a long-lost friend.

'I am Zita Adini,' Adini said. 'Welcome to freedom!'

22 : The naked truth

Captain Isaiah Muziringa of the Zambawian State Army, a.k.a. Captain Dubchek of the Black Boot Gang, sat back on his haunches, rested his shoulders against the rough bark of the baobab tree and drew hard on his hand-rolled cigarette. The damp tobacco that he'd procured from a local farmer popped and fizzed in his hand and the acrid smoke from the newsprint he'd used as cigarette paper stung his lungs. He made a face. This was the problem with patrolling the bush; not a chair to be sat upon, nor even a decent cigarette to be smoked.

Dubchek watched as his company bathed in the shallow water hole. He narrowed his eyes against the sun and pulled down the brim of his floppy hat so that the dangling corks bobbed around his nose. It was strange, but as his men splashed about, naked, in the muddy water, he found it hard to tell them apart. Was that Corporal N'dah ducking Private Amai? Was it Private Nyoka, the short-tempered company troublemaker, who lay floating on his back and spat a fountain of water into the air like a whale? Surely that was young Private Gudo – the butt of all the company's banter, who looked so unfortunately like his simian namesake – washing so conscientiously in the shallows?

Dubchek looked at the piles of civvies discarded on the water's edge and realized that these indistinguishable men were no longer Corporal This or Private Anything. For these were not naked soldiers at all but naked guerrillas. This was his company of naked revolutionaries, primed to overthrow the state. That was not Private Gudo but Samora Machel of the Black Boot Gang. And it was Mandela who floated like a whale and De Valera who was ducking Nehru.

Dubchek sighed. It was all just too confusing. Why couldn't they just be naked boys? Why did he have to answer all these tricky questions of identity? Hadn't that been his reason for joining the army in the first place, precisely to avoid such questions? Dubchek didn't know whether to laugh or cry. So he laughed. And the sound of his distinctive high-pitched giggle rang over the shouts and splashes of his boys and made him wince with embarrassment.

The Black Boot Gang, he reflected, had seemed like such a good idea in the beginning.

Dubchek remembered visiting his parents down in Simba Province about eighteen months before. He had just received his first commission as a captain and been granted three days' leave. He was so proud of the pips on his epaulette that he felt like the buttons on his uniform might burst with his swelling chest. He remembered getting off the bus – the 'Simba Dragon' with the multicoloured panelling and shining chrome headlamps – at Chipingi village, and his astonishment at the sight that greeted him.

The village looked like it had been buried in dust. Sand drifts piled up against the breeze-block walls of the bottle store and the butcher. The Simba River that ran to the west of the village was no more than a cratered trench of crusting mud, punctuated by the occasional shallow puddle. On its banks, island outcrops of coarse reeds stuck out from the eroded soil like heads that needed a comb. Where was the crowd of screaming kids who used to chase the bus like a pack of dogs? Where were the women selling mangoes, grilled maize cobs and scoops of ground nuts? Dubchek saw no one but a small boy with a distended belly and a carved wooden car in his hand. A couple of lazy flies settled in the traces of mucus that ran from the boy's nose to his upper lip. But the boy seemed too tired to brush them away.

Dubchek had walked to his family's kraal and found a similar deserted story. There was none of the usual bustle of a busy day on the smallholding. The chickens, scrawny and moulting, meandered slowly about the yard as if they were bored. There was no sign of his brother's goat, which used to stand meekly against the fence, just a stub of rope like a makeshift marker of what had been lost.

He remembered his father coming out to meet him. He remembered the way his heart had sunk when he saw the stoop of his father's posture and the wince of each stride. He remembered the way his father had greeted him with the traditional clapping, as if he was an honoured guest. He hadn't seen his dad for two years. It might as well have been twenty.

'Dad,' he said, 'what in the name of Tuloko has happened?'

'Ah! My son! A captain in the army! How proud I am!'

'Dad! Tell me. What's happened to our land?'

'Isaiah. My son. Surely you have heard in Queenstown? The rains do not come and the top soil is dead and blown away in the wind.'

'But what about the crop rotation?'

'You have been away a long time, Isaiah. Where are we to rotate the crops? We live in a desert. We eat *kiba* grass like the bushmen but it gives us cramps in our bellies.'

'What are you going to do?'

'Do not worry, Isaiah. Every Sunday we attend the mission and pray to the Lord Jesus Christ to have mercy on our eternal souls. And every evening we pray to the ancestors for the fecundity of our country. The Great Chief Tuloko will scold the *shamva* for us and soon it will flow freely once again.

'How can we worry with the gods on our side? Jesus died for our sins; he will take care of us. Tuloko is the father of our people; he will take care of us.'

Later that afternoon, as the shadows began to lengthen, Dubchek had walked out to the hills behind the village, where he had played as a boy. He found a familiar path – a path that he'd walked on many a baboon hunt – and picked his way up the slope through the brittle vegetation. Although his motives were not conscious, in his melancholy he knew exactly what he had come to see and when he reached the brow of the first hill, he looked down over the expanse of Boer farm land that stretched to the horizon. There, beneath him, was a green sea of fertility. Wind-waves rippled the lush sunflower crop before breaking on the barbed-wire boundary of the electric fence and the scent of abundance in the air was almost obscene.

For a moment or two Dubchek had felt sick and he wondered whether the *musungu* farmer prayed to any god at all. Let alone two.

When he returned to Queenstown, Dubchek had unburdened himself to one of his fellow new captains on their last night in the barracks. His confidant had listened attentively as he described what he had seen.

'It seems so unfair,' Dubchek had concluded. 'I thought our fathers defeated the *musungu* for control of our land. But what do we control? Nothing but desert. What kind of a victory is that?'

'You are an idealist,' his companion had said. Then he beckoned him closer and told him all about the nascent Black Boot Gang. Dubchek had signed up on the spot.

All these memories flooded Dubchek's mind eighteen months later as he sat under his baobab tree and smoked his disgusting cigarette. He remembered how exciting 'the revolution' had sounded. He remembered how passionate he had felt and the way his heart thumped against his ribcage. He remembered how his recruitment to the Black Boot Gang had felt like the most important decision of his life. But now he wasn't so sure. Those first ardent feelings of politization had been replaced by less certain, less noble sensations, nagging doubts and nervous questions. In fact, Dubchek now wondered whether he had ever been 'politicized' at all, or merely seduced by the delicious slogans of revolution that he barely understood: 'power is freedom', 'democracy is choice'; even 'Africa for the Africans' now seemed to throw up more questions than it answered.

The truth is, he thought, I am a coward. It's not that I'm scared to fight. Or even to die, come to that. But I am scared of change. And that can't be right for a revolutionary.

I don't believe that anyone in the Black Boot Gang knows what we are going to do. So we overthrow that fool Adini: what happens next? So we kick the whites out of our country: then what? We will only keep the support of the people so long as we know what we're doing. Look at my boys! They're not revolutionaries. It's all just a game to them: army uniforms one moment, looting villages the next. But will they stay true to the coup when the shit hits the fan? No way! They will just join the winning side! And, if I am honest, so will I.

The momentum is building and yet nobody has a plan. Shit! The first casualty of the revolution dies of a heart attack! Nothing but random chance! We kill a presidential guard in Queenstown and nobody knows why! We kidnap poor Enoch and nobody knows what for! It is a fiasco!

I am not a revolutionary. I am a fool. I am like the woodcutter who chops down a tree without even thinking where it might fall. I am like the host who kills his chickens before he's even invited the guests. I am like the farmer who dams the river and floods his village. And now the tree is falling, the chickens are fresh-killed and the river's about to burst its banks and there is nothing I can do about it!

'Sir?'

Disturbed from his thoughts, Dubchek looked up and found Samora Machel standing in front of him, saluting. He was completely naked and dripping wet.

'Is it customary to address an officer in that state of undress?' Dubchek asked.

'I apologize, Captain Muziringa . . .' began Samora Machel.

'Muziringa!' Dubchek exclaimed. 'How many times do I have to tell you? In civvies we are the Black Boot Gang and only use our revolutionary names! That kind of blunder could get us all killed!'

'Yes, sir. I'm sorry, sir.'

'What was your question, private?'

'Sir, I am confused. I don't know which clothes to put on. Are we the Black Boot Gang or are we the army?'

Dubchek stared at the naked man and suddenly felt himself moved by Samora Machel's trusting nudity and the innocence of the question.

'We are the Black Boot Gang,' he replied. 'For now.'

23 : Jim Tulloh's out-of-body experience

After Jim's mysterious meeting with Musa, the witchdoctor, his life at St Oswald's began to improve. He realized that something within him had changed and, though he couldn't put his finger on exactly what or why or when, he suspected that his conversation with Enoch in the Barrel, followed by his out-of-body experience, might have had something to do with it, and he now felt a definite and new sense of belonging. Or at least not belonging in a comfortable kind of way.

Jim explained it to himself like this: when I first came to St Oswald's, it was like a dream. Not a good dream or a nightmare, but one of those frustrating dreams when you know that you're asleep and can't do anything about it. But now, this Africa lark, it feels like my reality. Of course, I could be wrong about that and it could all be a dream after all. But the important thing is that I've stopped noticing the seams and fastenings.

This wasn't a perfect explanation, but it was satisfying enough to put Jim at ease and he began to throw himself wholeheartedly into the version of reality in which he found himself.

Where the classrooms had previously filled him with a claustro-phobic trepidation that upset his stomach, he now entered each form with a confident swagger and a breezy 'Who's ready to learn?' His cynical disregard for the slower pupils was replaced with attention and compassion. His lessons were no longer bloated with time-wasting tactics, but transformed into breakneck rides of vigorous enthusiasm. He eschewed the easy options of grammar and spelling for the challenges of literature, tackling the children's illiteracy with inspiration and spirit.

He scoured the cardboard box of tatty books that PK referred to as 'the school library' for reading material. He read aloud from an anthology of modern African poetry – Soyinka, Marechera and Angira – but the children quickly tired of the blank verse and dense, angry politicking. He borrowed a collection of Kipling from Musa's hoard and that went down a whole lot better. 'The Female of the Species' brought cheers from boys and girls alike. 'Another! Another!' they shouted and, before Jim knew what he was doing, he began to read the next poem, 'Fuzzy-Wuzzy'.

'So 'ere's to you, Fuzzy-Wuzzy, at your 'ome in the Soudan;
You're a pore benighted 'eathen but a first-class fightin' man;'

Jim flushed with embarrassment as he read but his pupils laughed and laughed, revelling in his attempts at a Victorian sergeant-major accent and the simple rhythm of the language. 'Where is the Soudan?' they asked. 'What is a night-time 'eathen?' 'What is a Fuzzy-Wuzzy?' And when he candidly explained, his class laughed all the harder and pointed at one another, hollering 'Fuzzy-Wuzzy!' at the tops of their voices.

Best of all, however, was Jim's discovery of a battered copy of *Macbeth*. He took it to his house one evening and painstakingly reproduced various scenes in ballpoint block capitals until his wrist cramped and his eyes ached in the meagre candlelight. The next day he distributed the handwritten scripts and his classes performed speeches and dialogue, with Jim explaining every word through context and comparison.

Soon Jim realized that many of the resonances of *Macbeth* echoed the pupils' own experiences. The description of the bearded witches provoked endless discussion of the widow who lived by the well and cackled like a raven and had sprouting hair on her cheeks like the long legs of a *shangu* spider. The story of 'Brave Macbeth' slashing his way through the enemy had the boys in the class whooping with delight, dancing on their desks and waving imaginary spears above their heads. Macbeth's murder of Duncan evoked the myth of the *shamva*'s betrayal of Father Sun. The blurred lines between physical and metaphysical fired the children's imaginations. The blurred lines between truth and fiction echoed their own experience.

This also presented the odd problem. On one occasion, in his GCSE class, Jim invited two pupils to play out a scene between Macbeth and Lady Macbeth: Lovemore, the shy boy who always sat in a corner at the back, and Gertrude. Jim had particular affection for Gertrude. Every morning she would sing past his house on her way to school, lost in the complexity of traditional melodies and the rhythmical accompaniment of her home-made rattle. Now she stared at the script and attempted the part of Lady Macbeth in a small voice as nervous as her singing was confident.

> 'I have given suck, and know
> How tender 'tis to love the babe that milks me:
> I would, while it was smiling in my face,
> Have plucked my nipple from his boneless gums,
> And dash'd his brains out, had I so sworn as you
> Have done to this.'

Gertrude finished the speech and looked blankly up at Jim. He smiled and nodded his thanks before launching into an explanation.

'Right!' he began. 'You remember what's going on? Lady Macbeth – Gertrude – has persuaded her husband to murder the chief so that he can take his place. But Macbeth is scared because he knows it is a bad thing to do and now he wants to change his mind.

'Here, Lady Macbeth remembers what it was like to nurse her child. She remembers that close bond that every mother feels with her baby. But Lady Macbeth is so driven by ambition that she says she would rather have smashed her baby's brains against a rock than go back on her word.'

Jim looked around the class and the faces of the pupils were as attentive as could be. Even those who struggled to understand his explanation were enwrapped in the thrill of his tone. Jim was enjoying himself.

'She would rather murder her own child!' he continued. 'She

would rather murder her own child than fail to keep such a promise!'

Lovemore and Gertrude were staring at one another. Gertrude's eyes were wide and defiant and her nostrils flared a little. Her lower lip was quivering like a butterfly's wing.

'So! Lovemore!' Jim enthused. 'What does Macbeth do?'

Lovemore glanced at the piece of paper he held in his hand and fixed his eyes on Jim for a moment. Jim misinterpreted the intensity of the boy's gaze.

'What does he do?' he said again and, before he could stop him, Lovemore drew back his hand and stung Lady Macbeth's face with a vicious slap that sent poor Gertrude tumbling to the floor.

'Fucking hell!' Jim shouted.

But Lovemore ignored him and bent over the prone figure of his stage wife. He thrust a jabbing finger at her head. 'My wife!' he said. 'Never talk to me like that again!'

Immediately the boys of the class launched into spontaneous applause and Lovemore sheepishly straightened up, acknowledging his audience with a humble smile. The girls huddled silently around Gertrude, clicking their tongues and whispering Zamba curses under their breath.

On another occasion Jim read out one of Macbeth's soliloquies.

'Methought I heard a voice cry, "Sleep no more!
Macbeth does murder sleep," the innocent sleep,
Sleep that knits up the ravell'd sleave of care,
The death of each day's life, sore labour's bath,
Balm of hurt minds, great nature's second course,
Chief nourisher in life's feast.'

He paused and looked around the blank faces of his GCSE class. He strode around the room, his eyes flitting from one pupil to another.

'So,' he said, 'any offers? What's Macbeth saying here?'

There was an uncomfortable moment or two of silence.

'Come on! "Sleep no more! Macbeth does murder sleep." What's happening?'

Eventually Kissmore, the brightest, naughtiest and most confident pupil in the class, spoke up.

'Macbeth cannot sleep,' he said.

'Exactly! And why can't Macbeth sleep? Well. What does he say? He says that sleep is for the innocent. He says that sleep is where *nature* mends the worries of the day. You see? Sleep is natural. When you plant the maize seed before the rains, it is *natural* for the crop to grow, isn't it?'

Kissmore spoke up again.

'Unless you are under a *shamva* curse,' he said.

'Well. Sure. But if you are not under a *shamva* curse . . .'

'And the Great Chief Tuloko blesses your harvest,' Kissmore interrupted and Jim sighed.

'And the Great Chief Tuloko blesses your harvest. Yes. Look. Sleep. Let's start again. When you work in the fields all day, you are tired. Yes? So at the end of the day it is *natural* that you go to sleep, isn't it? That is how your body recovers from a tiring day.'

'Unless a witch comes to you in the night.'

'Shut up, Kissmore!'

'Or a totem ancestor wishes to speak to you.'

Jim sighed and rubbed his eyes for a second. He was getting frustrated and the class had begun to chatter in Zamba. He took a deep breath, stood stock-still and waited for the hum to subside. It was a tactic that usually worked.

'Look,' Jim said. 'Forget everything I've just said. Gertrude, what has Macbeth done that was so evil?'

'He has murdered Chief Dunker, Mr Tulloh.'

'Yes. Good. He has murdered Chief Duncan. And tell me, Farai, why did he murder Chief Duncan?'

'Because he wants to be chief.'

'Right. So Macbeth has done an evil thing. Duncan was his chief, but, instead of supporting him, Macbeth has murdered him. This is not *natural*. It is against the *natural order*. So. Just as Macbeth has broken the *natural order* in the murder of his chief, so he is no longer allowed his *natural* sleep. OK? It's simple. Has everyone got that?'

But even as Jim spoke he knew that nobody had 'got it' at all. Some of his pupils nodded unconvincingly, others looked at one another in confusion and one or two lolled back in their chairs and stared brazenly out of the window. But not one face showed the slightest sign of comprehension. Jim looked at Kissmore, but he looked as baffled as the rest.

'This *natural*, Mr Tulloh,' Kissmore said. 'We do not understand this *natural*.'

That evening Jim related the events of this lesson to Musa as they sat in PK's house, drinking the witchdoctor's home-brewed millet beer ('This beer,' Musa said, 'is two parts alcohol to one part magic. Powerful stuff') and smoking an ingenious *gar* pipe, fashioned from a modified Coca-Cola bottle.

'I don't get it,' Jim concluded. 'At some levels, these kids understand Macbeth far better than I do. The witches and stuff like that. It rings true for them, doesn't it? Because there are witches in Zimindo Province.'

'And witchdoctors,' Musa interjected.

'Yeah. Of course. Like you.'

'You're very kind.'

'But when I tried to explain the idea that Macbeth's murder of Duncan was against nature, they looked at me like I was from another planet. I mean, it's not that complicated, is it?'

Musa smiled and sucked on the *gar* pipe until his eyes bulged. He exhaled lazily and turned to PK, who was sitting back to the wall and looking rather the worse for wear.

'He is a barbarian,' Musa said, 'and thinks that the customs of his tribe and island are the laws of nature.'

PK laughed and Jim felt slightly irritated and left out.

'What?' he said.

'Shaw,' Musa replied. 'George Bernard Shaw.'

'But what do you mean by it?'

'Mr Tulloh, in truth you are one of our number, but in mind you are still an Englishman. You are still a *musungu*. For these children, you try to distinguish between the real and the fantastical, the physical and the metaphysical. But there is no such distinction.

Our ancestors are with us at every moment. Our totem ancestors bless our families; the witches curse us with their spells; we *zakulu* pray to Zamba that the Great Chief Tuloko might look after us all. Do you understand?'

'Sure. Of course. It is your religion.'

'No! It is not religion! Religion is removed from life, is it not? This religion you speak of is a spirit that only exists side by side with the physical world and only – what is that word? – *interferes* with the physical on very rare occasions.

'Look at the Pope, for example! He visited Zambawi. Did you know that? The black people turned out in their thousands to be cured, to be blessed, to be honoured by his god. And what did he do? He did nothing! For us, the spirit is not just in church on Sunday. No! The ancestors are everywhere. You *musungu* divide what you know like a mother divides grain during famine so that all her children slowly starve. Frankly, Mr Tulloh, you must concede that we Fuzzy-Wuzzies understand life a good deal better than you.'

'I don't . . .'

'Of course you don't, Mr Tulloh. But you will. I have seen your fate. And you will.'

Although – as on this occasion – Musa's confident presumption sometimes verged on the annoying, Jim loved to listen to him speak. Whatever Musa said, the weight of his voice seemed to swell its wisdom. It was the kind of voice that Jim found himself nodding to, at times swayed by the argument but generally seduced by the depth of tone and the sincerity of phrasing. And PK, with his dry wit and bitter interjections, was Musa's perfect foil. So these meetings with the witchdoctor and the headmaster became a nightly ritual. The three of them would sit in PK's house, drink beer – either lager from the *shabeen* or the lethal millet brew – smoke *gar* and talk into the early hours.

Generally Musa and PK liked to discuss politics. Specifically they liked to discuss President Adini (or 'that fucking eunuch', as they referred to him) and Jim was always astonished by just how well-informed a pair they were. One might think that a nightly dissection of one man's character, motivations and policies would soon wear thin. But the two Zambawian friends always came up with new perceptions of his wrongdoings, new ways to insult him and new plans of how, one day, he would be made to pay.

'You see, Mr Tulloh,' Musa said once, 'in his speeches the eunuch continually refers to the importance of Zambawian tradition. As if he cares a fig for tradition! The eunuch does not have the support of a single witchdoctor. How can he be the chief of our people without the ratification of the *zakulu*? It is ridiculous. It is no wonder that he sides with the *musungu* farmers; the man is a coward and a charlatan. In fact, he is barely a man at all!'

Another time, late in the evening, Jim mentioned that he had met the President's son, Enoch. Musa and PK glanced at one another sharply and, for a moment, Jim felt uncomfortable, as though there was something passing between them that he knew nothing about. Maybe they despised him as a sell-out. But he reasoned that he was just being stoned and paranoid.

'Haven't you heard?' PK asked.

'Heard what?'

'The fucking eunuch's son has been kidnapped.'

'What? You're joking! That can't be true. It's not been in the paper.'

'It's true.'

'Who kidnapped him?'

'The Black Boot Gang.'

'How do you know?'

For a moment it appeared PK was about to answer. But the words seemed to catch in his throat. Instead he looked to Musa, then to Jim and smiled.

'Come on, Mr Tulloh. It is time to go outside.'

The three of them stumbled out of PK's house and propped themselves up against the wall. As usual the cool night air burst Jim's pinching lungs and made him giggle. And when Jim began to giggle, Musa and PK couldn't help but join in.

'What are you laughing at tonight, Mr Tulloh?' Musa asked.

Jim looked up at the huge breadth of black sky and the

uncountable stars that punctuated its canvas like a thousand different join-the-dot drawings. And he laughed until he could control his stomach muscles no longer and he knew that he had to break wind.

'I was just thinking that Cousin Zamba has cried a lot of tears tonight,' he spluttered. 'He must be down in the dumps.'

And Musa and PK bent double in uncontrollable laughter.

'Oh, *zakulu*!' Jim continued. 'I think the time has come to expel the evil spirits from within us.'

'Please, Mr Tulloh,' Musa said. 'Take the lead!'

Jim turned around and pressed his palms against the wall of PK's house. He bent his legs slightly and felt the enormous *gar* fart build in his stomach, rumble through his bowels and explode from his bottom with that incomparable, inhuman sound. And as he farted, just like every other night, Musa sang out his favourite lines from Chesterton.

'But since he stood for England
And knew what England means,
Unless you give him bacon
You must not give him beans!'

When Jim had finished, he rested his face against the cool concrete blocks and closed his eyes, as spent and happy as he'd ever known. He could still hear his two friends straining with laughter and he waited for what he knew was coming next.

'Ah, Mr Tulloh!' PK said at last. 'We will make a Zambawian of you yet!'

24 : Arrested development

Jim wondered how an English estate agent would describe his small house on the outskirts of the St Oswald's school grounds.

'A very attractive rural property in the heart of the sought-after Zimindo Province. Handily located for transport, water and the local conveniences, this is a cosy home and ideal first-time buy. It also benefits from an east-facing front door and marvellous view of the famous African sunrise. Boasting a host of modern features – including door, window and natural roof ventilation – we are proud to offer this post-traditional, African breeze-block shack.'

Something like that.

When Jim first arrived at St Oswald's, his heart had sunk at the sight of his lodgings. He hadn't really known what to expect, but the grey square box topped by an asbestos roof offered neither the comfort he was used to nor the romanticism of a mud-brick Zambawian home. What's more, the materials used in its construction seemed to be designed for maximum discomfort in the African climate. During the day Jim would look through his misting window and feel like a roasting joint peering out at the kitchen. At night the wind sang through the holes in the roof and no amount of bedclothes and blankets could keep him warm.

But, most of all, he struggled to get used to the teachers' washing block, which stood opposite his front door on the other side of the main path to the school. It was a dark, forbidding and unsanitary place. For all the rural Zambawians' ingenuity and invention in other areas – the remarkable refrigerators made from water-filled clay pots, the baffling irrigation systems that squeezed every last drop of goodness from the seasonal rains – they had drawn a blank when it came to clean toilet facilities. The aptly named 'long drops' were just two holes in a concrete floor laid over a vast subterranean crater. Concrete, roofless walls were erected around the holes and a wooden pole was set before each, so that you could hang like an abseiler from a cliff-face over the ominous shit-gobbling mouths.

Two washing cubicles were added to the same block, one next to each toilet, with smaller apertures to allow drainage into the cesspit. Sometimes, when Jim washed, he would hear a fellow teacher empty himself into the long drop next door and the sound would echo about the gaping cavity like a round of applause. Generally Jim would wash until he was clean or the smell got the better of him, whichever was the sooner.

Since the morning school assembly started at 7 a.m. prompt, most of the teachers would wash in the hazy light of dawn, processing two by two to the washing block with their buckets of icy water and towels thrown over their shoulders. As for Jim, he tended to leave his ablutions until the very last minute. This was due not to any laziness on his part, but to his early discovery that the rats did not retreat into their shit-hole until the morning sun was well-established in the sky. While the African teachers seemed to regard the rats as an occupational hazard, Jim could not stand the glimpses of dark shapes scurrying through the shadows and the touch of coarse, turd-caked fur against his bare ankles.

Unfortunately his desire to wash by sunlight meant that he tended to emerge from the washing block at precisely the time when most of the pupils were streaming along the path to school. Consequently he suffered the daily humiliation of dozens of taunting kids as he hurried back to his house with a towel wrapped around his waist. In particular there was a group of girls from his GCSE class who took to lying in wait for his appearance. And he regretted having ever taught them the use of comparatives and similes.

'Mr Tulloh! You are as naked as the day you were born!' they would shout.

'I am not naked!' Jim would insist, clutching his towel.

'*Eesh!* Mr Tulloh! You are as thin as a sick dog!'

'Oh, Mr Tulloh! You are as pink as the milk from a bloody udder!'

'Mr Tulloh! You need a wife to fatten you like a chicken before a feast!'

But Jim decided that the humble pleasure of rodent-free bathing outweighed the indignity of this morning run of the depictive gauntlet.

Lately, however, Jim had changed his ways and begun to wash at dawn, even before the other teachers. This, he thought, was another sign of the new confidence in his surroundings, his new sense of belonging. It wasn't that he learned to accept the company of rats with any grace, but he discovered in his character a vindictive seam that surprised him.

Now he traipsed out to the washing block at around a quarter to six in the company of PK. This pairing was the advanced party of morning bathers. The two of them would enter their separate cubicles and begin their vigorous bucket-wash, chatting boisterously all the while.

'And how are you this morning, Mr Tulloh?' PK would say.

'I am well, thank you, headmaster,' Jim replied. 'And how are you?'

'I am just fine. Thank you. And did you sleep comfortably?'

'Very comfortably, headmaster.'

'And were your dreams undisturbed by the witches, *shamva* and totem ancestors?'

'Quite undisturbed.'

All the while Jim's eyes were scouring the shadows for the unwelcome intruders. And, although PK maintained the conversation in that laid-back tone of his, Jim knew that he too was waiting for the appearance of a rodent.

Suddenly one of them, generally PK, would spot a rat.

'I have seen one, Mr Tulloh!' PK would shout. 'Fuckers!'

Jim would lift his head and crane his neck above the walls of the washing block to ensure a good view of what came next. In PK's cubicle there was a brief ruckus of ratty yelps and manly swearing, then Jim saw a small grey body fly over the top of the wall and heard it land on the hard earth with a dull thump and a pained squeak.

'Fucker!' PK shouted. 'One—nil, Mr Tulloh!'

And Jim looked for a rat of his own, caught it by the tail and swung it in one swift movement up and out of the washing block.

'One—all, headmaster!' he gasped, exhilarated by his nerve and cruelty.

Most mornings PK, aided by his remarkable lack of squeamishness, would win their game with something to spare. But Jim didn't mind because it wasn't the winning that mattered but the taking part. Besides, he would always cherish the memory of a particular high-scoring contest that he clinched five—four, expelling a rat in the last moments of the game just as PK had settled for a draw.

It was during one of these early-morning contests that a company of the Black Boot Gang decided to pay St Oswald's a visit. It had been a dull game, which PK had won with a single late score and the two of them sauntered out of the washing block, discussing whether the rats could possibly have learned to stay underground between a quarter to six and the hour. Their conversation was silenced by the sight of a bedraggled-looking bunch, thirty or forty in number, quick-stepping towards them. Dressed in scruffy civilian clothes, they could have been a company of convicts but for the rifles at their hips and the heavy webbing that crossed their chests. At their head was a small man wearing a bizarre floppy hat with dangling corks that bounced against his face. Jim noticed that most of the men were not men at all but boys, barely older than his pupils.

'Who the fuck?' said Jim.

'Shut up!' said PK.

So concentrated were the Gangers on the rhythm of their marching that they were within twenty yards before one of the young men looked up from his feet.

'*Musungu*!' the young man exclaimed and the company came to an abrupt and comical halt, bumping into the backs of one another like an accident in slow-moving traffic. The small man

in the Australian-style hat drew his pistol and approached Jim
cautiously. Jim felt ridiculous, naked but for a towel that he gripped
to his waist, with his empty bucket hanging at his side.

'Greetings from the Democratic People's Republic of Zambawi.'

'Hi,' said Jim.

'Who are you?'

'Jim Tulloh. And who are you?'

'Captain Dubchek of the Black Boot Gang,' said Dubchek and
he extended his hand to Jim.

Jim let go of the towel to return the courtesy, but he felt the
hurried knot slip down to his hip. Quickly he retracted his hand
and grasped the towel again.

'You do not wish to shake my hand, boss?'

'No! It's not that . . .'

But the captain tutted irritably and turned his attention to PK.

The other teachers were gathering at their doors and windows.
One or two early pupils were hurrying past, heading for refuge in
the classrooms.

'*Iwe*!' Dubchek began. '*Varasi chigwendere edu?*'

'I am the headmaster,' PK replied, his voice tinted with annoyance. 'Paul Kunashe. This is my school.'

'Well, Mr Headmaster. Do you always greet your guests in such
a state of undress?'

'At least I am clean,' PK observed and Dubchek smiled meanly.

'Indeed you are. And I am not. We have been marching for
three hours and, even in this cool morning, I am unbearably
hot. Will you not give me your towel so that I can dry my
forehead?'

Dubchek and PK looked at one another. PK's eyes flickered for
a second.

'Well, Mr Headmaster?'

PK unwound his towel from his waist and gave it to the captain.
He retreated a couple of paces and stood calmly naked, his back
straight and his chin high. Jim looked at PK and felt a novel sense
of angry solidarity. Slowly he slipped off his own towel and offered
it to the captain.

'Here, Captain Dubchek,' Jim said. 'You are sweating a lot. Take mine too.'

Dubchek accepted Jim's towel and looked at the two naked men in front of him. For a moment his eyes had a strange, regretful expression.

'Both of you!' he said. 'Return to your houses and, for God's sake, put some clothes on!'

The two men about-turned on their heels and marched slowly back to their respective houses. Jim's step never faltered, but, as soon as he closed the door behind him, he was overcome by a wave of nervous nausea and gingerly lay down on his mattress, hugging his arms across his chest. He could hear the sounds of the Black Boot Gang outside, helping themselves to what they pleased, the squawks of stolen chickens and the occasional crunch of breaking timber as resistant doors were kicked in. Eventually he got to his feet, slipped on a T-shirt and jeans, and peered fearfully through his window.

By now the sun was high and the majority of pupils were filtering into the school grounds, strolling unwittingly into the dangerous anarchy. Immediately outside his window Jim saw Gertrude confronted by one of the young Gangers. The Ganger shouted at her in Zamba and Gertrude cowered away as he pressed his forehead into hers. Behind her back Gertrude clutched a cloth bag. The Ganger shoved her to the ground and snatched the bag from her grasp. He then upturned it and emptied the contents into the dust: a charred maize cob, an exercise book, two pencils and a small seed-pod rattle. The Ganger picked up the cob and hungrily bit into it.

'I procure this maize on behalf of the Democratic People's Republic of Zambawi!' he announced in English, spitting food into Gertrude's face. Then, as Gertrude scrabbled in the dirt to reclaim her other paltry possessions, the Ganger sank the heel of his black boot into the rattle, smashing the seed pod and scattering its contents. Gertrude cried out pitifully, '*Aiwa!*'

The Ganger looked furtively around himself. Elsewhere his colleagues were murdering poultry and puffing on fresh tobacco for the first time since God knows when. For a moment the Ganger looked directly at Jim's window and Jim thought he'd been spotted. But the reflection of the bright sun preserved his cover. The Ganger caught Gertrude by the arm and swung her carelessly to her feet as if she were a sack of corn. Again he looked about himself and Jim spotted a terrifying, lustful menace in the curl of his mouth and the lascivious tongue that moistened his lower lip. Gertrude saw it too and began to scream.

Fuck! Jim thought. What do I do? And, although he knew the answer, he found himself frozen to the spot, staring helplessly at the unfolding drama.

'Iwe! Mandela! Aiwa!'

Captain Dubchek's voice rang out. Dubchek was standing by the washing block, his hat pulled low over his eyes and his feet set square. His pistol was drawn and trained on the Ganger.

'Aiwa!' Dubchek said again.

Reluctantly the Ganger let Gertrude go. It looked as though she might faint, but she managed to gather herself and ran off towards the school building as fast as she could. Briefly captain and soldier squared up to one another. Jim saw the junior's fingertips curling and uncurling around the butt of his rifle. Dubchek cocked his pistol and spat in the dust at his feet. Jim saw the young Ganger's shoulders relax a little. Dubchek smiled confidently, holstered his pistol and turned away.

Retreating from the window, Jim found that his heart was racing and his legs were jelly. His breathing was uneven and trickles of sweat stung his eyes and tickled his nose. He was scared and confused.

I don't get it! he thought. Musa and PK wanted rid of the President. But how could they support this mob?

He had an idea. He delved into his rucksack and found his small automatic camera. He had bought it especially for his travels and it had one of those mechanical long lenses that telescope from the front with a gentle whirring sound. All the time he had been in Zambawi and he was yet to take a picture. Now seemed like a good moment to start.

Sidling back to the window, Jim pressed the lens of the camera against the pane. But the glass was too dirty and he found that he couldn't see anything. Slowly he eased open the window and the hinges creaked. To him the noise was so loud that it could have woken the dead. But nobody looked his way. Quickly he pushed the camera's nose through the opening and rattled off an entire film: the headless chicken carcasses that the company collected in a macabre heap; the two young Gangers who counted dollar bills and laughed as they talked; the gargantuan thug who beat down locked doors with his fist; and maybe six or seven shots of Captain Dubchek – smoking a cigarette, fingering the brim of his hat, barking orders to his men.

The camera clicked to the end of the roll and began to rewind automatically. Again the noise seemed unbearably loud and, in his fright, Jim fell backwards and pressed himself against the wall beneath the window like an expert sniper. For a full minute he remained motionless, expecting a bang on his door or a bullet through the glass. But none came. Eventually he flipped open the base of his camera, stuffed the finished film deep into his pocket and dexterously reloaded. Gradually he inched his way up the wall again, sucked a deep breath and resumed his former position. But the Gangers were gone.

By the time Jim made it outside, most of the other teachers and pupils had already emerged from their hiding places. They seemed, Jim thought, remarkably unfazed by the morning's events. Somewhere he could hear the sound of a woman crying. But most of the St Oswald's community gathered into small groups and placidly bemoaned the loss of their food, their clothes, their savings. One teacher gathered the discarded chicken heads into a bowl – there was no point letting them go to waste; another tended a small boy whose chance remark had provoked a beating. Gertrude and her friends sat on the step of one of the classrooms and sang to themselves, a melancholy song that slipped from major to minor key like a shutting door.

In the midst of it all P K stood and calmly rolled a cigarette. Jim approached him and felt a wave of righteous, indignant rage bubble in his throat.

'Mr Tulloh,' PK said.

For a moment, Jim couldn't say anything. He looked into PK's eyes and was somewhat disgruntled by the glazed emptiness he found there. As if he were being shut out.

'What the fuck was that all about?' he asked and he heard his voice quiver like a taut bow string. 'Is that how you get rid of the fucking eunuch? With that bunch of hooligans! Did you see what they did to Gertrude?'

PK's gaze skipped to where Gertrude was sitting.

'She looks all right to me,' he said.

'Yeah. Well, I just don't get it. Is this what the Black Boot Gang want? It's hardly going to make them popular, is it? Wading into a small school, stealing the food and beating the kids. Fuck! You would have thought they wanted the people on their side, a bit of grassroots support, rallying the masses. Not this!'

'This is Zambawi, Mr Tulloh. You are a *musungu*.'

'I'm a *musungu*! So fucking what? What's that got to do with anything?'

'There is no such thing as a popular revolution.'

While they spoke, Jim was vaguely aware of the sound of an approaching engine. At first he thought nothing of it, assuming it had to be Number 17. Besides, the car-free plains of rural Zambawi carried the sound of an approaching bus for miles. Often it would be half an hour or more between hearing the first straining gear change and seeing the bus trundle into view. However, when PK delivered his pessimistic assessment of the nature of insurgency, Jim suddenly realized that a camouflaged army truck was driving towards them across the scrub land from the road, scattering the pupils and teachers, who disappeared back into their hide-outs like rabbits into a warren.

'Would you believe it?' Jim exclaimed. 'Twenty minutes too late!'

'Indeed,' PK said quietly.

The truck pulled up some ten yards away and a small man jumped down from the cabin. He was wearing a pristine khaki uniform and a peaked cap that seemed slightly too big for his head, resting low on his eyebrows. The pips on his shoulder marked him out as a captain.

Immediately he hit the ground, the captain shouted an order in Zamba and the tarpaulin flap at the back of the truck was pulled open. A company of the Zambawian State Army leapt out and aligned themselves in four smart rows of maybe eight soldiers each, standing rigidly to attention, chins jutting.

Shit! Jim thought. They look a damn sight more professional than the other mob. Look at the creases in their uniforms! They look like they've just been put on. Young, though. No older than the Gangers.

The captain approached PK, marching stiffly.

'I am Captain Isaiah Muziringa of the Zambawian State Army,' he said, extending his hand. 'Who are you?'

'Paul Kunashe,' said PK carefully, shaking the captain's hand. 'The headmaster. This is my school.'

'Jim Tulloh,' said Jim and warmly took his turn to shake hands. Was it his imagination or was there contempt in the captain's eyes? Jim suddenly thought that the captain looked somehow familiar. But, without any appropriate context for that idea, he put it out of his mind.

'You have had a visit from the Black Boot Gang. Which way did they go?'

PK pointed up the road that led to the main Zimindo township, some twenty miles away.

'Are you certain, Mr Kunashe?' the captain said. 'We have just come from that way and we saw no one.'

Without speaking, PK reversed the direction of his arm.

'Just as I thought. They have headed into the hills. We will pursue them straight away and I will be back to take a statement from you, Mr Kunashe.'

PK shrugged. The captain saluted, PK smiled thinly and Jim spoke up.

'Captain Muziringa,' Jim said, 'I have something to show you. I managed to take some photographs of the Black Boot Gang.'

Jim reached into his pocket, extracted the roll of film and held it out to the captain between thumb and forefinger. PK coughed noisily and Jim looked at him. PK's eyes were blazing with warning, but Jim assumed that this was from misplaced allegiance – as he now considered it – to the would-be revolutionaries. Ignoring the headmaster, he turned back to the captain. An emotion that Jim couldn't figure was fluttering about the soldier's face like a nervous tick. But before Jim could identify it, it was gone.

'That is very good of you, boss,' the captain said. 'Perhaps you would not mind accompanying us to the barracks at Zimindo township to answer a few questions?'

'Now?' Jim asked.

'Yes. Now.'

'I thought you were going after the Gangers.'

'When such important new evidence has come to light? I would prefer to question you as soon as possible.'

Jim felt proud and important and he was about to agree when PK interrupted.

'I am sorry, captain,' he said. 'But Mr Tulloh has some vital lessons to teach today and I really cannot spare him. Perhaps he could answer your questions tomorrow. I will accompany him to the township myself.'

Jim stared at PK in surprise and irritation. Some vital lessons? What the fuck was going on?

The captain pulled the peak of his cap even lower over his face, so that Jim could only see his mouth. He peeled his lips and ran a bored tongue over his teeth.

'Well, Mr Kunashe! You do want us to catch the Gangers, don't you?'

'Of course, but . . .'

'It is settled, then. The *musungu* is coming with us.'

'But, captain,' PK tried again, his voice as slippery as water on glass, 'surely you could take the *musungu*'s film and leave him here. After all, the pictures are the important thing. When you have the film, you can do what you like with it. You don't really need the *musungu* at all.'

'He is coming with us, Mr Kunashe,' said the captain with

incontrovertible finality. 'Corporal N'dah! Take the *musungu* to the truck!'

Throughout this exchange Jim's feelings of disquiet had been slowly increasing. He sensed a subtext that he hadn't noticed before, though he still couldn't figure its essence. What's more, he hadn't missed the way his epithet had slipped from 'Mr Tulloh' or 'boss' to 'the *musungu*'. Now the powerful hands of Corporal N'dah clutched his shoulders and began to manhandle him towards the truck, ignoring his 'Thank you, I can manage'. He looked back at PK and saw genuine panic spreading over the headmaster's face.

'Captain Dubchek! I must protest . . .' PK shouted and then his voice tailed off with the weight of the error he'd made. The words ran through Dubchek/Muziringa like a bitter-cold wind and froze him to the spot. Jim was overwhelmed by a terrifying wave of realization that filled his lungs and left him choking for breath. No wonder he had recognized the captain! And the strong-handed Corporal N'dah was none other than the enormous Ganger who'd smashed up the teachers' houses! And there, with the rifle to his shoulder, was the evil bully who'd threatened Gertrude!

Oh fuck! Jim thought. A rifle!

A single shot tore the air and Jim felt it fizz his cheek on its way past. For one brief instant, he wondered how the soldier had missed at such close range. Then he heard the dull clunk of bullet hitting bone and an appalling, sibilant sound of expelled air, like a dying balloon. Shrugging off the mammoth corporal with strength born of alarm, Jim spun just in time to see PK sink to his knees, his hands pressed to his chest, a curious look of pleasant surprise on his face.

'*Aiwa!*' Jim cried.

Jim ran to PK and caught him in his arms as he fell backwards. Vainly he tore PK's shirt open, only to find that the bullet wound was remarkably bloodless, innocuous-looking and as cleanly circular as a hole punched through paper. PK opened his mouth to speak but no words came out. Instead he coughed and a great fountain of warm blood burst from his mouth and splattered Jim's face.

'You'll be all right,' Jim said. Not because he believed it. But because that was the kind of thing they said on TV in England and he didn't know what else to say.

'Mr Tulloh, you look like shit,' PK whispered. And the words surfed out of his mouth on wave after wave of blood.

'So do you,' Jim said.

'Mr Tulloh, I thought you had learned to recognize us black people.'

'I have, PK!' Jim wept. 'Really I have!'

'Ah! You will always be a *musungu*, Jim,' PK said and his mouth split into a ghoulish smile. 'My friend.'

PK closed his eyes and died.

Around the pair of them, all hell had broken loose, although Jim was not aware of it. First of all, the gunman, Private Mandela/Nyoka had burst out laughing at the sight of the fallen headmaster. But he was soon shut up by the furious captain. '*Iwe! Kula kadoma zike valuka e gudo*,' the captain shouted (roughly, 'you bastard lovechild of a whore and a baboon'), before punching him in the face and shattering the bridge of his nose. Next the captain realized that an army of teachers and pupils – armed with sticks, broom handles and the odd saucepan – was beginning to encircle his men. Immediately he ordered the soldiers back into the truck and the driver to start the engine. Finally he ran to where Jim was cradling the headmaster's corpse, rocking backwards and forwards like a mother holding a baby.

'You must open his eyes,' the captain said quietly, 'so that the ancestors know that he is ready for them.'

Numbly Jim did as he was told.

'I'm sorry, *musungu*,' the captain said and drew his pistol.

Jim turned in time to feel the full weight of the gun's butt across his chin.

25 : Jim Tulloh wakes up four times and passes out five

Jim was dreaming about the loss of his parents. He was eight years old. A Tuesday lunch break.

The playground was full and the kids were bouncing off the mesh fences like excited pinballs. Some older boys were throwing conkers at a fat four-eyes in the corner by the netball court, others were swapping football stickers and the rest were running around like unwitting participants in an experiment in chaos. Jim was hiding behind a dustbin next to the shed because the girls were playing kiss chase and he knew he was a prime target. Aged eight, he was at the zenith of his sexual prowess.

He saw his grandmother talking to one of the dinner ladies on duty – Mrs Jayawardena, the dark-skinned woman with the sunny smile and orange-peel ankles. What was his grandmother doing there? Forgetting the threat of the lustful little girls in white pop socks and bright yellow dresses, Jim sauntered across the tarmac. His grandmother looked tense and sad, dragging on her cigarette with the concentration of a baby sucking a thumb. Her drawn face reminded him of the expressions she pulled at Grandpa's funeral when she clutched him to her mastectomized bosom and pleaded with him as if he were God himself. 'It's not true, is it, James?'

If anything, today his grandmother looked sadder still.

As soon as she saw him, she rushed forward and gathered him into her arms. Jim was embarrassed and struggled to get free. She smelled of cigarettes and lavender and her chest was bony and unwelcoming.

'There has been an accident, James,' she said.

'What kind of accident?'

'Mummy and Daddy are in hospital. But don't you worry because everything's going to be just fine. Now you run inside and fetch your duffel.'

Jim trotted off obediently to the boys' coat pegs in the school's front hall. But he knew that his grandmother was lying. And he was worried. And everything wasn't just fine.

At the doorway he was accosted by Suzie Bayliss, the mousy girl with braces on her teeth and snot slugs beneath her nose. She held him by the shoulders and planted a soggy kiss on his lips. Then she danced off around the playground singing 'I've kissed Jimmy Tulloh! Jimmy is my boyfriend!'

At this point Jim's dream skipped. So he missed out on the silent car ride to the hospital, the morbid sense of foreboding that was pungent in the air of the surgeon's office and that night spent between cold sheets in his grandmother's spare bedroom. Instead his dream jumped straight to the next day, when the 'just fineness' of everything had slid into the loss of both parents.

Jim accompanied his grandmother to the funeral parlour to view the bodies. 'To say goodbye' was how his grandmother had put it and he was too numb to argue. He thought that the skin on his mother's face was the most beautiful colour he'd ever seen and he wanted to touch it. His father, with an expressionless mouth and softly closed eyes, was barely recognizable as his father at all.

He heard the undertaker in the black suit talking to his grandmother.

'You wouldn't believe they were dead to look at their faces. They look like they're sleeping.'

The man put his hand on Jim's head and ruffled his hair affectionately. 'Poor mite!' he said.

But the undertaker was wrong because Jim looked at his parents' faces and he *did* believe they were dead. In fact, he believed that two waxwork dummies had maliciously taken the space that his parents had once occupied to try and fool him. But he wasn't going to fall for it. These motionless and emotionless corpses in their coffins were just mannequins. He knew that.

Jim was lying on the floor of an interrogation cell at the Zimindo township barracks. But he didn't know that's where he was and he didn't know how long he'd been there and he didn't much care. His head had been muddled by the crack of the pistol whip across his face and he was circling between consciousness and sleep as if he were stuck in a revolving door. One minute his mind was pinprick lucid with a kind of remote interest in his surroundings – the dull light of the windowless cell and the curious, musty cereal smell, like sweaty men who ate nothing but roughage – the next he was bombarded by druggy hallucinations and claustrophobic sensations, all closing walls and gasping lungs. One minute he dreamed of his dead parents with a precision that his wakeful mind would never sanction and the next his tender psyche was assaulted by images of PK's death that scared the shit out of him.

Gradually, however, the bouts of sleep began to recede until he was able to haul himself into a sitting position and address the absorbent walls with some confidence.

'I am awake,' he said and he immediately regretted the admission and the trap doors it opened in his memory.

When Mum and Dad were killed, he thought, I didn't feel like this.

In the weeks following his parents' death, Jim found that an empty bubble was swelling in his stomach. It was small at first but it soon grew into a dull ache, a hunger gremlin gnawing at his insides. In those early months Jim's bubble was delicately skinned and amorphous, shifting size and shape with the state of his mood and digestion. Later the bubble's surface hardened and bristled until he felt like he was carrying a coconut in his middle, with coarse hairs that chafed his soul. Ten years later and Jim's bubble was still there. Sometimes he managed to forget about it – when he'd eaten too much fried food or drunk too much beer – but it always bobbed to the surface again on drizzly days or sad nights, when memories came calling.

He shifted uncomfortably on the cold mud-brick floor and hugged his belly. He tried to feel whether a baby PK bubble might be hiding behind the mature bubble of his parents. But he couldn't feel anything down there. Instead PK was a twisting corkscrew that skewered deeper into his brain with every flashing recollection. Would his soul bubble ever burst? Would his brain cork ever pop?

Jim concluded that 'dead' and 'death' must be very different things. 'Dead' was a chronic illness that needed careful management with bacon and eggs and large quantities of alcohol. 'Dead' was an embedded feature in his character that was continually pasteurized, first through the funeral rituals and then through the ongoing euphemisms of 'loss'. 'Dead', Jim realized, was more than just a state of being 'not alive'. It was a cultural construction built around tiptoe language, dignified symbols and cosy, soft-edged mythology. But 'death'? The precise mechanics of 'death' were terrifying and inhuman! That moment when the victim is stripped of his personality, that moment when a man is no more than the sum of his parts, torn from a starring role in his own personal story to fill nothing more exciting than a bit part in a tiresome *opus magnum* that nobody would ever have the patience to read. 'Death' was shit!

Jim wondered whether he would have felt differently about his parents if he'd witnessed the moment of their death. Sitting in that claustrophobic interrogation cell, he tried to picture the detail of his parents' accident for the very first time, the steering wheel impacted in Dad's forehead, Mum's body sprawled at unnatural angles across the bonnet of the car. The snapshots that slideshowed across his mind were too much to bear.

And that brought him to PK. It was the first death that Jim had witnessed. Although, as it turned out, it was far from the last.

As clearly as the images of PK's last moments took their turns in Jim's mind – the eerie smile that spread across the headmaster's face, the innocuous bullet hole, the hot blood that splattered Jim's cheeks with almost concupiscent abandon – he simply couldn't get his head around their meaning. He couldn't fit the separate little instances together into any kind of coherent narrative. Because it was like trying to tell a short story using nothing but questions: whys, hows, and what the fuck fors. And these questions led to wordless answers consisting only of the basest desires and frustrations. Jim realized that he was hungry (for fried food), thirsty (for beer), tired and angry and lonely and sore all at once.

There was a knock on the heavy wooden door of the cell and Jim looked up. His ears were immediately alert, but there was nothing but silence to be heard. Perhaps he had imagined it. There was something blackly comical about the idea that his murderous captors should observe such etiquette. Another knock. Jim almost smiled, but the heavy welt on his jaw was too painful to allow his mouth much movement.

'What?' he grunted.

The door opened and Captain Muziringa/Dubchek entered. Framed in bright sunlight he was struggling to make out his prisoner in the unaccustomed murk. Jim coughed.

'Boss,' the captain said.

'What do you want?'

The captain locked the door behind him and pulled up a chair to the plain wooden table in the middle of the cell. He laid out some papers and extracted a pen from his top pocket. Jim stared at him but the captain refused to meet his eyes. Instead he bent over the desk and talked as he wrote his notes.

'Interview with Mr James Tulloh; 3.47 p.m.; those present Captain Isaiah Muziringa of the Zambawi State Army and the aforementioned Tulloh, James, Mr.'

'Is – what do you call yourself? Dubchek? – is Dubchek not joining us this afternoon?'

Still Jim stared at the captain and he noticed the way the soldier shivered a little at the mention of his alias. The captain bent further over the table and focused intently on the blank page in front of him. How little he looked like a soldier! His wiry frame seemed swamped in the capacious battledress, like a child playing at dress-up.

'Would you not like to sit on a chair, boss?'

'I'm fine.'

'You're comfortable?'

'I'm fine.'

'That is good.'

The captain was now so low over the table that his nose was practically brushing the paper. Jim couldn't be sure, but he thought he saw a single tear slip down the bridge of his nose and hang from the tip like a reckless skier clinging on for dear life. The captain retrieved a handkerchief from the pocket of his fatigues and blew his nose ferociously.

'The first thing to say, Mr Tulloh, is that you are not under arrest. You are here of your own free will to assist us in our investigation into this morning's . . . erm . . . incident. You can leave at any time.'

'It was this morning?'

'Quite.'

'Any time?'

'Exactly.'

'Then I'm going.'

Jim lifted himself gingerly to his feet and stumbled to the door. He found that the floor was unsteady beneath his feet. Irritating. The captain didn't look up but tapped his pen on the table in front of him.

'It's locked,' Jim said and he heard the slur in his voice.

'That is unfortunate.'

'So I'm not free to leave.'

'You are free to leave. But the door is locked. That is unfortunate.'

'I see.'

Jim sat down on the chair opposite the captain and stared at him some more. Again the captain avoided his eyes and Jim hazily resolved to be as confrontational as possible.

'So, Mr Tulloch, to your knowledge, how long was Paul Kunashe collaborating with the Black Boot Gang?'

'What?'

'Three months? Six months? A year?'

'You murdered him.'

'Six months it is. And did you try to dissuade him from such traitorous pursuits?'

'You shot him in cold blood! He died in my arms. A good man. A school teacher. And, you know, he supported you. He actually supported you and your fucking bunch of hooligans. Shit! You're all fucking mad, aren't you?'

'Of course you did. You are a good friend to the Zambawian state and your cooperation will be noted. But why did you not go to the police with your suspicions?'

So we're playing a game, Jim thought. Or is it an interrogation technique? Shame I'm feeling so woozy.

'He always said that you were fickle,' Jim stammered. 'Fickle! As if that covers it! You fucking Zambawians don't have a clue who you are! You love the English. You hate the English. You're soldiers. You're guerrillas. You're Christians. You're pagans. You're a nation, a tribe, a totem, a *gwaasha*. You're rich and poor, you get fat while you starve, you dance brilliantly to music that sounds like rodents being murdered, you smoke the best weed on earth and drink the shittest beer. You would die for a chicken and kill for . . . for what? Who the fuck are you people? You're nationalists, continentalists, Marxists, democratists, piss artists!'

Jim concluded his rant by banging his fist on the table. There was a moment or two of silence and he suddenly felt very awake. His heart was pumping and his mind was jumping from thought to thought. This was just too unreal! He felt both reckless and detached; maybe because his head was still humming from the blow of the pistol or maybe because his base fury was overwhelming any other emotions.

'So Paul Kunashe threatened you?' said the captain quietly.

That was it! Jim stood up abruptly and sent his chair tumbling backwards. He began to stalk around the room – hands in his pocket one moment, tearing his hair the next – berating the soldier with an unstemmable flow of concussed gibberish.

'No, you chump! Have you listened to one word I've said? How long was PK a Ganger? Shit! How long do you want? Twenty-five years! Since 1836! Ever since the Traveller first washed his tootsies in that pond that Musa keeps banging on about! Did I try to dissuade PK from his traitorous pursuits? Oh yes! Of course I did! I thought he'd make much better money in pest control! He was quite a rat catcher, you know! But the bastard threatened me, didn't he? If you say so! Yeah! PK threatened to be my friend until you decided to put a bullet through him! So fuck you and your bullshit revolution! Fuck the lot of you!'

While Jim harangued the captain, he circled the desk three or four times with a strange, uncoordinated step, like a foal getting to its feet for the first time. And the more he polemicized, the less breath he could devote to his unsteady movements. And as his breath shortened, the dizzy monster that had been paddling on the shores of his mind decided to take a dip and plunged into the rough waters with an almighty splash that bespattered the inside of his cranium with the delicate droplets of his reason.

'Oh God!' Jim mumbled. He covered his eyes with the palms of his hands and collapsed into a dead faint.

When Jim came to for the second time, precariously balanced on the poorly stitched seam between unconscious and awake, the first thing he noticed was a smell. Sleepily he remembered the time he had fainted at the feet of the naked boy with the razor-sharp teeth and he wondered vaguely if he was back lying on Musa's bull, transported slowly through the African night with the *zakulu* at his side. But there was none of the gentle rocking motion of the bull's gait beneath him and, besides, this smell was altogether different, comforting and familiar and difficult to pinpoint.

'Digestive biscuits!' Jim said and he opened his eyes to find the captain bent over him with a worried look on his face.

'What did you say, boss?'

'Digestive biscuits. Your breath smells of digestive biscuits.'

The captain furrowed his brow and bit his lower lip.

'I'm sorry, Mr Tulloh. I fear I must have hit you too hard.'

But Jim smiled and saw a drunken, dismissive hand that must have been his own wave in front of his face.

'Don't you worry, Isaiah Dubchek of the Black State Boot Army,' he mumbled. 'I'm sure I deserved it.'

Slowly the captain helped Jim up; first to his feet and then to the table. Jim slumped in the chair and looked about himself, puzzled. He was feeling very confused again and he wasn't quite sure what was going on. The captain sat opposite him once more and thrust a ballpoint pen between his fingers and a piece of paper under his nose.

'Sign at the bottom,' the captain said.

'What is it?'

'It's your statement.'

'What statement?'

'Your statement.'

'Oh. Right.'

Jim grasped the pen tightly and found that his hand was shaking. He wondered absent-mindedly what the hell he was doing there.

Absent-minded. That was it. His mind was absent. He looked at the spot on the floor where he had just lain prone and tried to see if his brain had rolled off into the shadows. No such luck. Resigned to his lack of mind, therefore, Jim decided to sign the paper. He stared at the captain's intricate handwriting. It was complete gobbledegook.

'Captain,' Jim said slowly, 'either I can no longer read or this is complete gobbledegook.'

'It's in Zamba.'

'Oh,' said Jim. 'I see.'

He stared at the page some more and he began to recognize some words. St Oswald's. Zimindo. Black Boot Gang. Paul Kunashe. James Tulloh. Gradually Jim's thoughts began to coalesce into something approaching order. He looked up at the captain and the captain looked away.

'My parents are dead,' he said randomly and the words seemed to float above the table like a child's mobile above a cot. 'You murdered my friend, didn't you?'

'No!'

'Yes, you did!' Jim heard his voice grow louder and more confident. 'Well! Fuck you!'

With that, Jim threw the ballpoint at the captain and just had time to see it bounce off the soldier's lapel before his eyesight began to blur. At last the captain turned to meet his eyes. But Jim's vision was now too squiffy to make out anything beyond vague pixilated shapes.

'You must sign it, boss!' the captain said and Jim was mildly aware of the sadness in his voice. Jim shrugged and sighed.

'No,' he said. 'I'm going to sleep.'

And he did, with his head lolling on to his shoulder, dribbles of saliva decorating his T-shirt and unremembered dreams of adolescent schoolgirls and soldiers fighting with water pistols.

The third time Jim woke up, he did so with a start. He was aware that someone else was in the room and he opened his eyes alertly to find himself staring at a belt-buckled midriff. He looked up the bright shiny buttons of the uniform to the underside of the proud chin that was covered in angry-looking shaving bumps. He would have been able to see right inside the soldier's wide nostrils but for the large wads of bloody cottonwool that filled them. Jim recognized the soldier by his broken nose. It was Private Nyoka/ Mandela. The thug who'd pulled the trigger.

'So you're awake now, eh *musungu*?'

Jim swallowed and found that his throat was dry and sore. He said nothing. This man reeked of evil like a father smells of cheap aftershave on Boxing Day.

The private held up Jim's 'statement' in front of his face.

'The captain says you won't sign your statement. I told him I was sure you'd sign it for me.'

The private crouched down so that his face was level with Jim's. Two black bruises circled his eyes and the whites were stained with burst blood vessels. The wads of cotton wool suspended from his nose looked like a pair of chrysalises, ready to hatch some kind of horrendous insect. He leered at Jim and his tongue spilled out of his mouth as if it had a lecherous mind of its own. His lips were thick and stupid and his teeth were uneven, his canines pronounced. He looked like the devil himself.

'Sign it,' he whispered and the soft breath on Jim's cheek turned his stomach upside-down.

Jim shook his head and the private smiled because this was clearly the answer he'd wanted.

'Open your mouth.'

'Fuck you!'

The private stared at Jim for a moment or more and the suspicion of a wink played around the corner of his eye. Then he straightened up and idled menacingly around to the back of Jim's chair.

'Have you heard of Zambawian roulette?'

Resting his elbows on Jim's shoulders, the private held a revolver in front of Jim's face and flipped open the barrel to reveal six full chambers. Carefully he extracted one bullet, snapped the barrel back into place and spun the revolver.

'The odds are not good, *musungu*. Open your mouth.'

Jim found that any response was paralysed in his throat, but he shook his head violently from side to side. With malicious dexterity the private grasped Jim's jaw with one hand, his thumb pressing hard into the painful sore left by the captain's pistol. Involuntarily Jim yelped with pain and his lips clamped down on a mouthful of steel.

'Sign it!'

Jim struggled for a moment, but, cross-eyed, he could see the private's finger twitching over the trigger.

'Sign it!' the private said again and Jim tried to speak, only to find the barrel of the gun pressed deeper to the back of his mouth, catching in his throat and making him gag. Jim gesticulated furiously. But the private tightened his grip on Jim's jaw until his eyes began to water and he was forced to sit still.

'Nnnngh!' Jim grunted from deep in his stomach.

Of course, he would have signed. If the private had offered him a pen.

'So you're a brave man, *musungu*,' he said with a grudging tone of respect. 'Of course, it doesn't matter.'

Still holding the gun in Jim's mouth, the private let go of Jim's face and his spare hand disappeared for a moment before returning across Jim's shoulder with its fingertips grasping a half-eaten ballpoint. Jim felt the weight of the soldier's body on his neck as he leaned across him and signed 'J. Tulloh' in unlikely, childish script at the bottom of the page. The private laughed – a cruel, soulless laugh – and his finger squeezed the trigger. The chamber clicked over. Empty. And Jim fainted.

When Jim woke up for the fourth time, he resolved to keep his eyes shut until he was absolutely sure of the situation. He had learned his lesson. The last thing he needed was another confrontation with a murderer, be they guilt-ridden and sombre or out and out evil. He could feel a soothing, damp cloth mopping his brow and he didn't want to spoil it by opening his eyes. Besides, his head was now painful and throbbing. He remembered a phrase that PK had used to describe a hangover: 'My head feels like it has a Nigerian living in it.' That was how he felt.

For about ten minutes Jim lay resolutely still, enjoying the tender application of the cold cloth, collecting his thoughts and trying to evict the typically stubborn and self-righteous Nigerian. Only when he heard his unknown nurse stand up and the footsteps recede from his side did he dare open his eyes the tiniest amount. He found that he was lying on a hard wooden board in a different murky room. Tilting his head surreptitiously to one side, he saw that one side of the room was open but barred from ceiling to floor, like a jailhouse in an old western. Gazing through the filter of his eyelashes gave his surroundings, he thought, the look of a black-and-white film. He heard the sound of dripping water and, turning his head a little further, he made out a tiny, hunched figure wringing a cloth over a bucket. The figure finished its job and began to turn around mechanically with stuttering footsteps, like a very old man. Jim squeezed his eyes tight shut and resumed his former position. The wooden board gave a little as his nurse sat down next to him once again.

'Ah, Mr Tulloh! What has happened to you?'

A man's voice, lullaby-soft and calm. Jim recognized the tone, but he couldn't place it. Slowly he opened his eyes.

'Jesus Christ!' he exclaimed and he shut his eyes once again, as if the man could possibly believe that he was talking in his sleep.

'No, Mr Tulloh!' the voice said with a concerned inflection. 'It is I, Taurai Murufu.'

Jim abandoned his pretence and opened his eyes to look up into Mr Murufu's ancient face. If anything, the old man looked even more old and knackered than he remembered. Such bad luck! His repeated fainting had allowed him to survive the attentions of two professional killers and now here he was, at the mercy of a geriatric amateur!

'What the fuck . . .' he began.

'I'm sorry, Mr Tulloh?'

'What are you doing here?'

'Ah, Mr Tulloh! You know what I am doing here! It is because I murdered *mbudzi*!'

'*Mbudzi*?'

Mr Murufu looked at Jim reprovingly as if here was being very stupid. Then he lifted his hands to his forehead, poked out his index fingers like two horns and made a strange braying noise that rattled in his nose.

'*Mbudzi*, Mr Tulloh. *Mbudzi!*'

Jim remembered his last brush with the old man and his machete.

'Oh!' he said. 'The goat.'

Mr Murufu beamed in satisfaction.

'On Number 17?'

'Exactly, Mr Tulloh! The goat on Number 17!'

The two men looked at one another and, in spite of himself, Jim found that he was smiling at the absurdity of it all. But then he remembered that Mr Murufu wanted to kill him.

'Look, Mr Murufu. If you still want to kill me, now's the time to do it. Because I really can't be fucked to care.'

The old man shook his head.

'Ah, Mr Tulloh! Now I learn to listen to the wisdom of the ancestors.'

'What do you mean?'

'In English?'

Jim shrugged and Mr Murufu got to his feet and pretended to unzip his fly and urinate. He made a whooshing sound through his teeth.

'What is this called?' he asked.

'Pissing,' said the puzzled Jim.

'Exactly! So. Revenge is like pissing on a snakebite to remove the . . .'

'Poison?'

'Revenge is like pissing on a snakebite to remove the poison. Sometimes it works. Sometimes it does not. But it always makes you feel disgusting.'

Mr Murufu nodded seriously for a moment before his face opened into a luxurious smile that Jim couldn't help but join in. Jim tried to raise himself on to his elbows, but he felt a cold sweat break out on his forehead and his stomach churn. Quickly he eased himself back down into a horizontal position because the Nigerian in his brain was now involved in a noisy argument with a melodramatic French woman and a brash American tourist. Mr Murufu's face was a picture of worry and he sat down at the head of the wooden board and cradled Jim's skull in his lap, his soft hands kneading the skin, the bulbs of his fingertips like ten little pillows that muffled the noise.

'Ah, Mr Tulloh! What has happened to you?'

Lying in the old man's lap, beginning to relax a little, Jim told him the whole story of the day's events (was it still that day? he couldn't be sure). He told him about the arrival of the Black Boot Gang, their brutal looting, the assault on little Gertrude and the well-intentioned roll of film. He told him of the appearance of the army, his naive self-importance and PK's fatal slip of the tongue. And, as Jim spoke, it was as if the corkscrew of PK's death began to disengage itself slowly from his brain. But it was such a painful operation that tears began to blur his eyes and streak his face and he wished for an anaesthetic.

When he had finished his story, Mr Murufu asked, 'Why did they do it?' And his voice sounded like it was calling from a long distance.

'It was my fault,' Jim said quietly and his mind began to float away on the trade winds of guilt.

The last thing he remembered hearing was another of the old man's Zamba sayings: 'When your family die, part of you dies with them. When a friend dies, part of them lives on in you.'

Then he passed out for the fifth time that day.

26 : Of card sharps and classicists

Academics have been known to argue about what is the greatest (or worst) legacy of British colonialism. And though the answers have varied with shifts in ideological fashion and changing personalities, the essence of the discussions has tended to remain the same: discussions of erudite formulae (simultaneously nebulous and rigid) that are indubitably proved by their countless exceptions. Thus bookish tea parties in Oxbridge Masters' gardens are enlivened by radical political theorists standing brogued toe to brogued toe with worthy anthropologists as they argue the merits of the 'rule of law' against the catastrophes of 'divide and rule'. Or revisionist historians in comfortable tweed who expound the unstoppable force of democracy to worthy sociologists with their backs pressed to the immovable object of inequality. Of course, the social function of such arguments in dry, university circles is as undeniable as the truth is elusive and they have long constituted the conversational ballast of such affairs, to be chewed over with the endless plates of finger sandwiches, lattice pastries and sausage rolls. However, the value of the answers on offer (in real terms) tends to be as meagre as the grant for the most junior fellowship.

One colonial legacy that has often been ignored – perhaps because it brooks no argument or maybe because it is so profoundly depressing to the nation's collective ego – is the great British pastime. At the end of the nineteenth and beginning of the twentieth centuries the crown's representatives sowed the seeds of various sports and games to all four corners of the globe, so that, in the latter years of the millennium, the former colonies could grind British noses into the dirt of the world's sporting arenas in a ritual, cathartic expulsion of oppressed angst (on one side) and suppressed guilt (on the other). So it is that Australians revel in their permanent ownership of the Ashes of the empire and the All Blacks crush England's oval balls in the grip of unfeasibly large Maoris with hands the size of saucepans. So it is that lithe Pakistanis rule the principality of the squash court with graphite sceptres and the schoolchildren of Barbados outwit their English counterparts in the International Junior Debating Championships. As for football? England's eleven finest tour the world in search of new depths of national humiliation at the hands of minor Balkan republics and tiny African nations with names that commentators can't pronounce.

Unfortunately for their national psyche Zambawians proved to be intrinsically unsuited to the procedures of organized games. Many Zambawian sportsmen *do* possess unusual natural gifts. But such genetic talents (when combined with a fundamental misapprehension of the nature of competition) tend to be more of a hindrance than a help when entering the field of play. The prevailing ethos of the Zambawian athlete – arrogant in the extreme – is a simple one: if I know that I am better than you, where's the fun in winning? And this ethos manifests itself in all kinds of bizarre ways: the Zambawian Davis Cup team were soundly beaten by Papua New Guinea because of a sinister insistence to play every match left-handed; the national cricket team lost five wickets to consecutive deliveries after a dressing-room bet as to who could break a window in the neighbouring presidential residence. Indeed, the only Zambawian athlete who ever made a name for himself on the world stage was a 1500-metres runner called Patrick Murufu. But even he had to make do with an Olympic silver after he trotted the first two laps to ensure 'a challenge' at the sounding of the bell.

Although Zambawians have never yet fulfilled their international sporting potential, there is one colonial pastime at which they cannot be beaten. Cards. For some reason, undoubtedly but inexplicably connected to the wider culture, Zambawians are born card sharps, counters and cheats. Every Zambawian will play his hand with a raised chin, thin lips and vacant eyes, remember at least fifty card combinations and palm, skim and noodle the pack with extraordinary dexterity. And, since the essence of great card play is to maximize your potential from a starting point of relative weakness, the Zambawians' self-defeating sporting ethos was – initially at least – redundant.

In some Las Vegas casinos, the expression 'poker-face' has been succeeded in the vernacular by 'Zamba mouth', and a famous Zambawian card magician ('the Great Tatenda') has spent more than a decade on the American chat-show circuit, baffling audiences, scientists and hidden cameras alike with his improbable sleight of hand. The tourist hotels that line the shores of Lake Manyika on Zambawi's western border have been forced to ban the use of local currency in their gaming rooms. Officially, this move was designed to encourage the loss of ForEx at their tables. In fact, it was to stop the unbeatable, indigenous gamblers from bankrupting the hotels on a nightly basis.

However, just as Zambawi seemed set to dominate the world in the shady field of professional gambling, the population as a whole lost interest in the basic staples of card schools worldwide: poker, gin and pontoon. It started about ten years ago, as the known Zambawian 'faces' began to fade from the gambling scene. At first they started to lose extravagantly, gambling small fortunes on a bluffed pair of twos. Then, little by little, they simply stopped showing up. The thing was, as the gamblers got better, so the Zambawian sporting ethos began to kick in. The best gamblers simply became so good that they got bored and it seemed preferable to lose in style than win with ease.

Consequently the only card game that was currently in vogue at the time of the Black Boot Anarchy was 'cheat', a game so easy, so difficult and so random that the most skilful player could lose to a simpleton while retaining the right to bask in his own brilliance. In fact, the only problem with cheat was that it frequently concluded with a punch-up. But nobody minded this too much. It was all part of the game.

Thus it was cheat that the two presidential guards were playing outside the door of Adini's office some two weeks after Enoch's kidnap. Generally they wouldn't have dared play such games for fear of invoking the President's renowned temper. But, these days, Adini had become something of a recluse, locked away in his office with his pipe and a wide selection of handguns.

'One seven!' declared the first guard as he set down the seven of diamonds on the pack with a flourish. Immaculately concealed beneath this card were six others. The first guard was proud of his deception. Inwardly the second guard smiled, but he maintained his Zamba mouth.

'Two eights!' claimed the second as he laid down the rest of his hand – some twelve cards. As his hand touched the pack, he skimmed the seven of diamonds to third from the top with a remarkably adroit, unseen flick of his index finger.

'Cheat!' the first cried. 'Pick up the pack!'

Casually the second fanned the top cards from the pack. There were his two eights. Then the seven of diamonds.

'You see?' he said.

'You cheated!'

'I did not.'

'You cheated.'

'That's the name of the game.'

'But I caught you.'

'You did not!'

The game would undoubtedly have come to blows but for the sound of echoing footsteps on the polished marble floor. '*Cave!*' said the first guard – a phrase he had picked up from the President himself – and he gathered the cards with one smooth cock of the wrist into the breast pocket of his uniform.

General Bulimi approached the door of the President's office with some trepidation. He was lost in thought. Nobody but he had seen the President for several days now and even their meetings had begun to follow a depressingly familiar pattern, with the President demanding 'Answers, Bulimi! Answers!' without asking any questions. Their every conversation was weighed down with heavy, unspoken agenda that hung in the air like putrid *gar* farts:

Adini's lack of concern about Enoch's kidnap, what was going to happen in the future and what had happened in the past.

When he reached the door, the two presidential guards on duty saluted magnificently.

'Sir!' they said in stereo, clicking their heels for good measure.

As the first guard lowered his elbow – longest way up, quickest way down – a single playing card fluttered out of his sleeve to land upturned on the floor. The ace of spades.

The death card, Bulimi thought gloomily.

General Bulimi knocked at the door of the presidential office and entered nervously. The President was sitting behind his heavy mahogany desk and he didn't look up. He was busy cleaning the chambers of a small revolver with a white silk handkerchief. His initials were embroidered in silver on the handkerchief's corner and embossed on the butt of the gun. Bulimi cleared his throat and the President looked up, his face breaking into a generous smile.

'Ah, Bulimi!' the President said. 'My old friend! Come and sit down.'

My old friend? Sit down?

Bulimi perched awkwardly on one of the high-backed chairs that lined the walls of the office. All those years of wishing to take a seat and now he felt as comfortable as if he had been sitting on a spike.

'Come closer,' the President said.

And Bulimi reluctantly obeyed.

'Guns. They're funny things. A devil to clean. Do you remember trying to scrub the sand from a 47?'

'I do, sir.'

'Do you remember what you said to me, Indigo? Do you mind if I call you Indigo? Of course not. We've seen some times, haven't we? You said to me, "It's hard to clean a gun because they do your dirty work for you." Do you remember, Indigo?'

'I do not, Mr President.'

'Well, you said it all right. Or something like that. Strange, because now a gun seems like the cleanest scalpel in the kit. Ha! Only a politician could say that, don't you think?'

'I don't know, Mr President. I am only a soldier.'

'A soldier? Yes. Of course you are.'

The President sighed and put the gun down. He sucked in his pot belly for a second and slid his hands into the waistband of his trousers in a movement that Bulimi knew so well. But everything else about the President's manner was new and unfamiliar, the first-name-terms nostalgia, melancholic reminiscences and unself-conscious chatter.

'You know, Indigo,' the President said, 'sometimes I feel that I could place my extracted testicles on a podium in front of the people and they would inspire greater loyalty and patriotic fervour than I ever could myself. Wouldn't you agree?'

He is paranoid, Bulimi thought. No. That's not right. He's always paranoid. He's a dictator, for God's sake! Paranoia comes with the territory!

paranoia. noun. a mental disorder which causes delusions of grandeur or of persecution. intense fear or suspicion, usually unfounded.

So that's it, Indigo, you old fool! He's not paranoid at all! He is having a reality attack! Surely this will drive him over the edge! But to what? To paranoia? That makes no sense!

'Let me tell you something about loyalty, Indigo. Because lately it is an idea that has been troubling me a great deal. One: you cannot create loyalty in an instant. Two: when loyalty is lost, it can never be recaptured. Three: one is never loyal to a man, only the ideas (or indeed testicles) he represents. Four – and this? For goodness' sake Indigo! This is the contradictory killer! – four: the only man to whom one owes undying loyalty is oneself. So what do you think of that?'

The President looked at his general with unswerving eyes. Bulimi blinked and had to look away. He felt an uncomfortable mass rising in the back of his throat.

'I don't know, Mr President,' he said. 'I am only a soldier.'

'And are you loyal to me, Mr Soldier? Have you been loyal to me all these years?'

'I have, sir.'

'Then, Indigo – my old friend – you are a fool.'

Again the two men stared at one another and, for the first time in more than fifteen years, their eyes connected as if they were friends. Or comrades at least. And before the President spoke again, Bulimi knew what was coming and he felt his jaw clench and the muscles in his back begin to spasm as if teased by a ticklish electric current.

'That day,' Adini began.

'Sir?'

'You remember that day?'

'I do not.'

'Yes, you do. It was your twenty-third birthday. Do you remember? We have never talked about that.'

Bulimi heard his breathing quicken. He ran his tongue over his lips and it felt like a dry twig.

'I do not remember, sir.'

The President held his gaze for a moment before raising his eyebrows and looking out of the window. Bulimi desperately tried to ride the rising swell of despair in his chest. Where had all this come from? You can't let a memory like that creep up on you unannounced!

'Loyalty to oneself, Indigo! Loyalty to oneself!'

'You can talk!'

The words just slipped out of Bulimi's mouth and he immediately regretted them. The President turned his head sharply and Bulimi thought he would explode. But again the President's face relaxed into an easy smile.

' "Now he goes along the darksome road, thither whence they say no one returns." Do you recognize that?'

'Catullus.'

'Indeed. Catullus.'

'But a poor translation. What is "darksome"? The road is not "darksome"! It is obscure.'

'Obscure! How right you are! The road is most definitely obscure! You remember how we used to do this around the camp fire? Classical allusions late into the evening when Cousin Moon was lighting up the sky? The comrades looked at us as if we were mad but we didn't care. Come on, Indigo! Try one out on me.'

'*Miser Adini, desinas ineptire, Et quod viedes perisse perditum ducas.*'

The President furrowed his brow in concentration for a moment and gave his balls a thoughtful squeeze before his face lit up in happy comprehension.

'How clever you are, Indigo! Though you never went to university, you always were a greater classicist than me. Cicero and Catullus. Both Plinys and Plautus. "*Dictum sapienti sat est.*" But for goodness' sake, Indigo! You were a poet yourself. Of course you were. Do you remember? "A leader without a cause is as a play with no applause . . ." How did it go?'

'I don't know.'

'You were an excellent wordsmith, Indigo. You were a poet. Are you still writing?'

'No, sir. I am a soldier.'

Again Adini sighed as if the word 'soldier' were a pinprick to deflate his growing enthusiasm.

'Of course you are. Look at you, general! Look at your loyalty! You were born to be a soldier!'

'I was born to be a soldier,' repeated Bulimi. And his feet were leaden on the floor and his eyes felt too big for their sockets and his teeth too big for his mouth and his skin was numb and his fingertips twitched and his soul cried out in its sleep.

27 : Stories from the Black Boot Anarchy

When he discovered that Enoch had been kidnapped, President Adini's first concern had been that the news should not get out. So he went straight to the press.

He telephoned the editor of the *Zambawi National Herald*, filled him in on the exact situation and promised the removal of his extremities if one word was printed.

'I understand, Mr President,' the editor agreed. 'For these are very sensitive areas that we are discussing.'

'Exactly.'

Adini returned the receiver to its cradle with a smug smile. State ownership of the one newspaper had been such a good idea!

Unfortunately Adini was so out of touch with the timbre of Zambawian society that he had no idea of the ways in which news was disseminated around the country. He still laboured under the naive illusion that governmental control of the media guaranteed the successful management of information. Nothing could have been further from the truth!

Adini had brought the *Herald* under the state umbrella in the aftermath of independence and, in the intervening decade, the circulation had gradually dwindled to less than five figures and its content had dumbed down until it was filled with nothing but government propaganda and advertisements for toxic skin-lightening cream from the state cosmetics factory (ZamLux). The *Herald* was ignored by anyone with half a brain and universally referred to as 'the eunuch's loo roll'. In fact, by the time of Enoch's kidnap Zambawi's one daily was brought only by government ministers (who liked to see their names in print), lazy Reuters correspondents and hardened *gar* smokers in search of a cheap alternative to cigarette papers.

Of course, the *Herald*'s editor, a thick-set man with a stubborn streak called Eddy Kotto, found the constraints of puppet publishing to be a constant source of frustration. He had learned about the principles of the free press on a correspondence course with the University of Wyoming and he longed to print damning headlines and searing editorials revealing all his knowledge of scandalous government incompetence. But he was attached to his extremities.

Instead, fired by a journalistic fervour that was tempered with a healthy dose of pragmatism, Eddy Kotto developed an inventive system for spreading the juiciest gossip. This system became known as the Pass It On. So, as soon as he'd been sworn into the President's confidence about Enoch's kidnapping, he went out into the small newsroom and announced at the top of his voice: 'Pass it on!' Immediately the clatter of typewriters subsided and the journalists stubbed out their cigarettes and raised their heads in hushed expectation.

'Enoch Adini has been kidnapped,' Eddy Kotto declared. 'Pass it on!'

Within twenty-four hours the whole of Queenstown was fully aware of the facts of Enoch's abduction and President Adini was inundated with phone calls from concerned government ministers. Within two days the news had spread throughout the whole of Zambawi and, with the perverse logic of the paranoiac, Adini ordered General Bulimi to search personally the entire presidential residence for hidden cameras, bugs and other clandestine devices.

'I want to know how it got out!' Adini said. 'I want to find the source of this gossip! Maybe there is a spy in our midst!'

It never occurred to him that he himself was the unwitting double agent.

The most serious consequence of the breaking news had been the impetus it gave to the Black Boot Gang. Minor *ter* companies that were lying low in far-flung corners of the country, knocking off the odd chicken and the occasional farmer's daughter, had known nothing of the kidnapping plot. So, on hearing of its successful completion, these rag-tag bands were imbued with renewed revolutionary vigour and a rising passion for bloodshed. Consequently Adini was forced to face up to a spate of violent crimes and even murders. In the eastern highlands (where the mountains kissed the sky), four German climbers were strung up by their belay lines. Just south of Lelani, Zambawi's second city, a Swedish archaeologist was found half-eaten by hungry jackals, his head bashed in with the femur of an Australopithecus that could have exploded the myth of Olduvai as humanity's cradle. But most disturbing of all was the Case of the Promiscuous American Women.

Forty miles or so north-west of Queenstown, on the borders of Chivu Province, there lived an obscure sub-sect of the Zamba called the Felati (that is, 'the adulterers') who were renowned for their fantastic fecundity. The women of the Felati were permanently pregnant and the men were feted for their unstoppable virility, elephantine penises and dubious sexual morality. Historically the Felati were a nomadic people, wandering naked through the bush of Chivu, living off *moshu* roots and mangoes and having sex at every opportunity. The Felati fucked like nicotine addicts smoke. They fucked while they worked to keep their nerves in check, they fucked after a heavy meal to aid digestion and, after they had fucked, they shared the intimacy of a post-coital fuck.

Nobody was quite sure of the Felati's ethnographic roots, but the general consensus was that they had been around a long time. An eminent American anthropologist (based at Cambridge University) who conducted a field study in the 1960s even went so far as to suggest that the men's gargantuan penises were no less than a product of natural selection. Since the entire population was forever naked, he argued, surely that implied that those with more averagely sized genitals had simply been priced out of the market.

Certainly it seemed likely that the Felati's occupation of that area of Zambawi predated the arrival of the *musungu*, since there was apparent mention of the sect in one of the most popular Zamba myths. The Great Chief Tuloko, so the story went, had fought a long war with the Men with the Spears between Their Legs (surely the Felati). Tuloko's people suffered many casualties at the hands of these gifted warriors until, unable to raise an army, the Great Chief was forced to turn to the women of his *gwaasha* to take up arms. Unsurprisingly Tuloko's remaining men refused to allow the widows of their fallen brothers, their own wives or the prettiest young virgins to go to battle. Consequently the chief ended up dispatching an army to meet the Men with the Spears between Their Legs that consisted entirely of *vakodzi mira chi gudo* ('women who look like baboons'). The myth tells how, at the sight of this fearsome bunch of simian amazons, the enemy's spears turned to squirming snakes and they threw themselves on the mercy of the Great Chief. At the sight of the vanquished warriors, the Great Chief Tuloko delivered the immortal line: '*Mapanga basa arinaka ku chitesha benzi.*' Literally this means 'A sharp dagger is more use than a floppy spear'. But a more artistic paraphrast might get away with 'size isn't everything'.

However long it was that the Felati had been living their unique lifestyle, their world was turned upside-down by Zambawi's independence and the subsequent arrival of wave upon wave of Western tourists in search of a taste of Africa. Within a year the fame of the Felati men had spread far beyond the continent through word of mouth and the occasional article in magazines like *Reader's Digest* and lurid American tabloids. Their story seemed to grip one American social stratum in particular: white, female, middle-class divorcees. Within two years of independence the Felati's corner of Chivu Province was awash with lusty, middle-aged middle-American women, for the Felati quickly replaced Kenya's Masai as the prime targets of Africa's sex tourists.

The American women were always the easiest to spot at Queenstown International Airport. The new arrivals resembled wedding cakes in their pale linen suits beneath newly tinted perms like decorative ribbons. Their lips were always set in pursed uncertainty and their hand luggage was jammed with enormous, industrial-strength condoms, specially purchased from seedy downtown 'adult' stores. The departing women, on the other hand, sat in the airport transit lounge with glazed eyes and surprised eyebrows or they walked to the toilet with an uncomfortable kink in their gait.

Initially the Felati men had been unimpressed by the influx of salacious divorcees and, with reference to the myth, they nicknamed the Americans '*musungu vakodzi chi gudo*' ('white women like baboons'). In the first months the women had offered the Felati money and gifts to try to bribe them into sex. But the general Felati response had been, 'I don't like clothes because I like to be naked. I don't want a car because I cannot drive and there are no roads. I don't need a goat because I suck on my wife's breast milk. I don't want a bull because it will make me – even me! – feel inadequate. And I don't want a hamburger or tinned soup because it is *moshu* porridge that makes my root thicken.'

Eighteen months or so after independence, however, one Felati man succumbed to an American gift. A sixty-year-old bottle-blonde called Candy-Jane, despairing at the failure of her advances, offered the Felati the paisley silk tie that she had bought as a present for her son in Newark duty-free. Why the young warrior accepted this gift above all others is unknown – perhaps he liked the yellow splashes, the colour of Father Sun, or maybe he enjoyed the swirling patterns that reminded him of the shapes he saw when he closed his eyes – but he began to wear the tie at all times, flapping against his naked belly.

An oft noted sociological feature of the invasion of primary economies by capitalism is the fetishization of Western commodities (Lawrence, P., 1964. Burridge K., 1969) and within months, collections of neckties had joined penis-size as the fundamental markers of Felati social status. Soon the most sought-after men owned hordes of the things, wide mauve kippers that hung from their necks like a baby's bib, conservative pinstripes and the occasional college alumni tie that had belonged to an ex-husband.

Since they were always fucking, the Felati had never been hard-working at the best of times. But the arrival of the sex tourists made them lazier than ever. They gave up digging for *moshu*, preferring to live off the pilgrims' knapsacks of savoury snacks and tinned meals, and hung out in the shade of the baobab trees like louche young men around a cocktail bar, stroking their ties with seductive fingertips. On top of their nakedness, their neck-wear and their enormous penises, the Felati men were soon recognizable by their poor complexions, the product of a diet that was so high in monosodium glutamate.

Eventually the Felati women tired of their men-folk's indolence and they took to wearing expansive clothes (tent-like dresses that dragged along the ground as they walked) and moved *en masse* to Queenstown, where they formed Afrocentric women's groups that demonstrated outside the Ministry for Tourism. Consequently, even before the onset of the Black Boot Anarchy and the Case of the Promiscuous American Women, the Felati were a dying breed.

When the news of Enoch's kidnap broke, there were about forty divorcees roughing it with the Felati in Chivu, making up for lost sexual time and dishing out ties with the enthusiasm of PR girls at a business convention. Also in Chivu at that time was a weedy bunch of Gangers, *temba* kids mostly, armed to the teeth and under the command of an insane former state army sergeant called (Mad) Banana, who had been court-martialled for beating one of his men to death with a saucepan.

It was a moonlit night when the Gangers chanced upon the Felati camp and at first the young *ters* feared that they might have stumbled into a dark *zakulu* ritual. All that could be heard was a cacophony of strange whining noises and pained yelps; all that could be seen was a circle of the backs of dozens of men who appeared to be doing bored press-ups on top of squeaking cushions the colour of pig fat. But the experienced Sergeant (Mad) Banana sized up the situation in an instant, drew his machine pistol and let off a couple of rounds. Immediately the kids in his charge, terrified and excitable, followed suit and, within seconds, forty of the Men with the Spears between Their Legs lay dead aboard their dry-docked white vessels with bullet wounds between their eyes or between their shoulder blades (depending on their position in the orgiastic circle).

The following morning an old Boer farmer who worked a

smallholding some twenty miles away and had never heard of the Black Boot Gang (since he dismissed all forms of media as 'the devil's own mouthpiece') was driving his clapped-out old Land Rover through the Chivu bush when he came across half a dozen clapped-out old white women, naked, shivering and totally lost. After several repetitions of the Our Father and a few Glory Bes for good measure, he agreed to help them and retraced their steps to the Felati camp. There, he found the site of a bloody massacre with around seventy blood-soaked corpses, some horrifically mutilated, gathering dust in the morning breeze. In the middle of the carnage sat a thirteen-year-old Ganger who called himself Washington. Left behind by his fellows, he had watched Father Sun rise on what he had done and he squatted on his haunches, clutched the barrel of his gun and dry-wept with witless, heaving sobs. When he saw the Boer farmer approaching, he held his gaze for a second before putting his gun to his head and blowing his own brains out, taking the death toll to seventy-one.

Exactly what happened at the Felati camp is uncertain. The culpable young Gangers were eventually discovered. Dead. They, like Washington, had found the call of the ancestors too powerful for their collective guilt. A year later Sergeant (Mad) Banana turned up, recognized by a former comrade, begging on the streets of Queenstown. But the sergeant was now deaf, dumb and blinded by cataracts so opaque that it appeared that his irises and pupils had completely disappeared. However, most people concluded that the sergeant's eyes had inverted and he could no longer see outwards because he was too busy examining the damage to his soul.

As for the surviving Americans, all bar one claimed memory loss of the night's events and the exception only managed to divulge one sentence of explanation before she too clammed up for good. 'They said they wouldn't hurt us if we promised to come quietly,' she whispered.

In the bars of Queenstown this phrase was quickly picked up by heartless foreign journalists with too much cynicism to censor their humour. And when they talked each other into sex over the last brandy of the evening – 'There's nothing else to do in this shit-hole excuse for a city' – one of the randy hacks would 'promise to come quietly' and both would dissolve into drunken giggles.

By the time the Case of the Promiscuous American Women had spread to every tip of the Zambawian grapevine the general consensus of opinion was that President Adini had lost control. At first the nation held its breath, awaiting the reaction of the White House to the murder of so many of its nation's sex tourists. But, despite a strongly worded statement from the departing American ambassador, it soon became apparent that the US government found the whole affair too embarrassing for effective action and wanted to hush it up as much as its Zambawian counterpart.

President Adini appeared on the front of the *Zambawi National Herald* promising tough action against 'those who wish to underline the state [*sic*]' and he immediately dispatched ranks of the state army to every Ganger black spot. Unfortunately, much to the President and General Bulimi's consternation, all of these companies promptly went missing. One company of loyal but overweight presidential guards was defeated in a brief skirmish with a newly confident bunch of *ters*. But most were easily persuaded of the merits of the Black Boot Gang cause, tempted by the 'Africa for the Africans' rhetoric and the opportunity to keep the guns and lose the uniforms.

Soon, with the threat of all-out civil war building in the national psyche like a weighty cumulus, Queenstown began to degenerate into something approaching anarchy. Vast hordes of urbanites started to flee the city for the perceived safety of the *gwaasha* at the same time as busloads of rural dwellers fled their homes for the perceived safety of the city. Queenstown didn't know whether it was coming or going and the crime rate spiralled. Deserted homes were squatted by the new arrivals, deserted businesses were looted by those left behind and mobs of bored kids aligned themselves with government or Gangers on the toss of a coin and fought violent pitched battles in car parks and bus stations. What's more, the government's attempts to 'manage' the situation only 'managed' to wind the unease that little bit tighter. When it became apparent that what remained of Queenstown's police force couldn't possibly contain the growing unrest, President Adini declared a 'state of national emergency' and recruited a thousand-strong Emergency Militia, kitted out with full riot gear, batons and pistols from the state armoury. Within twenty-four hours these guns had replaced bottles and sticks as the warring factions' weapons of choice.

The British High Commissioner, Alistair Digby-Stewart, summed up the Black Boot Anarchy better than most in an emergency e-mail dispatched by satellite phone to the foreign office in London: 'As in most cases of civil disturbance, the central issue is one of perception. The question facing the population is not whether life is unfair because life is always unfair. The question is whether the majority of the population perceive life's injustices acutely enough at any given moment to encourage them to set fire to their rubbish bins and throw bottles at one another. And at this point in time the streets of Queenstown are ablaze with burning garbage and a danger to bare feet.'

Like the other foreign diplomats Digby-Stewart quickly found himself submerged in the tiresome business of evacuating his fellow expatriates, commandeering local buses, chartering jumbo jets and the like. By and large it wasn't too difficult. He had no moral compunction in dismissing the tears and tantrums of bogus British citizens (screaming, snot-nosed brats and all) and he rather enjoyed the bumbling gratitude he encountered from recently retired middle-managers from Penge who had invested their savings in a once-in-a-lifetime safari. He was, however, becoming increasingly frustrated in his attempts to ship out a bunch of around forty students who were spending a year off as temporary teachers in the Zambawian bush. It was their attitude that was the problem. Half of them were public schoolboys with bucketloads of confidence and bugger-all commonsense – God knows what had happened to England's finest establishments since his day! As for the rest? Strange hippy types: effete young men with earnest lips and nostrils and strapping women with armour-piercing voices and prop forward's calves. One such girl had actually had the cheek to refuse to leave. As if she knew what was best for her! The size of a small hospital, the girl had gone native and shacked up with a black man. In the end Digby-Stewart had had little option but to leave her to it, with nothing for support but 100 quid, a smattering of Zamba and her King at her side.

Now he was on the trail of the last of these students, some little pillock called James Tulloh, who had managed to get himself caught up in a Ganger incident down in Zimindo Province and was currently sweating it out in an army jail cell. The High Commissioner had considered taking on the four-hour drive to Zimindo in person, but, frankly, he was buggered if he was going to set off into one of the main Black Boot Gang strongholds with a single bodyguard and his peashooter revolver. Besides, rumour had it that Zimindo concealed the base of the Black Boot Gang's commander, although Digby-Stewart found it difficult to see any evidence of leadership in the current chaos.

Instead, therefore, the British High Commissioner set out for the presidential residence – running the gauntlet of the Queenstown street riots – to confront Adini once again. He had little appetite for their meeting, but he needed to be seen to secure this boy's release and he was fully conversant with what was known in Whitehall as Reverse Foodchain Diplomacy: feed the top man a toxic line and you can watch the troublesome pond scum wither and die.

So what tone should he adopt? Angry? Too provocative. Patronizing? No. Africans hated being patronized. Patronizing only worked on the Japanese. Persuasive? Too much effort for little return. Indignant? That was it. Indignant. It had worked before and it would work again, especially when sweetened with some supportive noises and the trump card he had up his sleeve. So the Zambawians thought they could play cards, did they? It would take more than a Zamba face to break this diplomat's winning streak!

Stepping out of his Mercedes and walking slowly across the presidential residence's gravel drive, Digby-Stewart began to feel somewhat uneasy. Although he couldn't figure out exactly why. There was something about the atmosphere of the place, like a western saloon on the eve of a gunfight. The guards on the door looked as imposing as ever and there was the usual hubbub of activity in the front hall; though, if anything, the movements of the secretaries and support staff seemed even more frenetic, as if they were working to an impending and immutable deadline.

His feelings of disquiet only increased when he reached the top of the absurdly aureate double staircase and turned into the corridor of the presidential office. At the far end he saw two men wrestling on the floor. At first he assumed that he'd had the misfortune to walk in on an assassination attempt and his realization that both the men were dressed in the uniform of the presidential guard did nothing to disabuse him of this idea. For a moment he paused and wondered whether to run away. But then one of the men got on top and landed a full-blooded punch on his colleague's nose. The guard stood up, his chest heaving, and scattered a pack of playing cards over the prone body. 'Cheat!' panted the victor.

'Oh, for fuck's sake!' whispered Digby-Stewart under his breath.

The High Commissioner entered the presidential office to find Adini and General Bulimi sitting opposite one another on either side of the President's desk. On his entrance the two men looked round at Digby-Stewart, somewhat embarrassed. Digby-Stewart felt like he must have walked in on an acutely melancholy and intimate heart-to-heart and he was briefly knocked out of his planned stride. The general, in particular, looked as though he were weighed down by the cares of the world, as if someone had just called him an arsehole and he'd been forced to agree. And when the President's face creased into an unexpected smile, relaxed and welcoming, Digby-Stewart only felt more uncomfortable still.

'Alistair!' Adini said. 'Come and join us!'

'Thank you, Mr President.'

'Pull up a chair.'

Digby-Stewart sighed and stood up a little straighter. May as well get it over with.

'No, thank you, Mr President. I can hardly sit down with you when your army is holding one of my nation's citizens without charge, representation or any regard for the legal process. Frankly, Mr President, I am utterly disgusted and I will have my concerns heard! Let me tell you that Downing Street takes a very dim view of such shenanigans and, while the British government has long been your greatest supporter in both the Commonwealth and the United Nations, we will not tolerate such a gung-ho attitude towards human rights!'

He felt his top lip quiver as his temper bubbled. That was a nice touch. Nothing like a bit of emotional artifice to get the ball rolling! He was pleased to see the President's smile vanish, his eyes darken and his nostrils flare. Adini almost looked like his old self.

'What are you talking about?'

'A student teacher, Mr President. James Tulloh. He has been held for a whole week in the Zimindo township barracks and I demand to know the reason; I demand to know who's responsible and I demand action.'

Adini stared at the British High Commissioner and his eyes blazed for a second before they transferred their attention to General Bulimi, who studiously avoided them, preferring to gaze morosely at the floor. The President sucked his tongue and made a loud popping noise. He grunted. He coughed. And the desk creaked as he adjusted the position of his legs and hands.

'Why was I not told about this, Bulimi?'

'Because I did not know, sir.'

'Why did you not know?'

'Because I did not. We have received no communication from the Zimindo company for more than three weeks.'

'Who is in charge down there?'

'Captain Muziringa, sir'

'Isaiah? What the hell is he playing at? For goodness' sake!'

'I don't know, sir.'

'See to it, Bulimi. See to it that the *musungu* boy is released.'

'Yes, sir.'

'Now, Bulimi!'

'Yes, sir.'

Slowly General Bulimi got to his feet, saluted to the President with provocative apathy and tottered towards the door. His movements were tired and geriatric. Digby-Stewart absent-mindedly pondered the general's age. He could have been anything from forty to seventy-five.

When Bulimi had left the room, the President and the High Commissioner looked at one another. Digby-Stewart turned his head in that curious way of his and contemplated Adini from the corner of his left eye. Now that his indignation had proved so effective, he wasn't quite sure what faces to pull next.

'Please sit down, High Commissioner.'

'Thank you,' Digby-Stewart said and he assumed the general's chair and sat back with his legs languidly crossed. Nonchalant, he thought. Self-confident and nonchalant. That would do just fine.

'The situation is grave, High Commissioner.'

'It is.'

'May I speak frankly?'

'Please.'

'You have perceived the – what shall we call it? – civil unrest of the last two weeks?'

'It has come to my attention.'

'And you are advising your citizens to depart from Zambawi?'

'I am.'

'That is good.'

The High Commissioner nodded. The President nodded too. Get on with it, man! Digby-Stewart thought. Because if you want my help you're going to have ask for it.

The President leaned forward in his chair and clasped his hands together on top of the desk. Absent-mindedly, he removed a pubic hair that had been stuck beneath one fingernail and discarded it on the floor.

'Let me tell you something about myself, High Commissioner. I am a man of the people. That surprises you? It should not. These' – Adini waved a careless hand around the room – 'trappings of power are not for me. I would be happy to run this nation in a barn or a chicken coop out in the *gwaasha*. But the people, well, the people, they expect. You understand?'

'It's all a question of perception.'

'Exactly, High Commissioner! How right you are! Perception!

You see, I am not a rich man. No doubt you have heard the rumours of Swiss bank accounts and the like?'

'I have.'

'Of course, they are – how should I put it?'

'A misconception.'

'Indeed. Because it's all a question of misconception. I have given my life for this nation . . .'

Adini paused and for a moment his eyes seemed to blur and fill. Oh God! Don't start crying, you buffoon!

'I have given my life for the love of my country and it has cost me dear. I lost my wife, Sally – dear Sally! The doctors said it was cancer. But, after ten years of the independence struggle I believe it was the cancer of fatigue. And now my enemies have taken my son from me, my pride and joy. And you know why? Because they fear a man of the people. They fear a democrat. For all their slogans and their empty rhetoric, they have no grasp of the real issues. "Africa for the Africans," they say. As if I was about to give our nation away! Do you understand?'

'I do.'

'You see, they believe that politics is all a question of perception.'

'I'm sorry?'

'I know. It is a ridiculous notion, is it not? Beause the people will always see through such blatant populism! Politics is about representation. And as a man of the people, I represent the people. That was my one aim when I became life-President a decade ago; to create a one-party democracy that was both stable and representative. And – though I say so myself – I believe I have succeeded. Whether the people *perceive* themselves as represented or not is another question, but I am in the business of politics and not of public relations. Perception is not – I repeat, NOT – a foundation of democracy. That is why I say that perception is a ridiculous notion. *Quod erat demonstrandum.*

'My opponents? High Commissioner, what can I say? Their logic is as flawed as a farmer who lets his chickens run through his newly planted field, as watertight as Kaunda's string vest at the Pan-African Conference. How can you be an opposition party in a one-party democracy? For goodness' sake! And yet they say that I am suppressing free speech when I arrest them for treason! They want to have their cake and eat it too. It would be laughable if it wasn't so serious.

'I have made mistakes. I know that. Of course I have. There is nothing so powerful as the arguments of a martyr. I should have allowed them to dig their own toilet ditch, throw themselves in and drown in their own faeces. But you cannot cry over spilled blood! Let alone spilled shit!

'And now they rally against me, High Commissioner! The people, the army and the treasonous Black Boot Gang in a treacherous alliance of different agenda. Food, money and power. Ha! Do you know the story of the *shamva*, High Commissioner? You do not? No matter. It is enough to say that the *shamva* tried to trick Father Sun. Some wanted more food, some wanted precious stones and some wanted ritual objects that were . . . well! You would not understand. The point is that I – like Father Sun – I, Zita Adini, President of Zambawi, am facing an unholy alliance.'

As Adini spoke, Digby-Stewart watched him in growing fascination. Was this all plain bullshit or did he actually believe the incomprehensible bollocks he was spouting? He remembered the television pictures of Zambawian independence he had seen a decade earlier when he was First Secretary in Tehran; the proud, upright, Oxford-educated figure of comrade Zita Adini, brandishing a gun above his head and enthusing the cheering crowds with his righteous rhetoric. Of course, his voice had always rung with that curious falsetto – we all know why that is – but he was a man of principle and zeal. Or at least that was how he seemed. So what was the connection between that proud revolutionary and this puffed-up cocktail of complacency and neuroses? He had always wondered about the corruption of power and now he concluded that 'corruption' was the wrong word. Erosion. That was better. Adini's soul, his mind, his body – they had all been eroded by the circular currents of a decade of dictatorship. Either that or a pernicious seed had been sown somewhere in his past, a seed with roots that had slowly choked his soul, his mind, his body.

Perhaps it went back to his castration. Or perhaps to something else.

Digby-Stewart stared at the President and the more he stared, the more he imagined Adini's limbs knotting in their sockets. With every confused phrase and circular argument the threads of his arms and legs pulled tighter and the High Commissioner imagined him perched on his chair with twisted limbs like a Thalidomide victim. Now his tongue was knotting too until he pictured the President as no more than a tangled ball of string.

Lost in his bizarre fantasies, Digby-Stewart realized that he had missed the conclusion of the President's rambling diatribe. He was irritated with himself because it must have contained the real thrust of meaning. But no problem. He already knew what the President had been getting at. However circuitously.

'You want my help, Mr President?' he said.

'I . . . I mean to say . . . well . . .'

Adini looked uncomfortable. He picked up his pipe from its stand on the desk and, with intense concentration, he began to pack it full of sour-smelling tobacco.

'Obviously, Mr President, I would love to be able to help you with this problem. But I am an ambassador of the British government and, as such, I represent government policy. There is no way that they, that is to say we, that is to say I, could possibly be seen to interfere in the internal struggles of an independent African nation. So if you are asking for my help, I am afraid that I have to decline. If, on the other hand, you are asking for *my* help, I would be only too happy to oblige. As long as we understand each other.'

'Of course!'

'Because as an employee of the British government I couldn't possibly sanction outlining the options that you have available to you. However, as an employee of the British government, I am aware of certain options whose nature I would be prepared to discuss.'

'What options?'

'Mr President! Surely I have made myself clear! Surely you do not expect me to talk about specific options!'

'I'm sorry, High Commissioner, I thought . . .'

'I said that I would discuss the nature of the options available to you! For example, with the forces of the Black Boot Gang growing in direct proportion to the decrease in loyalty of the state army, you are faced with a difficult situation which requires immediate action. Now. As an employee of the British government, it would be utterly out of place for me to suggest that you looked to a mercenary force. I could, however, outline the nature of your options for you. So then. Let me do so. It seems to me that you could either look to a mercenary force or go mouse-hunting in the Black Forest with Little Bo Beep (I believe Bavaria is charming at this time of year) or you could sail to Waikiki on a vessel made entirely of matchsticks.'

Adini stopped his pipe-packing and stared at the High Commissioner. Come on, you fool! Digby-Stewart thought. Put two and two together.

'Have you gone mad, High Commissioner?' Adini asked.

'Not at all! That is the nature of your options.'

'So I should hire mercenaries?'

'Mr President! As an employee of the British government I couldn't possibly condone such a thing!'

'But where would I find mercenaries?'

'Really! I must insist! You are putting me in a very difficult position. But I should warn you – as a mark of mutual respect between my nation and yours – that I have heard rumours of a squad of Africa-trained British ex-marines that can be reached on 00 44 370 396882. Obviously I tell you this only as a consideration for your internal security. You can't be too careful these days.'

Adini replaced his pipe on its stand, picked up a pen and raised his eyebrows.

'Could you say that again?'

'Take a card,' said Digby-Stewart and, with a flourish, he produced a small business card from somewhere about his person. Adini accepted the card and studied it carefully.

'One thousand pounds per man per day!' he exclaimed.

'I believe that a discount can be negotiated for large orders.'

'Plus expenses!'

'War is a pricey business.'

'*Nervos belli, pecuniam infinitam.*'

'What's that?'

'Cicero,' said Adini as he reached for the telephone.

28 : The Poet (five)

For the first five years the Zambawian independence war wasn't really a *war* at all. More of an abusive relationship, like a hastily arranged marriage that seethed with bitterness and hatred from day one. It wasn't as though the Manyikaland state occupied the majority of the country and the ZLF the rest. There were no battles in open fields, no fighting for territory, no fronts and lines and no man's lands; just frequent spats of violence and assassination. In fact, the polarized lifestyle of colonial Manyikaland carried on pretty much as before. But the whites learned to avoid the black townships on cloudy nights and, before leaving for work, they checked under their cars with home-made devices constructed from a wing mirror and a broom handle. As for the blacks, they got used to being stopped in the street, intrusively searched and viciously beaten for the terrorism of others.

In those early years the battlegrounds were predominantly urban, concentrated on Queenstown and, to a lesser extent, Lelani (then known as Coppertown). And the bloodshed was mostly abstracted in its nature: faceless car bombs, nameless snipings and thoughtless drive-bys. After independence, when Indigo trawled the memories of his introduction to guerrilla warfare, he would often wonder whether this early detachment had been a good or bad thing. On the one hand it offered him a relatively gentle initiation into the practicalities of murder with none of the screaming gore of close combat. On the other, when the need for screaming gore arrived, Indigo found that he was largely inured to its horrors. At the time this had felt like a blessing. But now? Now the shame of his memories wrapped his heart in a hermetic blanket the colour of night itself.

At first there was no ZLF army as such, just Hit and Run Units of two or three people. In those days it was still Comrade Solo Maponga in charge, with Zita as his right-hand man (it wasn't until three years later that Maponga was caught and executed, his disembowelled corpse hung from a lamp-post in Mutengwazi bus station). Indigo remembered Maponga well: an old-school Marxist with a grandfatherly smile and a passion for *gar* that made him unbearably smelly company at the end of an evening. Maponga had appeared so old and wise that it seemed unbelievable that he had been just thirty-five at the time of his murder. Younger than Indigo was now.

It was Maponga who had teamed Indigo and Zita as a Hit and Run Unit, despite the future President's vociferous objections.

'Comrade Solo! You cannot pair me with an inexperienced, untrained boy!'

'Look at his eyes,' Maponga had replied. 'Look at the light in his eyes, Zita. You can't teach that!'

And Maponga had been right. Because back then Indigo's eyes had glistened like moonbeams on deep water with a surfacing passion; a passion born of injustice, a passion born of his parents' deaths, a passion born of the certainty of youth.

It did not take him long to prove his worth. On their first mission together – the assassination of a High Court judge – the Hit and Run Unit were approached by two uniformed policemen as they loitered uncomfortably on a suburban street corner.

'What the fuck are you two boys doing round here, munt?' asked one of the policemen, jutting his chin into Zita's face.

Indigo saw Zita's hand twitch to where the gun was concealed in the waistband of this jeans. 'What's it got to do with you?' Zita replied in his best Oxford English.

'What did you say? Jesus, kaffir! You are in for one *lekker* beating!'

Whereas Zita's pride clouded his judgement, Indigo was thinking on his feet. He shrunk his shoulders, bowed his head slightly and lowered his eyebrows, positioning himself between Zita and the scrawny young policeman who was pulling his *shambok* from his belt.

Addressing Zita, Indigo raised his voice: '*Urikusekayi futsek!*'

Then he turned to the policeman, bent himself smaller still and arranged his face in its most innocuous, fawning 'house nigger' expression.

'I'm sorry, boss!' he said. 'My brother forgets his tongue. *Mboko* sent him to school to learn to speak English good and now no one will give him a job because he has ideas! He's a strong worker, boss. Really he is. But with a mouth like that? *Eesh kabeesh!* Nobody wants him for houseboy. And our brothers and sisters go hungry in the *gwaasha*, so we come here for work; to sweep a drive or clear some rubbish.'

'I should beat some sense into him.'

'You do, boss!' Indigo agreed, nodding furiously. 'The ancestors will thank you. *Mboko* has tried, for he brings nothing but shame on our family.'

The policeman looked at his partner and laughed smugly.

'Kaffirs!' he said with a tut and the two of them continued their patrol up the street without another word for Indigo and Zita.

'Thank you, boss!' Indigo called after them. 'May Tuloko walk with you!'

Ten minutes later the High Court judge lay dead on his front porch and Zita was very impressed.

'You could talk an angry *shumba* to sleep.'

'Words are my weapons,' Indigo replied immodestly and the face of his partner suddenly darkened. Zita produced his gun and pressed it into Indigo's hand, so that he might feel its weight.

'This is a weapon, my colourful poet,' he said. 'Words do not kill people.'

Soon Zita and Indigo's Hit and Run Unit was infamous through-out Manyikaland. This was due to two reasons. First of all, Zita seemed to be driven by some kind of innate desire for publicity. The future President was not content with murder, he also wanted the nation to know who was responsible. So he christened their unit 'The Righteous Brothers' and, when practical, printed this unlikely moniker across the foreheads of each corpse in black felt-tip.

Since Indigo preferred to flee the scene of each crime with natural haste and he had no desire to confront the faces of his victims, it took him a long time to discover what his partner was up to. In fact, he only found out the truth when he nervously returned to check on the certain deadness of an unimportant internal security officer whom he'd assassinated leaving a *shabeen*. Indigo was sure that he'd shot the man cleanly between the eyes when Zita had marked him with a nod of the head and a raised eyebrow. But as he ran through the alleys, depositing his gun in a nearby sewer for later collection, he was filled with self-doubt. Had he actually seen the bullet enter the cranium? No. What if the drunken officer had simply passed out in an instant of coincidental good fortune? Indigo took a few deep breaths and returned to the street where the corpse lay face down in a dusty gutter. He could see caked blood on the back of the man's head but he had to make sure. Hesitantly he turned the body over and the first thing he saw was the clean bullet wound, bang in the middle of the man's forehead like an Indian woman's *bindi*. Around it was written, 'The Righteous Brothers' in a neat circle of block capitals.

Later, when he met up with Zita, Indigo berated him for the ridiculous indiscretion.

'For the sake of the Great Chief Tuloko! What were you thinking of? We are guerrillas. We are anonymous. What is it Comrade Solo tells us? We are the anonymous ghosts of the *musungu*'s past come back to haunt him.'

'You would not understand,' Zita replied dismissively. 'It is propaganda. Propaganda is a vital weapon of war.'

'What? Propaganda is just words. You said that . . .'

But Indigo's outrage was cut short by his partner's throaty guffaw, hearty slap on the shoulder and manly embrace.

'Come here, Indigo! We are the greatest team in the ZLF. Every *musungu* in Manyikaland will fear our Hit and Run Unit. We are the Righteous Brothers!'

Only much later, months after the name had been discarded under the weight of more pressing concerns, did Zita discover that the Righteous Brothers was the name of a twee American pop combo. And, when he thought about it, he was forced to admit that this particular assemblage of words must have embedded itself in his subconscious during a drunken stumble around a smoky Oxford dance floor. So, for years afterwards, this memory would twist his insides with the quick-fingered dexterity of an unforgettable embarrassment.

The second reason for the notoriety of the Righteous Brothers was Indigo's passion for the dramatic. After the first few assassinations it no longer seemed adequate merely to kill someone. Indigo felt that murder had to be done with an appropriate degree of drama, be it weighty and tragic, slapstick comedy or a combination of the two. This desire of his stemmed partly from his innate creativity but mostly from his need to see murder as artifice, a staged playette with coherent narrative structure, themes and character.

He used to console himself: 'Assassination is so similar to English poetry. Just raw meaning constructed from the language of emotions as opposed to emotions constructed from the language of raw meaning.'

Thus it was that the Righteous Brothers' terrorism became ever more audacious in its conception. To assassinate the Queenstown Chief of Police, an obese florid man called 'Kippie' Terreblanche, Indigo sneaked into the central precinct and stole his bodyguards' side arms. Undiscovered, he replaced them just before sunrise after a long night's welding and modification. Later that morning, as the Chief of Police walked down the steps of his luxurious home flanked by his bodyguards, the Righteous Brothers confronted him, pulling childish faces and shouting, 'ZLF! Ra-ra-ra! ZLF! Ra-ra-ra!' Immediately the two security men drew their weapons and simultaneously opened fire and their guns discharged at right angles, fatally penetrating each of their boss's lungs. And Indigo thrilled at the look of astonishment on Terreblanche's face as the last whistle of air was expelled from his chest, and he turned away before the body hit the ground with an ugly and prosaic 'thunk'.

After that success Indigo's imagination ran riot. A hang 'em-high politician was caught in a man trap that left him dangling from the beams of his son's tree house; a horny general blew himself up when his eager fingers tore open a parcel post-marked 'Amsterdam'; and the Bishop of Queenstown – renowned for his conservatism by most and his infidelity by those in the know – released a sensitive weight trigger during his Seventh Commandment sermon and exploded before the eyes of his terrified flock just as he was concluding with the words 'May God strike me down'.

By and large, Indigo rather enjoyed the urban era of the independence war. Assassination was made bearable by the creativity with which he imbued it. He developed an intimate camaraderie with his partner, Zita, and his poetry was published under various pseudonyms in the liberal British press, 'anthologies of empire' and complacent, worthy journals with boring titles like *Africa*, *Africa Today* and *The African*. In a sense the urban era was a honeymoon period (if civil wars can have such a thing), with each side inflicting just enough damage on the other to feel that it was probably winning. But it was a delicate balance. And it was always going to tip in the end.

It was the murder of the Queenstown Chief of Police that launched the violence to another level and forced the *ters* to flee into the bush. Solo Maponga had made a serious mistake in concluding that 'Kippie' Terreblanche was the most brutal and vicious bastard the *musungu* had been able to find. In fact, Terreblanche's old-fashioned brutishness and colonial arrogance – 'the kaffirs couldn't organize a *braai* in a butcher's shop' – had often worked to the *ters'* advantage since, despite overwhelming evidence to the contrary, he refused to accept that the guerrillas were capable of waging a sustained campaign. His replacement, however, was an altogether different animal, a younger, cunning man seconded from Internal Security whose career had flourished in the shadowy half-light of deception and double cross, intelligence and interrogation. When Indigo heard of the appointment, he felt the saliva in his mouth chill and congeal. The new Chief of Police was Frank Pienaar, the man responsible for his father's death.

As soon as he took up his new position, Chief Pienaar introduced a new concept that quickly brought the simmering unrest to the boil: 'stick and carrot policing'. Where his predecessor had essentially treated the *ters* as troublesome hooligans whose crimes were to be investigated using traditional police techniques, Pienaar understood that (whether the colonial administration admitted it or not) Manyikaland was already in a state of civil war and the guerrillas were 'the enemy'. In fact, more than that, *all* blacks were the enemy.

In a confidential memorandum to the head of Internal Security (unearthed after independence by an eminent Jamaican cricket writer and sometime historian for his book *A Colonial State of Mind*), Pienaar wrote as follows:

> . . . and the real point to grasp in this situation is that all blacks are potential guerrillas, be they subsistence farmers, city workers or even policemen. Our aim, therefore, must be to recognize the blacks as our enemy while retaining the trust and cooperation of the black majority. To retain our rightful position in Manyikaland society, we must be seen as the force of law and order, freedom and democracy. As soon as we lose the moral high ground, we can expect nothing less than anarchy and ultimately revolution.

It was with this in mind that Pienaar introduced 'stick and carrot' policing, the aim being to encourage and reward loyalty and frighten the living shit out of the *ters*. He negotiated a substantial slush fund from the Manyikaland parliament and turned the ethos of the Queenstown police force on its head. Where previously officers had been encouraged to investigate with a firm hand and a solid whack of the *shambok*, now they were furnished with pocketfuls of loosely defined 'expenses'. Suspects were no longer threatened and beaten but cajoled with hard cash, offered sums that often exceeded a month's wages in exchange for information.

Within weeks, the Hit and Run Units of the ZLF were in

complete disarray. Dozens of *ters* were caught, generally betrayed by dozens of others, overcome less by greed than the pragmatism of extreme poverty. Comrade Solo quickly ordered his men into hiding. But it was already too late for him. He was picked up at his *gwaasha*, not far from Coppertown, on the tip-off of a neighbour. Dragged back to Queenstown central police station, he was questioned and tortured for three days by Pienaar and his cronies. But he refused to divulge any of the names of ZLF members and Pienaar wondered at the beatific smile he maintained in the face of such excruciating pain.

Comrade Solo would surely have had to endure further suffering but for the broken dial on the interrogation suite's voltameter, which led to him being fried by a careless guard. Pienaar had ordered a light toasting, but his man only noticed that the cooking had gone too far when the stench of burning flesh began to trouble his nose.

Determined to make the best of a bad job, Pienaar had Comrade Solo's charred body removed to the police station at Mutengwazi. There he took out the Bowie knife that his father had given him for his eighteenth birthday and sliced open the corpse's chest so that its vital organs dangled decoratively from the wound. He then ordered two young constables to hang Comrade Solo from a lamp-post in Mutengwazi Bus Station. The stronger-stomached of the two asked him, 'What are we doing, Chief Pienaar, sir?'

'Advertising, mun,' Pienaar said with a toothless smile.

Many years later Indigo Bulimi chanced upon a copy of *A Colonial State of Mind* when shopping in Edinburgh during a Commonwealth Conference. Initially he had bought it as a present for young Enoch. But a browse through the chapter headings and the book's concentration on the Zambawian independence war had convinced him to keep it for himself. What had he bought for Enoch instead? A novelty cigarette lighter in the shape of James Bond's gun or some knick-knack like that.

Indigo read the book with growing fascination and within a day it was near-finished. But when he came to the quote from Queenstown Chief of Police, Frank Pienaar, his appetite faltered, partly with nauseating memories but mostly with Pienaar's words themselves.

As soon as we lose the moral high ground, we can expect nothing less than anarchy and ultimately revolution.

Indigo knew that Pienaar – that evil bastard! – had got it completely right. And that thought made him feel most peculiar. He realized – or at least feared – that the independence war had not been won by his own bravery, that of his fellow *ters* in the ZLF or the leadership of President Adini. No. Rather it had been lost by the stupidity of the *musungu* government and its determined alienation of the black population in the wake of Pienaar's death some two years after the murder of Comrade Solo. And Pienaar was not even killed by the ZLF! No! In fact, he was shot between the eyes by his long-suffering wife, who decided that she had taken one beating too many at the hands of her vicious husband. Indigo wondered whether this battered woman realized that her last black eye had changed the course of a nation's history. What a thought!

Indigo was shocked too that his own thinking should correlate so precisely with that of the dead police chief. What Pienaar was saying was that words held no truth, just morsels of meaning like the titbits of flesh that hang from a vulture's beak. And when a carcass has been torn apart by the scavengers, can you tell what creature it once held? Of course not. Words were no more than leaking vessels fired by an incompetent potter. And this was truly what Indigo believed. But how could a born wordsmith, a natural poet, have come to such a jaded conclusion? His twenty-third birthday! Oh God! His twenty-third birthday!

After the murder of Comrade Solo it took Zita Adini a couple of weeks to come to terms with the weight of the command of the ZLF. He had always thought of himself as born to lead. But now the opportunity presented itself, he wasn't so sure. Eventually, however, as with any man who regards leadership as his birthright, his ego swelled enough to fill the role and he called all the remnants of the ZLF together for a meeting at his *gwaasha* in Chivu Province. Their numbers had dwindled to something less than 200, but Zita's chest swelled with pride as he stood in the flickering light of the open fire to address his men. His trusted friend, the colourful poet, was at his side and he could see his wife and child hovering in the shadows at the back of the crowd. It was, in fact, the last time he saw Sally and Enoch before independence.

'*Tecum vivere amem, tecum obeam libens*,' he began. 'As the poet Horace said, "With you I should love to live, with you I am ready to die."'

Zita spoke for ten minutes and he felt his confidence grow with every syllable, as if the words themselves were building blocks that lifted him higher and higher above his audience. He talked about the death of Comrade Solo. He talked about the magnitude of the task facing them. He talked about honour and glory and justice. He talked about the burden of destiny that they carried on their shoulders. He talked about the blessings of the ancestors and the courage of the Great Chief Tuloko, which coursed through their veins. And the words were so powerful that he began to believe them himself and at the end of his speech the men cheered and waved their guns and clicked their tongues against the back of their throats in the traditional manner.

When the meeting was finished, Zita led his men into the night and they began their trek to Zimindo Province, the area that Zita had designated as their new base because of its geographical centrality, status in Zamba myth and pre-eminence among the *zakulu*. His small army was able to march all night on the adrenalin of Zita's lyricism and, as they marched, Indigo composed poetry on the spot, shouting it into the darkness to the rhythm of each stride.

'We march with the wind at our backs
      And the Great Chief in step at our side.
The ancestors sing us to glory
      Musungu has nowhere to hide!

Father Sun will rise in the east,
      Where the mountains kiss the sky,

Shining his light on our triumph.
   Musungu has nowhere to hide!

We taste the Great Lake in the west
   That drowned Zamba in its tide,
But as Cousin Moon lives on in the sky
   Musungu has nowhere to hide!

We march into the future
   Where only *zakulu* reside,
But this path is leading to freedom.
   Musungu has nowhere to hide!'

With their movement into the bush, the ZLF developed a new set of tactics, splitting into squads around forty strong under the central command of Zita. These squads formed a ring around Zita's primary stronghold (some thirty miles north of the main Zimindo township), with a remit to educate and recruit among the local population and terrorize the *musungu* farms in the surrounding area. Zita had chosen his location wisely, since these *musungu* farms were largely isolated – scattered over Zimindo's vast plains – making them easy targets for the ZLF raids, with little chance of calling on the Manyikaland state forces for support. What's more, the farmland in Zimindo Province produced a substantial part of Manyikaland's export crops, so it wasn't long before the government was forced to take notice.

The government, of course, immediately dispatched troops to Zimindo, but the area was too large and the ZLF too cunning for the army's deployment to present much of a threat. The troops tried Chief Pienaar's policy of 'stick and carrot'. But the rural population was simply too poor to be bought with wads of cash. What were they supposed to do with paper money, when there wasn't a shop for 100 miles? If the army had been able to deliver sacks of seeds or ground maize, maybe the response would have been different. But the success of the ZLF in their attacks on *musungu* farms had left even Queenstown feeling the pinch of food shortages.

Less fruitful was Zita's intention of indoctrinating the local population with revolutionary zeal. It simply didn't work. When the ZLF squads marched into remote villages spouting ideas of 'exploitation', 'capitalistic appropriation' and the 'profit of surplus value', they were greeted by nothing but blank stares and the occasional nervous chuckle.

Indigo could remember one conversation he'd had with an elderly farmer.

'Do you not want freedom in Zambawi?' he had asked.

'Where is Zambawi?'

'Here! This land is Zambawi!'

'Don't be silly! You talk like *a temba*! This is my kraal. This is my land.'

'Yes. But ultimately it is Manyikaland.'

'I thought you said it was Zambawi?'

'It is but . . .'

'You talk in circles like a dog chasing its tail or licking its testicles. And your breath is just as bad. You should try cleaning your teeth once in a while.'

'What I'm trying to say, *mboko*, is that ultimately this land belongs to the *musungu*.'

'That is ridiculous! How can this land belong to the *musungu*? In this life my kraal belongs to me and ultimately it belongs to the Great Chief Tuloko and is blessed by Father Sun and fertilized by the *shamva*. How can it belong to the *musungu*? The *musungu* is just a man and he will die like any other. Who will it belong to then? Only Tuloko and the *zakulu* are for all time.'

Initially, therefore, the ZLF's rural recruitment drive seduced few new revolutionaries. In fact, it was not until some time later, with the death of Chief Pienaar and the adoption by the colonial government of the absurd, counter-productive policy of 'example and reprisal', that the rural population joined the ZLF in their thousands, driven to insurrection by the astonishing thuggery of the Manyikaland army.

In those early days of the rural independence war, Zita (encouraged by Indigo) determined to retain a degree of traditionalism in his very modern revolution. He led the ZLF squads in nightly prayer to the ancestral spirits and he positively encouraged the telling of the stories of the Great Chief Tuloko's many victories and Indigo's rallying poetry, which was loaded with mythical imagery. He particularly enjoyed the poem 'The Authority of the Chief', which Indigo would recite most evenings around the camp fire, with its fiery verses of Tuloko's awesome personality and its call and response chorus.

'And the *shumba* they growled!' Indigo would say and the men would growl like lions.

'And the *gudo* yahooed!'

'Ooh ooh ooh!' yahooed the men.

'And the *boka* birds sang in the sky!'

'Fillipee! Fillipee!'

'But the *shumba* and *gudo* and *boka* were silent when the Great Chief Tuloko walked by!'

Before long, however, Zita began to tire of the endless references to the Great Chief and the constant harking back to the fairy stories of Zambawi's glorious past. Zita's impatience stemmed from various reasons. Some better than others.

At a rational level Zita was concerned that the myths should not overshadow the fact that there was a war to be won. He worried, for example, that some of his men were so intoxicated by the fateful atmosphere that effused through Indigo's poetry that they had lost sight of the fundamental truths of conflict. He had heard rumours of certain squads allowing *musungu* farmers to go free, saying, 'In the name of the Great Chief Tuloko, we show you mercy.' And that simply wouldn't do. Zita was sure that 'mercy' was not a vital ingredient of a successful revolution. Similarly, at an ideological level, Zita found it difficult to reconcile the new-found mysticism of his men with the Marxist principles he'd learned from the Socialist Workers Party in Oxford and during his spell in Moscow with Comrade Solo. At first the mythology seemed like an expression of an idyllic 'state of nature' of an economically backward people. But as Indigo's poetry spun new and resilient webs of magical reality, Zita began to fear his Marxist revolution was being subverted by 'false consciousness' and an insubstantial opiate that confounded his economic materialism.

More to the point, however, Zita was irritated that all the tales told were of the Great Chief Tuloko, since such heroic transference sat uncomfortably with his ever-burgeoning ego. Indigo certainly wrote poetry about the battles that they fought and the victories they won at the expense of the Manyikaland forces. But the realism of his description — however bloody — was always encased in a mythical structure that, to put it bluntly, allowed no room for mention of the magnificent Zita Adini.

One night, after a particularly close shave with a company of crack troops that had left him with the indignity of an arse full of lead and a hole in one of his rubber testicles, the future President had confronted Indigo over his poetic chronicle of the skirmish, an epic narrative that accurately portrayed the violence of the fighting before dissolving into fantastical nonsense about the spirit of Tuloko chasing the *musungu* away.

'For goodness' sake, Indigo!' Zita exclaimed. 'It's not the Great Chief Bloody Tuloko who's got a bum full of buckshot!'

It was, however, his meeting with the witchdoctor that finally convinced Zita to ban all ancestral worship, even all mention of Tuloko, from the ZLF camps. He received word, one day, that the local *zakulu* wanted to see him and, intrigued, he willingly made the day's journey to the *zakulu*'s kraal, an isolated smallholding on the borders of the Maponda plains. The *zakulu* met him at the kraal's gate with his head bowed, a small man, as bald as wind-polished stone and as old as the earth itself.

'Welcome,' the *zakulu* said. But he blocked the entrance to his home and showed no sign of moving.

For a moment Zita forgot himself and offered the man his hand. The *zakulu* would not accept it.

'Oh! Right!' Zita said and he bowed his head a little and began the traditional clapping.

'You are Zita Adini?'

'I am.'

'You lead the ZLF?'

'That's right, *mboko zakulu*. The Zambawi Liberation Front.'

'And in whose name do you fight this war?'

'In the name of the Zambawian people.'

For the first time the *zakulu* looked up and Zita was disturbed by his eyes. The irises seemed to fill the whole of his eyes and they were utterly black. This gave him a disconcerting appearance, as if he could be completely blind or all-seeing and you would never know. The *zakulu* shook his head slowly from side to side.

'Oh!' Zita said. 'What I meant to say is that I fight in the name of the Great Chief Tuloko.'

'And who gave you that name?'

'I . . . what do you mean?'

'It is the *zakulu* who give the blessing of Tuloko and Father Sun.'

'Of course. I'm sorry. May I ask . . .'

'And a man whose heart is full of pride fights for nobody but himself. Father Sun allows me to see many things. You will win your war, Zita Adini. But it is *your* war and yours alone.'

With that, the *zakulu* turned on his heels and tottered back into the kraal towards the small, circular building – presumably his house – that stood in the middle of the yard. Zita was very confused and somewhat disorientated. He felt like he wanted to laugh but his chest was empty. For a moment the wind picked up and the dust blew in baby whirlwinds and his eyes began to water. He rubbed them irritably with his knuckles and when he opened them again he saw a mangy dog with no hind legs dragging itself across the parched earth of the kraal and into the circular building where the *zakulu* stood at the door.

'What else do you see, *mboko zakulu*?' Zita called.

'I see that you have no testicles. Very unfortunate,' the *zakulu* replied before disappearing inside.

Zita stood staring at the doorway for a full further minute, disturbed and nervous. But there was no sign of the *zakulu*. His thoughts were disjointed. Who was this witchdoctor? How had he seen his rubber-filled scrotum? Why did the dog have no hind legs? Why could he not invoke the name of the Great Chief Tuloko, for goodness' sake! Slowly Zita turned and began the long walk back to the ZLF base. And when, some ten minutes later, his mind finally reassembled into something close to its usual order, he realized that his lips were moving and he was repeating a single phrase over and over again.

'There is my war to be won,' he said. 'There is my war to be won.'

29 : The Poet (six)

When Zita forbade ancestral worship and banned all storytelling and poetry recitation about the Great Chief Tuloko in the ZLF camps, it had a profound effect on all his men. But none more so than Indigo.

It wasn't just that Indigo had thrilled at the sight of dozens of intent faces staring up at him under the pale light of Cousin Moon as he stalked among them and the poetry fell from his mouth like droplets of magic potion. It was more than that. Unable to write about the Great Chief Tuloko, he tried to summon heroism from the day-to-day battles and the run-of-the-mill violence. But he could find none. Where once the death of a *ter* had been a heroic sacrifice, a courageous leap into the world of the spirits, now it was no more than a death, a loss, an ache, as prosaic and unsatisfying as the first mouthful of an unwanted meal. Though he tried to keep writing poetry, his work now seemed listless and uninspired. Bloody wounds were no longer 'crimson trails mapping the sacred path to Tuloko's side'. They were just 'bloody wounds'. The screams of the *musungu* were no longer the 'defiant shrieks of an ebbing soul'. But simply 'screams of agony'.

Indigo soon found that his perception of the independence war was shifting. How long had it been since he had witnessed his parents' deathly embrace? Almost five years. And he'd long since lost count of the number of men he had killed. Thirty? Forty? Eighty? He could remember the hunger for vengeance that had moistened his lips. But, without his noticing, it had passed and now he felt as bloated as the *musungu* glutton who guzzles the best part of the chicken and discards the head and feet. Twenty-two years old and he had killed more men than he could remember! Was this the wish of the Great Chief Tuloko? Was this what freedom demanded?

Guerrilla war, Indigo had discovered, was a curiously stop-start affair. You would fight for three hours – narrowed behind the inadequate protection of a sapling, burrowing your face into the dust as the bullets whistled over your head, desperately praying to any god that would listen – and time passed in a flash. Then you waited for a week, maybe two, for the next action and it seemed to stop like a lost note in the song of an *mbira*. In the lull after a battle hours became weeks became years, as if you were living the lifetimes of the soldiers you'd just killed.

During these times the men of the ZLF amused themselves in various ways. Some cleaned their guns with religious attention to detail; others visited the local prostitutes, sowing their seed in poor soil for fear that they would never win the battle for the land; most whiled away the days in endless games of cards, recklessly chancing fictitious cars, cows and cash with the same abandon with which they gambled their lives. But Indigo didn't believe that a pristine gun barrel would save his life (for that was in the hands of the ancestors); he'd never been with a woman and he'd no interest in games. Instead he used to find himself a quiet corner of the camp, sit down with his notebook and stubby pencil and write his poetry. Reams of the stuff. Or at least that was what he did before Zita's ban was imposed and the muse deserted him without saying goodbye.

Thereafter Indigo began to use these expanses of free time to take long walks through the Zimindo countryside. Assuming there was no reconnaissance to be done and it was not his turn to persuade the local farmers to part with their chickens on a promise, he would set out at first light with his notebook in his pocket, his pencil between his teeth and his revolver in his boot. Sometimes he would walk only a couple of miles to one of his favourite spots – the sandstone outcrop punctuated by higgledy-piggledy holes, home to *shangu* spiders and dusties (the small beetles that lived off baboon crap), or the secluded watering hole with banks lined with *muti* leaves (excellent for hornet stings), where the baby *nzou* came to play, repeatedly squirting water over one another as if their trunks were still a source of surprise and delight. On one occasion Indigo tried to bathe in the watering hole. But he emerged from his dive to find that he was covered head to toe in leeches that left painful welts all over his body. When he returned to the camp, the other *ters* mocked his extraordinary appearance.

'Look at Indigo!' one said. 'He has been with a crazy whore.'

'I hope you asked for your money back,' added another.

'You've been well and truly fucked!' said a third.

Indigo, of course, denied their accusations. 'I have not fucked anyone,' he insisted and to laughter. After that he became known as 'Indigo the Virgin' instead of 'Indigo the Poet'.

On other days Indigo ventured further afield. He walked until Father Sun reached his throne and then he found a patch of shade and sat down and produced his notebook and pencil. Then he wrote poetry. About the faces in the occasional clouds, the twisting shapes of the trees and the expanses of *kiba* grass that bit your bare shins. But it was all mundane stuff. He was like an artist knocking out a watercolour for the sake of something to do or a sculptor modelling a quick ashtray so that he has somewhere to stub his cigarette.

It was on one of these longer excursions, however, that Indigo chanced upon a *musungu* smallholding that had not featured on any of the ZLF's maps. He was walking to the west of the ZLF camp some two weeks after Zita had cut off his poetry, marching with a purposeful stride to find a suitable spot of shade before Father Sun could chase away all but the most resilient shadows. His hair was burning and he had taken off his baggy shirt and tied it around his head, so that the cloth flapped against the back of his neck like a legionnaire's kepi. But his small water flask was empty and nothing could stop the thirst spiders from crawling up the back of his throat and dancing on his tongue. He cursed his stupidity. How could he have set off into an unknown area trusting on a waterhole? He was beginning to experience the first nagging sensations of dehydration: the slight queasiness in his belly, the rasp in his chest and the blur before his eyes.

Concentrating as he was on the search for shade and water, he abandoned his usual caution. Generally his eyes and ears and nose were ever peeled and pricked up and sniffing for any sign of the Manyikaland army. But what good would it do to spot a patrol if he'd lost the strength to run away, climb a tree or even pull a trigger?

Indigo reached the crest of a sand-slipping ridge and looked down. Below him was a small *musungu* farmhouse. At least, that's what it had to be, though it was like no farmhouse that he had ever seen, with its freshly painted white brick-work, Mediterranean arched windows and flat roof served by external stone steps. A curse caught in his throat and he threw himself on to his chest.

Expertly he rolled himself behind the cover of a parched tree stump and, lying on his back, extracted his revolver from his boot and checked that it was fully loaded. Raising himself on his elbows, he peered around the stump and trained his gun on the farmhouse. Opposite the house was a small fenced paddock, where a sprightly chestnut mare chewed contentedly from a healthy bale of hay. The dusty earth of the paddock was punctuated by maybe forty small mounds – curious – that were aligned in symmetrical rows. In the yard a dozen plump chickens clucked officiously around each other like proud elders at a *temba* initiation. On the small wooden veranda a single figure was bent over a large metal basin. Indigo narrowed his eyes against the sun. It was a girl – maybe eighteen or nineteen – washing her hair, bare to the waist, with her loose white dress tied around her midriff. Her skin was the colour of milky coffee. She was either a very light-skinned Zamba or a very dark-skinned *musungu*.

Slowly Indigo got to his feet and, keeping his gun fixed on the girl, he descended the ridge towards her. He wasn't sure what he was going to do, but he knew that he had to get some water. When he was no more than five paces behind her, he stopped. Still she hadn't heard him, partly because she had water in her ears and partly because of the strange song that she had begun to sing at the top of her voice. It wasn't Zamba, that was for sure. At first Indigo assumed it was English, but he couldn't understand all of the words. Maybe it was another of those Northern European languages: German or Flemish or something like that.

'In the land of San Domingo!' the girl sang, 'Lived a filly, oh-by-jingo! Ay ay! Iddy iddy oompah oompah oompah! Pop it up your jumper!'

Indigo stood stock-still. He didn't know what to do next. Besides, he was transfixed by the chiming clarity of the girl's voice, which pierced the heat, the precise definition of her spine beneath her supple skin and the outline of her buttocks, which teased the damp cloth of her dress as she bent over. He inclined his head slightly and could just make out the gentle curve of the girl's right breast where it cast its shadow against the metal basin. He felt an uncomfortable twitch in his groin and his tongue seemed too big for his mouth.

'From the marshes in galoshes! Trumped the odelay by goshes! And every night, they'd trill the pale moonlight! Oh by gee, by gosh, by gum, by Jove! Oh by jimminy, can't you feel our love?'

The girl finished kneading her scalp and suddenly straightened up, tossing her head back and throwing a cascade of black curls tumbling between her shoulder blades down to her waist. A shower of water flew through the air and sprinkled Indigo's forehead and cheeks and mouth. He licked his lips and he was sure he could taste the girl's skin, and he felt lecherous and guilty.

In spite of himself he coughed and the girl spun round, clasping her arms across her naked chest. She stared at him, frozen with shock, and her eyes were like a startled bush buck's, wide and wet. She was mixed race, although she looked nothing like the Cape Coloureds that Indigo had seen working as foremen on the Queenstown building sites, with their piggy snouts and freckles and mean little eyes. Her forehead and cheekbones were high and handsome, with just enough pronunciation to suggest intellect and pride; her nose was long, slim and aquiline, with a slight hook in the middle, a charming imperfection that only seemed to accentuate her beauty; her lips were full and curiously two-toned, the top lip the luscious orange-pink of an ideal mango, the lower deep purple like the sky at dusk. Water droplets glistened in her hair like tiny beads of sun. For some reason, though they looked nothing like each other, she reminded Indigo of his mother.

'*Aiwakupe!*' he whispered.

'I'm not.'

'*Maoko ka!*'

The girl stared at him and an expression of fear and confusion fluttered across her eyes.

'I said, put your hands up!' he rasped.

'I know what you said.'

'Do it!'

Slowly the girl raised her arms above her head, exposing her breasts. Indigo hadn't quite latched on to the fact that her hands had been protecting her modesty and he suddenly felt terribly embarrassed. But he couldn't help but stare. The girl's breasts were perfect: small, high and utterly symmetrical and tipped with dark rosebud nipples that stiffened and goosebumped. Indigo found himself tracing a line with his eyes from the gentle undulation of her breastbone across her belly to the deep cavity of her button. And he noticed a soft line of silken hair that slid downwards from her navel before disappearing beneath the gentle folds of her dress.

'I'm sorry,' he said.

'Are you going to rape me? I would rather die than have a man rape me.'

The girl spoke with no discernible tremor in her voice. And Indigo was shocked by the brutality of the question.

'No! I . . . Of course not!'

'Then don't look at me as if that's what you want.'

Indigo was speechless. A single pearl of water was trickling down the girl's forearm. When it reached the bend in her elbow it paused for a minute, as if uncertain how to proceed, before continuing its gravity-defying path across the smooth mound of her triceps to her armpit.

'I'm sorry,' he finally said. 'Please put your hands down.'

The girl lowered her arms, quickly undid the dress that was

knotted around her hips and slipped her arms into the loose white sleeves. She reached for the zip at the back and, for a brief moment, it looked as though she might ask Indigo for assistance. But she managed to fasten her dress herself, with considerable dexterity and flexibility. All the while Indigo was unable to take his eyes off her. And she returned his gaze with interest. Her eyes radiated warmth, but there was a hard glimmer that told she wasn't one to be trifled with.

'Who are you?' Indigo asked.

'Ruth. My name is Ruth. Will you put the gun down?'

'Who lives here?'

'I do. Are you all right? You don't look very well.'

'No. I meant who else lives here apart from you.'

'My father. You really don't look well, you know.'

'Water,' Indigo said.

Suddenly he saw Ruth topple sideways and something big and hard hit him on the side of the head, knocking the gun from his grasp.

Ouch! he thought. My gun! Where's my gun?

He wanted to look for his gun, but he could still feel a heavy weight pressing against the side of his face. He stared at Ruth where she lay prone. Her eyes were open and she looked conscious. In fact, if anything, her expression held concern. Oh God! If only his mind weren't so fuzzy. Who the hell had hit him?

'Are you all right?' he tried to say. But he found that his mouth was full of dirt.

Ruth walked towards him – how did she manage that when she was lying on her side? – and crouched down next to where he stood, her face perfectly contrasting with the sky behind her head.

Gravity, Indigo thought, has gone wonky. And he tried to tilt his head to one side to align his face with Ruth's. The movement was curiously unnatural and painful. But at least it released the pressure on the side of his face and he found he was able to talk. Ruth laid her hand against his cheek and it felt like hot coal. She clearly had quite a fever.

'Are you all right?' Indigo managed to ask.

'*I'm* fine.'

'Who hit me?'

'The ground. You fell over.'

The next thing Indigo knew he was cradled in Ruth's lap, looking up at her face as she wiped his forehead with a cloth and drizzled water into his mouth from a small plastic beaker. Her hair brushed against his cheek as she worked. It smelled like fresh fruit juice squeezed into a chilled glass.

'You have beautiful eyes,' Ruth said. 'Not soldier's eyes at all.'

'I'm not a soldier. I'm a poet,' Indigo croaked.

'A what?'

'A poet. Po-et.'

'Oh! A poet? Since when did a poet carry a gun?'

'We are fighting for freedom.'

'Freedom? Of course you are. It's a just war, isn't it?'

'Yes.'

'My father says it's not a just war. He says it's just a war. And that's different.'

'I . . .'

'No. Don't try to talk.'

Ruth leaned forward slightly over Indigo and began to dab at his neck and shoulders with the cloth. She then rubbed over the ridges of his pectorals and the firm muscles of his belly. Indigo could see the shape and colour of Ruth's breasts just above his lips and he began to breathe deeply, intoxicated by the scent of fresh musk. Ruth pulled back, her face screwed in annoyance.

'Don't smell me without asking! Do you want me to leave you here to cook in the sun until you're as dry and crusty as a burnt-out kettle?'

'I'm sorry. It's just . . . you smell like my mother.'

'Like your mother? *Maiwe!*' Ruth exclaimed and her mouth twitched into an unwilling smile. 'You're overheated,' she said. 'Don't they teach you anything in this guerrilla army of yours? A fine bunch of soldiers you'll make if you don't drink enough water. What kind of *ter* do you think you are anyway?'

'I'm not a *ter*. I'm a poet.'

'Oh yes! Of course you are. So tell me, Mr Poet. Tell me what I look like in your best poetic language.'

Indigo looked up at Ruth and thought for a second. He wrinkled his nose in a way that she found completely charming.

'You are a goddess,' he began, 'expelled from the spirits on the breath of the Great Chief Tuloko. He cast you from the best the earth could offer. Your bones are shaped from the supple limbs of mother *shumba*; your hair was spun by the greatest *babayako*; your blood is the menstrual blood of Mudiwa herself; your flesh is ripe mango; your eyes two diamonds from the mountains in the East; your tears the gossamer that dances on the *kiba* grass; and your voice is the sound of creation, a voice that can speak only truth, a voice that wakes the love of our ancestors and sends a squawking baby to sleep.'

Ruth laughed in delight. 'You really *are* a poet!'

'I haven't finished yet. Your breasts . . .'

'Don't be rude,' she scolded. 'You'll spoil it.'

She lifted Indigo's head slightly in her hands and planted a soft kiss on his forehead. Indigo felt that all the sensation in his body was concentrated in that one square inch of skin and his toes curled and uncurled in the caps of his soldier's boots.

'That's for your poetry,' Ruth said. 'Do you have a name? Or do I just have to call you Mr Poet?'

'Indigo.'

'N'dgo? Ha! So what do you expect from me?'

'No. *Indigo*. The English word. It is a colour. The colour between blue and violet on the spectrum.'

Again Ruth bent forward. This time she kissed each of Indigo's cheeks in turn. Indigo did his utmost not to smell her. Or at least not too obviously.

'What were those kisses for?'

'They were for being just like me. You are neither blue nor violet. I am neither black nor white. We are neither one thing nor the other. My father says that this is a special kind of gift . . .'

Indigo finished her sentence. 'From the ancestors.'

'Exactly! How did you know? I am a special kind of gift from the ancestors. That's what my father says.'

'Who is your father?'

'My father is Gideon. He is a *musungu*. But not really. He is a Jew. Do you know about the Jews? They are *musungu* who are treated like blacks. That's what my father says and he is the wisest man in the whole of Manyikaland. That's what he says anyway. But I don't think he can be that wise because he is a terrible farmer and we have to barter for most of our food from the proper black people and buy it from the other *musungu* farmers, who don't like us.'

'Your chickens look healthy.'

'Of course they do! Because my father feeds them all the best grain and he refuses to eat them. He gives the chickens names and when you know someone's name, it's harder to kill them. That's what my father says. My mother – who was a proper black person – died in childbirth, you see. And since then my father hasn't killed any animal. He says that when you have killed someone you love, murder becomes too easy, so you must never kill again. So now he leaves me to tend all our crops while he just sits in the field and tells my mother all about me. We must be the only farm in the whole of Manyikaland where the chickens die of old age! Did you see the mounds in the paddock? That is our chicken cemetery. Did you see it?'

Indigo wanted to answer but he found that he was too confused, partly by Ruth's random chatter and partly by the thump-thump-thump of his heart, which was echoing loudly in his head. He could feel sweat on his forehead, which was beginning to dribble down the sides of his nose to sting his eyes.

'Listen to me blabber when you're so overheated!' Ruth said. 'I've got to cool you down, Indigo! Let me wash your body with cold water. But you must promise not to smell me without asking.'

'I promise,' Indigo whispered and Ruth stared down at him expectantly.

'Well?'

'Well what?'

'Well? Do you want to smell me?'

'Can I?'

'You can. But only on one condition. You must promise that when you smell me I remind you of your mother.'

Again Ruth leaned forward and began to wash Indigo's neck and shoulders and chest and belly with the gentlest of touches. And as the cool dampness seeped into his skin, the slightest breeze sent the most magnificent sensation through his whole body. As she bent over him, he could feel the fold of Ruth's belly against his head and the weight of her breasts rested on his chin. He inhaled hungrily, sucking in her ambrosial scent as if it was the most addictive narcotic. He heard his breathing quicken and the thumps of his heart accelerated to an irregular, jumpy patter. In spite of himself he felt his loins twitch and thicken and the little muscles at the base of his penis began to flex of their own accord. For a moment Ruth paused above him.

'Are you thinking of your mother?' she asked coyly.

How many years later was it? More than fifteen. More than fifteen years later! But Indigo Bulimi often thought of that day they first met and, when his dreams were strong, he could still conjure up her scent. If Ruth were alive, she would be past thirty now and maybe her glorious hair would be streaked with unforgiving grey and maybe her perfect breasts would sag a little. But she would still smell the same. Indigo was sure of that. If she were alive.

After that first meeting Indigo visited Ruth whenever possible. He helped her in the fields, dug graves for geriatric chickens and ate her maize porridge with barely a grimace. Ruth was very sensitive about her maize porridge since she had never had a mother around to teach her how to make it and she watched Indigo eat with avid concentration on every quirk of his expression.

Sometimes, when the work was finished, Indigo would read to her from his notebook full of poems. Sometimes she would sing him songs that she had been taught by her father, who, it transpired, had spent years playing the music-halls in London's East End. Sometimes the two of them would sit on the wooden veranda and she would nuzzle his chest or suck his fingers. But they never made love.

Ruth put it like this: 'Truth be told, Indigo, we cannot perform *gulu gulu* when you want to kill my father and take his land.'

'I understand. But maybe one day . . .'

'Of course one day! We are neither one thing nor the other! But together? That will be something!'

Indigo didn't mind. Everything he knew about sex had been gleaned from the gross bragging of his fellows in the ZLF and they made it sound like more trouble than it was worth. Besides, he might be killed any day and the idea of leaving his lover on her own was too much to bear. It never occurred to him that it could be the other way round.

Only once did Indigo see Gideon. Ruth took him to her father's favourite field and they tunnelled through the high corn so that they could watch him as he sat in his clearing and talked to his wife. He was a withered little man with hunched shoulders and wispy black hair that he pasted to his bald pate and his voice was the saddest voice that Indigo had ever heard. He said this to Ruth later and she agreed. 'Even when my father tells a good joke his voice makes me want to cry.'

'Ah, my wife!' Gideon was saying. 'How much I miss you. And *sisi* Ruth grows more like you every day. Sometimes it makes me angry that you could leave me to bring up our daughter alone. I know you love her where you are, but she needs a mother's hand. She is as impulsive as a hare and as frantic as a fly with no legs. Oyoyoy! She is beautiful too. One day she will break some poor boy's heart.'

When Gideon said this, Ruth tightened her grip on Indigo's hand and whispered 'I love you' in his ear before biting it affectionately.

Part of the reason why Indigo spent so much time with Ruth was the change in atmosphere at the ZLF camp. Since the prohibition of ancestral worship and praise-songs to the Great Chief Tuloko, the happy camaraderie of the ZLF units had begun to evaporate. In its place an attitude of cold violence began to seep into the contextless minds of the men. The endless games of cards were replaced by tests of strength and bare-knuckle fights; local hookers were dismissed with nothing but a slap for payment; and the obsessive gun cleaners began to modify their weapons and shells to inflict maximum damage and maximum pain.

Of course, it wasn't Zita's ban alone that caused this change. It was also a reaction to the escalation in the war and the pronounced increase in the viciousness of the *musungu* army. Soon after the ban was imposed, a missing ZLF patrol was discovered hanging in a copse, the scavenged remains of all eight men crucified on eight separate trees with bolts through their wrists and ankles and bloody gashes sliced into their sides. What's more, rumours began to circulate among the ZLF of new *musungu* tortures devised for their hostages: live burial in a mound of *zveko* ants, motorcycle helmets filled with *putsi* fly larvae and 'Welsh rabbit' (nobody knew what 'Welsh rabbit' could be but that just made it worse).

Now the ZLF went into battle with insane eyes and itching trigger fingers. Their heroic war songs were replaced by feral, bloodthirsty screams and the ceremonial smoke of the *gar* pipe gave way to chewing the mandrake root, which robbed the guerrillas of pain and pity. Many of the soldiers acquired bizarre fetishes and superstitions. One young *ter* carried the rotting head of a Manyika-land army sergeant in his backpack. Another took to stealing the personal photographs of his victims and taping them beneath his uniform around his back and chest, as if they might offer some kind of magical protection. One of the ZLF's most courageous warriors (who had hitherto picked up a flesh wound in every single skirmish) visited a whore before one battle and returned to camp unscathed. Thereafter he demanded a blow job before every encounter, which was fine if there was a whore on hand but otherwise led to terrible arguments and in-fighting. Nor was Zita, the ZLF's leader, immune to such eccentricities. Soon he began to refuse to question any *musungu* hostage unless the man had first been castrated, and he would commence every interrogation saying, 'So, *musungu*! You think that you're better than me?'

Initially Indigo managed to retain a degree of detachment from the growing barbarism. He reassured himself that the independence war was a just struggle and he continually harked back to the words of Cicero with which he had first challenged Zita: '*Silent enim leges inter arma.*' And he clung to his visits to see Ruth as little islands of innocence and altruism.

On one occasion Zita asked him, 'Indigo, my colourful friend! What has happened to your poetry? Do you not write any more?'

'Poetry is the language of truth, immutable and heroic,' Indigo replied. 'I see no heroism in this place.'

'*Multa fero, ut placem genus irritabile vatum.*'

'Horace,' Indigo said. 'And it doesn't please me at all.'

After a while, however, Indigo too began to be brutalized. With hindsight he tried not to blame himself for this, just to view his change in character with an odd sense of melancholy, as a reformed alcoholic might look back at his first drink. How could he have avoided being influenced by such a culture of violence? The poisonous blood ran so freely that he couldn't possibly escape unstained. But this thought could not stop the guilt from gobbling his soul.

The change was gradual and pernicious, so that, by the time Indigo noticed it, it was too late to rectify. At first he began to dream of severed limbs, decapitations, the *shamva* flowing with human detritus and the Great Chief Tuloko crying large bloody tears. Then his upper lip curled into a permanent snarl and he took to chewing the mandrake root before going into battle. One day he led an assault on a *musungu* farmhouse where the Manyikaland army had made a temporary base. Instructing twenty *ters* to lay down suppressing fire, he stormed the front door with a dozen screaming fellows. With a nod of his head and a pointing finger, he signalled to the majority of his men to secure the ground floor while he raced upstairs to take out the machine-gun in the front window. Issuing forth a mighty roar, he kicked in the bedroom door and, within seconds, the gunner and his loader lay dead in the window bay, though not before the loader had let off a couple of rounds that sent all kinds of shrapnel flying around the room. Looking down, Indigo saw a large shard of mirror glass embedded in his thigh and he collapsed to the floor with a curse. He laid down his sub-machine-gun at his side, gritted his teeth and tried to loosen the glass from his leg slicing the palms of his hands in the process. Despite the effect of the mandrake, the sound of chewing flesh turned his stomach. For a moment he closed his eyes and swallowed the bile that was filling his mouth.

I will not pass out, he thought. I will not faint.

When he opened his eyes, his mind was suddenly refocused by the reflection in the glass in his wound. A *musungu* soldier was standing just a yard or so behind him with his gun trained on the back his head. In one swift movement Indigo picked up his sub-machine-gun, rolled backwards and swung its butt with all his might. With an unreal crunch the gun embedded itself in the soldier's cheek and he fell dead to the floor. But Indigo wasn't done. Dragging himself up on his one good leg, he repeatedly battered the corpse, shouting, 'Die, *musungu*! Die!', not realizing that death was no longer enough for him. He wanted to grind the body to invisible, unidentifiable dust that might be swept under the carpet of his mind or scattered on the breeze of his future.

Eventually Indigo ran out of breath and looked down at the bloody mass at his feet. The corpse was barely recognizable as human, bar the tattered uniform and the mouth and jaw that had somehow escaped undamaged. On the soldier's upper lip were the first traces of an adolescent moustache and his teeth were latched together with heavy metal braces. He was just a buck-toothed kid!

Indigo screamed and fired again and again into the dead boy's chin until some of the other *ters* appeared and dragged him back to the ZLF camp.

After this incident he didn't manage to visit Ruth for three or four days. His wound made walking uncomfortable. But, more than that, he was overwhelmed by guilt and self-hatred. Whereas once his trips to Ruth's farm had been opportunities to be himself, removed from the heinous mire of war, as artistic and good-willed as he hoped himself to be, now he began to fear that the real Indigo Bulimi was the barbaric soldier, not the poet-lover who thrilled to a delicate phrase and the soft touch of his soulmate.

When he finally summoned the courage to see Ruth, it seemed that his worst fears were confirmed.

'What has happened to your eyes?' she exclaimed. 'You look different.'

'Soldier's eyes?'

'No. Your eyes look like my father's.'

'That's not so bad.'

'No? He is sixty years old and he has seen too much.'

Ruth unwound the field dressing from his leg and cried when she saw the deep laceration that jagged across his thigh, her salty tears pooling in the indentations of rough stitching.

'My Indigo! My Indigo!'

'Don't cry,' Indigo said and, before he knew what he was saying, he added, 'You should see the other guy.' And fearful images flashed across his mind and cold sweat clammed his palms and armpits.

'Don't say that,' Ruth said. 'Don't say that ever. I don't want to see. I don't want to know what kind of *ter* you are. When you are here, you are my Indigo, my poet, my love.'

Indigo held her then. He pulled her into his arms and held her so tight that she thought she might suffocate. She began to splutter and giggle and pushed him away.

'Enough! That's quite enough of that! There will be plenty of time for cuddling and canoodling on your birthday. You are coming to see me, Indigo, aren't you? You promised. I am making a new dress and baking a cake and I will make you a fine meal. Perhaps we might even kill a chicken!'

Indigo's twenty-third birthday was on the following Saturday and he planned to spend the whole day with Ruth. On the Friday night, however, Zita threw a huge party for him in the ZLF camp and there were gallons of home-brewed millet beer to be drunk, sacks of mandrake root to be chewed and dozens of local hookers to be fucked. Within an hour the men were singing filthy songs, fighting over *musungu* trophies and bragging of the soldiers they had impaled or carved or blown to smithereens. One man told how, when a *musungu* soldier shat himself with fear, he had forced him to eat his own excrement before killing him. Another boasted that he had blown up a wounded man's head, jamming a stick of dynamite down his throat. The brave warrior who demanded a blow job before each battle was in his element and he kept score of each oral conquest by nicking his forearm with the blade of his knife.

Though he was the guest of honour, Indigo tried to remain sober and aloof from the carnage. For starters he had no desire to have sex with a prostitute. According to the other *ters'* stories, the local hookers had teeth around their vaginas and mosquitoes in their pubic hair. And although Indigo knew this was a joke, one look at the hookers in question forced him to conclude that it wasn't worth the risk.

Indigo was not, however, able to remain sober. Every time the bucket of millet brew reached him, he was forced by some laughing colleague to drain its contents and he was soon too drunk to see straight and sick to his stomach. Seeing this, the *ters* filled his mouth with mandrake root and made him masticate until he felt better. In this way Indigo balanced his intake of drugs in an ever-teetering see-saw of intoxication.

It was at midnight that he felt himself being lifted to his feet, supported by a man under each arm. He was taken to the fire in the middle of the camp and left to stand on his own. He swayed gently on the spot, like a champion prize fighter who refuses to hit the canvas, and tried to focus on the laughing faces around him. Even in his toped state, he had the vague sensation that he was the subject of an unkind practical joke. He caught sight of the young *ter* who carried the fetid head in his backpack hurrying away from the main group like a kid with a new toy at Christmas. But now he was holding a fresh *musungu* head by its wispy black hair. Indigo licked his lips and blinked and the young *ter* and his grisly luggage disappeared into the darkness.

Trying to recapture his senses, Indigo realized that the *ters* around him were singing and shouting.

'Indigo the Virgin! Indigo the Virgin!'

'You cannot be *temba* for ever!'

'We have a surprise for you, Indigo.'

'Leave him alone. He's a poet. Aren't you, Indigo?'

'No wonder he's no lead left in his pencil!'

'Virgin! Virgin! Virgin! VIRGIN!'

At first Indigo laughed at the taunting and even waved his hands in encouragement to the crowd. But, as the voices rose into a crescendo of shouting and clapping hands, his mind started to clear and he began to feel scared. In the name of the Great Chief Tuloko, what was happening? He began to spin slowly on the spot, taking in the face of each baying *ter*. Their expressions were twisted and ugly, like the faces of the *shamva*, drunk for sure, as much on their evil as the alcohol.

Suddenly the crowd parted to one side and a battered figure was shoved forward into the makeshift arena with Indigo at its centre.

'A present for the virgin! A present for the virgin!'

Indigo stared at the woman in front of him and, though he recognized her, for a moment or two his brain refused to accept or process the information. He wiped the back of his hand over his clammy brow and stared at her again. Ruth! Was it Ruth? Or some macabre spirit approximating to her form?

'Oh Tuloko! No!' he screamed and the men laughed harder and the tide of the crowd swelled with excitement.

'Half-cast whore!' they shouted. 'She needs some more black in her and you're the man to give it.'

It was Ruth, all right. But they had set fire to her luxurious hair and her scalp was burnt, bald and pustulated. She raised her head and her eyes flickered with recognition before dying. Her charmingly wonky nose was now spread across her face and her jaw was skewed with one canine tooth protruding through the side of her cheek, giving her the look of a terrified spastic. Hanging from her body were the tatters of a white dress with dozens of indigo blossoms lovingly embroidered into the material. The lower half of her dress was stained red and blood was dripping from the hem, her vagina ruptured by repeated gang rape. Indigo didn't know what to say. He didn't know what to do. He wanted to hold her, to comfort her, to make it better, but somehow he thought that any concession to this reality might reinforce its truth. He felt more alive than he had ever been, but he knew that this was the moment of his death. So he just forced himself to stare at her – to accept the unacceptable – until he vomited violently all over his chest.

Ruth tried to speak but the pain of her jaw constricted her voice into an anguished yelp. The *ters* laughed expectantly. Ruth tried to speak again and this time the strength of her voice silenced the crowd, venting from her midriff like the final act of an indefatigable character.

'Are you going to rape me, Indigo? I would rather . . .'

Ruth's words were cut short by a gunshot and a poorly aimed bullet shattered her kneecap. Indigo walked towards her and quickly pumped more bullets into her prone body. For a second the *ters* were silent. Then they erupted into spontaneous cheering and her corpse was immediately swallowed up in the crowd's celebrations, even trampled beneath dancing feet. Indigo, apparently unnoticed, put the gun to his head, shut his eyes and prayed for forgiveness. But before he could pull the trigger, the gun had been taken from his hand and Zita was standing at his side.

'Rules are inoperative in war,' he said. 'You know that.'

Long before he was decapitated and his brain began to rot into the damp canvas of an insane young man's rucksack, the self-proclaimed wisest man in the whole of Manyikaland once said to his daughter that when you have killed someone you love, murder becomes too easy so you must never kill again. After he killed Ruth, Indigo often pondered the truth of these words, because killing then came to him as easily as *kapenta* to a *boka* bird's beak. Indigo killed *musungu* soldiers dispassionately. He shot them, he knifed them, he broke their necks in the crook of his arm and he ignored their pleas for mercy as if they were nagging children interrupting a busy schedule. Indigo was Zita's right-hand man. But he was more than that. He was the ZLF's champion; the champion warrior, the champion *ter*, the champion killer.

After his twenty-third birthday he was no longer a poet. He was a soldier. And English was no longer the precise language of poetry but a blunt knife that barely indented a bloody piece of meat, a rusting saw that disintegrated against rough bark, a fractured spade that snapped on scorched earth. Where was the truth in what he'd seen? Where was the truth in what he'd done? He did once try to describe the night he killed love, but the words were hollow and the reality was only ever touched in the spaces and the last full stop. Sometimes Indigo stared at a blank piece of paper for hours at a time and he would see the emptiness of truth. Eventually he always covered the page in incoherent doodles and shapes to hide the unwritten. But Ruth's voice would sing through every gap in his scribbles: 'You are my Indigo, my poet, my love.'

In time, of course, Indigo realized that his soul was not dead after all. Just paralysed and numb. And that was why he was not able to kill himself. In time, even the numbness began to pass and on warm nights he could smell Ruth's teenage musk and allow himself the faintest hint of a smile. In time, he was almost back to his old self, respected by his men for his fair mind and good heart. But the poet could never write poetry again.

30 : Enoch Adini doesn't know where he is when he wakes up. Then he remembers and feels depressed

When Enoch woke up, he did not know where he was. But he did know that he didn't want to be there. His back was hurting, his sleep-filled head was sore and he decided to keep his eyes shut until he figured out where he'd spent the night.

Tentatively he explored the spaces on either side of him, trying to locate whichever woman it was with whom he'd shared a bed. Was it one of the boring Noses? If so, which one? Or one of the Murewa sisters? If so, which one? Surely not the German ambassador's wife with the taste for rough fellatio! Instinctively Enoch reached one hand between his legs to check he was still in one piece and the other wiped the beading sweat from his forehead.

Such a headache! Last night he must have drunk the Barrel dry!

Gradually he perceived that he had been woken by the sounds of an argument. Two men were cursing one another in Zamba. Enoch was sure he recognized one of the voices, though he couldn't place it. One of the presidential guard perhaps? So he must be at home. That was a relief. But he wasn't in his bed after all.

Enoch realized that he was out in the open air. (No wonder there wasn't a woman beside him! The Noses would never accept less than a soft bed!) He could feel dry earth beneath his head and a pebble or something was digging into the small of his back and his skin was damp with morning dew. He figured that he was cold and he shivered and his teeth began to chatter. He hadn't fallen asleep in a flower bed again, had he? So embarrassing! And his Dad would go off the wall!

He opened his eyes a smidgen and looked down at his body. He found that he was wearing black tie. But his dinner suit was filthy and torn and there were mysterious stains all over his white shirt. Shit! It must have been quite a night!

The arguing voices approached and Enoch turned his head slightly to try and identify their owners. The single bass drum that was banging in his cranium was suddenly accompanied by a clanging high hat and a piercing snare. He looked at the two men standing above him just feet away and his gummy eyes tried to focus. Why weren't they in uniform? Perhaps it was a 'wear-your-own-clothes day', one of those pointless corporate Americanisms that Adini periodically introduced. Who was the tall Rasta in baggy jeans and trainers? One of the kitchen boys perhaps. The other guy? It was Isaiah Muziringa, the gate guard. Thank God for that! Though he was almost unrecognizable in that ridiculous hat with corks hanging from the brim.

Enoch struggled to lift himself on to one elbow and he rubbed his eyes and scratched his head.

'Isaiah!' he said and he was surprised to hear his voice sound so croaky. Either he was seriously thirsty or he must have smoked his way through a sackful of *gar*.

'Isaiah!' he said again, but Isaiah was deeply embroiled in his argument and completely ignored him. If only they'd speak English, he'd be able to understand what they were saying without having to engage his mind! Enoch found that he was beginning to get irritated. He was too thirsty and his throat was too sore to be forced to raise his voice.

'For God's sake, Isaiah! There's a Nigerian living in my head and a dog's done its business in my mouth. Get us some orange juice and a cup of coffee, would you? Better make it black. I feel terrible.'

Enoch sneezed and the jolt that shook his body left him fully awake. He opened his eyes wide and found Isaiah and the dreadlock staring at him in disbelief. What was so surprising? Had he puked on himself or something?

An insistent surge of realization surfaced in his mind like a *kapenta* diver coming up for air. He slowly turned his head round

180 degrees and there wasn't a building in sight, let alone the presidential residence. On one side undulating hills rolled to the horizon; on the other dusty plains stretched as far as he could see. Around him a dozen makeshift tents were erected between four baobab trees and several scruffy men lounged around smoking cigarettes and training their gun sights on the sky as if they were about to shoot down an imaginary aircraft. Enoch noticed a chafing pain in his ankle and looked down to find his leg shackled to a stake in the ground.

'Oh!' he said. 'Oh, fuck!'

Since his kidnap Enoch had lost track of time. He could certainly remember five nights of trying to get comfortable on his bed of dirt. But it may have been six or seven. Definitely no more than a fortnight. Trouble was, his perception of the passing hours had been thrown by a combination of intense hunger and thirst and the unbearable sun of the hottest part of the day, which sent him into a hazy stupor, and nights so chilly that he had to bang his feet on the ground to make sure they were still there. What's more, his time-keeping was further hindered by the fact that he was ignored by all the Gangers and consequently had few social markers with which to measure the rotations of the clock. Upon his kidnap he had at least expected to be interrogated or tortured or something. But the Gangers (who, as far as he could tell, were all members of Isaiah's company of the Zambawian State Army) seemed to regard him less as a hostage than an unwanted piece of old furniture, a lowly stool that barks your shins as you walk past or a warped coffee table with rickety legs. When the Gangers had to pass him to cross from one side of the camp to the other, they averted their eyes and their mouths curled contemptuously. Occasionally a clumsy soldier would trip over the chain that held Enoch fast, tugging at his leg and gnawing the raw skin of his ankle. When that happened, the Ganger would curse and perhaps kick the wooden stake. But he would never look at Enoch.

Thinking about it, Enoch could remember his father telling many stories of the ZLF camps during the independence struggle. Stories of happy singing, Marxist discussion and heroic poetry around the camp fire; stories of fellowship and mutual purpose. Those camps had been in Zimindo Province too. But by comparison this Black Boot Gang camp seemed remarkably apathetic. The men were unmotivated and listless and when Isaiah (who called himself 'Dubchek') or the strange Rastafarian asked a Ganger to complete a task, he would tut and drag his feet through the dust like a disobedient schoolboy. Enoch concluded that either his father was lying (looking back on the past with rose-tinted nostalgia and political licence) or these men felt little passion for their 'cause'. Probably a bit of both.

In fact, Enoch was so utterly neglected by his captors that he would surely have died of dehydration but for the occasional reluctant ministry of Lieutenant Gecko Tula, who brought him a cup of water every now and then and the odd chunk of dry bread. 'Drink!' she would say or 'Eat!' and she would stare at him spitefully as if he were somehow responsible for her birth into the amorality of presidential luxury rather than the revolutionary hotbed of a rural pigsty or an urban slum.

The only woman in the camp, Gecko had abandoned her swathes of cod-African Java print in favour of army fatigues and a tight peaked cap that she pulled low over her eyes. But her new outfit did nothing to help her fit in (not least because the rest of the Black Boot Gang favoured dirty jeans and T-shirts that declared support for local football teams). Enoch noticed that, like him, she was generally ignored by the other Gangers. Sometimes he would see her approach a group as they chatted by one of the tents. She would sidle up to them shyly and try to engage them in discussion about plans and politics in heavily accented Mozolan pidgin-Zamba that made even Enoch wince. But, as soon as Gecko opened her mouth, the men would shut theirs and stare at each other in silence, avoiding her eyes, until she gave up. Only then, as she walked away, would they look at her, watching the luscious roll of her arse in her tight combat trousers and nudging one another and laughing slyly. One of the men in particular – a big, brutal-looking bastard with a broken nose and protruding canines – would whistle through his teeth and throw crude shapes with his hands.

Though ignored by her comrades, Gecko still maintained their policy of ignoring Enoch and, even when she was offering him bread and water, he found it almost impossible to get her to talk or listen. Except on one occasion when she looked even more lonely and out of place than usual.

As he accepted her cup of water, Enoch asked Gecko for a cigarette. Mutely she produced one and Enoch took it with a smile, saying, 'You haven't got a Chesterman, have you? These local smokes taste like elephant shit.' He enjoyed the flash of Gecko's eyes and her sharp intake of breath.

'Only joking,' he said. 'Lighten up.'

'Exploitation is serious. Revolution is serious. Why should I lighten up?'

'That's the trouble with revolutionaries. So tight-lipped and sombre. Don't you think it would be fun to have a smiling revolution for a change? Now there's an idea! A revolution accompanied by laughing kids, street parties and fireworks displays! But that's moral righteousness for you. It's like a tight suit that pinches at your shoulders and groin and makes you feel uncomfortable.'

'Are you always so flippant?' Gecko asked with a sneer.

Enoch thought for a moment.

'Yes,' he said.

'Don't you care that most Zambawians haven't got enough to eat? Don't you care that more black people live below the poverty line ten years after independence than did in the years before? Don't you care that your father siphons off IMF loans into a Swiss bank account? Don't you care that the *murungu* still owns eighty per cent of Zambawi's prime agricultural land?'

'*Musungu.*'

'What?'

'It's not *murungu. Musungu.* And yes, I do care. I'm just not convinced that killing people (black people, mostly) and kidnapping people (me, for instance) is such a great thing either. You're so self-righteous! You look at me like I'm a piece of shit stuck to your heel! At least I know that killing people is wrong!

'You idealists! You're so bloody . . . idealistic! You're so idealistic that you won't let commonsense or basic human decency get in the way of your sacred dreams. It's all bullshit!

'How come you're such a revolutionary? Feeling guilty, are you? Daddy's genocide nagging your conscience, is it? Why? Did you give the order? Did you pull the trigger? Did you dig the mass graves? I tell you something. It's hard enough taking responsibility for your own actions without worrying about anyone else's.

'I just can't believe that you're so sure of yourself. I can't believe that you really think you know best for *my* country. You really think the rural population give a baboon's arse who the government is? Of course they don't! If the rains come with any degree of predictability, if their land is fertile and the chickens plump, then they are happy.'

'That is so . . .' Gecko huffed and her brow furrowed attractively. But Enoch didn't notice.

'Don't interrupt! You think that sounds patronizing? Fine! At least it's *my* country and I'm allowed to be patronizing. What is it you people bang on about? Equality of opportunity? Stupid idea! Leads to equality of aspiration and all that other materialist shit that strangled Western Europe and turned America into a twenty-four-hour, nationwide talk-show. Probably. I don't know because I've never been there. Even though I want to. Even though I know that aspiration is a terrible thing.

'I reckon good government is about making people happy. Not showing them the ways in which they can never be happier. So the *musungu* owns all the best land and it's not fair? So what? That's not the problem. The problem is that people are unhappy because they don't have enough to eat. People are unhappy because they don't even have the basic space to be who they are. That's it! Equality is not about people being what they want, it's about them being who they are! That's it. End of story.'

Enoch paused and looked at Gecko. He knew that he had more to say, but he was so surprised to hear this diatribe burst from his mouth that it took his brain a moment or two to catch up. He had never vocalized these kinds of thoughts before. There'd never been much point. Maybe, just like the courage of boredom, there was a certain fulfilling recklessness to be discovered in being kidnapped and tied to a stake and ignored and left to fry and die like an unwanted pet.

Gecko looked taken aback. She lit a cigarette of her own and opened her mouth. But Enoch wouldn't let her speak. Now that he'd got her attention he was determined to make the most of it.

'I'll tell you something, Ms Rujeko Tula, daughter of President Tula of Mozola. A social conscience is a luxury commodity and just because you can afford it, you shouldn't expect the average Zambawian to have one too.'

'And what about you, Master Enoch Adini, son of President Adini of Zambawi?' Gecko retorted. 'You can afford a social conscience. So where's yours?'

Enoch shrugged and looked as smug as he could (which wasn't very smug as he was chained to a stake and rather the worse for wear).

'Me?' he said. 'I haven't got one. Because, unlike you, I've always tried to retain the common touch.

'Look around you. The Black Boot Gang? Don't make me laugh! Where's the revolutionary zeal sparked by a driven passion for justice? This isn't a righteous army! Just a bunch of chancers who've seen the opportunity for some recreational rape and pillage. You don't fit into this mob any more than I do. In fact, less. At least I'm a hostage. To them you're just some self-righteous woman who doesn't speak their language and is overeducated and undersexed. You're even more expendable than I am.'

For a moment a shadow of acknowledgement and fear darkened Gecko's face like a presumptuous cloud that blocks the view of Father Sun. She took off her cap and absent-mindedly shook out her long plaits. And the shadow was gone in a second, thrown out by the proud lift of her chin and the indignant flaring of her nostrils, which granted her an expression that was almost as irritating as it was utterly sexy.

'Look,' Enoch said, 'I'll tell you something that General Bulimi once said to me. You know him, my dad's henchman? The one who looks dead on his feet. Anyway, he once said that if there are no ideals left to follow, then a man is the next best thing.'

'A *man*?'

'Or woman! Fuck! The point is that you lot need a leader. Look at you! What have you got at the moment? Isaiah? He's just a jumped-up gate guard, he couldn't lead a monkey to a tree or a rat to the toilet! And what about that Rasta? Who the hell is he anyway? You need a real leader'

'What? Like your father, you mean?'

Gecko was sneering again and Enoch felt his temper rise. If only her lips didn't look so ripe and her neck so kissable. The twisted braids of her hair deserved to be artistically arranged on a soft white pillow.

'Yes,' Enoch said. '*Like* my father. Or like he used to be.'

'What do you know about revolution anyway?' Rujeko replied and, deciding that their conversation was over, she turned on her heels and marched to where a group of Gangers were playing cards. She paused by them for a second before turning once again and stalking out of the Ganger camp into the bush, towards the sun.

Enoch recalled this confrontation with Gecko on the morning that he was woken by the argument between Isaiah and the incongruous Rastafarian. Because, whether he knew anything about revolution or not, the tone of their disagreement suggested that they shared his analysis.

With no orange juice and no coffee to be enjoyed and little else to do, he pulled his legs up to his chest and tried to unpick the rapid-fire argument that was cooking between the two Gangers. The only trouble was that they were speaking so fast and in such dense Zamba slang (loaded with curses and colloquialisms) that Enoch had trouble following the exchanges. Every time one of them paused for breath, he had to rerun their last sentence in his head and translate it into some kind of workable English. But by the time he'd done that to his satisfaction, the argument was a stage or two further down the line and it took him another minute to catch up. And so on.

As far as Enoch could tell, the Rastafarian was angry because Isaiah had killed a Black Boot Gang supporter and taken an unwanted hostage. (At first Enoch assumed this referred to him. But then he realized with some relief – because no hostage likes to be unwanted – that they were talking about a *musungu*.) In his turn Isaiah seemed furious because the Rastafarian '*kwenobva ake sadza kure china kure meme mukadzi*'. Literally this meant that the Rastafarian 'could not choose one bowl of maize porridge from four cooked by the same woman'. But Enoch concluded that the implication was that the Rastafarian was not as decisive as Isaiah would have liked.

'Look here, you bastard lovechild of a whore and a baboon! It's all very well for you to crease your face at me and moan like a grandmother because Mandela killed your headmaster friend. But if you won't give us any orders and any kind of lead, then how am I supposed to know what to do? These soldiers are just kids, barely out of *temba*, and they need a strong lead. And frankly, to be as blunt as a *garwe*' – Enoch thought this meant 'cabbage', but that didn't quite make sense – 'so do I! We need some kind of plan. When are we going to take Queenstown? The ancestors are with us but the men are getting restless.'

The tall dreadlock bared his teeth and spat in the dust at Isaiah's feet. Enoch had never seen him so animated. Generally the Rasta had appeared charismatic in a laid-back kind of way. But now his eyes were blazing and his voice rattled with barely suppressed fury.

'Don't you talk to me like that, penis nose! It is a mistake to start calling one of my kind rude names. You should know that we deserve to be treated with respect. And my "headmaster friend", as you call him, was a good man who had much to offer to our cause. I would be more furious still if I did not know that he was already living in one of the finest houses in the celestial *gwaasha* of the Great Chief Tuloko.'

'I am sorry for my disrespect but . . .'

'Do you not think I realize that we need a leader? Do you not think that this is known by Tuloko himself? But I have explained to you that I cannot lead. It is not for one of my kind to lead because we are the descendants of Cousin Moon. Do you not remember the story of the Traveller, the Child of the Horizon, even though it was told to you every evening by your father?

'And what about you? You can talk! You do not want to be a leader either because you are too much of a coward! You know that you were weak enough to betray the fucking eunuch and you fear that others may be as weak as you! So give me time and I will find us a leader. Tuloko will find us a leader!'

As the Rastafarian finished speaking, Isaiah's face fell. Enoch wasn't surprised. For all the Rasta's matted hair and shabby dress, he cut a daunting figure with his erect posture and broad chest. In some ways he reminded Enoch of the more impressive monks at St Ignatius' College who strode around the school ground with the confidence of unshakeable faith, eloquent and masculine with the smallest glint of madness in their eyes. But Enoch didn't really get the full texture of the Rasta's argument. For starters he was confused by all the stuff about the Great Chief Tuloko because, though he had learned some of the bones of Zamba myth, his father had never told *him* the story of the Traveller. Let alone every evening. What's more, he did not understand the dreadlock's repeated references to 'one of my kind', and to the fact that he could not be insulted and could not lead. Enoch had not realized that the Black Boot Gang held Rastafarians in such high regard.

'So what do you want me to do?' Isaiah asked, with his chin touching his chest. Now that his outburst was over, he was clearly feeling sheepish.

'The white kid you arrested. Release him and bring him to me.'

The Rastafarian's tone was ominous, as if he might eat this poor *musungu* for dinner. Enoch shivered unconsciously.

31 : The Great Chief Tuloko makes a surprise appearance

When the heavy barred gate of Jim's jail cell slid open, Jim immediately spun around and swung his legs on to the floor. Mr Murufu, however, remained squatting in the corner. At the gate stood Captain Muziringa/Dubchek, flanked by two men, one of whom Jim recognized as Private Nyoka/Mandela, the thug who'd forced him to play Zambawian roulette after shooting PK. The other looked especially young and naive, with gawky limbs that seemed too long for his body. Jim contemplated them for a second. Then he yawned – quite deliberately – and swung his feet back on to the hard wooden bed and lay down with his hands behind his head.

'I am Captain Dubchek of the Black Boot Gang,' Dubchek began.

But Jim interrupted him: 'I think I've figured out who you are by now, captain.'

'I am Captain Dubchek of the Black Boot Gang, boss,' Dubchek tried again. 'And I am here to rescue you.'

Jim laughed drily. 'You've come to save me from yourself, have you?'

'I do not understand you.'

'Nothing.'

'Look, boss. No time for little talk. We must hurry and get you out of here before the guards return. We will take you to the Black Boot Gang camp.'

'What about Mr Murufu?'

'Who?'

'Mr Murufu,' said Jim, nodding to his cellmate's corner.

Mr Murufu appeared from the shadows and approached the

captain with his head bowed and his hands clapping. He looked like he was about to say something, but the captain cut him short with a dismissive glance.

'Mr Murufu is not my problem,' Dubchek said flatly.

Jim sniffed and sighed. He'd had enough of being fucked around by this bunch of lunatics who couldn't make up their minds whether or not they were revolting and killed people for fun. He rolled his eyes up and stared at the ceiling. A large hornet was caught in the spider's web that he had been watching the whole day. The hornet was thrashing ferociously and he couldn't believe the delicate web would hold it. But it was stuck fast, all right.

The spider, a tiny thing, wandered absent-mindedly out from his hidey-hole and along one of the web's strands towards the hornet's head (giving the ferocious-looking sting a wide berth). When it reached the head, the hornet stopped thrashing, developed a rather resigned look in its strange compound eyes and merely twitched its tail occasionally in a sweet and melancholy way. Jim imagined that the spider must have said something to the hornet. Something like: 'Don't bother, mate. You and I both know that the game is up. Time to accept your fate like a man.'

Jim turned his head, looked at the captain once again and bit down on his bottom lip.

'You know what, captain?' he said breezily. 'I'm not going with you.'

'What are you talking about, Mr Tulloh? We are trying to set you free.'

'No, you're not! You want me to go with you to the Black Boot Gang camp and I don't want to go. Why the fuck should I trust you when you killed PK? How do I know that your camp is any better than your jail cell? At least here I'm a prisoner of the Zambawian state and, as such, the British government is bound to find out in the end and kick up some kind of fuss. Even for someone as lowly as me.'

'You do realize that we could take you by force?'

'Of course. You've done it before and you can do it again. But you're not a violent man, Captain Dubchek. You don't enjoy hitting me much more than I enjoy being hit. Besides, I've decided to be awkward. Prisoners don't have a lot of freedom, but they do at least have the freedom to be awkward. And I tell you something else: I'd have gone on hunger strike as soon as you stuck me in this joint if you'd ever bloody fed me.'

For the first time Private Mandela spoke up, baring his sharp canines and opening his bloodshot eyes a little wider than seemed natural.

'You know *I* enjoy hitting you, *musungu*!' he snarled. But Jim kept his eyes steadily focused on the captain.

'So, are you going to set your gorilla guerrilla on me again, captain?' he asked. 'Very courageous.'

Dubchek heaved a deep sigh and he seemed to shrink even deeper into his oversized clothes. He took off his ridiculous hat with the corks that bounced from the brim and scratched his scalp thoughtfully. Jim almost felt sorry for him. He certainly felt a degree of empathy. Dubchek clearly wasn't cut out for leadership; just a simple, decent soul who'd been caught up in a tricky situation.

'Mr Tulloh . . .' Dubchek began pleadingly.

But Jim had already relented.

'I tell you what, captain,' he said. 'I'll come with you and I won't give you any trouble so long as Mr Murufu goes free. Do we have a deal?'

'Why should I agree?'

'For two reasons. Firstly because I will give you no trouble (and believe me, captain, I'm learning how to be a stubborn bastard). But secondly because I am sure that somewhere beneath that uniform there is hidden the heart of a family man. Mr Murufu has a daughter who needs him and, as you well know, a daughter is like diarrhoea. She leaves you drained and empty but when she calls you have to answer.'

The captain stared at Jim for a moment or two, evidently impressed by his grasp of Zambawian proverbs, before nodding his head decisively.

'OK, boss. You have a deal. The *mboko* goes free.'

Jim smiled. He was pleased with himself. And he stood up and offered the captain his hand. But before he knew it, this gesture had been brushed aside by Mandela and a large maize sack was thrust over his head and bound around his shoulders with rope.

'What's going on?' Jim hollered.

'Don't worry, boss; it's just a precaution. We cannot risk anyone discovering the whereabouts of the camp. Just come this way.'

'Which way? I can't see shit.'

Jim felt himself being bundled towards the door. Unable to resist the opportunity, Mandela elbowed him twice in the ribs and thrust his knee into his groin, knocking the wind out of him. Jim gasped for air and realized that the maize sack's last cargo had certainly not been maize. The sack smelled of tiny dead creatures that had died eating little dead creatures that had died eating bigger dead creatures. Jim retched and his stomach felt like a twisting rubber band and the smell of bile on rank sackcloth competed for nose space with the other noisome odours.

Eventually he was dragged out of the cell like a dead weight with the parting words of Mr Murufu ringing in his ears.

'Goodbye, Mr Tulloh!' Murufu called. 'Remember the wisdom of the ancestors. Turn an enemy into a friend and at least you know who has stolen your chicken!'

Jim was unceremoniously slung into the back of a jeep that sped off with a squeal of spinning tyres and the whine of a dicky fanbelt. The next two hours were the most unpleasant of his life as the jeep tore over God knows what terrain and Jim, unable to see each approaching bump and dip, bounced around the back like popcorn in a pan. His digestive system was working reverse overtime and he puked in his sack every fifteen minutes or so. Then, when he'd puked once, the smell of his vomit made his stomach contort and hurl again and again for a further minute. When this happened, Jim would struggle manically and Mandela would kneel beside him and whisper in his ear, 'If you move, *musungu*, I will kill you.' And Mandela's cold words and evil delight made Jim sicker and sicker.

By the time they reached their destination, Jim felt slightly unreal, scared out of his wits and extremely sorry for himself. The acidic bile vapours stung his eyes and nostrils and left his lips feeling oversized and rubbery, his every movement uncovered a new bruise (courtesy of the blunt metal of the jeep and the careless fists of Mandela) and his thoughts had been whittled down from an endless series of questions (How did I get here? Where are we going? What's going to happen? Do you have to pull or push at death's door?) to just one (Why me? Why me? Why me?).

Someone (presumably Mandela) dragged Jim out of the back of the jeep by his feet so that his head bounced from the tail gate to the tow hook to the ground like a ball down some steps. He was then lifted upright – only to discover that his legs were unwilling to work – before being frog-marched between two Gangers with his feet pushing pedals above the ground. He heard some voices, but they sounded a million miles away and he couldn't understand them. Allowed to stand on his own, he immediately buckled and landed on his backside with a bump.

Somebody cursed next to his head and Jim felt eager fingers tugging at the ropes that bound him. The sack was dragged over his shoulders and head in one rough movement and the voice that had just cursed, cursed again and said, in English, 'For the love of Jehosephat, what have you done to him? Tula! Fetch some water!' Jim tried to open his eyes, but they were sore and his vision was blurred. He tried to move his arms but they were as stiff as the barred gate of his jail cell. He spat a mouthful of puke into his lap. He ran his tongue around his teeth, which felt like they had been shaved with a cut-throat razor. 'Yuck!' he said.

As he opened his mouth, Jim was hit full in the face by a bucket of water that made him splutter and sneeze. He managed to open his eyes a little wider and another bucketful was dumped over the top of his head, washing bedraggled hair into his eyes. Jim lifted a sore arm and combed his fingers back through his hair. He was beginning to feel more human. More water was splashed on to his head and into his lap.

'OK! OK!' Jim said and he opened his eyes wide. At first he thought that something had happened to his vision because the world was dark but freckled with countless specks of light.

I am seeing stars, he thought. But then he realized that this was exactly what he was doing. The shining, stone tears of Zamba, Cousin Moon.

Jim lowered his gaze and found two figures staring at him, each swinging an empty bucket at its side. One belonged to Dubchek, who looked concerned and nervous, and Jim was surprised to find a bubble of genuine hatred rising in his throat – the Ganger always looked so worried about what he was doing and still did it anyway! The other figure belonged to the most beautiful woman Jim had ever seen, a silk-skinned goddess with snaking black braids. She was dressed in army uniform, but, on her, it looked more like a fashion statement, slightly too tight and showing off her every curve.

Jim heard somebody laughing at his side and he turned his head. There, doubled-up in hysterics, sat Enoch Adini, the eunuch's son, chained to a stake in the ground and looking as battered as he felt. The sensation of unreality expanded.

'Enoch!' Jim said, wondering if his fellow hostage had recognized him. Enoch reined in his manic, reckless giggling and swung his eyes lazily in Jim's direction.

'Hey, Jim! Welcome to the fucking party!'

'Mr Tulloh!' a voice said above him. And Jim looked up to see Musa the *zakulu*'s face staring down at him, framed by dreadlocks.

'Musa!' exclaimed Jim.

Musa slipped his hands under Jim's armpits and lifted him to his feet with easy strength. Then, beckoning to Dubchek to join them, he said, 'Come this way, Mr Tulloh. We have much to discuss!'

Dubchek and Jim (the latter stumbling slightly) followed Musa away from the fire at the centre of the camp and between a couple of tatty tents until he stopped beneath the fat branches of an ancient baobab tree. Looking about him at the soft outlines of hills that dipped like sponges into the inky sky, Jim realized that he couldn't be too far from St Oswald's and, for a moment, his imagination was transported to that other place, which now felt like home. He could feel the weight of PK's dying body on his arms and a lonely breeze caught in his throat.

Musa and Dubchek were talking heatedly.

'*Ise!*' Musa was saying. '*Ise kupisa chinje ne Chenjera Tuloko!*'

'*Ise!*' Dubchek replied and his expression was a universal statement of incredulity. He pushed his finger into Jim's chest with disdain. '*Ise! Musungu! Chenjera! Zvakaoma zakulu! Zvinodhura pamusoi!*'

Musa shook his head impatiently and upturned his hand. His palm was covered with a thousand tiny grains of sand that, despite the absence of any light, sparkled like lovers' eyes. Gently he blew on the sand and it floated into the air in shifting fractal shapes that reminded Jim of ferns uncurling at dawn. One grain, however, caught in the wispy curls at Musa's temples. There was a pungent smell of burning hair and Musa cursed. He picked out the grain between his thumb and forefinger and, poking out his tongue, placed it carefully on the very tip. Musa's eyes popped comically and Dubchek looked alarmed. Jim, however, was beyond surprise.

'I tell you something, Dubchek,' Musa said, reverting to English. 'And I hope you do not take this amiss. But, as the great Sherlock Holmes himself so forcefully expostulated, "Mediocrity knows nothing higher than itself, but talent instantly recognizes genius."'

Dubchek looked puzzled. 'I don't understand, *zakulu*,' he said.

'Exactly,' Musa retorted triumphantly, beaming from ear to ear. 'Thus you must gather the men together in the most handsome location and prepare them for our address!'

For a second it looked as though Dubchek might protest, but he clearly thought better of it. He bowed low in front of Musa, acknowledged Jim with a curt nod and turned back to the camp, leaving the *zakulu* and the *musungu* alone. Jim, of course, didn't have the faintest idea what was going on. But that was OK. He didn't much care.

With Dubchek out of the way, Musa sighed melodramatically and sat himself down on the dirt beneath the baobab tree. Slipping his hand into the pocket of his baggy jeans, he retrieved a parcel of *gar* and a scrap of newspaper and he began to build a small joint with that knack of adroit fingertips and gummy saliva that could keep Jim fascinated for hours.

'I didn't know you were involved with this mob,' Jim said.

'Every army needs the ancestors on its side.'

'You know they killed PK?'

'It was a terrible happening,' Musa nodded. 'But it has been my good fortune to speak to him since his death and it is my pleasure to inform you that he is happy and well. He has a house next to Mudiwa, the wife of the Great Chief himself, and Tuloko has promised him the hand of his youngest daughter. PK tells me that he is excited by this but – the old rogue! – somewhat nervous. Although the girl is as fresh-faced as a sixteen-year-old debutante, she is fully 843 years old! Have you ever heard of such a thing? Such are the confusions of the spirit world of which we cannot hope to be cognizant. But what glorious felicity!'

While Musa spoke, his eyes were fixed on Jim and dancing with excitement. But then he lapsed into silence, concentrating on the precise dimensions of his joint and leaving Jim with a curious, buzzing feeling in his head, as if his brain were the vibrating key of an *mbira*. Listening to Musa always affected Jim like this. It wasn't just what he said but the extraordinary depth and sincerity of his voice and the Victorian formality and verbose vocabulary of his English. Jim stared at the *zakulu* and concluded that his speech patterns were altogether appropriate for a witchdoctor, detached from any realistic markers of place or time.

When Musa had finished skinning up, he sat back against the trunk of the baobab tree, sparked the joint and inhaled deeply. He gestured for Jim to come and sit next to him and Jim concurred, so that the two men leaned against the rough bark almost back to back. Musa passed Jim the reefer over his shoulder and Jim accepted it gratefully, enjoying the way the smoke flushed through his system like spring water.

'Mr Tulloh,' Musa said eventually, 'I have something to ask you. And if the tone of my voice sounds ominous, it is because it is a question of national import.'

Jim turned his head and looked at the witchdoctor. But Musa refused to meet his eyes. Jim shrugged.

'Fire away,' he said carelessly.

'Did you know that there are no chiefs in the whole of Zambawi?'

'No. I didn't know that. Is that the question?'

'Mr Tulloh! Before I ask that which must be answered, I must ensure that you are furnished with all information! Do you follow?'

'Yes,' said Jim, taken aback by the vigour of Musa's tone and scorching his fingertips on the fast-burning joint. 'Do you want to skin up again? I think I need some more *gar* for this.'

Musa took out his supply once again and began to build a fatter construction.

'There are no chiefs in the whole of Zambawi, Mr Tulloh,' he continued. 'Of course, there are local headmen who call themselves "chief" but they are not descendants of Tuloko and they do not care for the word of the *zakulu*. As for those who *are* descended from Tuloko, they are no longer chiefs, for they have all accepted – I know the word, but I do not fully understand its meaning – "sinecures" from Adini. What I mean is that they have become local government officials, provincial officers and the like, all in the pay of the fucking eunuch. Do you understand?'

'I think so.'

'Good. And as for Adini? During the independence war, he abandoned the praise of ancestors and thought of no one but himself. Have you not heard the rumours of castration and rape and murder? In the Black Boot Gang, of course, we too have our bad apples, but they will rot in the sunlight of our victory, for Tuloko and Father Sun are our forebears. Do you think that Adini is Tuloko's chiefly descendant? Of course not. Besides, he is *nyoka* totem, a snake. Which I believe is what you call in English "irony".'

'Right.'

'Right? Good. So you see the situation? There are no chiefs in the whole of Zambawi. But do you remember the story of the Traveller that I told you that night in my kraal, when your head floated around the ceiling like *gar* seed on the wind? Then you will remember that Tuloko himself, the first chief, was not *actually* a descendant of Father Sun. And what did Father Sun say to him? "What is a descendant but a man you can trust?"'

Musa stared at Jim with eyes so intent that the *musungu* felt like his very soul was under examination.

'Do you trust me, Mr Tulloh?' he asked.

'I do. Of course I do, Musa.'

'I trust you too,' Musa said and he then paused for a moment, as if those words were the richest of foods and required much digestion. 'Shall I tell you the problem of the Black Boot Gang?'

'Tell me.'

'The problem of the Black Boot Gang is that we have no leader.'

'What about Dubchek?'

'Dubchek?' Musa snorted, blowing the *gar* from its precarious position in the newspaper. He cursed: 'Damn and blast! That is the trouble with *gar* at this time of year. Too dry and flaky. Dubchek? You know what his totem is? *Mbudzi.*'

'The goat.'

'The goat! Exactly! Your Zamba is improving!

'Dubchek is a goat. He was not born to lead. Besides, like all the Zambawi State Army, he is too scared to – what is the expression? – put his balls on the line. He knows that the hearts of the men do not pump to the marching drum and he fears that the slightest setback will have them running back to the State Army, deserting the cause. Once you accept leadership of the Black Boot Gang, you accept political responsibility, and no soldier – for all his manly pretensions – is prepared to accept political responsibility and its consequences.

'Now, Mr Tulloh, I don't want you to misunderstand me. I am not saying that leadership of the Black Boot Gang is a difficult job. Heavens, no! Already we have nine out of ten soldiers on our side and the voice of the Great Chief Tuloko ringing in our ears. But we need the right figure to lead our march into Queenstown; someone that the men can support, perhaps an unknown who has no enemies; someone to accept all the praise and the favours of the beautiful young women.'

Musa and Jim looked at one another and Musa raised an eyebrow and then winked.

'Sounds like fun!' Jim agreed. 'Surely you're the man for the job.'

'Mr Tulloh! I am a *zakulu* and a *zakulu* can never be a chief. A *zakulu* has the blessing of Zamba, Cousin Moon. The chief needs the blessing of Tuloko and Father Sun. You know what *zakulu* means in the Zamba language?'

'Of course. Witchdoctor.'

'No! It is only the *musungu* who calls us that. A better translation would simply be "doctor". But the life of the *zakulu* is destined for the background; we are of the shadows, behind the door, secreted in the maize field. When the *musungu* missionaries arrived in Zambawi, they would visit the sick and find them cured and we would be hiding under the bed or disguised as a water jug or an old woman. And the *musungu* would say to the patient, "You are better already?" And the patient would reply, "The doctor cured me." And the *musungu* would look puzzled and shake his head in disbelief. "Which doctor?"

'And that is how we got our name, "witchdoctor". It is a corruption of "which doctor".'

Jim stared at Musa in disbelief and then began to giggle.

'Are you sure?' he said.

'Of course, I am sure. Do you not trust me, Mr Tulloh?'

'Yeah. But . . . but what about witches, then? How did they get to be called witches?'

Musa flared his nostrils in indignation and clicked his teeth dismissively. He did not like to be contradicted. This was a common character trait among the *zakulu*.

'Do not be . . . Ah! I do not know the word! Do not make mock of me, Mr Tulloh! For these are serious issues and not to be treated with a light heart and a whore's contempt! And it is not for me to explain to you the peculiarities of the English tongue!'

'I'm sorry . . .' Jim began.

But Musa was shaking his head and muttering beneath his breath. Jim couldn't understand what he was saying. But he did catch the words intended for his ears: '*musungu*', 'arrogant' and 'boy'. For a moment Musa buried himself in concentration on his joint-rolling exercise. He was building a whopper, nearly a foot long and as thick as a child's wrist. Eventually he sighed, looked up to the sky and whispered something indecipherable in Zamba. A prayer perhaps. Something along the lines of 'God give me strength!'

'Allow me to tell you something else,' Musa continued with an altogether more breezy air. 'You know that we witchdoctors – *zakulu* – we can talk to the ancestors. You know that, don't you? And also we can talk to the Great Chief Tuloko through the patient offices of Zamba, Cousin Moon. But, Mr Tullo, all this communication with the spirit world is a haphazard business, it is like trying to spot a particular city gent at Waterloo station among the sea of bowler hats! Sometimes I am able to find Zamba with no delay. But sometimes I call his name into the night, crying as a hyena over a kill, and there is no reply. Did you know that? It can be very embarrassing, I can tell you. Especially when an *mboko* has come to consult me about the problems of his ugly daughter or the cow that thinks it's a pig and will produce no milk. Imagine! I call to Cousin Moon and there is no reply! So I have to make something up. "Don't worry, *mboko*," I say. "One day your daughter will meet a powerful man with a face like a hippopotamus." Or, "You must allow your pigs to roam the land and keep your cow in the pigsty, then she will produce milk." It is a terrible thing to tell lies in the name of the ancestors, but even a *zakulu* has to do it sometimes.'

Musa finished rolling the joint and handed it to Jim, who lit up greedily. Jim had completely lost track of what Musa was going on about and concluded that he needed to be stoned. God knows where all this waffle was heading.

'My apologies, Mr Tulloh. I digress like a woman who listens to the wireless when she should be making your meat and two vegetables.

'My point is this. In recent weeks I have not been calling Zamba, Mr Tulloh – oh no! – for Zamba has been calling me with messages from Father Sun and the Great Chief Tuloko. Such a trial!'

'Isn't that a good thing?' Jim asked, tugging deeply on the *gar* and enjoying the nostalgic sensation of gas pockets building in his colon.

'A good thing? Well. Yes. Perhaps. But it can be very awkward when I am washing myself or going to the toilet or having *gulu gulu* with one of my lovers.'

'So what do Father Sun and Tuloko say?'

'Ah, Mr Tulloh! Now we come to the crux of it. They say they have decided who must lead the Black Boot Gang into Queenstown and return Zambawi to the rightful authority of the ancestors.'

'Cool!' Jim said. 'Who is it?'

'It is you.'

'I'm sorry?'

'You.'

'Who?'

'YOU!'

When Musa said this last 'you', the most extraordinary thing happened. Time stopped. Jim was in the middle of an enormous lug on the joint and his lungs were full to bursting. But, on hearing that he was the god-chosen leader of the Black Boot Gang, he found that he couldn't exhale. At first he panicked, thinking that he was going to suffocate. Then he realized, with relief tinged with apprehension, that he no longer needed to breathe. He looked at Musa and saw that the *zakulu*'s face was locked, his mouth circled into the last vowel. He noticed that the cicadas had stopped singing. In fact, there wasn't a sound to be heard. An inch in front of his nose, a large mosquito was suspended in mid-flight, its cellophane wings stilled and its hum caught in its throat. Jim got to his feet – an uncomfortable movement with lungs full of smoke – and looked over to the Black Boot Gang camp. The Gangers were assembled in one large group at the end of the central clearing, frozen in mid-argument, their individual faces variously contorted in anger and fear and disbelief. Jim walked slowly over to the open fire and he watched the flames that burnt bright orange and didn't flicker. His mind overflowed with random thoughts.

What the hell is going on? My lungs hurt. Or do they? Or do I just think that they should? Why me? I must lay off the *gar*. Those men will kill me before they follow me to Queenstown! Musa is a lunatic and he needs to cut his hair. Who could possibly want me as their leader? Look at that beautiful girl! She doesn't half look silly in her combat dress. What's that noise? It's funny, you don't appreciate silence until it's broken. If I were a Red Indian, I would put my ear to the ground and say 'Stampede' in that wise way that Red Indians have.

Jim turned to look towards the murky hills and, sure enough, a herd of unidentifiable animals was careering towards the camp. At first he thought they were horses because he could see human figures astride their backs. But as they got closer, he realized that the animals were gargantuan black bulls, perhaps a thousand in number, like the one Musa had been riding on the day they first met. Jim wanted to be scared, but since his heart wasn't beating, it couldn't beat any faster and his skin showed no signs of sprouting goose-pimples.

When the herd reached the fringes of the Black Boot Gang camp, the riders reined in their charges (not that they had any reins) and the bulls skidded and snorted to a halt before beginning slow circuits of the camp's perimeter. The majority of the riders were black men and women, but there were a few *musungu* too. Many of them were naked, but some wore clothes: loincloths or shirts and ties or just ties or dressing gowns or army uniforms. In fact, the only feature that all the riders had in common was that they were dead, and Jim wasn't sure how he knew this. But he was sure that he knew it none the less.

With some of the riders, the fact of their quietus was self-evident: there was a young black boy with a hefty gun that he fired repeatedly into his head to no effect shouting, 'Felati! What have I done?' until an irascible *musungu* in an ornate smoking jacket told him to shut up; there was the *musungu* soldier (in a pristine uniform that Jim didn't recognize) who had no head, but managed to turn on his mount as if he might somehow spot his missing appendage in spite of his handicap. By and large, however, this dead army looked remarkably cheerful and healthy and Jim had to wonder if it was, in fact, these very attributes that marked them out as deceased.

Gradually some of the dead retreated a little from the camp until the front line was left to a dozen, most of whom Jim recognized. P K sat upright on his bull with a beautiful young girl riding shotgun behind him with her arms around his waist. Catching Jim's eye, he waved ostentatiously and the girl looked annoyed and cuffed him around the head. Jim saw his parents holding hands as they rode side by side staring into one another's eyes like a young couple making love for the first time. Jim tried to call to them. But his lungs were full of smoke and no noise would come out. He saw his grandmother – shit! What had happened to his grandmother? When had she died? – smoking a cigarette like a film star. Behind her a dapper young man with slicked-back hair and a 1950s suit was digging his heels into his mount and desperately trying to offer her a bunch of flowers.

At last one of the dead broke ranks and rode into the camp. It was a young woman that Jim had never seen before, coffee-skinned and gorgeous, but as bald as an egg. The expression on her face was excruciating, as if breaking the living circle of the camp required the most extraordinary effort of will that none of the others could muster. In her hand she held a hairbrush and she tapped her bull – the largest beast in the herd, with steaming nostrils and balls the size of coconuts – on the side of the head, directing it towards Jim. When she reached the unflickering camp fire, she tweaked the bull by the ear and it came to a dead stop. Slowly she dismounted and tiptoed up to Jim, glancing furtively about herself for fear of discovery. Her nose, Jim noticed, had a charming hook in the middle and her eyes were the shape of almonds and the saddest eyes that he had ever seen.

The woman opened and closed her mouth a couple of times as if desperate but unable to speak. Jim knew that feeling.

'I . . .' she began. And her face creased in frustration.

Slowly, wretchedly, she stretched out her arms to Jim and clasped her hands behind his head.

'For . . . him,' she said and, shutting her eyes, she kissed Jim firmly on the mouth. Her lips were as cold as sheet metal in winter and Jim's, still sensitive from the puking, were immediately stinging and painful. She tried to slip her tongue into his mouth, but it felt like a dead snake and he kept his lips tight shut. After maybe thirty seconds of discomfort Jim tried to pull away but he found that their mouths were frozen together. The woman's eyes opened wide and Jim saw the look of alarm that quivered in her pupils. Closing his eyes, he jerked his head back as hard as he could and their mouths finally separated with a loud pop.

'Ouch!' Jim exclaimed, at last releasing the smoke from his straining lungs. He opened his eyes to find himself back beneath the baobab tree with Musa staring at him with the most curious expression on his face.

'Are you all right, Mr Tulloh?'

'Fine,' Jim said. He looked at Musa and away to the camp and everything seemed to have returned to normal. That *gar* was strong stuff! When was he going to learn his lesson?

Jim ran a rueful finger over his raw lips and then, noticing that the suspended mosquito had yet to continue its flight, he clapped his hands together on the insect. He looked at his palms and the squashed corpse and the stain of human blood (perhaps his own, perhaps another's) looked like a Rorschach test.

'So will you do it, Mr Tulloh?'

'Do what?'

'Will you lead the Black Boot Gang into Queenstown as the Great Chief Tuloko wishes?'

For a moment there was silence and Jim looked like he was deep in contemplation. But he wasn't. He was just feeling stoned and extremely disorientated. He shrugged.

'Sure,' he said. 'Why not?'

'Excellent, Mr Tulloh! We will make a Zambawian of you yet. This is excellent news indeed. But we must address the men without delay.'

'One thing, though, Musa,' Jim observed and he noticed the way his words were slurring. 'Just a thought. I kind of think that the Black Boot Gang might not want me as their leader.'

'Why do you think such a thing?'

'Come on, *zakulu*! You reckon that Tuloko and Father Sun want me to lead the coup. But who's going to believe that? In the first place I'm a *musungu*. Secondly I speak very little Zamba – *iwe, aiwa, mboko, dipayo wawa, gulu gulu, mbudzi* (fine if you want to have sex with a goat or buy beer for an old man, but otherwise pretty useless). And, most important of all, I've never had a fight in my life (unless you count bashing Suzie Bayliss when I was eight years old because she kissed me when I wasn't expecting it).'

'Your reasoning is excellent, Mr Tulloh,' Musa replied, furrowing his brow seriously. 'You see how you have already grown into the role of a chief? It is just as I expected.

'But how does this plan sit with you? I shall tell the men that you have been chosen by the Great Chief Tuloko and they shall surely protest. But then you will stand up and deliver a speech of such heart-stirring brilliance that the men will be won over.'

'But I don't speak Zamba!'

'Exactly! And here is the cunning of my plan. For you shall deliver the speech in English (using the modern vernacular and as fast as you can – so that nobody can understand you) and I shall translate it into the language of the spirits that will seduce the Gangers' minds and prepare them to follow you to the grave. (Never fear, Mr Tulloh! A metaphor. Nothing more.) And if that still fails? Well! Then I have other *zakulu* magic up my sleeve . . .'

'Magic?'

'Of course. Nothing too spectacular. But I am sure that I can summon a clap of thunder or a chimera or two. You know the kind of thing: a *shumba* with a chicken's head, or I do a very good *musungu* with *kapenta*'s scales and a *gudo*'s blue arse. Just enough to frighten the living daylights out of them until they'll believe anything we tell them. For lies are the mortar that bind the savage individual into the social masonry.'

Staring at Musa, listening to the solemnity of his tone, picturing the unearthly hybrid creatures he described, Jim began to feel very light-headed and somewhat swollen with irrational self-confidence.

'OK,' he said.

Only ten minutes later, when he found himself standing on an upturned weapons crate in front of forty shifty Gangers and he needed it most, did Jim's confidence evaporate, for their faces were pictures of distrust and some of them sucked their gums and some of them played with their bush knives in a threatening way. Musa was in among them, orating for all he was worth and slapping them on their backs and shoulders. At first a couple of the Gangers – one being Mandela – tried to subvert his speech with wry comments and the odd giggle and whistle and whoopee. But Musa confronted Mandela, hollowed his cheeks and blew on his chest, knocking the enormous man over with the magical power of his breath. And after that everybody listened.

Jim, of course, couldn't understand what Musa was saying, so he just stood on his crate and tried to look like leadership material. But he felt like the main event at a seaside cabaret: 'And now, ladies and gentleman, for your revolutionary delight, on this, the first date of his national tour, I give you your new chief, as recommended by Tuloko himself. Let me hear you give a big Zimindo welcome to the one, the only, James Tulloh!'

Every now and then Musa would raise his voice to a new intensity and point at Jim with a quivering finger. Then all the Gangers would look at Jim and he would feel embarrassed and wonder how standing on a crate two feet off the ground could make him feel quite so small.

Eventually Musa concluded his speechifying with an ostentatious wave of the hand and he made his way back to Jim's side. Jim, suffering a severe case of stage fright, smiled sheepishly and bent down to Musa's ear.

'Over to you, Mr Tulloh!' Musa said.

'I don't think I'm up to this.'

'Of course you are! You just start talking and I'll do the rest. Just remember to make it fast and, for the sake of the Great Chief Tuloko, try to look impressive!'

'Don't you think it's time for the *musungu* with the baboon's arse?'

'Mr Tulloh! The men are waiting. It is time for you to speak.'

Slowly Jim straightened up and gazed over the faces of the Black Boot Gang whose expressions seemed uniformly set in that ugly sneer that gives birth to jeering and contempt. He licked his lips, cleared his throat and opened his mouth. But the voice that emanated from the pit of his stomach and the words that echoed with assurance and authority were not his own.

'*Maganga!*' Jim boomed. '*Vakaurayi buzi musungu chi kopa tenda!*'

He heard the words. And he hadn't a clue what they meant. Effective, though! Damn, were they effective! For the Gangers, to a man, had dropped to their knees. Some of them covered their heads with their hands and others whimpered like children. Was this really happening? Surely not more *gar* hallucinations!

Get a grip! Jim thought. Get a grip!

But he felt a surge of adrenalin pumping through his veins and his back seemed to straighten and elongate of its own accord. His chest swelled and, to his surprise, his T-shirt split at the shoulder seams and his jeans pinched tight around the groin. His testicles positively throbbed with virility and he was certain he could feel his buttock muscles tense and lift. What's more, he felt every inch of his five foot nine plus two foot of crate and then some!

Sensing the potential of a dramatic pause, Jim turned to Musa.

'What the hell did I just say?' he whispered.

But for the moment Musa was dumbstruck and Jim thought that, for a very black black man, he looked rather pale.

'Tuloko!' Musa murmured.

You what? Jim thought. He licked his lips and they felt like two tyres set in the front of his face. He suddenly felt very peculiar and, for a second, he covered his eyes with his hands. He was surprised to find that his palms were the size of large pizzas. Taking his hands away, he inspected them in disbelief, turning them around in front of his eyes. His hands were the colour of dark chocolate, shiny and polished and rough with hard work. His fingers were long and thick and his nails – usually bitten to the quick – were as tough and sharp as an eagle's talons. Across the base of his right thumb, a jagged scar snaked to his wrist.

Where the terrible *shamva* spirit Bezi cut me with his flint, Jim thought. And then he thought, what the hell am I thinking?

'Did you do this?' Jim asked, turning to Musa again. Except the words came out in Zamba. And yet he understood them.

'No, Mr Tuloko!' Musa replied, shaking his head furiously from side to side as if he might jounce some sense back into it.

This, Jim thought, is very weird. Except he thought it in Zamba. And he thought it was weird to have a strange *musungu* living in his body. And he thought that he was looking in good shape for someone who'd been dead for a millennium. Even a dead god. And then he thought that maybe these weren't the thoughts he was supposed to be thinking because maybe they belonged to someone else. And then he realized he wasn't sure who he was and he thought it was better not to think about it at all. Better to get on with the job in hand.

'So, my children!' Tuloko said. 'You are surprised to see me and you bury your faces in the dust like burrowing *shangu* spiders and your voices catch in your throat and you whine like the stalks of the chincherinchee. Well you might! For the ever-watching eyes of Father Sun and Cousin Moon see nothing but shame on this land from the Mountains in the East That Kissed the Sky to the Great Lake in the West That Cooled My Feet. But don't be afraid, my little ones! For if I were here to punish you, I could kill you all with a flick of a bogey or a gob of my spittle. But a chief who punishes his people and takes no responsibility for their disobedience is no chief at all.

'I have been gone too long. So long, in fact, that you have given my land to the *musungu*. If you had called me a century ago, would I not have returned with an ancestral army to grind the little pricks into compost? Of course I would! But you did not call. I have been gone so long that you have forgotten the rituals of the *belabe* shuffle and you use your skills on the *musungu*'s gambling tables. If you had prayed to me to remind you of our most sacred rituals, would I not have done so? Of course I would! But you did not pray. I have been gone so long that you have learned to worship the *musungu*'s dead presidents. Did you not think that my image would look good on a dollar bill? Of course it would! But you did not worship me. I have been gone so long that you have allowed a *nyoka* with no balls to claim Zambawi in his name. Did you not think I would answer if you asked? Of course I would! But you did not ask. I have been gone so long that only a *musungu* boy is brave enough – or reckless enough – to accept my spirit into his body to lead you to the victory that you do not deserve. So the least you can do is treat his every order as derived from my mouth! His words are my words! His breath is my breath! His body – as puny as it is – is my body! For this *musungu* is the Traveller. He is the Child of the Horizon who came from far beyond the Great Lake in the West That Cooled My Feet!

'You think that glory is already yours, my children? Nothing could be further from the truth! The path you face is treacherous and some of you will not complete the journey. But remember that my soldier – and each and every one of you *is* my soldier – travels for the sake of all my people, not just for an extra five dollars taken from an *mboko* or a looted clock radio or a stolen motor car. So now I give you all the opportunity to leave the army. If you do not wish to fight for glory, then you can leave now and you shall not be punished.

'Does none of you wish to leave? Ha! Cowards, the lot of you. Remember the chance I gave you when you lie in a ditch with your guts spilling like a drunkard's beer!

'So, my army. You march to Queenstown for the land that is your body, for the people that are your blood, for Father Sun who is your beating heart, for Cousin Moon who is your soul, and for me, Tuloko, who has been, is now and always will be your head, your leader, your chief!'

Tuloko finished speaking and Jim found himself looking out over dozens of bent backs. He felt . . . well! He didn't know what he felt, but he'd certainly never felt it before. He vaguely wondered whether he had anything to add, but nothing sprang to mind. In fact, all he could think about was the enormous *gar* fart that was building in his bowels and he desperately tried to rein it in because he didn't want to undermine the words that he had spoken about himself, or Tuloko had spoken about himself, or Tuloko had spoken about him, or something.

In the silence that followed the Gangers began to look up and, when they saw the *musungu* atop the weapons crate, they felt rather silly and began to get to their feet and dust themselves down. Musa too looked up and, perceiving the uncertainty in the Gangers' faces, he had to think quickly.

'Tuloko!' Musa shouted. 'Tuloko! Tuloko!'

And immediately the men put their doubts to one side and they joined in and cheered and waved their guns and clicked their tongues against the back of their throats in the traditional manner. Unfortunately poor Jim, as confused and traumatized as he was, had now lost all control of his colon and he let rip with a fart of divine impetus. For a moment the men were silent again. But Musa cried out once more:

> 'But since he stood for England
> And knew what England means,
> Unless you give him bacon
> You must not give him beans!'

And soon the men were chorusing the words from Chesterton, belting them out like a battle cry, syncopating their rhythms, harmonizing their song and investing their nonsense with new and relevant meanings.

Only Gecko did not join in. She took a cup of water to Enoch and they shared a bemused cigarette.

32 : Mens cuiusque is est quisque

President Adini took his morning constitutional as usual. He liked to tour the presidential garden after breakfast, a brief lonely stroll that cleared his mind for the state business of the day and kept the staff on their toes. But this morning, as on the preceding three, Adini had the vague sensation that everything was not quite as he would have liked. Of course, it hadn't helped that he'd suffered another sleepless night. But it was more than that. Something, he wasn't sure what, impinged upon the tidy order of his mind.

Turning right out of the front entrance, Adini followed the gravel road around the west wing down the avenue of cherry trees and through the car park where the fleet of limousines were being given their morning buff by the team of bored-looking chauffeurs. For a moment Adini's eyes paused on Enoch's BMW, which was parked in one corner. As usual it was skewed across three parking spaces and the gravel bore the scars of two skidding back wheels, courtesy of his son's penchant for parking with a hand-break turn. Clearly the car had not been moved since the kidnapping.

From the car park Adini exited the rose-bordered gate to the flower garden (landscaped to the plan of the Masters' garden at Brasenose College, Oxford) and strolled up past the tennis court to the back of the presidential residence. On his left stood the new red brick of the large gymnasium that he'd had built a couple of years before. Since its opening Adini had never been inside. In fact, as far as he knew, the gym had only been used once, when Enoch had sneaked off from a presidential function with the daughter of the French under-secretary. Most awkward! For all their sexual reputation, the French were a conservative lot when it came to their teenaged offspring!

For the second time in as many minutes, Adini found himself forced to think about his son and he had a curious empty feeling in his pot belly, as though it were a large, foam-stuffed cushion that had been eaten from the inside by a thousand hungry moths. He wondered vaguely whether his son was still alive. And he realized that he didn't care and it was this lack of concern that he felt in his stomach. For goodness' sake, he thought. Am I really such a terrible father? Then he continued his perambulation (from the Latin *per ambulare*, to walk around, he thought), so that he didn't have to answer his own question.

Two mercenaries were guarding the back gate of the presidential residence. Huge men with shaved heads and misshapen noses, they were amusing themselves by flicking through the pages of an English pornographic magazine. One of them, Adini noticed, had a black spider's web tattoo that covered his neck and the underside of his chin. As he walked past, he slowed a little and waited for them to salute. But they paid him no attention. He stopped and stared at the pair questioningly. Eventually one looked up and acknowledged the President with a raised eyebrow.

'Keeping me safe and sound,' Adini said. Not as a question, merely a conversation starter that was easily ignored by the mercenaries. '*Qui vive!*' he said dramatically. And the two men looked at one another and harrumphed. But they did not smile or salute.

From the back gate Adini strolled across the expansive lawns on the east side and frowned at the patches of dead grass where the mercenaries had landed their helicopters. He walked through the Chinese water garden with the tinkling sounds that confirmed a good mood and exacerbated a bad one, and passed the pond in the shape of Lake Manyika. Finally he stopped at the statue of the Zamba warrior and, as usual, he stared at it contemplatively for a couple of minutes. He liked this statue, with its dreaming expression and rugged stone musculature. He had commissioned it from a renowned Zimbabwean sculptor in the first month after independence. Originally the warrior had been supposed to represent himself. But, even a decade earlier, the figure had been far too flattering to be a believable likeness. And now? And now Adini stroked his pot thoughtfully.

I suppose it is being surrounded by white soldiers in my own home, he reasoned. No wonder I feel slightly uncomfortable! Ah well! Needs must!

But he couldn't help but remember the last days of the independence war, when he had led the storming of this building (then the residence of the President of Manyikaland). The battle had been short and bloodless, with the dispirited *musungu* troops already resigned to defeat, and Adini had stood at the top of the staircase in the front hall and addressed the *ters*. 'Here are our headquarters!' he had announced. 'Never again will you see a *musungu* soldier in the presidential residence!'

What? Never? For goodness' sake! And now he'd hired the *musungu* to protect the crumbling structure of his one-party democracy. What was it the mercenary leader had said? 'The rule to end all rules, Mr President. You do what you gotta do.'

Deep in thought he left the statue locked in its expression of victorious ecstasy and wandered back to the front entrance. As he crossed the hall and ascended the staircase, two of the remaining presidential guard (those who had not deserted or switched their allegiance to the Gangers) stood up from the card school they'd formed with a bunch of mercenaries and stiffly saluted. But the President waved away their tribute with a tired hand. The remnants of his guard, he had noticed, were making a killing at the informal poker tables set up by their new *musungu* allies.

At the top of the stairs he turned right and headed down the long corridor towards his office. At the door, however, he paused with his hand on the knob. He could hear the vague mumble of a voice inside.

It has to be Bulimi, he thought, for no one else in allowed in my office when I'm not there. Ha! I knew he would come back to me with his tail between his legs!

Adini pushed open the door to his office and was ready with his most forgiving smile, but it was immediately wiped from his face. Instead of the missing general, Adini found two English mercenaries smoking cigarettes and playing catch with the paperweight that Enoch had made him for one birthday. And sitting in the presidential chair, with his feet on the presidential desk and his ear to the presidential telephone, was the mercenaries' leader, Terry Lamberton, known to all as Lambo, the terrifying thug recommended by the (now-deceased) British High Commissioner.

At the sight of President Adini, Lambo raised a silencing index finger like a boss to his young secretary. But he showed no signs of ending his phone call.

'Look, love,' he was saying, 'what do you mean, it's too much money? How much does it cost? Forty quid?'

Lambo rolled his eyes at President Adini and then winked conspiratorially.

'Come on, sweetheart! He's only eight years old once and if he wants the new Arsenal away strip, let's get him the new Arsenal away strip.'

Adini cleared his throat loudly.

'Yeah. Sure. Whatever. Better go. Of course. Speak to Denny, he'll sort out the accounts. Call me on the satellite. Gotta go. Yeah. You too.'

Lambo replaced the receiver and casually lit a cigarette.

'Kids,' he said with a shrug and he blew half a dozen perfect smoke rings into the air.

Adini felt his temper rise in his throat and tighten the seams of his lips. He turned to the two mercenaries.

'Get out!' he spat.

The mercenaries paused in their game of catch and looked at him, unimpressed. Then they looked at one another. Then they looked at Lambo, who held their gaze for a moment with sleepy eyes before nodding towards the door. The two men left the room. But not before the one holding the paperweight could drop it to the floor, sending the small crustacean shells that Enoch had affixed as decoration splintering across the marble.

Left alone with Lambo, Adini struggled to control his temper.

'For goodness' sake!' he exclaimed. 'For the sake of Tuloko, what do you think you're doing?'

Lambo smiled coolly. Whenever Adini spoke to him, he seemed to pull that smile (so cool it stripped his face of any emotion). And it was very disconcerting.

'Sit down, Mr President.'

'You're sitting in my chair.'

'I am? So I am. Would you like me to move? It's just I'm waiting on a phone call. You don't mind, do you?'

'Have you given the number of my direct line to just anyone?' Adini asked in astonishment.

'Calm down, Mr President! Not just anyone. Only my accountant and the missus. You know how it is. The little lady tends to worry. I'm sure yours is just the same.'

'Sally is dead.'

'Dead? Course she is. Cancer, wasn't it? Terrible thing, cancer. Terrible.'

Lambo nodded seriously for a moment or two. Then his face cracked into that same cool smile. ·

'Sit down, Mr President. We've got a lot to discuss.'

Adini sat grumpily in a high-backed chair and caught one of his prosthetic testicles beneath his right thigh. He shifted in the seat and it slipped under his buttock, denting at first and then expanding with a pop that pulled uncomfortably at his scrotum.

I should remind this bastard who's in charge, he thought. But his logical mind immediately countered this thought with two others (though divided into sub-paragraphs where appropriate).

One: I have no one to back me up. One A: most of my ministers have fled the country. One B: most of the presidential guard has deserted and the rest are too busy gambling to care. One C: Sir Alistair Digby-Stewart, the British High Commissioner, is dead and buried. One D: General Bulimi – Indigo! The disloyal bastard! – has not been seen for three days.

Two: I don't know who's in charge any more.

Of course, it was points One C and One D that did most

damage to Adini's self-confidence and contributed to the depressing conclusion of point Two.

Certainly the shooting of Digby-Stewart had undermined the President's management of the mercenaries, since it was Digby-Stewart who had organized their commission, briefing and transport (albeit in that roundabout way of his, all elliptical language and circular arguments – 'My "help", so-called, is more a question of perception than actual fact. And since perception is a misconception that may be given a hostile reception, let us keep my remuneration as our little deception').

Unfortunately Digby-Stewart was shot by his houseboy, Thomas, the day before the mercenaries arrived. He had appeared from the shower wearing his monogrammed white bathrobe (by Raith of Bond Street) to find Thomas pointing a revolver (his own, it transpired) at his head. With the unwavering arrogance of the English upper classes, Digby-Stewart didn't break stride, but continued to towel his hair as he chastized the servant.

'What the hell do you think you're doing, Thomas? Just put the gun down and get back to work, would you?'

But Thomas wasn't prepared to listen and he shot at once. Having never fired a gun before, he found that his hands were shaking and he chose to close his eyes. Consequently the bullet didn't hit Digby-Stewart in the head but the lower-left abdomen (extremely painful but missing all vital organs).

'Oh! Fuck!' Digby-Stewart exclaimed as he slid to his knees. 'Thomas! You little arse!'

Thomas didn't hear him, because as soon as the gun had discharged, he'd dropped it smoking on the shag pile and run from the house, appalled by what he'd done.

Police reports on the murder (compiled, because of the Black Boot Anarchy, some weeks later) described Thomas variously as a member of the Democratic People's Republic of Zambawi Party, a Black Boot Gang activist, a Ganger and a Ginger (*sic*). Unsurprisingly he was actually none of these, but an ordinary young man from a rural *gwaasha* who was caught up in the heady madness that had intoxicated Queenstown. In fact, a few days later, when

Thomas confessed all to his father in their local *shabeen*, he put it like this: 'It wasn't that he was a *musungu* or a friend of Adini. It was just . . . well . . . the gun was lying on the sideboard and he was such a penis nose.'

Shocked to discover that his first son was a murderer, Thomas's father immediately packed him off to the local *zakulu*. Fortunately this witchdoctor was a wise man who heard Thomas's explanation with sympathetic understanding of the weight of such existential moments of definition. And, besides, he possessed a second sight that allowed him to see that Thomas wasn't solely to blame. So the *zakulu* prescribed him a week's course of *zvoko* thistles that was painful enough to expunge any lasting guilty conscience and terribly good for the anaemia that he diagnosed from one glance at the young man's fingernails.

What Thomas never discovered was that Digby-Stewart didn't actually die on the bathroom floor. For, after the houseboy's flight, the British High Commissioner struggled to his feet, patched up the wound with a dishcloth and masking tape and gingerly dressed himself in an old jumper and a pair of tatty slacks. Then, with teeth gritted and upper lip suitably stiff, Digby-Stewart drove himself to the private Chisipite Clinic and booked himself in at Accident and Emergency.

'Name?'

'Digby-Stewart.'

'And what seems to be the problem, Mr Digby-Stewart?'

'I have been shot.'

The young receptionist looked up in surprise at the starch-voiced middle-aged man at the counter. He was standing up very straight and, though a little pale, showed no signs of any pain.

'Do you need to see a doctor immediately?'

'I'll wait my turn.'

The receptionist shrugged and said, 'The triage nurse will see you shortly.'

Whereupon the High Commissioner sat down, stiffly, in the gawdy waiting room that reminded him of the kosher fast-food restaurants in Tel Aviv.

Unfortunately for poor Digby-Stewart, that day's coincidence of the Black Boot Anarchy and a rugby match involving the lunatics of a South African provincial side (who had refused to cancel their tour despite the social unrest) meant that the Accident and Emergency department was stretched to capacity. And he found himself at the back of a long queue including broken limbs, bottle cuts, stab wounds and a pair of torn ears.

He watched the seemingly endless comings and goings with growing dismay, a fading heart and stoical silence (save the odd mutter of 'Fucking Africa'). What's more, when it was finally his turn to be seen, the High Commissioner was bumped to the back of the queue again on the admission by air ambulance of a rugged-looking little boy suffering from ruptured testicles. As the boy was stretchered straight into surgery, Digby-Stewart felt his head loll heavily to one side and he watched with detached amusement as a little side-drama played itself out in the waiting room. A young man was chastizing a weeping small boy.

'Ach! Scotty, mun!' the young man was saying. 'What the hell have you done?'

'Grant! You told me to pinch Chip in the privates!'

'Yeah, mun! Pinch him! Not squash the bloody things!'

Scotty turned away sulkily and looked, through his tears, directly at Digby-Stewart. The boy's eyes widened in amazement.

'Grant,' he said. 'That man's dead.'

Digby-Stewart stared at the small boy in surprise and tried to say something or blink to affirm his life. But he realized his mouth wouldn't open and his eyes wouldn't work and, worst of all, his heart wasn't beating.

So Alistair Digby-Stewart bled to death in a hospital waiting room, killed by Thomas's bullet, his private education (and conse-quent fear of matron's dismissive mockery) and his very English love of queuing.

I am dead, he thought. Then he thought, death is merely a question of perception. And after that he didn't think anything else.

When he heard about Digby-Stewart's demise, Adini immediately summoned General Bulimi and told him to arrest someone.

'Who?' the general asked.

'For goodness' sake, Bulimi! Anyone you like. Or, preferably, someone you don't like.'

Then Adini got on the phone to Downing Street, made suitable placatory noises and told the British prime minister that the investigation was ongoing but they already had someone in custody.

Since it had been Digby-Stewart who put the whole mercenary package together, Adini considered cancelling the deal (after all, the rent-an-army was due to arrive the next day and their first point of contact was dead). However, there were a couple of factors that mitigated against such a decision. One: how did you call off a deal with a bunch of mercenaries? Adini remembered full well how shirty the Koreans had got when he pulled out of negotiations to buy three Mig fighters. Two: the need for the mercenaries was now greater than ever (as proved by the murder of Digby-Stewart).

Instead, therefore, Adini summoned Bulimi to his office (again) so that he could fill him in on the mercenary plan. Adini did this because somewhere in an ignored spot of his conscience, he knew that hiring mercenaries was not a good thing to do and he trusted the general to offer some amoral support.

'So, Bulimi,' he began, lighting his pipe with a flourish of a match and a jaunty expression. 'Who did you pick up for the Digby-Stewart murder?'

'The cook,' Bulimi replied shortly.

The general was, Adini thought, looking rather tired. His face twitched with irritation and he shifted from foot to foot as though he needed to sit down. Adini made a mental note to relieve him of his duties after this rebellion was quashed. Time for some fresh blood.

'Does he have any known Black Boot Gang associations?'

'He was wearing a pair of black boots.'

The general and the President contemplated one another. Bulimi laughed a hollow laugh like a bad actor, which the President found perplexing.

'Good,' he said, nodding. 'Hold him until further notice.'

'On the evidence of his footwear?'

'Exactly.'

Bulimi shrugged and the President's breezy mood was undone and he began to bristle with irritation. Why did the general have to appear quite so detached? What was his problem?

'Bulimi,' the President continued, struggling to control his temper, 'what is your opinion of the current situation?'

'I am a soldier.'

'What?'

'I am a soldier. I don't have an opinion.'

'For goodness' sake! What the hell is wrong with you? Just tell me what our situation is.'

'Our situation?'

'Yes, our situation. Are we winning? Are we losing? Assuming we're losing, how long can we hold out?'

'Our situation? That is not my opinion. I just point that out. Our situation is different. I am a soldier. I don't have an opinion.'

Adini stared at the general. Maybe the time for some fresh blood had already arrived. But who? Anyone who sprang to mind was already deserted, dead or disappeared. Roll on the mercenaries' arrival! Now was not the time to start implementing personnel changes. That could wait until the war was won and the best people came back with repentant smiles and renewed loyalty. They'd soon see they'd backed the wrong dog! It would take more than a rag-tag bunch of hooligans to shift Adini.

'The situation is like this, Mr President,' Bulimi was saying. 'Outside Queenstown and Lelani, it is impossible to know because we have lost communication with the majority of our troops. It is, however, safe to conclude that this is because they have either been killed or, more likely, joined the Black Boot Gang. One may assume, therefore, that the majority of Zambawi is in the Black Boot Gang's hands (at least, insofar as it is in anybody's hands). Of course, I do know of several State Army companies that have remained loyal to your name, sir. So certain pockets of land are still within our control.'

'That is good,' Adini interrupted.

'Good? Yes. I suppose. Unfortunately such companies are largely commanded by bloodthirsty madmen who enjoy the lengthening odds and look forward to a glorious (if ultimately pointless) final scrap. Generally these company leaders are battle-scarred veterans of the independence war who have been waiting for a decade for an excuse to kill more people. Often they have been joined in an unholy alliance with the local *musungu* farmers (their former enemies) to repel the Black Boot Gang. I suppose one might see this as a happy sign of racial reconciliation. But I think not. Perhaps, therefore, I was wrong to describe these companies as loyal to your name. They are, rather, loyal to the lottery and lunacy of war.'

'Oh!' Adini said. Did the general really have to be so negative? And what was this stuff about lottery and lunacy? Just occasionally he could still see the poet inside the general, struggling to get out.

'What about Queenstown and Lelani, then? If we hold the cities, then we still hold all the best cards!'

'Hold the cities?' Bulimi said. And for a moment, the President thought that the general might start crying. 'Well. Yes. I suppose we hold the cities inasmuch as anyone does. The rule of law has broken down in both Lelani and Queenstown and been replaced by the law of the gun. And at the moment we've still got the biggest guns. So in that sense, yes, we hold the cities.'

'So what do we do, Bulimi?'

'Do? As I explained, Mr President, I am a soldier. I do not have an opinion.'

Adini stared at his right-hand man of the past twenty years and he felt a presidential moment coming on, a moment of definition, a moment to show his mettle, a moment like the night some seventeen years before, when he had stood up in front of the remnants of the ZLF and enthused their hearts for honour and glory and justice. When all had lost faith (even his oldest ally, for goodness' sake!), this was the time for him to demonstrate just what kind of man he was! And he squeezed his prosthetic balls for reassurance.

'Take a seat, Indigo,' Adini said and the general sat down with a tired sigh in one of the high-backed chairs opposite the President's desk. 'You're right. You are a soldier and, as such, you do not have an opinion. But me? I am the President. And I am blessed with opinions. The people look to me for decisions and it is my privilege to take them.

'You are down-hearted, Indigo, are you not? You are overwhelmed by a growing cynicism and fear of defeat. That's OK. Perhaps if I, like you, served on the front line of this sorry mess, then I too would feel down-hearted. But I do not. For it is not my place to be subsumed into the nitty-gritty of this bloody power struggle so that I cannot see the wood for the trees (or the corpses for the blood! Ha ha!).

'Perspective. That is what politics is all about, seeing the whole picture with a detached eye and no thought for personal gain. And it is my perspective that allows me to tell you exactly what we are going to do.

'I have sent for reinforcements. You seem surprised? Do not be! Instead you must be filled with renewed vigour for our righteous struggle. Tomorrow a band of British mercenaries arrive to aid our fight. They will soon show the amateurs of the Black Boot Gang what war is all about! For the sake of Tuloko, I'm quite tempted to dig out my uniform myself! The victory will be glorious!

'I see you shaking your head. You are concerned by the thought of *musungu* soldiers fighting in our name. But it is not for you to worry! As you said, you are a soldier and it is not for you to have an opinion. I believe mercenaries did an excellent job for President Tula of Mozola. Before his eventual overthrow, anyway.

'*Omnia mutantur, nos et mutamur in illis!*

'Besides, you must recall the pragmatism of the independence war. We fought the *musungu*, we fought for social justice, we fought for the freedom to determine our own destiny. But you remember full well that we made choices that we no longer talk about. Certainly *you* did things that we no longer talk about. But now, as then, the end justifies the means!'

Adini concluded his little polemic with a flourish, his high-pitched voice singing ever higher and his arms gesticulating enthusiastically. But Bulimi was unmoved. By the end he was just sitting limply in his seat and blank-staring at the President. He got to his feet and began to unbutton his army uniform.

'What the hell are you doing?' Adini asked. He hadn't expected his words to have this effect!

Bulimi removed his gun from its holster and laid it on the President's desk. He took off his general's jacket and laid it neatly over the back of the chair. He walked slowly towards the door in an almost trance-like state.

'Bulimi!' the President shouted. 'Where the hell do you think you're going?'

Bulimi turned and looked at him with eyes that seemed to be evaporating and his hands were trembling madly at his sides.

'I used to be a special kind of gift from the ancestors,' he began obtusely and then paused. His forehead creased a little. 'As a wise man never got the chance to tell me, this is not a just war. It is just a war. I fought – how did you put it? – for the freedom to determine my own destiny. Only to find, in victory, that my destiny was pre-determined, my freedom revoked and that uniform' – his voice began to quiver – 'that uniform was my jail cell.'

With that, Bulimi opened the door of the presidential office and walked out. Adini had not seen him since.

With Digby-Stewart infuriatingly dead and Bulimi infuriatingly AWOL, it was left to Adini to meet and greet the mercenaries on his own and, all things considered, he felt he handled the situation admirably.

When the Hueys touched down on the eastern lawns of the presidential residence, Adini was there in full dress uniform with his heart working overtime and his pot belly straining against the brass buttons. Immediately the choppers hit the ground, the mercenaries spewed out, weapons in hand, and dispersed to left and right, taking up positions with their backs against walls, flat on their tummies or crouching with their rifles to their shoulders. As the beat of the propellers slowed to silence, Adini heard them shout to one another: 'Briggsy. Secure!' 'Capper. Secure!' 'Nutjob. Secure!' Only then did Lambo appear from the central helicopter.

He wore a pair of dark glasses and smoked a cigarette and looked like a minor villain from an American movie.

While all this was going on around him, Adini watched with some bemusement. They were in the presidential residence, for goodness' sake! Where was the perceived threat? But he was suitably impressed by their immaculate drilling and he wondered if this was the point, to make him feel that he was getting his money's worth. Especially since 250 men looked a lot fewer in real life than they had on paper, when he'd signed the cheque.

Later he met Lambo in the presidential office and they discussed what Lambo described as his 'requirements'. The way Lambo talked about his job reminded Adini of a meeting he'd once had with a PR company in London (the President had considered hiring them to improve his personal image in the Western media). Lambo described the task in hand as 'coup management' and he asked questions like 'What is your blue-sky end-state scenario, Mr President?' and he kept referring to 'the necessary wastage statistics' (only later did Adini realize that this meant the percentage of the population that he was prepared to see killed). Adini disliked Lambo's euphemistic language, since it sat uneasily with his own vainglorious perception of war.

In fact, Adini disliked Terry Lamberton. He found him intimidating and arrogant and clearly slightly deranged. But this didn't worry him at first, since, the way he saw it, an intimidating, arrogant, deranged mercenary was exactly the kind of mercenary one wanted.

Certainly the mercenaries' work seemed impressive enough. Within forty-eight hours they had Queenstown returned to some kind of order with the rigorous application of Lambo's 'four-S policy' ('shout at 'em, shoot 'em, scare 'em, silence 'em'). In practice this meant driving through the main Queenstown thoroughfares in convoys of Land Rovers rigged with loudhailers. 'I am Acting General Lambo of the Zambawi State Army,' Lambo would announce. 'Return to your homes or we will kill you.' They then let off a few rounds, wantonly killing the slowest runners and those who spoke no English (mostly old women and children and Felati widows, who tripped over their capacious skirts).

Sometimes they stopped their Land Rovers in public spots like the Adini Shopping Mall and Independence Square and continued their speechifying to the terrified looters and looted who cowered in doorways and behind the ornamental fountains that had never worked.

'In accordance with President Adini's declared state of national emergency, we are imposing a twenty-four-hour curfew. Anyone seen on the streets will be shot on sight.'

When Lambo made this announcement at Mbave Bus Station (still jam-packed with people fleeing to and from the city), a cocky young man called Seventeen, who thought himself invincible because his father owned a bus company, strode out of the crowd and harangued the mercenaries.

'What are we supposed to do if we need to go outside?' he shouted.

'That is a good question,' the loudhailer replied.

'How are we supposed to do our shopping?'

'Carefully!'

Inside the front Land Rover, Lambo nodded to Briggsy, one of his more trusted marksmen, who promptly felled Seventeen with a single shot between the eyes. The mercenaries laughed and exchanged high fives and the loudhailer laughed too.

From one of the stationary buses, an orphan street urchin (maybe seven years old), who had found a pistol in a toilet ditch (where it had been dropped by a drunken member of Adini's Emergency Militia), fired off its last bullet in the vague direction of the Land Rover convoy and it scored a direct hit on the loudhailer and piercing electrical feedback screamed across the bus station and made the crowd cover their ears. For a moment or two there was silence and then the loudhailer began to curse. From the back of the second Land Rover the crowd saw an enormous man jump out, carrying what appeared to be a drainpipe on his shoulder. Suddenly the end of the drainpipe erupted, flashing with fire and booming with an echoing sound that one observer described as 'like a *gar* fart of the Great Chief Tuloko'.

The bus from which the shot had been fired immediately leaped from its tyres in shock, burst into flames and fell on to one side in a dead faint. Then the petrol tank exploded and a mushroom of smoke was thrown into the sky. After a second or two the smoke cleared and the crowd saw a small figure flying through the air with its arms and legs whirling. The junior gunman hit the tarmac hard and the crowd communally winced. But, to everyone's astonishment, he got to his feet with no worse damage than grazed knees, skinned palms and a ringing in his ears, and he ran away as fast as he could and hid in a dustbin.

Those who had seen the small boy's remarkable escape from the exploding bus repeated the story to their families in hushed voices. And their families asked to hear the story again and again because, what with the curfew, there was no other entertainment. At the end of each telling, the *mboko* would say stuff like 'that boy must have the blessing of Father Sun'. And, being wise old men, the *mboko* were proved right. Because some months later the boy was recognized by the locals as Zambawi's youngest *zakulu* (probably the first to live in a city and certainly the first to appear from unknown lineage).

Unfortunately the boy was never very successful because the tinnitus drowned out the messages of Cousin Zamba and sometimes, when he heard a door slam or an ancient car backfire, he would prophesy the end of the world by mistake. What's more, his only unerring gift proved to be for the prediction of his patients' impending deaths. And, although this was undoubtedly an impressive and spooky talent, it generally made him very unpopular with the so-afflicted. Though rarely for long.

For the most part Adini knew little of the mercenaries' arbitrary violence and he certainly had no desire to hear Lambo's 'natural wastage statistics'. As far as he was concerned, the main thing was that he was in charge of Queenstown again. Or at least he thought he was. At first.

But, if Adini was impressed with the mercenaries' results, he was less enamoured of their house training. It had never occurred to him that Lambo and his men would expect to stay in the presidential residence. And yet they did. And he didn't have the guts to ask them to leave.

For three days Adini had suffered sleepless nights as the mercenaries drank and sang their way through his collection of malt whisky (bought at a knock-down price at a Commonwealth Conference in Edinburgh). When he went to his bathroom, he would find the shaven bristles of a *musungu*'s beard in a scummy circle around the sink and the presidential rest rooms had been turned into dens of iniquity where the mercenaries watched Dutch skin flicks and masturbated incessantly.

'When you call out the plumber,' Adini muttered, 'you do not expect to find him sleeping in your bed, shitting in your toilet and performing the tight-fisted *gulu gulu* in your favourite chair.'

And, as he sat down in front of Lambo on the wrong side of the desk in his own office, he realized that it was these invasions of privacy as much as the death of Digby-Stewart (point One C) and the desertion of Bulimi (point One D) that led him to the depressing conclusion of point Two.

I don't know who's in charge any more, he thought.

He stared at Lambo and was shocked to find that the mercenaries' leader must have been talking for some minutes. But he had been so lost in his own head that he hadn't heard a word that was said.

What has happened to my tidy mind? Adini wondered. I never used to lose concentration like this and now it's becoming something of a habit.

But then he realized that he was doing it again and he ticked himself off and forced himself to focus on Lambo.

'With Queenstown secure,' Lambo was saying, 'we've got to look towards the next object focus, and, as far as I'm concerned, to strike at the very core of the rebels is the first principle of coup management. It minimizes necessary wastage and can often lead to a speedy resolution of this hostile takeover. There are risks. Of course there are risks! But my bet is that, with the security cordon around Queenstown, the Gangers don't even know of our arrival yet and, as I often say to the blouses under my command, there are three principles that guarantee success in battle . . .'

Lambo paused for dramatic effect, blew cigarette smoke from his nose so that he looked like a bull, and tilted his head enquiringly. But Adini was struggling even to follow what he was on about and he didn't know what he was supposed to say.

'You know what they are, Mr President?'

'No.'

'Surprise, surprise and surprise!'

'Oh. Good.'

'Now a little birdy tells me that the Black Boot Gang are gathering their forces just north of Zimindo in Maponda township, ready for their final push on your capital, Mr President. And you know what?'

'No.'

'I think we'll pay them a little visit. A courtesy call, if you will.'

'Oh. Good.'

'Show them a few fireworks and we'll have them running like niggers, pardon my French.'

Adini stared at the hog-like figure of Lambo, with his short limbs, barrel chest and pinking complexion, and he felt very old. He wanted to say something, something like, 'For goodness' sake! Who the hell do you think you are, you crazy bastard!', but he didn't have the will for it. At that moment, in his spirit, Adini knew it was all over, that he wasn't in charge, that – whether the mercenaries won or lost – he would never be in charge again. But his all-consuming pomposity and self-importance had rendered his spirit dumb and wrapped his ego in the cotton wool of vanity and wallpapered his mind with the soundproof cork of 'I'm so great'. And, besides, all he could think about was his desperate need for a decent night's sleep.

'Does that mean you're going?' Adini asked.

'I'll leave a skeleton patrol under Nutjob's command – you'll like him. He's a nutjob. Just to ensure your safety, Mr President. But the rest of us will ship out tonight.'

'Oh,' Adini said. 'Good.'

That night Adini went to bed early and settled into his soft pillows like a mother hen on her nest. He could hear Nutjob's patrol groaning in mutual selfish pleasure in the rest rooms down the corridor, but they were never going to keep him awake. And Adini was asleep within seconds and dreaming the most peculiar dream. Like all dreams it was part memory, part fantasy and part prophesy.

He dreamed that he was back at St Ignatius' College, in the communal showers with the chilly tiled floors, being dragged by his penis from wall to wall by those racist bullies who had made his life a misery. Suddenly another *musungu* boy appeared, but he was carrying a traditional Zambawian spear and he chased off the bullies with fierce threats in fluent Zamba. Adini wanted to thank him. But the boy sneered when he spoke and thrust the spear through his guts so that it poked out on the other side. Adini sank to the ground as the *musungu* walked around the showers, turning off every tap. As the steam began to clear, Adini made out a young black boy, dressed like a beggar, who had his hands over his ears and his eyes tight shut. His mouth was opening and closing but no sound was coming out. 'I can't hear you,' Adini wailed, even though he knew that the news couldn't be good. And he pulled agonizingly at the spear in his belly. The boy opened his eyes and removed his hands from his ears. '*Mens cuiusque is est quisque*,' he said.

33 : Of semen and acid and bile and tears

Jim Tulloh had been having some weird dreams too.

Since the bizarre (if brief) experience of becoming the Great Chief Tuloko inside the Great Chief Tuloko's body (if that makes any sense; it didn't to Jim), he had returned to being scrawny, monolingual little Jim during the day. But at night his sleep was overrun by all kinds of fantasies (both full-length stories and vivid set pieces) that could have no other root but in magic. In one dream he hovered above the viscous fluidity of the immature earth and watched it coagulate in the heat of Father Sun. In another he was dragged into a clear river, where he fought a fearless battle with invisible water men, cutting himself with a long hunting knife so that their figures stood out in the opaque mist of his blood. He dreamed of his grandmother's bathroom in Dorset, where President Adini reclined in the bathtub. He impaled the President on a huge spear, only to find him turn into a snake that circled with the water down the drain, leaving two rubber balls blocking the plug hole. He dreamed that he ate dinner with the irresistible bald girl who'd kissed him with dead lips. She fed him disgusting maize porridge and she cried when he couldn't finish it, saying, 'But you have to be strong!' He dreamed that he fell head first into the enormous vagina of a giant black woman who bounced up and down on top of him crying, 'Woo! woo! woo! woo!' And when he woke up, he was mortified to find he had the softening aftermath of a spent erection and his underpants were soggy with semen.

Jim concluded that he was dreaming the dreams of the Great Chief Tuloko and, while he didn't object to this *per se*, it did mean he woke up more exhausted than he'd been on going to bed.

Besides, now that he no longer spoke Zamba and he had an army to run and a coup to organize, he felt that any intrusion of the Chief's personality into his own would be a hell of lot more use in his day-to-day decision-making than the lost time of his sleep.

Of the early decisions that Jim took as leader of the Black Boot Gang, some worked better than others. Among the better orders that he issued, these are just a few:

Following Musa's advice that 'everybody wants to be important', Jim abolished the rank of private in the Black Boot Gang and promoted every Ganger by at least one rung (sometimes two), so that Private Nkrumah became Lieutenant Nkrumah, Lieutenant Tula became a captain and Dubchek leaped several strata to be installed as general and chief of staff. This order boosted morale and increased Jim's fragile authority, which had previously been based only on metaphysical fear. The Gangers' clandestine, subversive mutterings were replaced by good-humoured remarks about the *musungu* being an 'excellent judge of character'.

Of course, this wholesale promotion also meant that there was no longer a rank junior enough to be ordered to fill in the old toilet ditches and dig the new, so Jim and Musa were obliged to take up the spades themselves. But Jim considered this a small price to pay for camp harmony and, besides, this demonstration of his democratic sensibilities made him more popular among the Gangers than ever.

Flushed with the success of his first order, he followed it with two others, which (though they both required modification) proved to be equally inspired. Jim commanded the Gangers to return all looted property (that hadn't already been eaten, sold or otherwise disposed of) to its rightful owners. Initially this order provoked resentment among the ranks, but, with quick wits, Jim adjusted the order's wording so that the property was only to be returned to those who agreed to join the Black Boot Gang. In this way he swelled the numbers of local recruits (bribing them with what was already theirs), returned the personal knick-knacks that were of sentimental value to their owners and retained the vital supplies (the stolen chickens, maize and the like) as common property of the Gang.

Next Jim forbade the smoking of *gar*, partly because of his growing conviction (based on extensive and terrifying personal experience) of its dangerous hallucinogenic properties and partly because he figured that an army that was permanently stoned would be no use to anyone. Again this decision was predictably unpopular and required minor modification. Instead of banning *gar*, therefore, Jim forbade the Gangers to indulge in their luxuriant bouts of post-joint farting on the grounds that it fouled the atmosphere for everyone. At first a few of the hardened smokers kept up their habit and desperately tried to control their bowels. But such anal constraint stripped the whole experience of most of its pleasure, and soon the camp had transformed (relatively painlessly) into a *gar*-free zone.

Finally Jim ordered that any new recruit to the Black Boot Gang would have to serve a spell in the most junior rank (now lieutenant). The majority of these recruits were local villagers who were too thrilled by the return of their tin whistles, suede boots and ancient foreign magazines with pictures of unknown footballers to care about their lowly status. Of the rest, however, many were Queenstown refugees, former bigwigs who were determined to join the winning side before it was too late. And these city slickers were less than pleased to be ordered around by snotty-nosed, traitorous young soldiers. The senior partner of Queenstown's largest law firm, for example, was distressed to find himself boiling water for General Dubchek's bath. And, for all his democratic principles, Eddy Kotto, erstwhile editor of the *Zambawi National Herald*, didn't see why he should take dictations of lurid love letters (full of *double entendres* and morally dubious suggestions) on the aggressive order of Captain Mandela.

But Jim didn't worry about the opinions of his new recruits, since their lowly ranking was another popular decision on his part. And, in fact, this humbling experience of service was the making of many an arrogant urbanite. Though none of them would ever admit as much.

However, while Musa congratulated Jim on such undeniable evidence of a leader's intuition, other orders proved to be less successful. Jim decided that the Black Boot Gang should march to Maponda township, approximately fifty miles north of Zimindo, to join forces with the other disparate Black Boot Gang companies. While Jim knew that his fame had already spread nationwide in the aftermath of the Tuloko stunt, he reasoned (quite correctly) that he would have to gather his forces in one place if he was to maintain any kind of unified purpose. Therefore he immediately sent word to all the other Black Boot Gang captains, demanding their presence for the final push on Queenstown. At the time this seemed like an excellent idea. In retrospect Jim would regret it as rash and thoughtless.

The other rash and thoughtless decision that Jim took (though in retrospect it turned out to be an excellent idea) was the order to release Enoch Adini. Jim was pilloried by Musa (who regarded Enoch as adequate insurance against defeat) and Dubchek too (who had been scared of Enoch since his days as a presidential guard). But Jim refuted their criticism.

'You can't install me as chief,' he said, 'and then question my orders. Insurance against defeat? We're not going to lose!'

But even Enoch seemed surprised to find the chains removed from his ankles and, as he smoked a joint (since he was not a member of the Black Boot Gang) and finally changed out of his now-rotting dinner suit, he quizzed Jim in a puzzled tone of voice.

'Look, Jim. Very good of you to let me go, Mr Musungu, but what if I run back to old Daddy No Nuts and tell him exactly what you're up to?'

'Well,' Jim replied. 'One: you're not going to do that, are you?'

'No.'

'Right. Two: if you did, we'd catch up with you long before you made it to Queenstown. And three: I reckon we've got this coup all sown up, so you're a hell of a lot safer here where I can protect you than you'd ever be in the presidential residence.'

Jim found that Enoch was looking at him with a curiously wry expression on his face, all angular eyebrows and twitching lips.

Jim lit a cigarette, dragged deep and puffed smoke in irritation.
'What?' he said.

'What's all this "one", "two", "three" business?' Enoch asked,
barely suppressing a laugh. 'You sound exactly like my father.
Maybe even more cocksure and pompous. I tell you something,
Jim, you want to make sure this Chief Tuloko stuff doesn't go to
your head. I think I preferred you when you were a bullshit *musungu*
teacher who knew he didn't know what he was doing.'

Jim knew that Enoch was right, though he didn't like to hear
it, and he suddenly felt very small and inadequate. But, whereas
once such feelings would have made him hunch his shoulders and
shrink into self-pity, he now bristled with false confidence, swelled
his chest and sighed in a patronizing way.

'You should join us, Enoch,' he said. 'We could use someone
like you on our side.'

'Thanks but no thanks. As hard as it may seem to believe (and
believe me, I'm surprised), I have moral difficulties with the idea
of joining a plot to overthrow and undoubtedly murder my father.
He's never done much for me. But then I've never done much for
him either.'

'We're not going to murder your father!' Jim protested.

'Oh no? My mistake. So what exactly are you going to do?'

What *were* they going to do? It was a good question and Jim
didn't have an answer. This made him feel smaller and stupider
and more inadequate. Consequently he began to behave as if he
were bigger and cleverer and supremely competent.

It was not, however, Enoch's canny dissection of Jim's manner
that made his release suddenly seem so rash and thoughtless. No.
The real problem came when Enoch killed Captain Mandela.

It was a couple of days after Enoch had been unchained and the
Black Boot Gang camp was starting to get twitchy. They were
waiting on the order to mobilize, their numbers were swelling all
the time and food was fast running out. What's more, the former
Queenstown elite were beginning to threaten desertion as a couple
of the younger captains continually ordered them to perform the
most mundane and demeaning tasks just for the hell of it: 'Ah, Judge

Zvozvo, there you are! Light my cigarette for me!' or 'Reverend Bombazi! I've got a job for you. Squeeze the pimples on my shoulders. That's an order!' In fact, they would surely have upped and left if Musa hadn't pointed out that they'd nowhere to go.

Worse still, one of the local *musungu* farmers had discovered the whereabouts of the camp. Generally the *musungu* population had watched the rise of the Black Boot Gang with paranoid alienation and haunting memories of the independence war. They barricaded themselves into their luxurious estates, dismissed their shifty-eyed servants and armed their children, only to find that they were largely ignored. And when they ran out of milk, they had to dismantle their barricades just so they could get down to the local dairy.

What attacks there were on the *musungu* were mostly arbitrary in nature: Black Boot Gang patrols that stumbled on to the farms with no sense of direction and a taste for a bottle of cold Coke. Or disgruntled former employees, determined to make their bosses pay for their dismissal. But even these random acts of violence had subsided in the wake of Jim's appointment and the new sense of unity and purpose.

One *musungu* farmer in the Zimindo area, however, felt that he had an old score to settle. Not with the Black Boot Gang particularly, but with the Afs, munts, niggers, kaffirs in general. His name was Tom Kelly and, after ten years as one of the Manyikaland army's most-decorated soldiers, he had moved into the countryside from Queenstown in the aftermath of independence. He had joined the army upon the murder of his father, a Queenstown civil rights lawyer, by the embryonic ZLF ('He was trying to help the bloody munts and they shot him like a dog'). The bubbling coup, therefore, gave Kelly the sniff of a chance for further empty revenge, which he'd been dreaming of for more than a decade.

When he discovered the whereabouts of the Black Boot Gang ('Fucking *ters* on my own bloody doorstep, mun!'), he considered arming himself to the teeth and wading into the camp all guns blazing. But, though he was eaten up with bitterness, he knew that such an action would be suicidal and he valued his existence more than that, if only to perpetuate the bile that had replaced red blood as his life force. Instead, therefore, Kelly filled up his prop-driven old crop sprayer and flew low over the Black Boot Gang camp, drowning the ramshackle base in a homemade cocktail of household acids and toxic pesticides.

Fortunately for the Gangers, Jim had ordered the majority of his force out into the bush on pointless exercises to quell their growing frustration. Of those left behind, however, many were burned to differing degrees and their lungs corroded, and the food stores were largely ruined. One who was affected was Enoch, who was sitting on the outskirts of the camp when the plane made its pass. He missed the worst of the virulent deluge, but two droplets that caught on the breeze splashed him just below his left eye and scalded two tiny scars into the smooth skin of his handsome face, so that, from then on, a stranger might think that he was forever crying.

When the Gangers returned to camp to find there was no food to be eaten and their comrades were struggling for breath, the unease that had been building sparked full-blown arguments and even the odd punch-up. Jim knew there was nothing else for it and he informed the Gang that they would be marching to Maponda at first light.

Among the frustrated Black Boot Gang, Captain Mandela was more bad-tempered than most. It simply wasn't in his thuggish nature to sit around on his arse with the prospects of a good fight apparently receding. He didn't like taking orders from a *musungu* (even one who'd promoted him) and, as far as he was concerned, he should have blown Jim's head off when he had the chance instead of giving him the one-in-six odds of Zambawian roulette. The one thing worse than taking orders from Jim, however, was to serve in the same army as a woman. And not just any woman, but a dirty Mozolan whore who spoke English like a *musungu* and paraded around the camp with her breasts pressing against her shirt and her arse straining the seams of her trousers. Gecko Tula! What kind of a name was that? She called herself after a lizard, did she? Well, he'd give her a fine Zambawian *nyoka* that would have the little gecko begging for mercy! And that night – since every tent had been corroded with acid and the *musungu* had banned the lighting of fires for fear of another attack – would be the perfect opportunity.

It was around 2 a.m. when Gecko was woken up by the warm breath of Mandela on her ear and his cold dry hand clasped firmly across her mouth. A horrified shriek caught in her throat as her shirt was torn open and her right breast kneaded as if it were the soft dough for maize pancakes. Instinctively she raised her left knee and caught Mandela full in the genitals. He cursed next to her ear and bit down with his sharp canines, shredding the flesh of her lobe. 'Don't move, you little bitch!' he said in Zamba. 'You've got two choices. Either I fuck you then kill you, or I kill you then fuck you.' Fortunately Gecko didn't understand the true evil of his words – although rape is a universal language.

With the full weight of his body on her chest and one hand still covering her mouth, Mandela struggled to pull down first her combat trousers and then his rough jeans and soiled underpants. Gecko whined through his fingers as she felt the warmth of his penis nudging against her pubic bone and the ugly slime of his growing excitement dribble down the inside of her thigh. Mandela caught one of her hands, which were beating unnoticed against his shoulders and face, and thrust it down between his legs. 'That's what you've got coming, whore!' he said. Gecko took his testicles between her fingers and squeezed as hard as she could until Mandela brought his elbow crashing down on the top of her head, knocking her senseless.

When Gecko came to, she was overwhelmed by a peculiar sense of unreality. Mandela was kneeling over her with his penis in his hand, jerking himself lazily to an erection. The look on his face was not so much scary, she thought, as almost laughable; so grotesque and inhuman and evil that it looked like the Mozolan *koko* mask that her mother had used to frighten her children before Tula had her put to death for rumoured infidelity. Gecko tried to hit Mandela in the face as he knelt above her. But she found that she had no arms (or at least that's what it felt like). She discovered that her hands were bound behind her back and supporting her beneath her waist. Her arms were completely numb and immobile.

Something was in her mouth, something cold and metallic that tasted like the coins that you lick when you're a kid, just to see how they feel on your tongue. She opened her mouth a little wider to try and scream. But the gun barrel slid deeper into her throat, pressing against her palate and making her choke.

Suddenly Gecko's mind came rushing back to her and a terrified wordless sound squealed not from her mouth but from her very essence. 'Oh God, no! My virginity will be taken by a rapist!'

When he heard this sound, Mandela laughed (proving beyond doubt that he was a personification of evil) and sank his penis deep between Gecko's legs, plugging the scream with every vicious poke.

If he had been asleep, there's no way that Enoch would have been woken by Gecko's muffled cries. But he was not asleep. He had not slept properly for several days with the pain of ulcerating sores where the manacle had been secured to his ankle now joined by the sting of his permanent tears and the melancholy sensation of his spoiled good looks. So, as soon as he heard the sounds of the rape, he went to investigate.

In fact, Enoch watched the sordid wrestling for some moments. He was frozen, not by fear but the sight of the gun between Gecko's lips. He didn't know what to do. Only when he saw Mandela force himself inside her, only when he saw the evil bastard quiver as he pumped his semen into her, did Enoch act, and that was a spur-of-the-moment decision prompted by revulsion. He had no idea what he was going to do until he did it. He had no idea what he was going to say until he said it.

Enoch found himself standing by Mandela's head, Gecko's panic-stricken eyes staring up at him.

'What are you doing?' he said casually and Mandela swung round, his grip tightening on the gun's handle and his finger itching on its trigger.

The expression on his face was, Enoch thought, quite ridiculous.

Kind of embarrassed. As if he'd been caught with his finger in the maize porridge.

'The son of the fucking eunuch!' he exclaimed. 'Get out of here, you Nose!'

'I'm going to kill you,' Enoch said. And he noticed that his voice was barely above a whisper.

'I said get out of here or I'll shoot the little bitch!'

'I'm going to kill you,' Enoch said. And then again: 'I'm going to kill you.'

Mandela adjusted his position slightly on top of Gecko and, having regained his thug composure, he taunted Enoch by gently, playfully, squeezing the trigger. As he moved, Enoch saw his flaccid penis slide out and droop against his thigh. In an instant, before he realized what he was doing or had time to think of the possible consequences, Enoch swung his foot and caught the rapist flush on the cheekbone. Mandela lost his grip on the gun and tumbled off Gecko into the dusty scrub. He shook his head and began to laugh, as if this was what he'd wanted all along.

'Come on, boy!' he spat.

But Enoch was on him in a flash and the ferocity of the assault caught him by surprise. Enoch kicked him in the ribs again and again until he managed to catch his leg and unbalance him. For a moment Mandela was on top of him in a bizarre kind of 69 position and Enoch saw his penis swinging before his eyes. But Enoch sank his teeth into Mandela's thigh and punched his fist repeatedly into his testicles. The fading thug rolled off in agony and Enoch straddled him, beating his fists into his face, gouging his eyes and rupturing arteries until warm blood was spraying from the sockets. Mandela had stopped struggling, but Enoch didn't stop hitting him. He broke his windpipe, he smashed his jaw, he punched his nose (still tender from its breaking by Dubchek) until it splintered, sending shards of bone into the rapist's brain. And he only stopped when his eyes were blinded by blood and tears.

Numbly Enoch rolled off Mandela's corpse to find that Gecko hadn't moved; partly because her hands were still bound, partly because the gun was still in her mouth, and partly because she was in such a nauseous state of shock. Enoch lifted the gun slowly from her mouth and delicately unbound her aching wrists. Now his movements were as gentle and humane as they had a moment earlier been brutal and inhuman. Enoch tried to wrap Gecko's naked, shivering body in his arms. She pushed him away. She reached down between her legs and lifted her hand with her fingers splayed and dripping with Mandela's glutinous semen. She dissolved into tears, huge, hungry sobs that left Enoch breathless, as if they were somehow sucking all the air from the atmosphere. But still she wouldn't let Enoch comfort her.

'I'm spoiled,' she wept at last and Enoch tenderly pushed back one of her braids from her face.

'We're all spoiled,' he said. 'It's our birthright.'

Gecko looked up at him and her innocent eyes flashing with the steel of nobility were the most beautiful and unspoiled eyes he'd ever seen.

'No man will want me,' she said.

Enoch thought for a moment.

'You're Gecko Tula!' he said. 'You don't need a man! And you will never want a man as much as he wants you.'

Gecko collapsed into Enoch's chest, digging her nails into his flesh, clinging on to him for dear life, as if he was an olive branch suspended over the deepest chasm. And then they lay cheek to cheek until morning, the juice of their tears mingling as if they were making the saddest kind of love.

34 : The battle of Maponda

EXTRACT FROM EDDY KOTTO'S NOTEBOOK
For a proposed feature for the Sunday Times, London. *On spec?*

Zambawi is a nation founded upon myth: the myth of the *shamva*, the first chiefs, who betrayed the people for food, precious stones and ritual objects; the myth of Zamba, Cousin Moon, who challenged Father Sun atop the Mountain in the East That Kissed the Sky; the myth of the Great Chief Tuloko (the Traveller and the Child of the Horizon), who came from beyond the Great Lake in the West to save our nation from the wrath of Father Sun. Of course, the ritual objects are now forgotten, the mountain scaled and the lake a playground for the tourists, lined with casinos and five-star hotels. But the myths live on in our children's stories, our ancestral worship, the very essence of our culture.

No myth, however, is more powerful than that of the *musungu* (the Zamba word for 'white man') James Tulloh, an English student who was chosen by Tuloko to lead the coup against President Adini.

As with all myths, the details of 'Tulo' (as James Tulloh became known to the Black Boot Gang) are, at best, sketchy, with eyewitness accounts as divergent as they are numerous. Some say that the spirit of the Great Chief Tuloko entered Tulo and caused him to speak in the magical language of the ancestors, firing the Gangers' hearts with the spirit of dead warriors. Others say that Tuloko himself flew down on the back of a mighty eagle; or that Tulo spoke from his backside (a sure sign that the nation would be turned on its head); or that they bowed into the dirt and dusties crawled into their ears with messages from the Great Chief. But the myth of Tulo is just that: a myth. It is not to be analysed as though it were a document of law or a scientific equation. Suffice it to say that the Black Boot Gang chose to follow a nineteen-year-old *musungu* from rural Dorset. Surely that fact alone will resonate for everyone.

EXTRACT FROM EDDY KOTTO'S NOTEBOOK
For a proposed feature for the Sunday Times, *London. On spec?*

Every revolution has its heroes and ours were the *musungu* Tulo, Enoch Adini (the President's son), Rujeko Tula (the President's daughter) and Musa the *zakulu*. But above them all, bestriding events like the Colossus of Rhodes, stood another whose actions have already passed into the fluid rivers of fable . . .
NOTE TO SELF: If in doubt, set it out! There's no 'Pass It On' here! Tell the story chronologically, Eddy!

ENOCH

You know he had it coming, Jim. You know he did. He was nothing but a fucking bully. I've heard what he did to you. I know he killed your friend and beat you to shit. Don't look at me like that. You think I knew I was capable of that kind of behaviour? Oh God! You think I'm proud of myself?

But he raped her! So don't look at me like that. This is what violence does to people and it's not my fault. You're way out of your depth, white boy, whether you know it or not. You'll find out. You can sit there in silence as if you're the Great Chief Tuloko himself. But you'll find out.

What are you going to do with me? Chain me to a stake? They have done that already. Execute me for murdering a rapist? To be honest, I'm past caring.

I'm spoiled, Jim. You know that? We're all spoiled.

Did you know there's no Zamba word for rape? Your *zakulu* friend told me that. Make what truth of it you can. *I* make it all the *musungu*'s fault at some level. You can't rape a country for a century and then start sneering when the bastard rape-child turns out to be a hooligan.

Look at my face, Jim! I'm going to be crying for ever. So do what you want with me, Jim. But remember, there's no principles in this. It's not about power and politics. Just people. And I don't know about you, but I've always thought they were a great deal more important.

EXTRACT FROM EDDY KOTTO'S NOTEBOOK
For a proposed feature for the Sunday Times, *London. On spec?*

We were up to march at first light, but already the stench of death hung over the camp like some prescient sign of what was to come. Enoch Adini, then just the President's son and a hostage of the Black Boot Gang (*How strange it feels to write those words!*), had killed a Ganger captain for the alleged rape of Rujeko Tula (the daughter of the 'Butcher of Ikbo'). As you may gather from this information, the make-up of the Black Boot Gang by this time was very cosmopolitan in nature. Rural farmers rubbed shoulders with the ex-army, who bickered with former High Court judges, bishops and the like. As well as me, Eddy Kotto, your intrepid reporter (*Too much self?*). Truly, ours was to be a popular revolution!

In the wake of the murder there was some disquiet among the men, who were waiting to see what action Tulo would take. Soon it became apparent that Enoch was to be pardoned and the Gangers were uneasy; not because of any affection for the victim (who was deeply unpopular) but because of the disturbing dithering that such inaction implied in our leader . . . (*NB: What is this sentence? This is the* Sunday Times, *for God's sake!*)

In retrospect, of course, Tulo's forgiveness of Enoch proved to be a decision that saved our bacon. But Tulo could not have known this at the time. Is this another example of the all-seeing wisdom of the Great Chief Tuloko? It is just for me to report the facts.

We marched from our base on the outskirts of the main Zimindo township fully thirty miles across the dust bowl that now scars this central area of Zambawi. In years gone by this was fertile land that supported numerous Zamba villages. But decades of over-farming, necessitated by the appropriation of great chunks of land by the *musungu* commercial farmers, have left it as little better than a desert, dotted with sparse baobab trees that point accusing fingers from the sand and criss-crossed by dry rivers like the arteries of a dead man.

Our band was hungry and tired (for our food stores had been destroyed in an aerial attack), but not dispirited. At the head of the men marched Musa, the *zakulu*. Though he walked with an easy loping stride, Tulo struggled to keep pace with him. Some of the men sang songs remembered from the independence war and taught them to the younger Gangers, adjusting the words to the new situation.

'We march with the wind at our backs
    And the Great Chief in step at our side.
The ancestors sing us to glory,
    The eunuch has nowhere to hide!'

I noticed that Enoch Adini walked at the back of the Gang alongside Rujeko Tula, whose face was battered and bloody and footstep faltering. Within ten miles Rujeko could walk no further and Enoch carried her in his arms for the rest of the way (a supreme effort of strength and will!). None of the other Gangers offered to share the burden. But Enoch did not complain.

We reached Maponda township in mid-afternoon to find most of the disparate Black Boot Gang companies already there. A tiny hamlet of maybe four or five buildings (a general store, a butchery and two *shabeens*) either side of the dirt track that eventually meets the Queenstown tarmac road, Maponda was jam-packed with Gangers. The army was now some 3,000 strong and they greeted our arrival with expectant faces, crowding around us to catch a glimpse of Tulo, hanging on our every word with hushed respect for the stories of the Great Chief Tuloko. Tulo, however, disappeared into a *shabeen* with Musa, the *zakulu*, and armed guards were posted at the door. Many of the men were disappointed.

At around 5 p.m. Tulo appeared on the roof of the *shabeen* and the Gangers were called to hear him speak. Some of them remarked on how small Tulo looked and others who had worked in *musungu* households said he looked like 'Madam's youngest'. One man said, 'We must be crazy to follow this boy!' Another retorted, 'Look how pink his face is! *He* must be crazy to be out in the sun with skin like that.' But when Tulo began to speak, everyone was silent apart from the troop of baboons that frolicked in the nearby trees.

Addressing the Gangers in English, Tulo spoke with his head bowed and his voice was low and racing, so that some people said that he must be very nervous and others that he must be very wise. But nobody could hear what he was saying. This did not matter, however, because few of the Gangers spoke English anyway and, in each pause in Tulo's speech, the *zakulu* who stood next to him translated his words with a booming voice and vigorous gestures. It was a worthy speech full of justice and democracy and the Gangers seemed satisfied enough. But it was hardly the magical language of the ancestors.

JIM

I guess you've all heard by now that I'm to be your leader. I've been appointed by the Great Chief Tuloko to lead you on the final push into Queenstown. I know that some of you must find that hard to believe. Well, if it's any consolation, I have trouble believing it myself. All I can say is that I'll do the job as well as I can.

To be honest, I'm not really used to speaking in public. So I'm kind of glad that none of you can hear what I'm saying. I wish that Tuloko would speak through me again like he did the other night (if that is what happened, I'm not even sure myself). But I suppose that's not really my call. Mine is not to reason why and all that . . .

God alone – or Tuloko, rather – knows what we'll do when we get to Queenstown. But I would ask that if we're going to have a coup, it be a peaceful one. I mean, it's been weird for me, but in the last couple of months I've seen more violence than in the whole of the rest of my nineteen years. I think I'm just about getting used to it now. But I'm not sure I want to.

Oh yeah. Another thing. I suppose a lot of you must quite resent the idea that a *musungu* should be your leader. Well, it's weird for me too. But it seems like what the Great Chief Tuloko says goes. As you all know, I had a brush with him a few days ago and he didn't seem like the kind of guy to pick a fight with. Anyway, the point is that, although you might not like me being the chief or whatever, I hope you'll follow my orders. Because it seems to me that if we're going to get this coup right, someone's got to be in charge. And I suppose Tuloko's thinking is that it's better me than no one.

Still. That's about it, really. Do I have to keep talking, Musa? OK.

Well. I'll tell you something interesting. When I told my grandmother that I was coming to Zambawi, she said it would make a man of me (this was before she died, of course, and I saw her riding a black bull with all the other dead people; but that's another story). I tell you this because . . . well . . . now I'm the leader of the Black Boot Gang and that has to make me a man, doesn't it? It's strange, though. Because I don't feel like a man.

MR MURUFU

Have you heard, Innocence? Mr Tulloh is leading the Black Boot Gang to Queenstown! And still you say he made you perform *gulu gulu*? As the ancestors say, 'You cannot judge a chief by the size of his mouth any more than you judge a chicken by the size of its brain.'

All right, girls, this is the story, and forgive me if I piss myself laughing. The Gangers are holed up in Maponda township and they don't have a fucking clue that we're here. There's about ten sentries in a circle around the central buildings and what have they got? A few rusty AKs! Fuck knows what kind of nick they're in, but I wouldn't be surprised to see them blow up in the poor niggers' faces.

So this is what we do; a straightforward night attack, a shake and bake by the numbers. Capper, you take the aerial. Fly the Hueys in low and hit them with the Snebs. Trust me, when those babies blow, the Gangers will be running around like a bunch of headless niggers. After that, we just march in and mop up the mess.

Briggsy, you take the buildings with the Jimpies (I tell you what, you might want to take a couple of M79s with you 'n'all) and the rest of us will follow in behind. No point taking hostages, so if they run we don't go after them. But otherwise, ladies? It's all the fun of the fair. Last girl out buys the drinks.

EXTRACT FROM EDDY KOTTO'S NOTEBOOK
For a proposed feature for the Sunday Times, *London. On spec?*

Interview with 'Tulo'?

- What exactly happened that night with the Great Chief Tuloko?
- What qualifies you to lead the Black Boot Gang?
- What ambitions did you have as a child? (*Waste of time: get to the point!*)
- Assuming Adini puts up no resistance, what are we actually going to do when we get to Queenstown?
- Who will be the next President? You? A *musungu*? A nineteen-year-old white kid?!? (*Don't piss him off, though! (1) You need to get the interview, Eddy. (2) He might put a curse on you.*)

- Are you going to call democratic elections?
- Is it possible to create a sense of 'national identity' in Africa that is not founded in totalitarianism?
- What are you going to do about the land issue? Would you expropriate the *musungu* land?
- Are we looking at a South African 'rainbow nation' model?
- Why has the 'wind of change' blown us here?

What are you going to do? What are we doing this for? Why? Why? Why?

GECKO

Anybodygottamirror? Anybodygottamirror? Can you see it in the mirror? Can you see it in the mirror? Little Gecko climbs the mirror with sticky feet. Sticky feet.

You can spoil me, but I won't fall down for long. Geckos climb the mirror and you can see the underside, but they still keep climbing. Keep climbing.

EXTRACT FROM EDDY KOTTO'S NOTEBOOK
For a proposed feature for the Sunday Times, *London. On spec?*

When night fell on Maponda township, none of us Gangers was in the mood to go to sleep, so the *shabeen* stayed open into the early hours and we drank millet beer and listened to the dirty jokes of the rural farmers (the one about the Felati woman with the biggest pawpaw in the world springs to mind). The mood was high and soon everyone was singing traditional songs and bemoaning the lack of pretty girls. And yet the atmosphere was fateful too, as though we were standing on the doorstep of the future with no idea what lay inside. So we got drunk to dull the doubts and wallow in the carefree machismo that says, 'Everything's going to be fine.' There was a sense of fraternity, for sure. But we were brothers in uncertainty, drowning out our fears with ribald humour and truthless bragging.

In fact, I left the *shabeen* long before the night was done, unable to bear the weight of what was to come, which sat heavily upon my shoulders. I looked to the sky and found that Zamba's tears were nowhere to be seen and Cousin Moon himself was hiding behind the clouds that are his breath. My heart turned to ice, as though our gods had deserted us, consigned us to our fate. I returned to my corner of the Maponda store, where I had laid out my sleeping mat, and I tried to put these thoughts to the back of my mind as I wrote out questions for a hoped-for interview with Tulo by the light of a candle stub. Then I slipped into a fitful sleep for maybe two hours.

In retrospect I think it would be best to compare the atmosphere in Maponda township that night to that of an army on the eve of battle. But, although armed, we were no army in the usual sense (a ragtag collection of apathetic soldiers and under-trained civilians, we were united less by shared purpose than shared discontent and the spell of our own King Arthur). Certainly none of us realized that the door of the future opened on to blood and death.

ENOCH

The first time I saw you, you were talking to your father on the stairs of the presidential residence. Do you remember? I thought you were his wife and I loved the way you dismissed him with a glance. I said to myself, 'Even the Butcher of Ikbo is under the thumb of a tough woman.' You caught my eye across the room and if I were an artist, I'd be able to paint your face at that moment, so deeply is your expression burned on my mind. Since then I've often wondered what was in your head. Your proud manner oozed contempt. But I like to think that it was the kind of contempt you can't help but show someone who interests you.

That was only a few weeks ago, but it feels like a lifetime away.

We talked in the gardens. Was it always your plan to lure me outside for the kidnapping?

You told me about Chesterman cigarettes. You were an idealist. I'd never associated idealism with beauty before; I'd always assumed it was a position that someone adopted in place of fine features or a personality, a bitter sense of general injustice born of personal experience. But you? Your skin shone with the light of the moon and your scent mingled with the flowers as if they were on your side, determined to suck me in.

I know what you're thinking. But I'm not explaining myself properly, because it wasn't just your looks.

What I'm saying is that your ideals . . . no! . . . your *self* burst through your features and gave you a beauty I've never seen before: the proud tilt of your chin, the dignity of your neck, the woman in your walk, the passion of your eyes, the tenderness of your lips – it's all still there, Rujeko Tula. I wish I could express myself better. But I was expelled from school. I wish I had a mirror so you could see for yourself.

I thought that . . . I know that you don't want to hear this now, but I have to tell you . . . I thought that we would get together then. Ha! And I knew that we would when you pulled a gun on me!

Don't look at me like that! My father looks at me like that. Like I'm some kind of surprise package, a disappointing birthday present or something.

You say you are spoiled. But we're all spoiled at some level. Often it's the spoiling that makes us who we are. So what if Mandela's baby is growing in your stomach? If it happens, I will take the child as my own.

But you have to be strong now. I know that your ideals have been fucked out of you . . . I'm sorry . . .

I know that your idealism is gone. But that's O K. One day soon all this shit will be over and we'll find ourselves in a new place and we'll have to deal with it. But I need you and you need me. Come on, smile for me. The two presidential offspring together. Our fathers will be pleased. If they're still alive.

Judging by the pitch darkness, it must have been around 4 a.m. when the township was woken by the beating of wings. Groggily we came to into that half-state of the unnaturally disturbed drunkard's sleep. And the sound was getting ever louder, as if we were being invaded by a squadron of giant bats. The Gangers who shared my room in the store and me looked at one another quizzically. Some men were terrified and others nauseous. Suddenly, above the cacophony, came another sound, a high-pitched whine, as though the bats had been joined by a similarly disproportioned mosquito. The sound came ever faster and closer and then, for a moment, it stopped. A youngster was being violently sick in one corner of the room. A huge man with arms that bulged like maize sacks shut his eyes and held his hands over his ears, mouthing silent prayers. There was an explosion and a flash of light and an instant of intense heat followed by an eerie sucking noise that felt like it might tug our eyeballs from their sockets. That was it. We ran outside and found that the *shabeen* where Tulo had spoken was no longer there. In its place was a dump of blazing rubble that illuminated the night sky and gave us our first glimpse of the helicopters. There must have been some 100 men in the *shabeen*. But there was no sign of a single corpse, let alone a survivor.

I found that I could now hear screaming. I'm sure that these terrified sounds had been tearing the night for some moments, but it was as if my soul were able to deal with the horror only one sense at a time.

From every building, men streamed forth, and from the make-shift shelters that had been erected around the township too. We stared at one another with fixed eyes and we grasped our guns to our chests. As if they were any kind of protection! I felt a gust at my back and turned to see the shadow of a copter barely ten yards away, hovering just above the ground. One Ganger let off a few rounds in its general direction. Others tried to stop him because they feared he might anger the beast!

Instinctively I threw myself back through the door of the general store just as the RAT-TAT-TAT of the copter's machine-gun kicked in. I cowered under a table with my head buried in my arms and I wet myself in abject fear. RAT-TAT-TAT! RAT-TAT-TAT! RAT-TAT-TAT!

Machine-guns, I discovered, are not as loud as you might think. The sound is precise, almost clinical, and chilling.

The gunfire faded as the beasts lifted and turned for another pass and I exited my hidey-hole, so scared of death that I wanted to die. This time I could see bodies. Hundreds of dead littered the street: blown to bits, unnaturally contorted, frozen in death with their eyes wide open and their cheeks clenched. I found the youngster who had vomited moments earlier. I recognized him by the sick on his shirt. He must have been hit ten times in the head and, where his face had been, there was nothing but a mash of gore, like offal or mince.

I remember being surprised, even in my dazed state, by the lack of wounded. There was no agonized groaning, no reaching limbs or desperate clinging to life. They were all dead. Maybe half the Black Boot Gang had been wiped out in under three minutes. There was an all-consuming ridiculousness about it that only the hopelessly macabre can ever muster.

For the survivors the next . . . (*How long? Who cares? Time is irrelevant in death.*)

For the survivors there followed a bizarre and horrifying series of gambles. The copters held their position above the carnage – almost mocking, arrogant – and engaged us in a terrible game of tag. We would dive into a building only to hear the whine of a missile that would kill us on impact. We would flee for the open spaces only to be outrun and cut down by speeding bullets. How did I survive? Someone had to tell the story. That is what the ancestors tell me in my prayers.

I saw Tulo kneeling in the dust, his pink features charred and blackened. I ran to him shouting, 'What do we do? What do we do?' As if the poor kid had a clue! Tulo seemed stuck to his spot. His eyes were unblinking and there was no sign of life bar the tremor of his lips. Musa, the *zakulu*, appeared from nowhere at his side (*Literally 'from nowhere'. Make that clear*) and swept up the *musungu* over one shoulder as if he were as light as a sack of grain. He ran down the road towards the end of the township and then I realized that all the surviving Gangers were doing the same, desperate to flee the rubble for the darkness of the surrounding country. The copters had vanished. But there was no thought of regrouping, no orders to be given, nothing else for it but to run away from this slaughter. I began to run too.

Only when we reached the outskirts of the township – some 500 men – did we see our mistake. Ahead of us, approaching from the pitch night, was a line of *musungu* armed with huge guns they could barely lift. Who the hell were they? Surely even Adini would not have gone to mercenaries!

We Gangers stopped in our tracks. Some of us screamed with terror; others froze as if for a photograph. Some of us turned and ran the other way, others sank to the ground as if pre-empting the bullet. And they shot us where we stood with the bored efficiency of a secretary typing a letter. I looked for Tulo and the *zakulu*, but they were nowhere to be seen.

MUSA

Oh, Cousin Moon that knows my past and my future, do not leave me when I need you most. Only the *gudo* deserts his children and every creature despises him for it. Even the lazy *buju* flower that sleeps through morning will offer its seeds when Father Sun is high because she knows that her eternity depends on her sons and daughters. So envelop us, my ancestor, in your darkest shadow and light our escape route with the pale shine of your face.

And, Cousin Moon, you must wake Father Sun! How can you be afraid to disturb him? Even when you were cast into the Great Lake in the West That Cooled the Traveller's Feet, he could not destroy you because you are as a child to a full breast. So do not fear his bad temper now, when his anger will be ten times as great when he rises in the morning to a scene of such murder. The *musungu* needs the Great Chief Tuloko! Mr Tulloh needs the Chief's balls between his legs, his wit between his ears and his courage between his teeth! Oh, Cousin Moon! Why do you not answer me?

JIM

Incensed. Undeterred. Instinctive. Underdog. Inspirational. Unleashed. Ineluctable. Unearthly. Insurgent. Unbeatable.
Thank you.

EXTRACT FROM EDDY KOTTO'S NOTEBOOK
For a proposed feature for the Sunday Times, *London. On spec?*

Suddenly, amid the commotion and carnage, I saw one *musungu* soldier collapse into the dust. The *musungu* on either side of him looked at one another in surprise before they too fell, dropped by bullets from unseen guns. Frantically those of us who were still alive looked around for the source of this fightback and, from behind the debris of the butchery, the two presidential offspring appeared with AK47s to their shoulders.

Now the *musungu* had seen them too and they turned their attention upon them, spraying bullets in their direction like wedding guests throwing confetti. (*Strange simile. But appropriate?*) But Enoch Adini and Rujeko Tula did not attempt to take cover. They continued to march forward, their backs upright and their faces blazing with mutual courage and purpose as their guns spat flames. Enoch was unrecognizable as the loafing young man who used to hang out in the Barrel (*Explain: Queenstown bar*) and Rujeko looked every inch the Amazon, her mouth twisted with the kind of feminine scorn that undermines a man in the bedroom.

At the sight of such fearlessness the Gangers found new heart and those who had held on to their guns began to return the *musungu* fire. For a moment or two the *musungu* were on the back foot and many of us had time to crouch down behind the piles of rubble and retrieve weapons from our fallen comrades. Rujeko and Enoch joined us too and they were shouting and chivvying us to fight like the warriors of old. I can't remember what they said, but I remember the look of them. When the rest of us were gaunt with fear, their cheeks were fat with anger and their teeth gritted as if struggling to contain the venom that rose in their throats.

The *musungu* did not falter for long, though. They dropped back into the night and formed a new line behind rocks and in ditches, hidden by the darkness and the contours of the terrain. The gunfire began to subside into sporadic bursts as the two sides locked in a stand-off and, for the first time since the attack began, we had time to consider what we were going to do. We knew that the stand-off would be short-lived, for the *musungu* began to lob grenades in our direction with closing accuracy, and we feared the return of the copters. Enoch said that we had to try to outflank them because we could be sure that they were already doing the same to us and soon we would be surrounded. The Gangers were keen to follow him, but they looked to General Dubchek for confirmation. Dubchek squatted behind an isolated wall and handled his gun nervously. His face was washed with confusion and fear. At first I thought he was scared to die (as we all were), but it was soon clear that he was scared of the responsibility of such a decision.

One minute. Two minutes. Maybe three minutes were lost as Dubchek shook his head ponderously from side to side and Enoch trembled with agitation. Then the *musungu* gunfire receded completely, there was a moment of silence and we knew what it meant and we weren't surprised to hear the strange beat of the bats' wings approaching from a distance. We Gangers looked at one another with crazy, frantic eyes.

Impending death, however, forced Dubchek's hand. He may have been no leader, but he was, I realized, every inch a soldier. Dubchek stood up behind his wall, his face fixed in grim resignation, and he adjusted his strange hat with the corks that hung from the brim like a businessman adjusts his tie before entering an important meeting.

With his gun at his hip and an extraordinary high-pitched giggle on his lips, he ran from cover into the no man's land between the two sides, firing wildly into the *musungu* lines. We saw two, maybe three, white faces thrown towards the sky in the last ambition of death. And then the *musungu* guns cut loose, slowing Dubchek's advance, shredding his body as he stumbled forward. His torso whiplashed as a bullet bit his chest. But still he kept moving and firing. His legs buckled beneath him as the flesh of his thighs was peppered with lead. But he crawled on and kept firing. He can't have been more than ten yards from the *musungu* when he was finally repelled by a bullet in the forehead. And he lay on his back and tried to locate the welcoming face of Cousin Moon.

DUBCHEK

I am a coward. I fear responsibility and decisions and change. But I'm not scared to fight and die. So keep your eyes open, Isaiah! Keep your eyes open so that the ancestors know you are ready!

EXTRACT FROM EDDY KOTTO'S NOTEBOOK
For a proposed feature for the Sunday Times, *London. On spec?*

We had no time to mourn Dubchek's death.

As soon as he sank to the ground, a groan caught in our throats as sighting bullets began to spit in the dust just behind us. The copters were settling into their range. We were surrounded. All was lost. But at the precise moment that we Gangers knew we were going to die, so we saw our redemption. Ahead of us, in the distance, we heard the echoless sounds of gunfire, maybe some 400 yards from our position. At first we assumed that they were picking off any last Gangers who had escaped from the township. But then we saw Tulo, brandishing a *musungu* gun (clearly lifted from a victim) and standing exactly where the *musungu* had established their line. Next to him the *zakulu* swung another powerful machine-gun from side to side, laying down a veil of covering fire. For the first time we could see the backs of the *musungu* soldiers as they scattered into the night. Tulo punched the air in exhilaration and signalled to us to make our escape. We sprinted across the no man's land and, although the copters caught up with the stragglers, most of us escaped into the darkness and only stopped running when the air was quiet and our legs had turned to jelly.

In the aftermath of the battle of Maponda, some of the Ganger survivors have told how impressive Tulo looked as he saved us from certain death. Others have even claimed that Tulo assumed the form of the Great Chief Tuloko and the mercenaries fled in terror from a god. As an eyewitness, however, I can confirm that neither of these images has any foundation in truth. As I remember it, Tulo looked more like a terrified young man who handled the gun as uneasily as a peasant handles a pencil. In Zambawi, these days, any observation that undermines the myth of Tulo is regarded as near-blasphemy. But, for me, the fear that I saw in James Tulloh's eyes and his panicked gesticulations of pure adrenalin make his return to save the remnants of his army seem all the more heroic.

THE POET

    – Fruits then to your lips; haste to repay
    The debt of birth. Yield man-tides like the sea
    And ebbing, leave a meaning on the fossiled sands.

Only when morning broke did we see the full extent of the devastation. As the dawn sun painted the sparse landscape with its golden light, we gathered in the oxbow lake of a dry river and we looked at each other in disbelief. Some of the Gangers were hideously wounded, their guts spilling through their shirts, their skulls holed and festering. But they died only when Father Sun awoke and reminded them of their mortality.

As for the rest of us, though uninjured, we couldn't speak. Because there were no words to be spoken. Even the former State Army soldiers were struck dumb with the horror of it all and one of their number could not stop weeping. Eventually he was silent and we assumed that he had cried himself to sleep. In fact, he had cried himself to death.

In the space of half an hour this *musungu* force had depleted our numbers by ninety per cent. The Black Boot Gang? It seemed like a sick joke. Whereas yesterday we were a 3,000-strong army buoyed by the courage born of knowing we would never fight, we were now no more than 300. More than 2,500 dead! Just 300 survivors! No. Not even survivors. We were merely the fossiled shells where men once lived, human flotsam washed across the sands by the pitiless tide of war.

Only the four heroes – Tulo, Enoch, Rujeko and Musa – seemed capable of speech. And though we Gangers loved them for their courage, we hated them for their plans.

Enoch wanted immediate retribution. 'There can't be more than 200 of them left!' he said. 'Attack now and we have surprise! They think we're beaten!'

If I'd had the heart to speak, I would have said, 'We *are* beaten!' But there was no fight left in me. And certainly no words.

I don't know how long we sat in that dry lake after sun-up. But it must have been a good hour that we dressed each other's wounds, sipped on our depleted water flasks and opened the eyes of the dead. We were there long enough for the vultures to begin circling and Rujeko shot them down with her gun. Tulo harangued her.

'You'll let the *musungu* know where we are!' he said.

'They already know,' she replied flatly and my blood ran cold.

It was about then that we first heard the distant splutters of an approaching vehicle. Our immediate thought was that it must be the *musungu* in jeeps or tanks or armoured cars. But there was definitely only one vehicle and its choking engine marked it out as Zambawian. Gradually those of us who could stand began to get to our feet and we watched as an ancient bus bore down on us from the horizon, crossing the dust bowl with plumes of sand circling in its wake.

(*NOTE TO SELF: Don't forget to mention the light of Zambawi mornings: unreal/fantastical. 'As if easing you into the day from the miasma of your nightmares.' GOOD!*)

It took ten minutes or so for the bus to reach us from the horizon and we were transfixed by its slow progress. As it got closer, I realized it was one of those rickety affairs that you see at Mbave Bus Station and Tulo clearly recognized it because he said: 'Number 17!' And all of we Gangers looked at him in bewilderment.

When the bus finally arrived in our midst and pulled to a halt on the bank of the dry lake, we gathered around it in curious incomprehension. At first it seemed to bring no one but the driver, a well-dressed man in a two-piece suit whose hair was in tufts that showed he had been sweating for hours. He jumped out of the driver's seat and his eyes circled our little group (what must we have looked like?).

'Are you the Black Boot Gang?' he asked. And someone laughed wryly. But this only seemed to give him confidence.

'They killed my son!'

He said this with such emphasis on the injustice and horror of the fact that I could have put a bullet in him there and then. Couldn't he see what had happened? Couldn't he look into the dead men's eyes? But I still had no heart to lift a gun and, besides, his passenger appeared beside him and all our attention immediately switched to him.

'I am a poet,' the passenger said quietly and no one knew what to say to that. Though we couldn't speak anyway.

Being a journalist, I should have spotted General Indigo Bulimi, Adini's lackey, immediately (for that's who it was). In fact, I had even pumped him for quotes a number of times before: about the threat of the Black Boot Gang and their long-defunct political wing, the People's Democratic Republic of Zambawi Party (it was too much of a mouthful anyway). But the combination of my distressed state, the general's bizarre appearance and his even more bizarre introduction threw me off the scent and I recognized him only when he greeted Enoch like a long-lost son and they shared an incomprehensible Latin joke (presumably at the expense of Adini).

Of course, none of the other Gangers recognized Bulimi, but they, like me, were quite transfixed by his presence. He was a tall man, which helped the authority he exuded. And his features were even and handsome and, above all, ageless, which gave him a serene, spiritual air, as if he were a patient on the mend from a supposedly terminal illness. But it was neither his height nor his looks that really impressed. The Poet was utterly calm and his face was set with the charismatic certainty of a man on a mission. And when he spoke . . .

(*GET THIS RIGHT! GET THIS RIGHT! GET THIS RIGHT!*)

THE POET

'*Indiligens cum pigra familia*' – Plautus!

ENOCH

You want Plautus? '*Tandem impetraui ut egomet me corrumperem*!'

LAMBO

All right, ladies. Well, we got most of them. But that was still an absolute fucking disaster. How many funerals are we looking at? Twenty? Fuck! Who let that white kid break our line? I swear I know him from somewhere. Capper? Where's Capper? You're shitting me! Twenty-one it is, then. I am not impressed.

The way I see it, we've got two choices: we've done our job and we jet, or, just as a matter of professional pride, we finish the bastards off. And I know what I want to do.

But no risks this time. This time we do it all from the Jimpies. So Briggsy, you saddle 'em up and the rest of us will swill it. Watches for twelve noon. The bastards won't run far in that heat.

And one of you big girls tell me what that lot are doing up on the hill? What lot? *That* lot! The cows, for fuck's sake!

THE POET

So this is the Black Boot Gang, the army that strikes fear into the heart of the President! That terrifies the *musungu* with morals as bankrupt as the state! That threatens to destabilize our nation! That offers empty slogans in the place of integrity! That summons the Great Chief Tuloko with the cheek of a boy calling a dog! That promises much and delivers nothing!

Africa for the Africans! Oh, of course! And all that other bullshit besides.

Tell me, someone. What are you really fighting for? Ha! I see your faces are as blank as the pages of my manuscripts.

So come and listen to me, my friends, and I will tell you a story that you want to hear. For I am a poet and, though I no longer write poetry, I know a lot about words. And though I am no soldier, I know a great deal about war. And this is a story that is as old as language itself (for it was told to me in the womb by the Great Chief Tuloko) and it reminds you of the truth that you can find in your hearts. So gather round, my friends, gather round –

you too, *musungu*; you can hear the spirit if not the meaning! – and listen to the story of Great Chief Tuloko and the rogue *shumba*.

Many years ago, when the Great Chief Tuloko was still a young man (before he married the beautiful Mudiwa), a great trouble came to his village. It started one night in the rainy season, when the wind howled like a spirit, rivers fell from the sky and Cousin Moon offered no comforting light. The villagers huddled together in their houses, fearful that they must have offended the ancestors. Perhaps this is how you feel now? How easy it is to break the bravado of the Black Boot Gang!

In the morning, when Father Sun rose and made the mud smoke like a fire, a terrible discovery was made. One of the *chinjuku* girls' houses was destroyed and all the children were gone. At first the villagers thought that the spirit of the wind had carried them away. But, in the rubble where the house once stood, the Great Chief Tuloko found a *shumba*'s claw the length of a hunting knife. 'There is a rogue *shumba* on the prowl,' he said.

The Great Chief Tuloko addressed the men of the village just like he addressed you through the person of the *musungu*. (I see surprise on your faces. But yes, I have heard about that.)

'My brothers,' he said, 'we must hunt this *shumba* down before he kills any more of our families. We do not know who will be next. But every *shumba* returns to the scene of its last kill. Who will come with me?'

But the men of the village were afraid. 'Tuloko,' they said, 'father Sun appointed you chief of our people and he protects you. So you must protect us.' And they refused to join the hunt.

That night the air was still and silent and Cousin Moon shone down and the fearful villagers huddled together in the dark corners of their houses. They stayed awake all night and nothing could be heard but the echoing snores of the Great Chief Tuloko. And yet, when Father Sun rose in the morning, another villager had been seized by the terrible rogue *shumba*, a widow called N'tendu.

Again the Great Chief Tuloko appealed to the men of the village to join him on the hunt. Again they refused. 'Tuloko,' they said, 'you are protected by Father Sun, but who will protect us?' But the men were hiding their cowardice behind their words.

(Ha! You Gangers are silent! Does that mean you are ready to be brave? We will find out when the story is ended.)

A small boy of *temba* age came forward. His name was N'kimwi. He was the widow's son.

'Great Chief Tuloko,' N'kimwi said, 'five winters ago my father was taken by disease. Now my mother is gone too. There is nothing left for me in this village. Allow me to accompany you on this hunt, for I am entitled to vengeance.'

The Great Chief Tuloko looked at the small boy and admired the courage that fired his eyes and the pride that straightened his spine. 'Your heart beats well, N'kimwi,' Tuloko said. 'Stronger than that of any man in this village. But I cannot take you on this hunt, for you are just a small boy and the last of your line. Think how angry your ancestors would be if you too were killed! No! I must hunt alone.'

When Father Sun drew himself up to his full height, the Great Chief Tuloko took up his spear and his hunting knife and packed himself a small knapsack of mealy biscuits and fruit. 'I will kill the *shumba*,' Tuloko said, 'or I will die in the attempt!' And he marched into the bush in search of the rogue *shumba*. The sun was unbearably hot, but Tuloko, the Great Chief, the Traveller, was accustomed to such hardship.

All day Tuloko marched, following the *shumba*'s trail. He hoped to catch the *shumba* sleeping off the widow in the heat of the afternoon sun. But the trail wound on until even Tuloko, even the Traveller, found himself in unfamiliar country. Indeed, the Great Chief Tuloko was about to return home, for the shadows were biting his ankles, when he heard the *shumba*'s roar. Ahead of him on the path he saw the rogue *shumba*, as tall as a house, as wide as this bus, with a mane that was as silver as a waterfall at dawn. The air was heavy with the smell of death.

The Great Chief Tuloko stopped still and drew his hunting knife. But already the terrible beast was charging towards him. 'Father Sun!' Tuloko cried. 'Grant me the strength of the light!'

But Father Sun had reached the doorstep of the West and could not hear him. 'Cousin Moon!' Tuloko cried. 'Grant me the cunning of the night!' But Cousin Moon was not yet risen in the sky.

Before he knew it the *shumba* was upon him. The Great Chief Tuloko threw his spear, but it bounced from the *shumba*'s muscular flank. He thrust his hunting knife towards the *shumba*'s face, but the beast struck down with a paw, like a gun ship picking off a Ganger. In seconds the rogue *shumba* had pinned the Great Chief to the ground and its claws cut five long gashes across his chest. Tuloko could smell the scent of the *chinjuku* girls on its breath and he could taste the blood of the widow on the saliva that dripped on to his face from the *shumba*'s mouth. 'Oh, my people,' the Great Chief Tuloko cried, 'have you deserted me?' And he prepared himself for death.

Suddenly another voice cut through the murky light like the striking of a match. 'Stop!' There, at no further distance than a small boy could piss, stood the widow's child, N'kimwi. 'Stop!' he said again.

For a second the *shumba* paused and turned his attention to this intruder to his kill. The *shumba* showed N'kimwi its teeth. It showed N'kimwi the confident wag of its tail and the evil terror of its eyes. But N'kimwi did not run away.

'You do not scare me, *shumba*!' N'kimwi said. 'For you are nothing but a foolish animal. You have taken my mother, but you do not scare me. You have captured the Great Chief Tuloko, but you do not scare me. For you have no honour. Your ancestors do not protect you, for you cannot pray to them. Your family do not respect you, for you can tell them nothing of your fighting and your conquests. Your descendants will never sing praise-songs to the glory of your courage. Your blood is as thin as the water of a *shamva* river, your life as joyless as a stagnant pond, your existence as meaningless as a shallow puddle that vanishes in the morning sun. You do not scare me, *shumba*, for one day you will die and nobody will mourn. Your corpse will be eaten by the jackals, but they will leave your heart because it is blackened stone. Your eyes will be pecked out by vultures, but they will leave your heart because it is blackened stone. The maggots will strip your bones, but they will leave your heart because it is blackened stone. Even the smallest of the creatures of Father Sun will find no sustenance in your heart and it will be the only monument to your life until the summer winds blow and cover it in dust. Then you will be nothing.'

When the *shumba* heard this, it let out a roar so terrifying that it could be heard by the fearful villagers a full day's walk away. The villagers looked at one another and said, 'What can this mean?' But N'kimwi wasn't scared. And as the *shumba* roared, the Great Chief Tuloko saw his chance. Taking up his hunting knife, he plunged it deep into the *shumba*'s neck and, before the *shumba* fell dead in the dust, the roar was strangled in its throat. And, for just one instant, it sounded like a screaming child.

So, my brave Gangers! What do you think of that? Let me ask you: are your hearts as blackened stone like that of the *shumba* (or the *musungu* mercenaries)? Are they as shrivelled and cowardly as those of the men of Tuloko's village? Or do your hearts beat with the integrity of the *temba* boy? Perhaps you expect the Great Chief to flash down in the body of the *musungu* and win your battle for you. Yes? Then prepare to die like the lame bushbucks that you are!

We must fight, my friends! We have to fight!

I once knew a young man who believed that truth was found in freedom; freedom at all costs. And he put this truth above all others until he forgot who he was and he forgot what freedom was too. I once knew a young man who believed that truth was found in language. And he hid behind his words until they no longer held meaning and no longer held truth. I once knew a young woman who taught me that truth is neither one thing nor the other. It is a special kind of gift that you must find in yourself.

So tell me, my friends! Are you prepared to fight for the truth of who you are? We must fight the *musungu*! Not their colour or their politics or the feeble President they represent and his neo-colonial tastes. Not for the land or for justice or the neo-Western concept of democracy. No! We fight for who we are! We fight for our hearts!

My friends, I call you for your own sakes! We fight as men, as Zambawians, as children of the Great Chief Tuloko! We fight for our truth!

EXTRACT FROM EDDY KOTTO'S NOTEBOOK
For a proposed feature for the Sunday Times, London. *On spec?*

The sun had been up for maybe two hours when we moved out and the light added to the sense of unreality, of destiny even, with which we marched. Its magical golden wash seemed to ease us into the day from the miasma of our nightmares. The Poet led us with our four heroes at his side (though Tulo struggled to keep up) and within half an hour we were on a ridge overlooking the *musungu* camp. None of us had realized that we'd been so close!

In the camp some men were eating while others busied themselves around the four copters, reloading missile racks and patching the fuel tanks that had been punctured by lucky bullets. In the daylight their armoury was awesome. But none of us was scared. The Poet's words had made this confrontation a moral necessity rather than a choice. And I would have preferred to die than lose the new sense of certainty that bolstered my will and made my bones feel like unbreakable steel.

We set upon the *musungu* with no great plan. We sprinted down the slope towards them, firing our guns as we ran and hollering at the tops our voices. No one moved faster than the Poet, who stretched his legs like a man who has been stuck in a wheelchair for more than a decade through a mistake of fate.

Initially the *musungu* were surprised and we killed many of their number in those first few seconds. But they soon gathered their thoughts and weapons and began to return our fire. I saw men fall either side of me, but still I survived for the sake of the Great Chief Tuloko, so that I could tell this story.

When we reached the camp, our weapons were discarded as we were embroiled in close-quarter combat. For all our new-found courage, we were no match for a bunch of highly trained mercenaries! And I saw my fellows have their throats slit and their necks broken as I clung desperately to a large, sweaty man, biting and pinching and grabbing and squeezing. Only the Poet seemed able to hold his own, driven by the cold fury of conviction.

Enoch too would have coped with the onslaught but for his desire to protect Gecko and sing an unfamiliar song at the top of his voice with a manic look in his eyes. As he battered the mercenaries, he bellowed out the words with savage intent that terrified his victims. But, every now and then, he would pause in each assault as if he had forgotten the lyrics and give the mercenaries a chance to pull their knives and swing their fists.

(*NOTE TO SELF: 'We're leaving together. But still it's farewell. And maybe we'll come back to earth, who can tell?' The rest? Research needed. English traditional perhaps?*)

In fact, Gecko needed far less protection than most others, scratching with her sharp nails and taking on all-comers with her flailing elbows and knees. At one point she was confronted by a terrifying square figure that clearly belonged to the *musungu* leader. But she spat in his face and kneed him viciously in the groin with the expertise and pleasure of someone who'd done such a manoeuvre before.

That we Gangers eventually triumphed goes without saying (for surely, had we lost, I would not have lived to tell the tale). But the way in which we won is more difficult to explain. Suffice it to say that we would certainly have been beaten without the intervention of the herd of black bulls that stampeded into the camp in the first minutes of the fight.

Survivors have claimed that the bulls were sent by the Great Chief Tuloko or called by Musa, the *zakulu*. I know nothing of that. Similarly they say that the animals homed in on the *musungu* for their trampling and goring. But I think that these English mercenaries, naive in the field of animal behaviour, simply didn't treat the approaching stampede with the respect it merited. Though I must admit that I prayed thanks to Tuloko when my assailant was impaled on a butting horn.

As the adrenalin began to subside in my body and my new

courage began to wane in the face of such trauma and immense fatigue, I remember little of the closing moments of the battle of Maponda. I do, however, remember the *musungu* leader pressing a knife to the Poet's throat and then seeing Tulo put a precise bullet through his brain at some ten yards' distance.

'Rule Number Ten,' Tulo snarled, 'you do what you gotta do.'

I have no idea where this rule came from. Perhaps he learned it from the Great Chief Tuloko himself.

When Tulo said this, he looked just like a macho American film star. But then he collapsed trembling to the ground and had to be comforted by the thankful Poet and Musa, the *zakulu*.

Tulo was, I remembered, just a boy.

35 : The greatest good

By the time the Black Boot Gang reached Queenstown, almost a week later, the efficiency of the Pass It On ensured that the whole nation knew the myth of Jim Tulloh (sometimes referred to as 'Tulo', sometimes simply as 'the *musungu*'). They knew too of the powerful *zakulu* who had invoked the Great Chief Tuloko into Tulo's body and conjured a stampede of black bulls to trample the hated mercenaries. The *mboko* told stories to their grandchildren about the mysterious poet who had inspired the tired Gangers with the passion of his language. And the urban *shabeens* were full of discussions of the merits of Enoch. Some people protested, 'But he's an Adini!' But most agreed with the old Zamba proverb: 'You can never judge the fertility of *nzou* by the length of its trunk.' When one man said this, all the others would nod. Though none of them was quite sure what it meant.

Soon reports arrived in Queenstown that Enoch's girlfriend had been violated by a *shamva* spirit and his cheeks were permanently streaked with tears. This silenced any doubters for good because Zambawians in general (and Queenstownians in particular) are a romantic lot. So some said, 'He cries for lost innocence.' And others added, 'And he cries for the state of the nation.'

What's more, while the majority of the Black Boot Gang elected to march into Queenstown for the sake of solidarity, Eddy Kotto chose to catch a lift with Mr Mapondera aboard Number 17. In his first issue back at the *Herald*'s helm Eddy wrote an impassioned account of the battle of Maponda beneath the headline 'Living Legends' (a status conferred upon Jim, Musa, Indigo and Gecko).

Enoch, on the other hand, was granted a different moniker. He was the 'President-elect'.

Of course, there were dissenting voices, even among what was left of the *Herald*'s staff. But these quickly subsided. When the *mboko* complained that Enoch was 'just a boy', they were pooh-poohed by others who emphasized the 'need for fresh blood'. When revolutionary citizens protested about the 'importance of radical change', the commonsense thinkers reminded them, 'For goodness' sake! He has just masterminded a coup.' When the reactionaries fretted that 'change is dangerous', they were shouted down by loudmouths: 'He's Adini's son! How much continuity do you want?'

Enoch, unknown to himself, was therefore the compromise candidate and he was effectively installed as President before arriving in Queenstown by a vibrant surge of national unity. Surely this was the most democratic vote that Zambawi (perhaps even the world) had never held. Certainly it outdid the actual election that followed a month later, which was marred by corruption and rioting. Not because there was any argument about who should be President (Enoch, of course), but because, in Zambawi, corruption and rioting were vital elements of suffrage.

The remnants of the Black Boot Gang had heard that Queenstown was theirs for the taking before they entered the city. After much discussion, the four 'Living Legends' and the President-elect had concluded that they should send scouts ahead because they knew that their bruised company (wounded and dehydrated and riddled with *n'kuli* rash, a nasty bovine parasite) wasn't up to any more fighting, and the report came that Nutjob's patrol (which had been guarding Adini) had skulked out of the country some days previously. However, even the Black Boot Gang, who had long since learned to find a certain piquancy in anarchy, were surprised by the mayhem that greeted their arrival in Queenstown.

Of course, none of the Gangers expected to be met at the outskirts of the capital by a ticker-tape parade. But they did assume (what with the front cover of the *Herald* and the success of the Pass It On) that there would be some recognition of their famous victory at the battle of Maponda. Unfortunately they found Queenstown immersed in the tail-end of a three-day party that made the preceding political unrest seem as raucous as a candlelit dinner for two. Released from the constraints of the mercenaries' rigorously applied curfew, the Queenstownians had set about expressing their freedom in what was little more than a good-natured riot. Shopkeepers who had fought tooth and nail to protect their merchandise during the dark days of the Black Boot Anarchy now smashed their own windows and looted their own store rooms and distributed alcohol to the cheering masses. Rival gangs who had fought over guns from the state armoury now shot *boka* birds from their lamp-post perches and set fire to parked cars for makeshift *braais*. Even *gar* growers and prostitutes entered into the hedonistic spirit, handing out freebies to all and sundry in the hope of repeat business when the chaos died down. Indeed, some young Queenstownian men drank so much beer and ate so much barbecued *boka* bird and smoked so much weed and had so much sex that they never quite recovered. In the following months these young men could be spotted lying in Queenstown's gutters with bloodshot eyes and semi-smiles. They became known as *panzve kulaka*. Literally this translates as 'the lazy ploughs' (apparently something to do with their permanently horizontal state and seemingly permanent erections).

Consequently, when the Black Boot Gang marched into Queenstown down the wide thoroughfare of the Lelani road, with their chests bursting with the pride of their accomplishments, nobody took much notice. In other circumstances such a ragtag band of gun-wielding ruffians might have provoked some comment, but, by this stage in the party, young men with guns were two a penny and everybody – not just the Gangers – looked rather the worse for wear.

At one point the Gangers passed through Queenstown's red-light district and prostitutes of all shapes and sizes hung from their windows and wolf-whistled and cat-called.

'Who are you, boys?' called one middle-aged hooker with crooked teeth and blonde hair.

'We are the Black Boot Gang,' shouted a proud young Ganger.

'And what size boots do you wear?' the woman asked and she began to laugh helplessly until her wig slipped off her head and fell into the street.

Further on, Indigo approached a group of men who were grilling meat around a burning truck.

'I am Indigo the Poet,' he announced self-importantly.

The men looked at one another and their eyes were smiling.

'I am Job the Chef,' replied one. 'Do you want a leg or a wing?'

Eventually the Black Boot Gang reached Independence Square in the centre of Queenstown. Independence Square had been the hub of the three days of party-cum-riot and it looked so like a battlefield that many of the Gangers began to experience the first flashbacks of post-traumatic stress. The well-kept lawns were scorched and scarred, groaning bodies lined the paths, someone had decapitated the statue of President Adini and one of the mercenaries' Land Rovers was parked in one of the ornamental fountains that had never worked. The smell of *gar* smoke was heavy in the air and every now and then a man's voice rose up, wailing prayers to the Great Chief Tuloko for relief from his aching head and swearing never to touch another drop. For a moment or two, the Black Boot Gang stared at the carnage and at one another because they didn't know what to do.

It was Musa who had an idea and he climbed on to the mercenaries' Land Rover and picked out the microphone from the cabin that was attached to a loudhailer on the vehicle's roof.

'I am Musa, the *zakulu* of the Black Boot Gang,' he announced and agonizing feedback screamed across Independence Square, provoking a swell of angry groans.

'Shut up, Mr Zakulu!'

'Can't you see we're dying?'

'Who is this penis nose? Tell him I'm trying to sleep.'

'If you're a *zakulu*, give me something for my headache.'

Indigo climbed up next to Musa and took the microphone. 'Let me have a go,' he said. He aimed an AK47 high into the air and fired three or four shots until even the most determined hangovers were forced to sit up and take notice.

'I am Indigo Bulimi,' he proclaimed. 'I am the Poet of the Black Boot Gang and you shall listen to what I say because I tell you of the freedom that we bring you, of the truth that you will find in your hearts, and I speak words that were taught to me in the womb by the Great Chief Tuloko himself.'

As Indigo began to speak, so the casualties in Independence Square felt compelled to listen. His rich tone soothed headaches and stilled churning stomachs and his simple wisdom cleared lungs and vision. His speech reminded grown men of bedtime stories told by their mothers. It reminded mothers of their children's first words and prostitutes of pillow-talk from a time when they still believed in love. Long-time *gar* smokers felt the same rush of blood that they'd experienced with their first joint and boys heard Indigo's stories of the battle of Maponda and wished they'd been there to see such glory. And, as all fell quiet in rapt attention, so revellers throughout the surrounding streets heard the weighty silence and wondered what was going on and flocked into the square until there was standing room only.

Gradually, as Indigo spun his stories (of the leadership of Tulo, of the magic of Musa, of the heroism of Gecko and the President-elect), the listeners began to find their voices. At first they merely murmured their approval. But soon they were cheering his every word, clapping their hands and confirming every tale as if they'd been there themselves ('Oh yes indeed!', 'I heard about this one!', 'That's how it happened, all right!'). Overexcited by the rapturous reception, Indigo began to recite the reams of his own poetry, which he knew by heart (mostly almost twenty years old and utterly inappropriate). 'This one is called "The Tesseract"!' he shouted. 'Or: "A Poem for My Father!"' And the crowd greeted each poem with whoops of delight, though few of them spoke English and those who did had no idea of Indigo's family history or the meaning of the word 'tesseract'.

In the end, of course, the crowd's interest waned and they began to fidget on the spot and talk among themselves and uncork bottles and roll new joints and laugh at the English words that sounded like lavatorial Zamba. Indigo was sensitive to this and so he abandoned his poetry and began to introduce the individual Gangers with witty biographical anecdotes.

'This is Our Father,' he hollered. 'We call him Our Father because he used to be a Catholic priest. But we can forgive him for that, can't we?'

And the crowd laughed and cheered (apart from the old Catholic women who crossed themselves repeatedly and tried not to smile).

'Nkrumah is the son of a Felati! So can the women please queue to the left! Mapondera drove the bus of freedom! It was late, of course. But what do you expect? Musa the *zakulu* has a dreadlock for every mercenary he killed!'

Of course, the Gangers that the crowd really wanted to see were Tulo, the President-elect and Gecko. But, when Indigo looked for them, they were nowhere to be seen. Jim had managed to sneak off without too much difficulty since, away from the centre of attention, the people assumed he was just a stranded tourist. Enoch and Gecko, however, had to struggle to get out of Independence Square and, even when they did, they were repeatedly stopped in the street by passers-by who, in the spirit of the party, offered Enoch their handkerchiefs to dry his acid tears.

From the moment Jim entered Queenstown he had felt uncomfortable. In fact, he had not felt anything else since he shot Lambo dead and made an embarrassing fool of himself by crying like a baby. He was overwhelmed by mixed feelings of fraudulence and anticlimax and he kept thinking, what the hell am I doing here? Which, as far as he remembered, had been exactly the question he'd asked himself before all *this* began.

Since then he had been an English teacher (of sorts), a political prisoner (in a way), a prophet (of a kind) and a military leader (well . . . *ish!*). But now, as he marched down the Lelani road, he realized that he was still the same Jim Tulloh. And that thought depressed him. Of course, he had done stuff that he could never have done before. He had seen men killed (his fault) and killed men himself. But, the way Jim saw it, the weaknesses he had displayed had been very much his own, while the courage had been that of the Great Chief Tuloko. And he was left with both the depressing consequences of his weakness and – unfair, this – the depressing consequences of his courage, whatever its original source may have been.

When the Lelani road wound its way through Queenstown's red-light district and the whores leaned out of the first-floor windows of the seedy hotels and cat-called and wolf-whistled and flashed the Gangers their breasts or bottoms and smiled coyly and stuck out their tongues, Jim decided to make his getaway. One obese prostitute with pillar-box red lipstick and unashamed alopecia beckoned to him as the Gangers marched by and he stepped out of the parade, more because he didn't want to spoil the mood than from any great lust.

'*Gulu gulu, musungu?*' the whore asked.

'I'm afraid I'm a virgin,' he replied and then felt faintly ridiculous.

'That's good. So am I!' the woman said and then she laughed more deeply than any man.

'But I haven't got any money.'

'It's OK, I've been giving free love for the last three days. Besides, I've never done a *musungu* before. It will be good practice and I will put it up in my window: "I sleep with *musungu*." It will be excellent for business. Do we have a deal?'

'Sure.' Jim shrugged and they went inside and lay on a bed that smelled of urine and squealed under their combined weights.

When it was over, the woman patted Jim on the head and told him not to worry. This made Jim worry and he rolled off her and stared at the ceiling.

'Do you mind if I lie here for a bit?' he asked.

'Of course, my little *gudo*!' the whore cooed. 'Every man, whether he pays or not, has twenty minutes. You still have fifteen to go.'

The woman lit a cigarette and passed it to Jim sympathetically. He took a hungry drag on it and enjoyed the dizzying sensation. Then, quite unexpectedly, he found himself smiling and then giggling and then laughing so hard that he thought he might faint.

Now I'm a man! he thought. And he enjoyed his fifteen minutes of peace and quiet, little knowing that he'd picked up a healthy batch of crabs.

As for Enoch and Gecko, they criss-crossed the quiet streets and headed for the presidential residence. At the gate they were challenged by a terrified-looking presidential guard who clearly expected a rampaging mob to turn the corner at any second. But he recognized Enoch and his face broke into a comical expression of relief, all popping eyes and puffed cheeks.

They walked up the gravel driveway and Enoch led them for a moment into the presidential car park. There was his BMW, left where he'd parked it all those weeks ago. But Enoch's attention was drawn to one of the presidential limousines, which still had the sticker affixed to its rear bumper: 'Just because you're paranoid, they're still out to get you.' He pointed it out to Gecko.

'I did that.'

'Very mature,' she sneered. And then she winked at him and they both laughed.

As they approached the house, Enoch felt his heart quicken, his palate dry and his stride begin to falter. Noticing this, Gecko squeezed his hand in encouragement.

'What are you going to say to him?' she asked.

'I've no idea.'

In the presidential office Adini could feel his life slipping away from him. In one way, of course, this was what he'd wanted. But now that he was nearly dead, there was none of the accompanying peace for which he'd hoped. All he experienced was intense pain. His head felt like it might burst like a ripe spot and his vision had darkened and all he could hear was the crowd in Independence Square, who seemed to be cheering him to his death.

But it was the blackness that scared him most. He had expected to see Sally waiting for him on the other side, maybe flanked by the Great Chief Tuloko's honour guard. He had expected to strip naked and look down to find two fresh testicles, filled with twenty years of frustrated virility. He had expected to meet classical leaders for discussions of tactics and matters of state; maybe Priam, Demosthenes, Alexander and Caesar. Instead he saw nothing but closing blackness, like a pebble sinking to the bottom of a deep pool.

Desperately he struggled to get a foothold on the desk with the very tips of his toes. But every time he moved his legs he seemed to swing further into the middle of the room. Panicking, he tried to slip his fingers inside the tightening noose. But his fingers were not strong enough and now his arms were beginning to go numb.

When Enoch knocked and then entered the presidential office, he was dumbstruck and frozen by the sight of his father swinging from a makeshift noose attached to the chandelier. So it was Gecko who clambered up on to the presidential desk and cut Adini down. With Enoch still motionless and nobody to catch him, Adini's body hit the floor with quite a thump and one of the polished floorboards cracked under his weight. Enoch now approached the apparent corpse with a steady expression and felt for a pulse in his father's neck as if it were the most routine action in the world. Adini opened his eyes and found that his vision was clearing a little.

'Who is that?' he asked and Enoch was taken aback by the sound. His father's voice was higher and more incongruous than ever, now that his vocal chords had been further tightened by the noose.

'It's me, Dad.'

'Enoch? Are you still alive?'

'Yeah. I am. Thank you for your concern.'

'I am dead.'

'No, you're not . . .'

'Listen to me, Enoch! I have been dead without realizing it for only Tuloko knows how long. This is just the last step on a long journey for me. *Summum bonum*, Enoch. *Summum bonum!*'

For a moment Adini's expression seemed to open a little and he stared into his son's emotionless face with fading, misty eyes.

'You're crying for me, Enoch?' he said and then the expression locked, a growling gasp caught in his throat and he died.

As soon as Adini was dead, Enoch stood up and sighed and

looked at Gecko and he shrugged. He opened his arms, but she would not go to him at first. The coldness in his face disturbed her.

'I suppose my father's dead too,' she said.

'I'm sorry.'

'The thing is, Enoch, I really don't care.'

Now Enoch went to her and hugged her where she sat on the presidential desk, pressing his face into her breast. And she was relieved to feel his shoulders tremble as she wrapped him in her arms and planted soothing kisses on the top of his head.

It was some two weeks later, at Adini's funeral, before the five heroes of the battle of Maponda met again. Four of them had been living at the presidential residence (with Musa installed as the acting President's chief adviser in the run-up to the forthcoming elections and Jim an honoured guest). But the fifth, Indigo, had not been seen since the end of the celebrations in Independence Square. The others heard that he'd left Queenstown. But none of them knew where he'd gone.

In fact, when the crowds began to thin in Independence Square as night fell and many concluded that, after three days, it was about time they went to bed, Indigo was left holding his microphone with no audience and he started to feel very lonely. The other Gangers shook him by the hand and some embraced him affectionately. Then they too melted into the night, returning to their families or heading for the nearest *shabeen* or brothel to carry on the party and play a hand of cheat or two. A couple of the older Gangers asked Indigo if he would like to accompany them to their homes for a bite of food and a drink. But Indigo could see the fatigue in their faces and their need for a night's peace with their wives and children. And he thought about Ruth.

On a whim, he headed down to Mbave Bus Station and caught the first bus to Mutengwazi (a free trip courtesy of Mr Mapondera). There he took a room in the *shabeen* next to his childhood home with a window that overlooked the lamp-post from which Comrade Solo Maponga had hanged.

For the first two days of his chosen exile Indigo was in a daze and he couldn't do anything. He didn't eat or drink or wash or sleep. He said to himself, 'I must sort things out in my head.' But that was as far as he ever got. And he was plagued with such terrible headaches and such terrible memories that sometimes he couldn't tell where the headaches ended and the memories began.

On the third day Indigo ventured down into the *shabeen*, where he found an ancient *mboko* entertaining the young men with the tale of how the Great Chief Tuloko travelled to Zambawi on the back of a mighty eagle. Indigo listened in rapt attention, for the *mboko*'s language and phrasing and mannerisms were identical to those of his father.

When the story was concluded, Indigo approached the *mboko* and offered to buy him a drink.

'What is your name?' the *mboko* asked.

'Indigo.'

The *mboko*'s face registered mild surprise and he sucked on his beer bottle with a gummy mouth and a popping noise.

'Years ago there was a man who lived next door that we called N'dgo. We called him that because his wife was barren, but he still expected a child. He was a fantastic storyteller. In the end they had a son. Strangest thing. Some people said it was a miracle.'

'The son,' Indigo murmured, 'that was me.'

'And he called you N'dgo too, did he? Funny name. So what is it *you* expect?'

'No. My name means "a special kind of gift".'

The *mboko* looked at Indigo and laughed sarcastically and drank some more of his free beer as if he were afraid this stranger might take it away from him.

'Of course it does, N'dgo. So what do you expect?'

'Nothing,' Indigo said.

Indigo returned to his room and didn't emerge for a further ten days. He took out his notebook and pencil and stared at the blank page for hours at a time. Then he began to write poetry, really bad poetry that made him feel like a mechanic trying to milk a cow or a young boy trying to breastfeed a baby. He wrote rhyming couplets that ended in the word 'orange', blank verse that ran off the side of the page and love poems that read like the message in a greetings card.

Worst of all, on the fifth day of isolation, Indigo was overcome by the most terrifying realization. He was sitting quietly, chewing the stub end of his pencil, which splintered between his teeth, and he shut his eyes and found that he could no longer picture Ruth's face. Indigo sighed and inhaled and he could no longer smell Ruth's scent. Desperately he stared at the spaces between his words and listened to the silence. But he could no longer hear Ruth's voice.

'Indigo, my poet, my love.'

He spoke the words himself, but they were as soiled and empty as a beer bottle after a party. He tried to cry, but he didn't have the emotion for tears. Indigo was not filled with what *was*, he was filled with what was *not*.

When Adini's funeral was over, Musa and Gecko and Enoch and Jim gathered on the steps of Queenstown Cathedral and shook hands and hugged and kissed and tried not to snap at one another. Because they were all feeling irritable. They were irritated with each other, with themselves, with the state of things.

Musa was annoyed primarily with Enoch. He was annoyed that Enoch forbade him to smoke *gar* in meetings with the Emergency Cabinet (a majority of Gangers plus a few sheepish former ministers) and forced him to wear shoes. Next he'd be telling him to get his hair cut!

But mostly he was annoyed that the President-elect should have chosen to stage his father's funeral in a Christian church, when it was surely Musa's rightful place to conduct a traditional burial. After all, what the hell had they been fighting for?

Gecko's irritations were similarly focused. She was put out that Enoch had not mentioned her new outfit and she was piqued to see him shake the hands of so many foreign dignitaries.

'I can't believe it!' she exclaimed. 'The way you greet the African dictators and Western colonialists as if they were your best friends!'

'What do you want me to do?' Enoch protested. 'Would you rather I spat in their faces or insulted their mothers?'

As for Enoch, he was infuriated both by Musa's sulking and,

particularly, by Gecko's determined piety. He had only been a politician for two weeks and he was having to learn on the fly! What's more, he didn't understand why Gecko insisted on wearing a maternity dress embroidered with baby pink flowers when she was only a month gone. And he resigned himself to a difficult pregnancy.

On top of that he was smoking local-brand cigarettes that tasted like elephant crap and gave him a sore throat and, when he looked at Jim, he found the *musungu* was continually scratching his groin (fitting for the occasion on one level, but entirely inappropriate on another).

And where the fuck was Indigo? Enoch had spent the entire service craning his neck for his father's right-hand man. But he was nowhere to be seen.

Jim was immune to the others' irritations because his own were of a more personal nature that seemed to alienate him from the respectable mourners who smiled grimly and placed reassuring hands on one another's shoulders. He was distressed to find that he no longer fitted in. His feeling of belonging, which had taken so long to cultivate, was now evaporating like spilled spirits. *And*, for some unknown reason, his genitals were maddeningly itchy. *And* he was plagued by the acute sense of an unfulfilled promise. Though he had no idea what it could be.

Suddenly there was a commotion at the foot of the cathedral steps that caught the four mourners' attention. They saw an ancient, withered man with a grubby beard and dishevelled clothes scuffling with the newly appointed presidential security (who were keen to impress the boss with their efficiency).

'Let me through!' the man insisted. 'I am General Indigo Bulimi.'

Indigo approached the little group with a tottering step and vacant eyes. He looked as though he might faint at any second. At first, to his shame, Enoch felt embarrassed and he backed off a pace. But Gecko and Musa rushed forward and supported Indigo by the arms.

'Your father,' Indigo said, and his voice sounded as insubstantial as a tissue on the breeze. 'I am sorry.'

Enoch didn't know what to say. And there was a moment or two of awkward silence as Gecko and Musa looked at him quizzically.

But it was Jim who broke the spell. Unthinking, unknowing, possessed by the spirit of the forgotten promise, he pushed forward and cupped Indigo's cheeks in his two hands. 'For you,' he said. And he kissed Indigo firmly on the mouth, feeling the chill of his lips and the tickle of his sprouting moustache. Jim pulled away and immediately felt very stupid, and the two of them looked at one another in astonishment. Then Indigo's eyes rolled to the sky and his arms shot out at his sides and he tumbled back down the steps. As dead as his dreams.

36 : The Poet (seven)

When I first saw Ruth, she was talking to a young *musungu* with dark skin and sprightly eyes. Initially I was jealous. But it turned out to be her father. I didn't know what to say to her, so I just stood and watched for a moment. I was embarrassed to be an old man and I smelled like death. I said this to Tuloko and he told me that I would be young again soon. But I didn't believe him. I would have run away, but Tuloko called out her name and I had no choice but to meet her.

When she looked up, she knew me at once and she covered her mouth with her hand. It was strange to see her with no hair, rubbing her scalp self-consciously. I did not know what to do, but she pre-empted any action by running towards me and flinging her arms around my neck.

'Where have you been?' she cried.

I wanted to answer, but I was overwhelmed by the scent of her musk, which was as familiar as my face in the mirror and as exotic as the spice from the eggs of the *putsi* fly.

Ruth pulled away and looked at me coyly.

'Don't smell me without asking!' she said.

I laughed.

'You smell like my mother,' I replied.

We kissed then, locked together as intimately as twins in the womb. And Tuloko lent us his bed, which was as big as you needed and as soft as the pillows with which a duck lines her nest. When we woke up, we looked at each other and said at exactly the same moment, 'That was something!' And I noticed that her bald head was now covered in downy black hair.

Being dead is not at all what I expected. I suppose I am just getting used to it. But, since time is skewed here, I'm not sure how much more used to it I will get. Sometimes, when I walk with Tuloko (everybody does this, once a day, although sometimes he looks different), I try to ask him questions. He's not always very cooperative.

On one occasion I asked him if this was paradise and he took me to the clear Pool of Tears, where we swam. When we got out, we lay on the bank to dry off in the sun and I was nearly eaten alive by ants. Tuloko was untouched. He laughed at me and said, 'Even the *zveko* ant needs somewhere to go.'

Another day we walked to the top of a great hill that looked down into the most beautiful valley I have ever seen. In the middle of the valley stood a magnificent walled city with crystal skyscrapers that parted the clouds.

'Who lives there?' I asked.

'The Americans.'

'Why are they on their own?'

Tuloko shrugged.

These were the typical patterns of our conversations.

I asked Tuloko about my theory that truth could be found in language. He did not want to talk about that. But I pushed him because I had been thinking about trying to write poetry again.

'Language is the bastard child of truth and lies,' he said.

I told Ruth about this. I asked her if this meant that I'd got it right by the time I died. I asked her if this meant that truth was neither one thing nor the other. But she pulled faces and then kissed me, biting hard on my bottom lip. 'Write some poetry now or I'll divorce you!' she said. So I did.

I've seen all kinds of people since I died. I've seen Comrade Solo Maponga, who smokes *gar* all day and farts so badly that even Tuloko won't speak to him. I've seen my mother and father, and they look so happy together that I've only watched from a distance so far. Soon I'll have to introduce myself before they recognize me. Because I'm getting younger every day.

I've seen Indigo too, Enoch's son, who is growing in Gecko's womb and will be named after me. We've talked long and hard about his natural father (no sign of Mandela round here! – though I never met him when we were alive) and I've told him to love Enoch as Enoch will surely love him. Of course, he won't remember any of that when he's born. But there's no harm in trying and he seems like a good boy anyway.

Today I saw Adini for the first time. He is a pebble on the shore of the Pool of Tears, though he doesn't know it. Every time somebody walks by he greets them with an indignant cry of 'Don't you know who I am?' A lot of people consider this presumptuous on the part of a stone and Adini often finds himself thrown into the pool and it takes weeks for him to be washed back to the shore (which is why I didn't see him when I was swimming with Tuloko).

I asked Tuloko, 'How long will Adini be a pebble?'

'Until he knows who he is.'

'How long will that take?'

'Who knows?' Tuloko said with a smile. 'I hope he finds out before the tide wears him away to nothing.'

I hope so too.

Appendix 1: Map of Zambawi

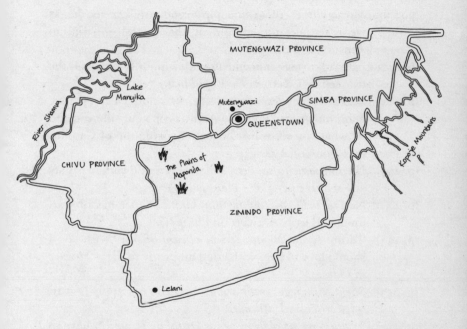

Source: Kotto, E. (1991), 'Musungu Takes the Myth', in Rose, A. and Lash, S. (eds.), *New African Outlooks*, New York: Camstead Press.

Appendix 2 : Translation notes

(p. 20)   *Moriamur et in media arma ruamus*: 'Let us die as we rush into the middle of the battle' – Virgil in *Aeneid*.

(pp. 156, 292, 310)   *Mens cuiusque is est quisque*: 'The spirit is the true self' – Cicero in *De Republica*.

(p. 205)   *Miser Adini, desinas ineptire, Et quod viedes perisse perditum ducas*: 'Poor old Adini, drop your silliness, and let what you see is lost be lost' – corruption of Catullus in *A Book of Airs*.

(p. 205)   *Dictum sapienti sat est*: 'What's been said should satisfy any sensible person' – Plautus in *Persa*.

(p. 223)   *Nervos belli, pecuniam infinitam*: 'The sinews of war, unlimited cash' – Cicero in *Philippic*.

(p. 233)   *Tecum vivere amem, tecum obeam libens*: 'With you I should love to live, with you I am ready to die' – Horace in *Odes*.

(p. 253)   *Silent enim leges inter arma*: 'Laws do not apply in war' – Cicero in *Pro Milone*.

(p. 253)   *Multa fero, ut placem genus irritabile vatum*: 'I have to put up with a lot, to keep the sensitive poets happy' – Horace in *Ars Poetica*.

(p. 303)   *Omnia mutantur, nos et mutamur in illis*: 'Times change, and we change with them' – Unknown.

(p. 341)   *Indiligens cum pigra familia*: 'You're a waster with a messed up family' – Plautus in *Miles Gloriosus*.

(p. 341)   *Tandem impetraui ut egomet me corrumperem!*: 'At last

I've managed to completely screw up my life!' – Plautus in *Mercator*.

(p. 358)   *Summum bonum*: 'The greatest good' – Cicero in *De Officiis*.

Appendix 3 : Glossary of select names and terms

Adini, Enoch   Zita Adini's son.

Adini, Sally   Zita Adini's wife (d. 1983).

Adini, Zita   Also known as 'the eunuch'. President of Zambawi. Former revolutionary leader of the ZLF (1975–81).

babayako   *Zamba*. Silk worm.

Banana, Zike   Also known as '(Mad) Banana'. Sergeant in the Black Boot Gang. Former soldier in the Zambawian State Army. Former ZLF *ter*.

Barrel, The   Non-residents' bar at the Queenstown Sun Hotel, popular meeting place for rich young Zambawians and expatriates.

belabe **shuffle**   Archaic Zamba ritual, believed to be the source of the Zamba's innate talent for card games (ref. Edison Burrows, 1965).

Black Boot Anarchy   Period of social unrest throughout Zambawi following the rise of the Black Boot Gang (coined by Eddy Kotto, *see below*).

Black Boot Gang   Revolutionary guerrilla army determined to overthrow President Adini, their major grievance being the 'land issue' (*see below*).

braai   *South African*. Barbecue.

Bulimi, Indigo   Also known as 'the Poet'. General in the Zambawian State Army. Former ZLF *ter*.

Burridge, Kenelm   Anthropologist. Author of *New Heaven, New Earth* (1969), Oxford, Basil Blackwell.

Burrows, Edison   American anthropologist based at Cambridge

University. Author of *The Zamba* (1965), London, Penguin Books.

Case of the Promiscuous American Women 1 Murder of twenty-nine American sex tourists during the Black Boot Anarchy (*see above*). 2 *Slang.* Any similarly horrific event that, for reasons of political expediency, provokes no governmental response, e.g. 'It's just another case of the promiscuous American women'.

cheat Zambawi's most popular card game, the basic premise being to cheat as much as possible.

chinjuku Zamba. Age grade for pubescent Zamba girls.

Chivu Province Province to the west of Queenstown (Local Government Act, 1982).

Cohen, Gideon Jewish smallholder in Zimindo Province (d. 1976).

Cohen, Ruth Gideon Cohen's daughter (d. 1976).

Digby-Stewart, Sir Alistair British High Commissioner to Zambawi.

Felati *Zamba.* 1 Adulterers. 2 Zamba tribal grouping from Chivu Province famed for their fertility and the size of their penises (*see above*: Case of the Promiscuous American Women). Also known as 'the Men with the Spears between Their Legs' (*Traditional Zamba*). 3 *Slang.* To binge, e.g. 'I'm going to felati all weekend'.

ForEx Foreign exchange.

Ganger *Slang.* Guerrilla soldier, usually a member of the Black Boot Gang.

gar Zamba. Marijuana.

garwe Zamba. Cabbage.

gudo Zamba. Baboon.

gulu gulu Zamba. 1 Sexual intercourse between consenting partners within marriage. 2 Other types of sexual intercourse.

gwaasha Zamba. Rural homeland.

Heroes Acre Queenstown graveyard reserved for those who died in the independence struggle, currently used as a vegetable patch by the local townships.

Hit and Run Unit Small urban terrorist unit employed by the ZLF in the early days of the independence struggle.

Ikbo Mozolan tribal grouping largely wiped out by the genocidal Anderson Tula (*see below*).

independence struggle 1 Fight to free Zambawi from colonial rule, culminating in civil war, 1970–81. 2 *Slang.* Dilemma for which there is no solution because of mutually conflicting conditions, e.g. 'This is a real independence struggle' (ref. Catch 22).

kapenta Zamba. Zambawian freshwater fish similar in appearance to sardine.

Kelly, Edward Manyikaland civil rights lawyer, assassinated by the ZLF (d. 1970).

Kelly, Tom Edward Kelly's son. A farmer in Zimindo Province.

Kola, Musape Headmaster of State Boarding School 063, 1961–8 (d. 1972).

Kopoje Mountains Also known as 'the Mountains in the East That Kissed the Sky'. Mountain range on Zambawi's eastern border.

Kotto, Eddy Editor of the *Zambawi National Herald*. Black Boot Gang sympathizer.

Kunashe, Paul Also known as 'PK'. Headmaster of St Oswald's School, Zimindo Province. Black Boot Gang sympathizer.

Lake Manyika Also known as 'the Great Lake in the West That Cooled the Traveller's Feet'. Lake on Zambawi's western border.

Lamberton, Terence Also known as 'Lambo'. English mercenary leader. Sometime outward-bound instructor.

land issue Primary source of Zambawian political tension arising from President Adini's refusal to redistribute white-owned land.

Lawrence, Peter Anthropologist. Author of *Road Belong Cargo* (1964), Manchester.

Lelani Zambawi's second city (formerly Coppertown).

Lévi-Strauss, Claude   Eminent anthropologist and essential commentator on the interpretation of myth. Author of 'Religions comparées des peuples sans écriture', in *Problèmes et méthodes d'histoire des religions: mélanges publiés par la section des sciences religieuses à l'occasion du centenaire de l'École pratique des Hautes Études* (1968), Paris, Presses Universitaires de France.

mandrake   Indigenous Zambawian plant possessing a root with narcotic properties similar to cocaine. Often chewed by the ZLF *ters* during the independence struggle.

Manyikaland   Colonial name for Zambawi (changed after independence).

Mapondera, Edward   Owner of the Mapondera Bus Company, Zambawi's largest, serving Zimindo Province.

Mapondera, Seventeen   Edward Mapondera's seventeenth child.

Maponga, Solo   First leader of the ZLF (d. 1975).

Mbave   1 Queenstown's bus station. 2 *Zamba slang*. Prison.

mbira   *Zamba*. Zambawian string instrument, usually fashioned from a large seed pod or shoe box.

mboko   *Zamba*. 1 Old man. 2 A respectful form of address to any elder male.

mbudzi   *Zamba*. Goat.

Mozola   African republic to the north-east of Zambawi (*see below*: Tula, Anderson).

Mudiwa   Mythical wife of Tuloko (*see below*).

Murufu, Innocence   *Chinjuku* pupil of James Tulloh at St Oswald's School.

Murufu, Taurai   Innocence Murufu's father. A subsistence farmer.

Musa   The most important *zakulu* (*see below*) in Zimindo Province. Black Boot Gang sympathizer.

musungu   *Zamba*. A white person.

Mutengwazi   High-density suburb north of Queenstown in Mutengwazi Province.

Muziringa, Isaiah   Also known as 'Dubchek'. Captain in the

Zambawian State Army. Member of the Black Boot Gang.

n'dgo   *Zamba*. One who expects.

Nose   *Slang*. Rich black Zambawian who speaks with a nasal accent.

Number 17   Mapondera bus serving St Oswald's School, Zimindo Province.

nyoka   *Zamba*. Snake.

Nyoka, Thomas   Also known as 'Mandela'. Private in the Zambawian State Army. Member of the Black Boot Gang.

nzou   *Zamba*. Elephant.

Order of the Ark   Obscure monastic order expelled from England in 1906. Founders of St Ignatius' College, Queenstown (*see below*).

Pass It On   Reliable news grapevine emanating from the newsroom of the *Zambawian National Herald* (coined by Eddy Kotto, *see above*).

pfanje   *Zamba*. Porcupine.

Pienaar, Frank   Queenstown Chief of Police 1974–6 (d. 1976).

Preston, Tyrone   Eminent Jamaican cricket writer and sometime historian. Author of *A Colonial State of Mind* (1981), London, Black List Publishing.

Queenstown   Capital city of Zambawi.

Radcliffe-Brown, Alfred   Eminent anthropologist and proponent of structural functional anthropological theory. Former tutor of Edison Burrows (*see above*).

Righteous Brothers, The   Nickname of the ZLF Hit and Run Unit (*see above*) of Zita Adini and Indigo Bulimi.

St Ignatius' College   Predominantly white private school in Queenstown. Founded by the Order of the Ark (*see above*).

shabeen   *South African*. 1 Bottle store. 2 Pub.

shambok   *South African*. Heavy wooden staff.

shamva   *Zamba*. 1 River. 2 Corrupt chiefs of Zamba tradition, eventually overthrown by Tuloko.

shumba   *Zamba*. Lion.

Simba Province   Province to the east of Queenstown (Local Government Act, 1982).

sisi *Zamba slang.* Generic term for a young woman. Sometimes daughter, sometimes sister, sometimes with sexual overtones (when accompanied by kissing teeth).

63 *Slang.* Pupil of State Boarding School 063, Mutengwazi Province (pre 1981: all state schools were renamed after independence).

Soyinka, Wole Celebrated Nigerian poet. A favourite of Indigo Bulimi.

'stick and carrot' policing Policy of bribing informants adopted by the colonial administration during the independence struggle (coined by Frank Pienaar, *see above*).

temba *Zamba.* Age grade for pubescent Zamba boys.

ter *South African slang.* Terrorist (usually a member of the ZLF).

Terreblanche, Kippie Queenstown Chief of Police (1958–74) assassinated by the ZLF (d. 1974).

Tribal Trust Lands Arid land set aside for 'native settlement' in Manyikaland (*see above*).

Tula, Anderson Also known as 'the Butcher of Ikbo'. Former Mozolan dictator living in exile in Zambawi.

Tula, Rujeko Also known as 'Gecko Tula'. Anderson Tula's daughter. Member of the Black Boot Gang.

Tulloh, James Also known as 'Tulo'. English teacher at St Oswald's School, Zimindo. Black Boot Gang sympathizer.

Tuloko Also known as 'the Great Chief Tuloko', 'the Traveller' and 'the Child of the Horizon'. Mythical first chief of the Zamba who secured the people's release from the tyrannical reign of the *shamva* (*see above*).

Van De Horse, Horst Afrikaans farmer in Zimindo Province. Former pupil of St Ignatius' College.

Walker, Grant Farmer in Zimindo Province. Former pupil of Ignatius' College. Son of Stanley Walker.

Walker, Scott Thirteen-year-old son of Stanley Walker and brother of Grant. Usually referred to by his father as 'the little ponce'.

Walker, Stanley *Musungu* farmer in Zimindo Province. English citizen and the first victim of the Black Boot Gang uprising.

zakulu   *Zamba*. Witchdoctor (ref. Edison Burrows, 1965).

Zamba   1 The people of Zambawi. 2 Indigenous language of Zambawi. 3 *Zamba*. Moon. 4 Mythical founder of the Zamba people and cousin of Tuloko.

Zamba mouth   Impassive countenance appropriate to a successful card player (ref. 'poker face').

***Zambawi National Herald*, the**   Also known as 'the eunuch's loo roll'. State-owned Zambawian newspaper. Before independence, simply the *Herald*.

Zambawian roulette   Threatening act in which one squeezes the trigger of a revolver held to another's head with one chamber empty (ref. 'Russian roulette').

Zimindo Province   Province to the south of Queenstown (Local Government Act, 1982). Mythical birthplace of the Zamba people.

ZLF   Zambawian Liberation Front. Revolutionary *ter* army in the independence struggle.

Acknowledgements

Lyrics from 'Fight The Power' by Public Enemy (Ridenhour/Shocklee/Sadler) © 1989 by kind permission of Universal Music Publishing Ltd.

Lyrics from 'Final Countdown' by Europe (Words and Music by Joey Tempest) © 1986 by kind permission of EMI Music Publishing Ltd, London WC2H OEA.

Extract from 'The Englishman' by G.K. Chesterton by kind permission of A.P. Watt Ltd on behalf of The Royal Literary Fund.

Extract from 'Fuzzy Wuzzy' by Rudyard Kipling by kind permission of A.P. Watt Ltd on behalf of The National Trust for Places of Historic Interest or Natural Beauty.

Extract from 'Dedication' by Wole Soyinka (from *Idanre and Other Poems*) by kind permission of Methuen Ltd.